New York Times and *USA TODAY* bestselling author RaeAnne Thayne finds inspiration in the beautiful northern Utah mountains, where she lives with her husband and three children. Her books have won numerous honors, including RITA® Award nominations from Romance Writers of America and a Career Achievement Award from *RT Book Reviews*. RaeAnne loves to hear from readers and can be contacted through her website, raeannethayne.com.

New York Times Bestselling Author

RaeAnne Thayne

Outlaw Hartes

Recycling programs
for this product may
not exist in your area.

ISBN-13: 978-0-373-40107-9

Outlaw Hartes
Copyright © 2015 by Harlequin Books S.A.

The publisher acknowledges the copyright holder
of the individual works as follows:

The Valentine Two-Step
Copyright © 2002 by RaeAnne Thayne

Cassidy Harte and the Comeback Kid
Copyright © 2002 by RaeAnne Thayne

Printed in U.S.A.

CONTENTS

THE VALENTINE TWO-STEP

To Lyndsey Thomas, for saving my life
and my sanity more times than I can count!

Special thanks to Dr. Ronald Hamm, DVM,
animal healer extraordinaire,
for sharing so generously of his expertise.

Prologue

"It's absolutely perfect." Dylan Webster held her hands out imploringly to her best friend, Lucy Harte. "Don't you see? It's the only way!"

Lucy frowned in that serious way of hers, her gray eyes troubled. In the dim, dusty light inside their secret place— a hollowed-out hideaway behind the stacked hay bales of the Diamond Harte barn loft—her forehead looked all wrinkly. Kind of like a shar-pei puppy Dylan had seen once at her mom's office back in California.

"I don't know…" she began.

"Come on, Luce. You said it yourself. We should have been sisters, not just best friends. We were born on exactly the same day, we both love horses and despise long division and we both want to be vets like my mom when we grow up, right?"

"Well, yes, but…"

"If my mom married your dad, we really *would* be sisters. It would be like having a sleepover all the time. I could ride the school bus with you and everything, and I just know my mom would let me have my own horse if we lived out here on the ranch."

Lucy nibbled her lip. "But, Dylan…"

"You want a mom of your own as much as I want a dad, don't you? Even though you have your aunt Cassie to look after you, it's not the same. You know it's not."

It was exactly the right button to push, and she knew it. Before her very eyes, Lucy sighed, and her expression went all dreamy. Dylan felt a little pinch of guilt at using her best friend's most cherished dream to her own advantage, but she worked hard to ignore it.

Her plan would never work if she couldn't convince Lucy how brilliant it was. Both of them had to be one-hundred-percent behind it. "We'd be sisters, Luce," she said. "Sisters for real. Wouldn't it be awesome?"

"Sisters." Lucy burrowed deeper into the hay, her gray eyes closed as if, like Dylan, she was imagining family vacations and noisy Christmas mornings and never again having to miss a daddy-daughter party at school. Or in Lucy's case, a mother-daughter party.

"It *would* be awesome." That shar-pei look suddenly came back to her forehead, and she sat up. "But Dylan, why would they ever get married? I don't think they even like each other very much."

"Who?"

"My dad and your mom."

Doubt came galloping back like one of Lucy's dad's horses after a stray dogie. Lucy was absolutely right. They *didn't* like each other much. Just the other day, she heard her mom tell SueAnn that Matt Harte was a stubborn old man in a younger man's body.

"But what a body it is," her mom's assistant at the clinic had replied, with a rumbly laugh like grown-ups make when they're talking about sexy stuff. "Matt Harte and his brother have always been the most gorgeous men in town."

Her mom had laughed, too, and she'd even turned a little bit pink, like a strawberry shake. "Shame on you. You're a happily married woman, Sue."

"Married doesn't mean dead. Or crazy, for that matter."

Her mom had scrunched up her face. "Even if he is… attractive…in a macho kind of way, a great body doesn't make up for having the personality of an ornery bull."

Dylan winced, remembering. Okay, so Lucy's dad and her mom hadn't exactly gotten along since the Websters moved to Star Valley. Still, her mom thought he was good-looking and had a great body. That had to count for something.

Dylan gave Lucy what she hoped was a reassuring smile. "They just haven't had a chance to get to know each other."

Lucy looked doubtful. "My dad told Aunt Cassie just last week he wouldn't let that city quack near any of his livestock. I think he meant your mom."

Dylan narrowed her eyes. "My mom's not a quack."

"I know she's not. I think your mom's just about the greatest vet around. I'm only telling you what he said."

"We just have to change his mind. We have to figure out some way to push them together. Once they get to know each other, they'll have to see that they belong together."

"I'm not so sure."

Dylan blew out a breath that made her auburn bangs flutter. Lucy was the best friend anybody could ask for— the best friend she'd ever had. These last three months since they'd moved here had been so great. Staying over- night at the ranch, riding Lucy's horses, trading secrets and dreams here behind the hay bales.

They were beyond best, best, best friends, and Dylan

loved her to death, but sometimes Lucy worried too much. Like about spelling tests and missing the bus and letting her desk get too messy.

She just had to convince her the idea would work. It would be so totally cool if they could pull this off. She wanted a dad in the worst way, and she figured Matt Harte—with his big hands and slow smile and kind eyes—would be absolutely perfect. Having Lucy for a sister would be like the biggest bonus she could think of.

Dylan would just have to try harder.

"It's going to work. Trust me. I know it's going to work." She grabbed Lucy's hand and squeezed it tightly. "Before you know it, we'll be walking down the aisle wearing flowers in our hair and me and my mom will be living here all the time. See, I have this plan...."

Chapter 1

"They did *what?*"

Ellie Webster and the big, gruff rancher seated beside her spoke in unison. She spared a glance at Matt Harte and saw he looked like he'd just been smacked upside the head with a two-by-four.

"Oh, dear. I was afraid of this." Sarah McKenzie gave a tiny, apologetic smile to both of them.

With her long blond hair and soft, wary brown eyes, her daughter's teacher always made Ellie think of a skittish palomino colt, ready to lunge away at the first provocation. Now, though, she was effectively hobbled into place behind her big wooden schoolteacher's desk. "You're telling me you both *didn't* agree to serve on the committee for the Valentine's Day carnival?"

"Hell no." Matt Harte looked completely horrified by the very idea of volunteering for a Valentine's Day carnival committee—as astonished as Ellie imagined he'd be if Ms. McKenzie had just asked him to stick one of her perfectly sharpened number-two pencils in his eye.

"I've never even heard of the Valentine's Day carnival until just now," Ellie offered.

"Well, this does present a problem." Ms. McKenzie folded her hands together on top of what looked like a grade book, slim and black and ominous.

Ellie had always hated those grade books.

Despite the fact that she couldn't imagine any two people being more different, Ellie had a brief, unpleasant image of her own fourth-grade teacher. Prissy mouth, hair scraped back into a tight bun. Complete intolerance for a scared little girl who hid her bewildered loneliness behind defiant anger.

She pushed the unwelcome image aside.

"The girls told me you both would cochair the committee," the teacher said. "They were most insistent that you wanted to do it."

"You've got to be joking. They said we *wanted* to do it? I don't know where the he—heck Lucy could have come up with such a harebrained idea." Matt Harte sent one brief, disparaging glare in Ellie's direction, and she stiffened. She could just imagine what he was thinking. *If my perfect little Lucy has a harebrained idea in her perfect little head, it must have come from you and your flighty daughter, with your wacky California ways.*

He had made it perfectly clear he couldn't understand the instant bond their two daughters had formed when she and Dylan moved here at the beginning of the school year three months earlier. He had also made no secret of the fact that he didn't trust her or her veterinary methods anywhere near his stock.

The really depressing thing was, Harte's attitude seemed to be the rule, not the exception, among the local ranching community. After three months, she was no closer to breaking into their tight circle than she'd been that very first day.

"It does seem odd," Ms. McKenzie said, and Ellie chided herself for letting her mind wander.

Right now she needed to concentrate on Dylan and this latest scrape her daughter had found herself in. Not on the past or on the big, ugly pile of bills that needed to be paid, regardless of whether or not she had any patients.

"I thought it was rather out of character for both of you," the quiet, pretty teacher went on. "That's why I called you both and asked you to come in this evening, so we all could try to get to the bottom of this."

"Why would they lie about it?" Ellie asked. "I don't understand why on earth the girls would say we volunteered for something I've never even heard of before now."

The teacher shifted toward her and shrugged her shoulders inside her lacy white blouse. She made the motion look so delicate and airy that Ellie felt about as feminine as a teamster in her work jeans and flannel shirt.

"I have no idea," she said. "I was hoping you could shed some light on it."

"You sure it was our girls who signed up?"

Ms. McKenzie turned to the rancher with a small smile. "Absolutely positive. I don't think I could possibly mix that pair up with any of my other students."

"Well, there's obviously been a mistake," Matt said gruffly.

Ms. McKenzie was silent for a few moments, then she sighed. "That's what I was afraid you would say. Still, the fact remains that I need two parents to cochair the committee, and your daughters obviously want you to do it. Would the two of you at least consider it?"

The rancher snorted. "You've got the wrong guy."

"I don't think so," the teacher answered gently, as if

chiding a wayward student, and Ellie wondered how she could appear to be so completely immune to the potent impact of Matt Harte.

Even with that aggravated frown over this latest scheme their daughters had cooked up, he radiated raw male appeal, with rugged, hard-hewn features, piercing blue eyes and broad shoulders. Ellie couldn't even sit next to him without feeling the power in those leashed muscles.

But Sarah McKenzie appeared oblivious to it. She treated him with the same patience and kindness she showed the fourth graders in her class.

"I think you'd both do a wonderful job," the teacher continued. "Since this is my first year at the school, I haven't been to the carnival myself but I understand attendance has substantially dropped off the last two years. I'm sure I don't have to tell you what a problem this is."

"No," the rancher said solemnly, and Ellie fought the urge to raise her hand and ask somebody to explain the gravity of the situation to her. It certainly didn't seem like a big deal to her that some of the good people of Salt River decided to celebrate Valentine's Day somewhere other than the elementary school gymnasium. Come to think of it, so far most of the people she'd met in Salt River didn't seem the types to celebrate Valentine's Day at all.

"This is a really important fund-raiser," Ms. McKenzie said. "All the money goes to the school library, which is desperately in need of new books. We need to do something to generate more interest in the carnival, infuse it with fresh ideas. New blood, if you will. I think the two of you are just the ones to do that."

There was silence for a moment, then the rancher sat forward, that frown still marring his handsome features. "I'm sorry, Miz McKenzie. I'd like to help you out, honest. I'm all in favor of getting more books for the library and

I'd be happy to give you a sizable donation if that will help at all. But I'm way out of my league here. I wouldn't know the first thing about putting together something like that."

"I'm afraid this sort of thing isn't exactly my strong point, either," Ellie admitted, which was a bit like saying the nearby Teton Mountain Range had a couple of pretty little hills.

"Whatever their reasons, it seemed very important to your daughters that you help." She shifted toward Matt again. "Mr. Harte, has Lucy ever asked you to volunteer for anything in school before? Reading time, lunch duty, anything?"

The rancher's frown deepened. "No," he finally answered the teacher. "Not that I can think of."

"All of her previous teachers describe Lucy as a shy mouse of a girl who spoke in whispers and broke into tears if they called on her. I have to tell you, that is not the same girl I've come to know this year."

"No?"

"Since Dylan's arrival, Lucy participates much more in class. She is a sweet little girl with a wonderfully creative mind."

"That's good, right?"

"Very good. But despite the improvements, Lucy still seems to prefer staying in the background. She rarely ventures an opinion of her own. I think it would be wonderful for her to help plan the carnival under your supervision. It might even provide her with some of the confidence she still seems to be lacking."

"I'm a very busy man, Miz McKenzie—"

"I understand that. And I know Dr. Webster is also very busy trying to establish her practice here in Star Valley."

You don't know the half of it, Ellie thought grimly.

"But I think it would help both girls. Dylan, as well,"

the teacher said, shifting toward her. "I've spoken with you before with some of my concerns about your daughter. She's a very bright girl and a natural leader among the other children, but she hasn't shown much enthusiasm for anything in the classroom until now."

The teacher paused, her hands still folded serenely on her desk, and gave them both a steady look that had Ellie squirming just like she'd been caught chewing gum in class. "It's obvious neither of you wants to do this. I certainly understand your sentiments. But I have to tell you, I would recommend you would put your own misgivings aside and think instead about your daughters and what they want."

Oh, she was good. *Pour on the parental guilt, sister. Gets 'em every time.*

Out of the corner of her gaze Ellie could see Harte fighting through the same internal struggle.

How could she possibly do this? The last thing on earth she wanted was to be saddled with the responsibility for planning a Valentine's Day carnival. Valentine's Day, for heaven's sake. A time for sweethearts and romance, hearts and flowers. Things she had absolutely no experience with.

Beyond that, right now she was so busy trying to salvage her floundering practice that she had no time for anything but falling into her bed at the end of the day.

Still, Dylan wanted her to do this. For whatever reasons, this was important to her daughter. Ellie had already uprooted her from the only life she'd known to bring her here, to an alien world of wide-open spaces and steep, imposing mountains.

If being involved in this stupid carnival would make Dylan happy, didn't she owe it to her to try?

And maybe, just maybe, a selfish little voice whispered,

this might just be the ticket to help you pile drive your way into the closed circle that is the Star Valley community.

If she could show the other parents she was willing to volunteer to help out the school, they might begin to accept her into their ranks. Lord knows, she had to do something or she would end up being the proud owner of the only veterinary practice in Wyoming without a single patient to its name.

"I suppose I'm game," she said, before she could talk herself out of it. "What about you, Harte?"

"It's a Valentine's Day carnival. What the hell do I know about Valentine's Day?"

She snickered at his baffled tone. She couldn't help herself. The man just rubbed her wrong. He had gone out of his way to antagonize her since she arrived in town. Not only had he taken his own business elsewhere, but she knew he'd convinced several other ranchers to do the same. It hurt her pride both professionally and personally that he made no secret of his disdain for some of her more unconventional methods.

"You mean nobody's sent you one of those cute little pink cards lately? With that sweet disposition of yours, I'd have thought you would have women crawling out of the woodwork to send you valentines."

She regretted the snippy comment as soon as she said it. Whatever her views about him, she should at least try to be civil.

Still, she felt herself bristle when he glowered at her, which seemed to be his favorite expression. It was a shame, really. The man could be drop-dead gorgeous when he wasn't looking like he just planted his butt on a cactus. How such a sweet little girl like Lucy could have such a sour apple of a father was beyond her.

Before he could answer in kind, the schoolteacher

stepped in to keep the peace with the same quiet diplomacy she probably used to break up schoolyard brawls. "There's no reason you have to make a decision today. It's only mid-November, so we still have plenty of time before Valentine's Day. Why don't both of you take a few days to think it over, and I'll talk to you about it next week."

Ms. McKenzie rose from behind her desk. "Thank you both for coming in at such short notice," she said, in clear dismissal. "I'll be in touch with you next week."

Left with no alternative, Ellie rose, as well, and shrugged into her coat. Beside her, Lucy's father did the same.

"Sorry about the mix-up," he said, reaching out to shake hands with Ms. McKenzie. Ellie observed with curiosity that for the first time the other woman looked uncomfortable, even nervous. Again she thought of that skittish colt ready to bolt. There was an awkward pause while he stood there with his hand out, then with a quick, jerky movement, the teacher gripped his hand before abruptly dropping it.

"I'll be in touch," she said again.

What was that all about? Matt wondered as he followed the city vet out of the brightly decorated classroom into the hall. Why did Miz McKenzie act like he'd up and slapped her when all he wanted to do was shake her hand? Come to think of it, she'd behaved the same way when he came in a month earlier for parent-teacher conferences.

She and Ellie Webster ought to just form a club, since it was obvious the lady vet wasn't crazy about him, either. Matt Harte Haters of America.

He didn't have time to dwell on it before they reached the outside door of the school. The vet gave him a funny look when he opened the door for her, but she said nothing, just moved past him. Before he could stop himself, he caught a whiff of her hair as her coat brushed his arm. It smelled clean and fresh, kind of like that heavenly lemon cream pie they served over at the diner.

He had absolutely no business sniffing the city vet's hair, Matt reminded himself harshly. Or noticing the way those freckles trailed across that little nose of hers like the Big Dipper or how the fluorescent lights inside the school had turned that sweet-smelling hair a fiery red, like an August sunset after an afternoon of thunderstorms.

He pushed the unwanted thoughts away and followed Ellie Webster out into the frigid night. An icy wind slapped at them, and he hunched his shoulders inside his lined denim coat.

It was much colder than normal for mid-November. The sky hung heavy and ugly overhead, and the twilight had that expectant hush it took on right before a big storm. Looked like they were in for a nasty one. He dug already cold fingers into his pockets.

When he drove into town earlier, the weatherman on the radio had said to expect at least a foot of snow. Just what he needed. With that Arctic Express chugging down out of Canada, they were sure to have below-zero temperatures tonight. Add to that the windchill and he'd be up the whole damn night just trying to keep his cattle alive.

The city vet seemed to read his mind. "By the looks of that storm, I imagine we'll both have a busy night."

"You, too?"

"I do still have a few patients."

He'd never paid much mind to what a vet did when the weather was nasty. Or what a vet did any other time, for that matter. They showed up at his place, did what he needed them to do, then moved on to their next appointment.

He tried to imagine her muscling an ornery cow into a

pen and came up completely blank. Hell, she looked hardly big enough to wrestle a day-old calf. He'd had the same thought the first day he met her, back in August when she rode into town with her little girl and all that attitude.

She barely came up to his chin, and her wrists were delicate and bony, like a kitten that had been too long without food. Why would a scrawny city girl from California want to come out to the wilds of Wyoming and wrestle cattle? He couldn't even begin to guess.

There were only two vehicles in the school parking lot, the brand spankin' new dually crew cab he drove off the lot last week and her battered old Ford truck. He knew it was hers by the magnetized sign on the side reading Salt River Veterinary Clinic.

Miz McKenzie must have walked, since the little house she rented from Bob Jimenez was just a couple blocks from the school. Maybe he ought to offer her a ride home. It was too damn cold to be walking very far tonight.

Before he could turn around and go back into the school to make the offer, he saw Ellie Webster pull her keys out of her pocket and fight to open her truck door for several seconds without success.

"Can I help you there, ma'am?" he finally asked.

She grunted as she worked the key. "The lock seems to be stuck...."

Wasn't that just like a city girl to go to all the trouble to lock the door of a rusty old pickup nobody would want to steal anyway? "You know, most of us around here don't lock our vehicles. Not much need."

She gave him a scorcher of a look. "And most of you think karaoke is a girl you went to high school with."

His mouth twitched, but he refused to let himself smile. Instead, he yanked off a glove and stuck his bare thumb over the lock.

In the pale lavender twilight, she watched him with a confused frown. "What are you doing?"

"Just trying to warm up your lock. I imagine it's frozen and that's why you can't get the key to turn. I guess you don't have much trouble with that kind of thing in California, do you?"

"Not much, no. I guess it's another exciting feature unique to Wyoming. Like jackalopes and perpetual road construction."

"When we've had a cold wet rain like we did this afternoon, moisture can get down in the lock. After the sun goes down, it doesn't take long to freeze."

"I'll remember that."

"There. That ought to do it." He pulled his hand away and took the key from her, then shoved it into the lock. The mechanism slid apart now like a knife through soft wax, and he couldn't resist pulling the door open for her with an exaggerated flourish.

She gave him a disgruntled look then climbed into her pickup. "Thank you."

"You're welcome." He shoved his hand into his lined pocket, grateful for the cozy warmth. "Next time you might want to think twice before you lock your door so it doesn't happen again. Nobody's going to steal anything around here."

She didn't look like she appreciated his advice. "You do things your way, I'll do things mine, Harte."

She turned the key, and the truck started with a smooth purr that defied its dilapidated exterior. "If you decide you're man enough to help me with this stupid carnival, I suppose we'll have to start organizing it soon."

His attention snagged on the first part of her sentence. "If I'm man enough?" he growled.

She grinned at him, her silvery-green eyes sparkling,

and he fought hard to ignore the kick of awareness in his stomach. "Do you think you've got the guts to go through with this?"

"It's not a matter of guts," he snapped. "It's a matter of having the time to waste putting together some silly carnival."

"If you say so."

"I'm a very busy man, Dr. Webster."

It was apparently exactly the wrong thing to say. Her grin slid away, and she stiffened like a coil of frozen rope, slicing him to pieces with a glare. "And I have nothing better to do than sit around cutting out pink and white hearts to decorate the school gymnasium with, right? That's what you think, isn't it? Lord knows, I don't have much of a practice thanks to you and all the other stubborn old men around here."

He set his jaw. He wasn't going to get into this with her standing out here in the school parking lot while the windchill dipped down into single digits. "That's not what I meant," he muttered.

"I know exactly what you meant. I know just what you think of me, Mr. Harte."

He sincerely doubted it. Did she know he thought about her a lot more than he damn well knew he ought to and that he couldn't get her green eyes or her sassy little mouth out of his mind?

"Our daughters want us to do this," she said. "I don't know what little scheme they're cooking up—and to tell you the truth, I'm not sure I want to know—but it seems to be important to Dylan, and that's enough for me. Let me know what you decide."

She closed the door, barely missing his fingers, then shoved the truck into gear and spun out of the parking lot, leaving him in a cloud of exhaust.

Chapter 2

Matt drove his pickup under the arch proclaiming Diamond Harte Ranch—Choice Simmentals and Quarter Horses with a carved version of the brand that had belonged to the Harte family for four generations.

He paused for just a moment like he always did to savor the view before him. The rolling, sage-covered hills, the neat row of fence line stretching out as far as the eye could see, the barns and outbuildings with their vivid red paint contrasting so boldly with the snow.

And standing guard over it all at the end of the long gravel drive was the weathered log and stone house his grandfather had built—with the sprawling addition he had helped his father construct the year he turned twelve.

Home.

He loved it fiercely, from the birthing sheds to the maze of pens to the row of Douglas fir lining the drive.

He knew every single inch of its twenty thousand acres, as well as the names and bloodlines of each of the three dozen cutting horses on the ranch and the medical history of all six hundred of the ranch's cattle.

Maybe he loved it too much. Reverend Whitaker's sermon last week had been a fiery diatribe on the sin of excess pride, the warning in Proverbs about how pride goeth before destruction.

Matt had squirmed in the hard pew for a minute, then decided the Lord would forgive him for it, especially if He could look down through the clouds and see the Diamond Harte like Matt saw it. As close to heaven as any place else on earth.

Besides, didn't the Bible also say the sleep of a laboring man was sweet? His father's favorite scripture had been in Genesis, something about how a man should eat bread only by the sweat of his face.

Well, he'd worked plenty hard for the Diamond Harte. He'd poured every last ounce of his sweat into the ranch since he was twenty-two years old, into taking the legacy his parents had left their three children so suddenly and prematurely and building it into the powerful ranch it had become.

He had given up everything for the ranch. All his time and energy. The college degree in ag economy he was sixteen credits away from earning when his parents had died in that rollover accident. Even his wife, who had hated the ranch with a passion and had begged him to leave every day of their miserable marriage.

Melanie. The woman he had loved with a quicksilver passion that had turned just as quickly to bitter, ferocious hate. His wife, who had cheated on him and lied to him and eventually left him when Lucy wasn't even three months old.

She'd been a city girl, too, fascinated by silly, romantic dreams of the West. The reality of living on a ranch wasn't romantic at all, as Melanie had discovered all too soon. It was hard work and merciless weather. Cattle that didn't always smell so great, a cash flow that was never dependable. Flies in the summer and snowstorms in the winter that could trap you for days.

Melanie had never even made an effort to belong. She had been lost. He could see that now. Bitterly unhappy and desperate for something she could never find.

She thought he should have sold the ranch, pocketed the five or six million it was probably worth and taken her somewhere a whole lot more glitzy than Salt River, Wyoming. And when he refused to give in to her constant pleading, she had made his life hell.

What was this thing he had for women who didn't belong out here? He thought of his fascination with the California vet. It wasn't attraction. He refused to call it attraction. She was just different from what he was used to, that's all. Annoying, opinionated, argumentative. That's the only reason his pulse rate jumped whenever she was around.

A particularly strong gust of wind blew out of the canyon suddenly, rattling the pickup. He sent a quick look at the digital clock on the sleek dashboard, grateful for the distraction from thoughts of a woman he had no business thinking about.

Almost six. Cassie would have dinner on soon, and then he would get to spend the rest of the night trying to keep his stock warm. He eased his foot off the brake and quickly drove the rest of the way to the house, parking in his usual spot next to his sister's Cherokee.

Inside, the big house was toasty, welcoming. His stomach growled and his mouth watered at the delectable smells coming from the kitchen—mashed potatoes and Cassie's amazing meat loaf, if he wasn't mistaken. He hung his hat on the row of pegs by the door, then made his way to the kitchen. He found his baby sister stirring gravy in a pan on the wide professional stove she'd insisted he install last year.

She looked up at his entrance and gave him a quick smile. "Dinner's almost ready."

"Smells good." He stood watching her for a moment, familiar guilt curling in his gut. She ought to be in her own house, making dinner for her own husband and a whole kitchen full of rug rats, instead of wasting her life away taking care of him and Lucy.

If it hadn't been for the disastrous choices he made with Melanie, that's exactly where she would have been.

It wasn't a new thought. He'd had plenty of chances in the last ten years to wish things could be different, to regret that he had become so blasted dependent on everything Cassie did for them after Melanie ran off.

She ought to go to college—or at least to cooking school somewhere, since she loved it so much. But every time they talked about it, about her plans for the future, she insisted she was exactly where she wanted to be, doing exactly what she wanted to be doing.

How could he convince her otherwise when he still wasn't completely sure he could handle things on his own? He didn't know how he could do a proper job of raising Lucy by himself and handle the demands of the ranch at the same time.

Maybe if Jesse was around more, things might be different. He could have given his younger brother some of the responsibilities of the ranch, leaving more time to take care of things on the home front. But Jess had never been content on the Diamond Harte. He had other dreams, of catching the bad guys and saving the world, and Matt couldn't begrudge him those.

"Where's Lucy?" he asked.

"Up in her room fretting, I imagine. She's been a basket case waiting for you to get back from the school. She broke two glasses while she was setting the table, and spent more time looking out the window for your truck than she did on her math homework."

"She ought to be nervous," he growled, grateful for the renewed aggravation that was strong enough to push the guilt aside.

Cassie glanced up at his tone. "Uh-oh. That bad? What did she do?"

"You wouldn't believe it if I told you," he muttered and headed toward the stairs. "Give me five minutes to talk to her, and then we'll be down."

He knocked swiftly on her door and heard a muffled, "Come in." Inside, he found his daughter sitting on her bed, gnawing her bottom lip so hard it looked like she had chewed away every last drop of blood.

Through that curtain of long, dark hair, he saw that her eyes were wide and nervous. As they damn well ought to be after the little stunt she pulled. He let her stew in it for a minute.

"Hey, squirt."

"Hi," she whispered. With hands that trembled just a little, she picked up Sigmund, the chubby calico cat she'd raised from a kitten, and plopped him in her lap.

"So I just got back from talking with Miz McKenzie."

Lucy peered at him between the cat's ears. She cleared her throat. "Um, what did she say?"

"I think you know exactly what she said, don't you?"

She nodded, the big gray eyes she'd inherited from her mother wide with apprehension. As usual, he hoped to heaven that was the only thing Melanie had passed on to their daughter.

"You want to tell me what this is all about?"

She appeared to think it over, then shook her head

swiftly. He bit his cheek to keep a rueful grin from creeping out at that particular piece of honesty. "Tough. Tell me anyway."

"I don't know."

"Come on, Luce. What were you thinking, to sign me up for this Valentine's carnival without at least talking to me first?"

"It was Dylan's idea," Lucy mumbled.

Big surprise there. Dylan Webster was a miniature version of her wacky mother. "Why?"

"She thought you'd be good at it, since you're so important around here and can get people to do whatever you want. At least that's what her mom says."

He could picture Ellie Webster saying exactly that, with her pert little nose turned up in the air.

"And," Lucy added, the tension easing from her shoulders a little as she stroked the purring cat, "we both thought it would be fun. You know, planning the carnival and stuff. You and me and Dylan and her mom, doing it all together. A bonding thing."

A *bonding thing?* The last thing he needed to do was *bond* with Ellie Webster, under any circumstances.

"What do you know about bonding? Don't tell me that's something they teach you in school."

Lucy shrugged. "Dylan says we're in our formative preteen years and need positive parental influence now more than ever. She thought this would be a good opportunity for us to develop some leadership skills."

Great. Now Ellie Webster's kid had his daughter spouting psychobabble. He blew out a breath. "What about you?"

She blinked at him. "Me?"

"You're pretty knowledgeable about Dylan's views, but what about your own? Why did you go along with it?"

Lucy suddenly seemed extremely interested in a little spot on the cat's fur. "I don't know," she mumbled.

"Come on. You can do better than that."

She chewed her lip again, then looked at the cat. "We never do anything together."

He rocked back on his heels, baffled by her. "What are you talking about? We do plenty of things together. Just last Saturday you spent the whole day with me in Idaho Falls."

She rolled her eyes. "Shopping for a new truck. Big whoop. I thought it would be fun to do something completely different together. Something that doesn't have to do with the ranch or with cattle or horses." She paused, then added in a quiet voice, "Something just for me."

Ah, more guilt. Just what he needed. The kid wasn't even ten years old and she was already an expert at it. He sighed. Did females come out of the box with some built-in guilt mechanism they could turn off and on at will?

The hell of it was, she was absolutely right, and he knew it. He didn't spend nearly enough time with her. He tried, he really did, but between the horses and the cattle, his time seemed to be in as short supply as sunshine in January.

His baby girl was growing up. He could see it every day. Used to be a day spent with him would be enough for her no matter what they did together. Even if it was only shopping for a new truck. Now she wanted more, and he wasn't sure he knew how to provide it.

"Wouldn't it have been easier to tell me all this *before* you signed me up? Then we could have at least talked it over without me getting such a shock like this."

She fidgeted with Sigmund, who finally must have grown tired of being messed with. He let out an offended mewl of protest and rolled away from her, then leaped from the bed gracefully and stalked out the door.

Lucy watched until his tail disappeared down the end of the hall before she answered him in that same low, ashamed voice. "Dylan said you'd both say no if we asked. We thought it might be harder for you to back out if Ms. McKenzie thought you'd already agreed to it."

"That wasn't very fair, to me or to Dr. Webster, was it?" He tried to come up with an analogy that might make sense to her. "How would you like it if I signed you up to show one of the horses in the 4-H competition without talking to you first?"

She shuddered, as he knew she would. Her shyness made her uncomfortable being the center of attention, so she had always avoided the limelight, even when she was little. In that respect, Miz McKenzie was right—Dylan Webster had been good for her and had brought her out of her shell, at least a little.

"I wouldn't like it at all."

"And I don't like what you did any better. I ought to just back out of this whole crazy thing right now."

"Oh, Dad, you *can't!*" she wailed. "You'll ruin *everything.*"

He studied her distress for several seconds, then sighed. He loved his daughter fiercely. She was the biggest joy in his life, more important than a hundred ranches. If she felt like she came in second to the Diamond Harte, he obviously wasn't trying hard enough.

Lucy finally broke the silence. "Are you really, really, really mad at me?" she asked in a small voice.

"Maybe just one really." He gave her a lopsided smile. "But don't worry. I'll get you back. You'll be sorry you ever heard of this carnival by the time I get through with you."

Her eyes went wide again, this time with excitement. "Does that mean you'll do it?"

"I guess. I think we're both going to be sorry."

But he couldn't have too many regrets, at least not right now. Not when his daughter jumped from her bed with a squeal and threw her arms tightly around his waist.

"Oh, thank you, Daddy. Thank you, thank you, thank you. You're the best."

For that moment, at least, he felt like it.

"No way is Matthew Harte going to go through with it. Mark my words, if you agree to do this, you're going to be stuck planning the whole carnival by yourself."

In the middle of sorting through the day's allotment of depressing mail, Ellie grimaced at SueAnn Clayton, her assistant. She had really come to hate that phrase. *Mark my words, you're not cut out to be a large animal vet. Mark my words, you're going to regret leaving California. Mark my words, you won't last six months in Wyoming.*

Just once, she wished everybody would keep their words—and unsolicited advice—to themselves.

In this case, though, she was very much afraid SueAnn was right. There was about as much likelihood of Matt Harte helping her plan the carnival as there was that he'd be the next one walking through the door with a couple of his prize cutting horses for her to treat.

She sighed and set the stack of bills on SueAnn's desk. "If he chickens out, I'll find somebody else to help me." She grinned at her friend. "You, for instance."

SueAnn made a rude noise. "Forget it. I chaired the Halloween Howl committee three years in a row and was PTA president twice. I've more than done my share for Salt River Elementary."

"Come on, SueAnn," she teased. "Are you forgetting who pays your salary?"

The other woman rolled her eyes. "You pay me to take your phone calls, to send out your bill reminders and to hold down the occasional unlucky animal while you give him a shot. Last I checked, planning a Valentine's Day carnival is nowhere in my job description."

"We could always change your job description. How about while we're at it, we'll include mucking out the stalls?"

"You're not going to blackmail me. That's what you pay Dylan the big bucks for. Speaking of the little rascal, how did you punish her, anyway? Ground her to her room for the rest of the month?"

That's what she should have done. It was no less than Dylan deserved for lying to her teacher. But she'd chosen a more fitting punishment. "She's grounded from playing with Lucy after school for the rest of the week *and* she has to finish reading all of *Little Women* and I'm going to make sure she does a lot of the work of this carnival, since it was her great idea."

"The carnival she ought to be okay with, but which is she going to hate more, reading the book or not playing with her other half?"

"Doesn't matter. She has to face the music."

SueAnn laughed, and Ellie smiled back. What would she have done without the other woman to keep her grounded and sane these last few months? She shuddered just thinking about it.

She winced whenever she remembered how tempted she'd been to fire her that first week. SueAnn was competent enough—eerily so, sometimes—but she also didn't have the first clue how to mind her own business. Ellie had really struggled with it at first. Coming from California where avoiding eye contact when at all possible could sometimes be a matter of survival, dealing with a terminal busybody for an assistant had been wearing.

She was thirty-two years old and wasn't used to being mothered. Even when she'd *had* a mother, she hadn't had much practice at it. And she had been completely baffled by how to handle SueAnn, who made it a point to have her favorite grind of coffee waiting very morning, who tried to set her up with every single guy in town between the ages of eighteen and sixty, and who brought in Tupperware containers several times a week brimming with homemade soups and casseroles and mouthwatering desserts.

Now that she'd had a little practice, she couldn't believe she had been so fortunate to find not only the best assistant she could ask for but also a wonderful friend.

"What's on the agenda this morning?" Ellie asked.

"You're not going to believe this, but you actually have two patients waiting."

"What, are we going for some kind of record?"

SueAnn snickered and held two charts out with a flourish. "In exam room one, we have Sasha, Mary Lou McGilvery's husky."

"What's wrong with her?"

"Him. Sasha, oddly enough, is a him. He's scratching like crazy, and Mary Lou is afraid he has fleas."

"Highly doubtful around here, especially this time of year. It's too cold."

"That's what I tried to tell her. She's convinced that you need to take a look at him, though."

Dogs weren't exactly her specialty, since she was a large animal veterinarian, but she knew enough about them to deal with a skin condition. She nodded to SueAnn. "And patient number two?"

Her assistant cleared her throat ominously. "Cleo."

"Cleo?"

"Jeb Thacker's Nubian goat. She has a bit of a personality disorder."

"What does that mean?"

"Well, let's put it this way. Ben used to say that if she'd been human, she'd have been sent to death row a long time ago."

Ellie grinned, picturing the old codger who had sold her the practice saying exactly that. Ben Nichols was a real character. They had formed an instant friendship the first time they met at a conference several years ago. It was that same bond that had prompted him to make all her dreams come true by offering her his practice at a bargain basement price when he decided to retire, to her shock and delight. He and his wife were now thoroughly enjoying retirement in Arizona.

"What's Cleo in for?"

"Jeb didn't know, precisely. The poor man 'bout had a panic attack right there when I tried to get him to specify on the paperwork. Blushed brighter than one of his tomatoes and said he thought it was some kind of female trouble."

A homicidal goat with female trouble. And here she thought she was in for another slow morning. "Where's Jeb?"

"He had to go into Afton to the hardware store. Said he'd be back later to pick her up."

"In that case, let's take care of the dog first since Mary Lou's waiting," she decided. She could save the worst for last.

It only took a few moments for her to diagnose that Sasha had a bad case of psoriasis. She gave Mary Lou a bottle of medicated shampoo she thought would do the trick, ordered her to wash his bedding frequently and scheduled a checkup in six months.

That done, she put on her coat and braved the cold, walking to the pens behind the clinic to deal with the cantankerous goat. Cleo looked docile enough. The brown-and-white goat was standing in one of the smaller pens gnawing the top rail on the fence.

Ellie stood near the fence and spoke softly to her for a moment, trying to earn the animal's trust. Cleo turned and gave her what Ellie could swear was a look of sheer disdain out of big, long-fringed brown eyes, then turned back to the rail.

Slowly, cautiously, she entered the pen and approached the goat, still crooning softly to her. When she was still several feet away, she stopped for a cursory look. Although she would need to do a physical exam to be certain, she thought she could see the problem—one of Cleo's udders looked engorged and red. She probably had mastitis.

Since Cleo wasn't paying her any mind, Ellie inched closer. "You're a sweet girl, aren't you?" she murmured. "Everybody's wrong about you." She reached a hand to touch the animal, but before her hand could connect, Cleo whirled like a bronco with a burr under her saddle. Ellie didn't have time to move away before the goat butted her in the stomach with enough force to knock her on her rear end, right into a puddle of what she fervently hoped was water.

With a ma-aaa of amusement, the goat turned back to the fence rail.

"Didn't anybody warn you about Cleo?" a deep male voice asked.

Just what she needed, a witness to her humiliation. From her ignominious position on the ground, she took a moment to force air into her lungs. When she could breathe again, she glanced toward the direction of the voice. Her gaze landed first on a pair of well-worn boots just outside the fence, then traveled up a mile-long length of blue jeans to a tooled silver buckle with the swirled insignia of the NCHA—National Cutting Horse Association.

She knew that buckle.

She'd seen it a day earlier on none other than the lean hips of her nemesis. Sure enough. Matt Harte stood there just on the other side of the pen—broad shoulders, blue eyes, wavy dark hair and all.

She closed her eyes tightly, wishing the mud would open up underneath her and suck her down. Of all the people in the world who might have been here to watch her get knocked to her butt, why did it have to be him?

Chapter 3

Matt let himself into the pen, careful to keep a safe distance between his own rear end and Jeb Thacker's notoriously lousy-tempered goat, who had retreated to the other side of the pen.

"Here, let me help you." He reached a hand down to the city vet, still sprawled in the mud.

"I can do it," she muttered. Instead of taking his hand, she climbed gingerly to her feet by herself, then surreptitiously rubbed a hand against her seat.

Matt cleared his throat. "You okay?"

"I've had better mornings, but I'll live."

"You hit the ground pretty hard. You sure nothing's busted?"

"I don't think so. Just bruised. Especially my pride," she said wryly. She paused for a minute, then smiled reluctantly. "I imagine it looked pretty funny watching me get tackled by a goat."

She must not take herself too seriously if she could laugh about what had just happened. He found himself liking her for it. He gazed at her, at the way her red hair had slipped from its braid thingy and the little smudge of dirt on her cheek. Her eyes sparkled with laughter, and she was just about the prettiest thing he'd seen in a long time.

When he said nothing, a blush spread over her cheeks and she reached a hand to tuck her stray hair back. "Did you need something, Mr. Harte?"

He was staring at her, he realized, like some hayseed who'd never seen a pretty girl before. He flushed, astounded at himself, at this completely unexpected surge of attraction. "You might as well call me Matt, especially since it looks like we'll be working on this stupid school thing together."

Her big green eyes that always made him think of new aspen leaves just uncurling in springtime widened even more. "You're going to do it?"

"I said so, didn't I?" he muttered.

She grinned. "And you sound so enthusiastic about it."

"You want enthusiasm, you'll have to find somebody else to help you."

"What made you change your mind?"

He didn't know how to answer that, and besides, it wasn't any of her business. He said he'd do it, didn't he? What more did she need? But somehow the sharp retort he started to make changed into something else.

"Miz McKenzie's right," he finally said. "Lucy's done better in school this year than she ever has. She never would have wanted to organize something like this last year. I don't want to ruin the improvement she's made. Besides, she usually doesn't ask for much. It's a small price to pay if it's going to make her happy."

Ellie Webster cocked her head and looked at him like she'd just encountered a kind of animal she'd never seen before.

"What?" he asked, annoyed at himself for feeling so defensive.

"Nothing. You're just full of surprises, Mr. Harte."

"Matt," he muttered. "I said you should call me Matt."

"Matt." She smiled suddenly, the most genuine smile she'd ever given him. He stared at it, at her, feeling like he'd just spent a few hours out in the hard sun without his hat.

"Is that why you stopped?" she asked. "To tell me you decided to help with the carnival?"

He shrugged and ordered his heartbeat to behave itself. "I had to drop by the post office next door anyway. I thought maybe if you had a second this morning, we could get a cup of coffee over at the diner and come up with a game plan. At least figure out where to start."

Again, she looked surprised, but she nodded. "That's a good idea. But if you're just looking for coffee, SueAnn makes the best cup this side of the Rockies. We can talk in my office."

"That would be fine. I've already had breakfast. You, ah, need to get cleaned up or anything?"

She glanced down at her muddy jeans, then at the goat with a grimace. "Can you wait ten minutes? Since I'm already muddy, I might as well take a look at Cleo now."

He thought of the million-and-one things he had to do at the ranch after he ran to the parts store in Idaho Falls—the buyers he had coming in later in the afternoon, the three horses waiting for the farrier, the inevitable paperwork always confronting him.

He should just take a rain check, but for some reason that completely baffled him, he nodded. "Sure, I can wait." His next question surprised him even more. "Need me to give you a hand?"

She smiled again, that sweet, friendly smile. "That would be great. I'm afraid Cleo isn't too crazy about her visit to the vet."

The next fifteen minutes were a real education. With

his help, Ellie miraculously finessed the ornery goat into holding still long enough for an exam. She murmured soft words—nonsense, really—while her hands moved gently and carefully over the now docile goat.

"Okay, you can let go now," she finally said. He obeyed, and the goat ambled away from them.

"What's the verdict?" he asked.

She looked up from scribbling some notes on a chart. "Just as I suspected. Mastitis. She has a plugged milk duct. I'll run a culture to be sure, but I think a round of antibiotics ought to take care of her."

"Just like a cow, huh?"

"Just like. Same plumbing involved."

"Cleo's a hell of a lot uglier than any of my ladies."

She grinned at him again. "Beauty's in the eye of the beholder, Harte. I imagine Jeb Thacker wouldn't agree. Anyway, thanks for your help."

She led the way inside the small building where she worked. While she went in the back to change her clothes, he shot the breeze with SueAnn, who went to high school with him and whose husband ran the local nursery in town.

In a surprisingly short time, Ellie returned wearing a pair of surgical scrubs. He figured she probably was supposed to look cool and professional in the scrubs, but instead they made her look not much older than one of Lucy's friends on her way to a sleepover, especially with her auburn hair pulled back in that ponytail.

"Sorry to keep you waiting," she said, sounding a little out of breath.

"No problem."

SueAnn hopped up and poured a cup of coffee for Ellie. "Here you go, sugar."

"Thanks. We'll be in my office if you need me."

"Take your time."

Matt didn't miss the not-so-subtle wink SueAnn sent the vet or the quick frown Ellie volleyed back. Before he could analyze the currents going on here, she walked into a cluttered office with books and papers everywhere. Dominating one wall was a window framing a beautiful view of the Salt River mountain range that gave the town its name. On the other was a big print of a horse—a Tennessee walker, if he wasn't mistaken—running across a field of wildflowers, all grace and power and beauty.

"Thanks again for helping me with Cleo," Ellie said as soon as he was seated.

"No problem. It was interesting to see you working on her."

She raised an eyebrow. "Interesting in what way?"

He shrugged. "I kept waiting for you to pull out the needles or whatever it is you use for that stuff you do."

"That stuff I do?"

There were suddenly as many icicles in her voice as he had hanging from his barn. "You know, that acupuncture stuff. You don't do that all the time, then?"

Whatever friendliness might have been in her expression faded away, and she became guarded once more. "Just when the situation calls for it."

"And this one didn't?"

Her smile was paper-thin. "See that diploma on the wall? I'm a board-certified vet with several years' experience in traditional veterinary medicine. The acupuncture stuff, as you call it, was just extra training to supplement my regular skills. I only use it as an alternative when some of the more orthodox treatments have failed or aren't appropriate."

"And when would that be?"

"A lecture on veterinary acupuncture is not the reason you stopped by, Mr. Harte."

"I'm curious about what you do."

She hesitated for a moment before answering. "Animals I treat most often are horses with performance problems, like short stepping or mysterious lameness. I've treated moon blindness successfully and also older horses with degenerative conditions like arthritis or joint disease. You'd be surprised at how effective acupuncture can be."

He didn't doubt that. He didn't want to sound too skeptical, not when they were going to have to work together for the next few months, but he thought the whole thing was a bunch of hooey. Her California crowd might buy all this New Age crap, but folks in Wyoming looked at things like this a little differently.

For a minute, he thought about keeping his mouth shut and changing the subject, but she and her kid had been good for his daughter. He didn't want to see her practice go under, since Lucy would just about wither away if Dylan moved.

He cleared his throat. "Don't take this the wrong way, Dr. Webster, but it seems to me you might be better off focusing on those more traditional things you were talking about and leave the rest of that, er, stuff back in California."

She pursed her lips together tightly. "Thank you for the advice," she said, in a tone that left him in no doubt of her real feelings. And they probably didn't include gratitude.

He should have stopped right there, but something made him push the issue harder. "Look, it's no secret around town that you've lost a lot of customers in the last few months to Steve Nichols, Ben's nephew. Hell, I've been using him myself. A lot of people don't understand why Ben sold his practice to you in the first place instead of to Steve. Anyway, I'm pretty sure you could lure some of those folks back if you didn't focus so much on the acupuncture side of things in your ads and all."

"I don't tell you how to run your ranch," she said quietly, folding her hands tightly on the desk. "So please don't tell me how to operate my practice."

He sat back in the chair, aware he sounded like an idiot. Bossy and arrogant, just like Cassie always accused him of being. "Sorry," he muttered. "It's none of my business what you do. Just thought you should know that out here we tend to prefer the things we know, the way we've always done things, the way they've been done for generations. Especially when it comes to our stock."

"Tell me about it."

"Sorry if I offended you."

She shrugged. "You're only saying to my face what I'm sure everyone else has been saying behind my back. I appreciate your frankness. Now can we talk about the carnival?"

"Uh, sure." Who would have dreamed twenty-four hours ago that he would consider a Valentine's Day carnival a safe topic of conversation?

"So I was thinking about calling it A Fair to Remember," she said. "What do you think?"

He scratched his cheek, not quite sure where she was going with this.

"From the movie. You know, Deborah Kerr, Cary Grant. Empire State Building. The one Meg Ryan bawled about in *Sleepless in Seattle*."

At his continued blank look, she shrugged. "Never mind. We can talk about it later. We have ten weeks to work out all the details."

Ten weeks working closely with Ellie Webster, with her green eyes and her wisecracks and her shampoo that smelled like lemon pie. He knew damn well the idea shouldn't appeal to him so much.

Chapter 4

"So we're agreed then," Ellie said fifteen minutes later. "Given our mutual lack of experience, we need to delegate as much as humanly possible. Our first step is to set up committees for booths, decorations, refreshments and publicity. Once we get some other willing victims, er, parents on board, we can go from there."

Matt scratched the back of his neck. "I guess. You know as much about this as I do. I just hope we can pull this off without making complete fools of ourselves. Or having the whole thing go down in history as the worst carnival ever."

He looked so completely uncomfortable at the task ahead of them that Ellie had to smile. He must love Lucy very much to be willing to put himself through it despite his obvious misgivings. Not many men she knew would be willing to take on such a project for their ten-year-old daughters, and she felt herself softening toward him even more.

"I can talk to Sarah this afternoon if you'd like and tell her we've both agreed to do it," she said.

"I'd appreciate that. I've got to run over to Idaho Falls

to pick up a part for the loader, and it might be late before I get back in." He unkinked his considerable length from the low chair and rose, fingering his hat.

He was so tall she had to crane her neck to look into those startling blue eyes. Just how did the man manage to make her little office shrink to about the size of a rabbit hutch by his presence? The awareness simmering through her didn't help matters one bit.

"Sure you're not too busy to talk to Miz McKenzie?" he asked.

"I should be able to carve out a few moments," she murmured dryly. Her appointment schedule for the rest of the day was woefully empty, as she was fairly certain he must realize.

Sure enough, he looked even more ill at ease. After a moment, he cleared his throat. "Think about what I said before, would you? About folks around here being more comfortable with what they know. Your business might pick up if you keep that in mind. You never know."

Any soft feelings she might have been harboring toward him fluttered away like migrating birds. Before she could snap at him again to mind his own business, he shoved his hat on his head and walked out of her office with that long, ground-swallowing stride.

She might be annoyed with him, but that couldn't keep her from wandering out of her office to the reception area to watch through the window as he climbed into a shiny new pickup that probably cost as much as her entire practice.

He drove out of the parking lot with deliberate care, as she was sure he did everything.

She had a sudden wild desire to know if he would kiss a woman that way. Thoroughly. Studiously. Carefully exploring every single inch of her lips with that hard mouth until he memorized each curve, each hollow. Until her knees turned to jelly and her body ached with need....

"Dreamy, isn't he?"

Ellie whirled and found SueAnn watching her, mouth twitching with amusement. She swallowed hard and fought the urge to press a hand to her suddenly trembling stomach. "I don't know what you're talking about," she lied.

SueAnn just laughed. "Right. Whatever you say. You want me to pick that tongue off the floor for you?"

She snapped said tongue firmly back into her mouth. "Don't you have some work to do?"

"Oh, watching you go weak in the knees is much more fun."

"Sorry to ruin your entertainment, but one of us *does* have some work waiting. If you need me, I'll be in my office."

"No problem. Looks like we'll see plenty of Matt Harte between now and Valentine's Day."

That's exactly what she was afraid of. She sighed and headed for her office. She had only been at her desk for a few moments when the cowbell on the door jangled suddenly. From her vantage point, she couldn't see who came in, but she could watch SueAnn's ready smile slide away and her expression chill by several degrees.

Curious as to who might have earned such a frosty glare from the woman who invented congeniality, Ellie rose and walked to the door of her office for a better look.

Steve Nichols, her main competition in town and the nephew of the vet who had sold her the practice, was just closing the door behind him.

She should have known. SueAnn had a good word to say about everybody in town except for Ben's nephew. When it came to Steve, she was as intractable as Jeb Thacker's goat.

Ellie couldn't understand her animosity. From the day

she arrived, Steve had gone out of his way to make her feel welcome in Salt River—treating her as a friend and re- spected colleague, not as a business rival who had bought his uncle's practice out from under him.

"Steve." She greeted him warmly to compensate for SueAnn's noticeable lack of enthusiasm.

His mouth twisted into a smile underneath his bushy blond mustache, then he gestured toward the parking lot. "Was that Matt Harte I just saw driving out of here?"

For no earthly reason she could figure out, she felt a blush soak her cheeks. "Er, yes."

"Is there a problem with one of his animals? Anything I should know about?"

"Oh, no. Nothing like that." She would have left it at that, but Steve continued to study her expectantly. Finally, she had to say something. "Our girls are in the same class and we're working on a school project together," she fi- nally said. "We were just discussing some of the details."

"Really? What kind of project?"

She didn't understand this strange reluctance to divulge any information—maybe she was just embarrassed—but couldn't bring herself to answer.

"They're cochairs for the annual Valentine's Day car- nival." SueAnn finally broke the silence, her voice clipped and her expression still cool.

His mouth sagged open, then a laugh gurgled out. "You've got to be kidding me. Matt Harte planning a school carnival? That's the most ridiculous thing I've ever heard. Next thing I know, you're going to tell me he's open- ing up a beauty salon in town."

Steve's reaction matched her own when she had first heard about the carnival, so why did she feel so annoyed at him for it? And so protective of a bossy, arrogant rancher who couldn't seem to keep his nose out of her business?

"He's doing it for his daughter," she said with a cool-ness to match SueAnn's. "What's so ridiculous about that?"

"It just doesn't seem like his thing. Matt's not exactly the PTA type, you know what I mean?"

She didn't want to get into this with him, so she abruptly changed the subject. "Was there something you needed, Steve?"

He shrugged, letting the matter drop. "Do I need a rea-son to stop by and visit my favorite vet?"

Behind him, SueAnn made a rude noise that she quickly camouflaged behind a cough. Ellie didn't need to phone a psychic hot line to read her mind. She was fairly sure SueAnn thought Steve's favorite vet looked back at him in the mirror each morning.

The other woman opened her mouth to say something snide along those lines, Ellie imagined. She quickly gave her a warning glare. To her relief, after a moment SueAnn clamped her lips tightly shut.

"You don't need a reason to visit, Steve. You know that." Ellie spoke quickly to head off any more trouble. "You're always welcome here. But surely you wouldn't have dropped by during the middle of your busy time of day just to chat, right?"

He sent her that boyishly charming smile of his. "You caught me. Actually, I did have an ulterior motive for drop-ping by. I'm in a bit of a bind. I ran out of brucellosis vac-cine this morning and I'm scheduled to inoculate the herd at Paul Blanchard's ranch in an hour."

Paul Blanchard! He was another of her regular clients, one of the few who had stayed with the clinic after she took over from Ben. Ellie's heart sank. Another deserter. They were dropping like flies.

SueAnn sent her a speaking glance, but before she could answer, Steve went on. "I've ordered a rush job on more but it won't be here until tomorrow. You wouldn't happen to have a few doses to tide me over until the shipment arrives, would you?"

"You want me to loan you some of my brucellosis vaccine for Paul Blanchard's stock?"

Steve seemed completely oblivious to the sheer audacity of asking a favor for an account he had just appropriated. He gave her a pleading smile. "If it's not too much of a bother. You won't need any before tomorrow, will you?"

She might have, if she had been the one treating Blanchard cattle. As it was, it looked as if she would have vaccine to spare. She ground her teeth in frustration. Her first instinct was to say no, absolutely not. He could find his own damn vaccine. But in her heart she knew it wasn't really Steve's fault her practice was struggling.

She also couldn't blame him for setting up his own competing clinic after Ben unexpectedly sold this one to her. If their roles had been reversed and she'd been the one left out in the cold by a relative, she would have done exactly the same thing. And probably wouldn't have treated the usurper with nearly the kindness Steve had shown her.

She forced a smile. "I'll go check my supply."

Trying hard not to mutter to herself, she pushed through the swinging doors that separated the front office and waiting room from the treatment area.

The refrigerator in the back was well-stocked, and she found a case immediately. For one moment, she debated telling him she couldn't find any but she knew that was petty and small-minded so she picked it up and shouldered her way through the swinging doors again.

Steve wasn't where she left him by the front desk, and she lifted a curious eyebrow at SueAnn, who scowled and jerked her head toward Ellie's office. Steve was sitting behind her desk, browsing through her planner where she meticulously recorded appointments and scheduled treatments.

With great effort, she swallowed her irritation. "Here you go," she said loudly. His gaze flew to hers, and he didn't seem at all embarrassed to be caught nosing around in her office.

"Thanks, Ellie. I really appreciate this." His mustache twitched again with his smile.

"Glad to help," she lied, and was immediately ashamed of herself for the ugly knot of resentment curdling in her stomach. "Read anything interesting in there?" she asked pointedly.

"Sorry. Professional curiosity. You don't mind, do you? I'm intrigued by the improvement you've noted here in that thoroughbred of Jack Martin's. I thought nothing would cure her. She's a beauty of a horse, and it would have been a real shame to have to put her down, but I thought she would always be lame."

"She's responded well to a combination of treatments. Jack and I are both pleased."

"So are things picking up?"

Not with you stealing my clients one by one, she thought. "Actually, it's been a pretty busy day."

"Have you given any more thought to my offer?"

She blew out a breath. She absolutely did not want to go into this with him today. "I have. The answer is still no, Steve. Just like it's been for the last month."

He rose from the chair and walked around to the other side of the desk. "Come on, Ellie. Think about it. If we combined our practices, we could each save tens of thousands a year on overhead. And pooling our workload would ease the burden on each of us."

What burden? She would kill for a little workload to complain about. Ellie sighed. His offer made common sense and, heaven knows, would help boost her meager income, but it also held about as much appeal to her as being knocked on her rear end by a hundred goats.

She didn't want to be partners, not with Steve or with anyone else. She wanted to stand on her own, to make her own decisions and be responsible for the consequences.

She had spent her entire adult life working for others, from volunteering in clinics while she was still in high school to the last seven years working for an equine vet in Monterey.

She was tired of it, of having to play by others' rules. Constantly having someone else tell her what animals she could treat and how she should treat them had been draining the life out of her, stealing all her satisfaction and joy in the career she loved.

It went deeper than that, though. If she were honest, her ferocious need for independence had probably been rooted in her childhood, watching her mother drink herself to an early grave because of a man and then being shuttled here and there in the foster care system.

She learned early she would never be able to please the endless parade of busybody social workers and foster parents who marched through her life. She couldn't please them, and she couldn't depend on them. Too often, the moment she began to care for a family, she was capriciously yanked out and sent to another one. Eventually, she learned not to care, to carefully construct a hard shell around her heart. The only one she could truly count on was herself.

This was her chance. Hers and Dylan's. The opportunity to build the life she had dreamed of since those early days cleaning cages.

She wasn't ready to give up that dream, patients or none.

Besides that, she had SueAnn to consider. With the animosity between the two, she and Steve would never be able to work together, and she didn't want to lose her as a friend or as an assistant.

"I'm not going to change my mind, Steve," she finally said. "It's a good offer and I appreciate it, really I do, but I'm just not interested right now."

If Dylan had given her that same look, Ellie would have called it a pout. After only a moment of sulking, Steve's expression became amiable again. "I'll keep working on you. Eventually I'll wear you down, just watch."

He picked up the case of vaccine and headed for the door. "Thanks again for the loan. I'll drop my shipment off tomorrow, if that's all right with you."

"That would be fine," she said.

At the door he paused and looked at her with a grin. "And have fun working with Matt Harte. The man can be tough as a sow's snout, but he's a damn hard worker. He's single-handedly built the Diamond Harte into a force to be reckoned with around here. I'm not sure that will help when it comes to planning a school carnival, but it ought to make things interesting."

Interesting. She had a feeling the word would be a vast understatement.

He was hiding out, no denying it.

Like a desperado trying frantically to stay two steps ahead of a hangin' party and a noose with his name on it.

A week after visiting Ellie at her clinic, Matt sat trapped in his office at the ranch house, trying to concentrate on the whir and click of the computer in front of him instead of the soft murmur of women's voices coming from the kitchen at the end of the hall.

As usual, he had a hundred and one better things to occupy his time than sit here gazing at a blasted screen, but he didn't dare leave the sanctuary of his office.

She was out there.

Ellie Webster. The city vet who had sneaked her way into his dreams for a week, with that fiery hair and her silvery-green eyes and that determined little chin.

He thought she was only driving out to the Diamond Harte to drop her kid off for a sleepover with Lucy. She was supposed to be here ten minutes, tops, and wouldn't even have to know he was in here.

Things didn't go according to plan. He had a feeling they rarely would, where Ellie Webster was concerned. Instead of driving away like she should have done, she had apparently plopped down on one of the straight-backed kitchen chairs, and now he could hear her and Cassie talking and laughing like they'd been best friends for life.

They'd been at it for the last half hour, and he'd just about had enough.

He wasn't getting a damn thing done. Every time he tried to focus on getting the hang of the new livestock-tracking software, her voice would creep under the door like a sultry, devious wisp of smoke, and his concentration would be shot all to hell and back.

Why did it bug him so much to have her invading his space with that low laugh of hers? He felt itchy and bothered having her here, like a mustang with a tail full of cockleburs.

It wasn't right. He would have to get a handle on this awareness if he was going to be able to work on the school thing with her for the next few months. As to how, he didn't have the first idea. It had been a long time since he'd been so tangled up over a woman.

Maybe he should ask her out.

The idea scared him worse than kicking a mountain lion. He wasn't much of a lady's man. Maybe he used to be when he was younger—he'd enjoyed his share of buckle bunnies when he rodeoed in college, he wouldn't deny it—but things had changed after Melanie.

He had tried to date a few times after he was finally granted a divorce in absentia after her desertion, but every attempt left him feeling restless and awkward.

After a while he just quit trying, figuring it was better to wake up lonely in his own bed than in a stranger's.

He wasn't lonely, he corrected the thought quickly. He had Lucy and Jess and Cassidy and the ranch hands. He sure as hell didn't need another woman messing things up.

He cleared his throat. The action made him realize how thirsty he was. Parched, like he'd been riding through a desert for days.

The kitchen had water. Plenty of it, cold, pure mountain spring water right out of the tap. He could walk right in there and pour himself a big glass and nobody could do a damn thing about it.

Except then he'd have to face *her*.

He heaved a sigh and turned to the computer until the next wisp of laughter curled under the door.

That was it. He was going in. He shoved back from the desk and headed toward the door. He lived here, dammit. A man ought to be able to walk into his own kitchen for a drink if it suited him. She had no right to come into his house and tangle him up like this.

No right whatsoever.

Chapter 5

As soon as he walked into the big, warm kitchen, he regretted it.

He felt like the big, bad wolf walking in on a coop full of chickens. All four of them—Ellie, Cass and both of the girls—looked up, their cutoff laughter hanging in the air along with the sweet, intoxicating smell of chocolate chip cookies baking in the oven.

"Sorry. Didn't mean to interrupt," he muttered. "I, uh, just needed a drink of water and then I'll get out of your way."

"You didn't interrupt," Cassie said. "Sit down. The cookies will be done in a minute, and I know how much you love eating them right out of the oven."

Information his baby sister didn't need to be sharing with the whole damn world, thank you very much. Made him sound like a seven-year-old boy snitching goodies after school. "I've got things to do," he muttered.

"They can wait five minutes, can't they?"

His jaw worked as he tried to come up with a decent-sounding excuse to escape without seeming rude. How was a man supposed to think straight when he had four females watching him so expectantly?

Finally, he muttered a curse under his breath and pulled out a chair. "Just five minutes, though."

Like a tractor with a couple bad cylinders, the conversation limped along for a moment, and he squirmed on the hard chair, wishing he were absolutely anywhere but here. He was just about to jump up and rush back to the relative safety of his office—excuse or none—when Lucy ambushed him.

She touched his arm with green-painted fingernails—now where did she get those? he wondered—and gazed at him out of those big gray eyes. "Daddy, Dylan and her mom aren't going anywhere for Thanksgiving dinner since they don't have any family around here. Isn't that sad?"

Keeping his gaze firmly averted from Ellie's, he made a noncommittal sound.

"Do you think they might be able to come here and share our family's dinner?"

Despite his best efforts, his gaze slid toward Ellie just in time to catch her mouth drop and her eyes go wide— with what, he couldn't say for sure, but it sure looked like she was as horrified as he was by the very idea.

"I don't know, honey—" he began.

"That's a great idea," Cassie said at the same time. "There's always room at the table for a few more, and plenty of food."

"Oh, no. That's okay," Ellie said quickly. "We'll be fine, won't we, Dylan?"

Dylan put on a pleading expression. "Come on, Mom. It would be so cool. Lucy's aunt Cassie is a great cook. I bet she never burns the stuffing like you do."

Ellie made a face at her daughter, and Matt had to fight

a chuckle. And he thought *Cass and Lucy* were bad at spilling family secrets.

"Be that as it may," Ellie said, her cheeks tinged slightly pink, "I'm sure the Hartes have a lovely family dinner planned. They don't need to be saddled with two more."

"It's no problem," Cassie said. "We'd love to have you come. Wouldn't we, Matt?"

He cleared his throat. Again, he couldn't seem to make his brain work fast enough to come up with an excuse. "Uh, sure."

Ellie raised an eyebrow at his less-than-enthusiastic response. He obviously didn't want to invite her for Thanksgiving any more than she wanted to accept.

"Good. It's settled," Cassie said, oblivious to their objections. "It's usually really casual. Just family— Matt, Lucy, our brother Jess and whichever of the ranch hands stick around for the holidays. We eat around two but you're welcome to come out any time before then, especially if you're into watching football with the guys."

What she knew about football would fit into a salt-shaker. Ellie sighed heavily. And what she knew about big rowdy Thanksgiving family dinners wouldn't even fit on a grain of salt.

It looked like she was going to be stuck with both things. So much for her good intentions about having as little as possible to do with the man who somehow managed to jumble up her insides every time she was around him.

What choice did she have, though? She didn't want to hurt his daughter or sister's feelings by refusing the invitation. Lucy was a dear, sweet and quiet and polite. Exactly Dylan's opposite! It was a wonder they were friends, but somehow the two of them meshed perfectly. They brought out the best in each other.

To her surprise, she and Cassie had also immediately hit it off. Unlike Matt, his sister was bubbly and friendly and went out of her way to make her feel welcomed.

She would sound churlish and rude if she refused to share their holiday simply because the alpha male in the family made her as edgy as a hen on a hot griddle and sent her hormones whirling around like a Texas dust storm.

"Can I bring something?" she finally asked, trying to accept the invitation as gracefully as she could manage.

"Do you have a specialty?" Cassie asked.

Did macaroni and cheese count as a specialty? She doubted it. "No. I'm afraid not."

"Sure you do, Mom." Dylan spoke up. "What about that pie you make sometimes?"

She made pecan pie exactly twice, but Dylan had never forgotten it. Hope apparently springs eternal in a nine-year-old's heart that someday she would bake it again. "I don't know if I'd call that a specialty."

"Why don't you bring it anyway?" Cassie suggested. "Or if you'd rather make something else, that would be fine."

I'd rather just stay home and have our usual quiet dinner for two, she thought. But one look at Dylan revealed her daughter was ecstatic about the invitation. Her eyes shone, and her funny little face had the same kind of expectancy it usually wore just before walking downstairs on Christmas morning.

She looked so excited that Ellie instantly was awash in guilt for all the years they had done just that—stayed home alone with their precooked turkey and instant mashed potatoes instead of accepting other invitations from friends and colleagues.

Why had she never realized her daughter had been missing a big, noisy celebration? Dylan was usually so vocal about what she wanted and thought she needed. Why had she never said anything about this?

"Whatever you want to bring is fine," Cassie assured her. "Really, though, you don't have to bring anything but yourselves. Like I said, there's always plenty of food."

"I'll bring the pecan pie," she said, hoping her reluctance didn't filter into her voice.

"Great. I usually make a pumpkin and maybe an apple so we'll have several to choose from. Knowing my brothers, I doubt any of them will last long."

She looked at Matt out of the corner of her eyes and found him watching her. What was he thinking? That she was an interloper who had suddenly barged her way in to yet another facet of his life when he had plainly made it clear she wasn't welcome? She couldn't tell by the unreadable expression in those startling blue eyes.

The timer suddenly went off on the oven.

"That would be the cookies." Cassie jumped up and opened the oven door, releasing even more of the heavenly aroma.

A smell so evocative of hearth and home that Ellie's heart broke a little for all the homemade cookies she never had time to bake for her daughter. She had shed her last tear a long time ago for all the missing cookies in her own childhood.

Cassie quickly transferred at least half a dozen of the warm, gooey treats onto a plate for Matt, then poured him a glass of milk from the industrial-size refrigerator.

She set both in front of him, and he quickly grabbed them and stood up. Ellie smiled a little at the blatant relief evident in every line of his big, rangy body.

"Thanks," he mumbled to his sister. "I'll let you ladies get back to whatever you were talking about before I interrupted you."

The girls' giggles at being called ladies trailed after him as Matt made his escape from the kitchen.

* * *

"Wow, Mom. You look really great," Dylan said for about the fifth time as they made their way up the walk to the sprawling Diamond Harte ranch house.

Ellie fought her self-consciousness. Matt's sister said Thanksgiving dinner would be casual, but she didn't think her usual winter attire of jeans and denim work shirts was quite appropriate.

Instead, she had worn her slim wool skirt over soft black leather boots and a matching dove-gray sweater—one of her few dressy outfits that only saw the light of day when she went to professional meetings. Was she hideously overdressed? She hoped not. She was nervous enough about this as it was without adding unsuitable clothes to the mix.

She shouldn't be this nervous. It was only dinner, nothing to twist her stomach into knots over or turn her mouth as dry as a riverbed in August.

She cleared her throat, angry with herself, at the knowledge that only part of her edginess had to do with sharing a meal with Matt Harte and his blue eyes and powerful shoulders.

That might be the main reason, but the rest had more to do with the holiday itself. She had too many less-than-pleasant memories of other years, other holidays. Always being the outsider, the one who didn't belong. Of spending the day trying to fit in during someone else's family celebration in foster home after foster home.

This wasn't the same. She had a family now—Dylan. All she could ever want or need. Her funny, imaginative, spunky little daughter who filled her heart with constant joy. She was now a confident, self-assured woman, content with life and her place in it.

So why did she feel like an awkward, gawky child

again, standing here on the doorstep, hoping this time the people inside would like her?

Dylan, heedless of her mother's nerves, rushed up the remaining steps and buzzed hard on the doorbell, and Ellie forced herself to focus on something other than her own angst.

She looked around her, admiring the view. In the lightly falling snow, the ranch was beautiful. Matt kept a clean, well-ordered operation, she could say that for him. The outbuildings all wore fresh paint, the fences were all in good repair, the animals looked well-cared for

Some outfits looked as cluttered as garbage dumps, with great hulking piles of rusty machinery set about like other people displayed decorative plates or thimble collections. Here on the Diamond Harte, though, she couldn't see so much as a spare part lying around.

It looked like a home, deeply loved and nurtured.

What must it have been like to grow up in such a place? To feel warm dirt and sharp blades of grass under your bare feet in the summertime and jump into big piles of raked leaves in the fall and sled down that gently sloping hill behind the barn in winter?

To know without question that you belonged just here, with people who loved you?

She pushed the thoughts away, angry at herself for dredging up things she had resolved long ago. It was only the holiday that brought everything back. That made her once more feel small and unwanted.

To her relief, the door opened before she could feel any sorrier for herself, sending out a blast of warmth and a jumble of delectable smells, as well as a small figure who launched herself at Dylan with a shriek of excitement.

"You're here! Finally!"

"We're early, aren't we?" Ellie asked anxiously. "Didn't your aunt say you were eating at two? It's only half past one."

"I don't know what time it is. I've just been *dying* for you to get here. Dylan, you have *got* to come up to my room. Uncle Jess bought me the new 'N Sync CD and it's so totally awesome."

Before Ellie could say anything else, both girls rushed up the stairs, leaving her standing in the two-story entry alone, holding her pecan pie and feeling extremely foolish.

Okay. Now what did she do? She'd been in the huge, rambling ranch house a few times before to pick up Lucy or drop off Dylan for some activity or other, but she had always entered through the back door leading straight into the kitchen. She had no idea how to get there from the front door, and it seemed extremely rude to go wandering through a strange house on her own.

She could always go back and ring the doorbell again, she supposed. But that would probably lead to awkward questions about why her daughter was already upstairs while she lingered by the door as if ready to bolt any moment.

She was still standing there, paralyzed by indecision, when she heard loud male groans at something from a room down the hall, then the game shifted to a commercial—somebody hawking razor blades.

"You want another beer?" she heard Matt's deep voice ask someone else—his brother, she presumed, or perhaps one of the ranch hands. The deep timbre of it sent those knots in her stomach unraveling to quiver like plucked fiddle strings.

Seconds later—before she could come up with a decent place to hide—he walked out in the hall wearing tan jeans and a forest-green fisherman's sweater. She was still ordering her heart to start beating again when he turned and caught sight of her standing there like an idiot.

"Doc!" he exclaimed.

"Hi," she mumbled.

"Why are you just standing out here? Come in."

She thought about explaining how the girls had abandoned her for their favorite boy band, then decided she would sound even more ridiculous if she tried. She held up the pie instead. "Where's the best place for this?"

"Probably in the kitchen. I was just heading there myself, I can show you the way. Here. Let me take your coat first."

She tensed as he came up behind her and pulled her coat from her shoulders while she transferred the pie from hand to hand. Despite her best efforts, she was intensely aware of him, his heat and strength and the leathery smell of his aftershave.

After he hung her coat in a small closet off the entry, he took off down the hall. She followed him, trying fiercely not to notice the snug fit of his jeans or those impossibly broad shoulders under the weave of his sweater. Something was different about him today. It took her a moment to figure out what. He wasn't wearing the black Stetson that seemed so much a part of him, nor was his hair flattened from it.

The dark waves looked soft and thick. They would probably be like silk under her fingers, she thought. The impulse to reach out and see for herself was so strong, she even lifted a hand a few inches from her side, then dropped it quickly in mortification.

It was much safer to look around her. This part of the house was one she hadn't seen before, but it had the same warmth of the rest of the house, with family pictures grouped together on one wall and a huge log cabin quilt in dark greens and blues hanging on the other.

As they neared the kitchen, the smells of roasting turkey and vegetables grew stronger, and her stomach gave a loud, long rumble. She pressed a hand to it, hoping no one else could hear but her.

When she looked up, though, she found Matt giving her a lopsided grin, and she flushed.

"Oh, Ellie! You made it!" Matt's sister looked pretty and flustered as she stirred something on the stove with one hand while she pulled a pan of golden dinner rolls out of the oven with the other. "When it started to snow, I was afraid you'd decide not to make the drive."

"It's not bad out there. A few flurries, that's all. Just enough to make everything look like a magic fairyland."

"Wait until you've lived here for a few years. You won't describe the snow quite so romantically. Oh, is that your famous pie? Does it need to go in the refrigerator?"

"No. I don't think so."

"Good. I'm not sure I could find room for it." Cassie blew out a breath and tucked a stray strand of hair behind her ear just as the timers on the stove and microwave went off at the same time. The frazzled look in her eyes started to border on panic.

"Uh, anything I can do to help?" Matt asked suddenly.

His sister sent him a grateful look. "Actually, there is. Can you finish chopping the raw vegetables to go with that dip you like? Oh, rats," she exclaimed suddenly. "I forgot to bring up the cranberry sauce from the store room. Ellie, would you mind stirring this gravy for me? I think most of the lumps are out of it—just make sure it doesn't burn on the bottom."

"Uh, sure."

She set her pie on the only bare patch of countertop she could find and took the wooden spoon from Cassie, who rushed from the room, leaving her and Matt alone.

He immediately went to work on the vegetables. The cutting surface was on a work island in the middle of the kitchen with only a few feet separating it from the stove, forcing them to stand side by side but facing opposite directions.

Again she felt that sizzle of awareness but she sternly tried to suppress it. They lapsed into an awkward silence while they did their appointed jobs.

"Everything smells divine," she finally said.

He seized on the topic. "Yeah, Cassidy's a great cook. I've always thought she should have her own restaurant."

"I didn't know Cassie was short for Cassidy." She paused, remembering something SueAnn had told her about the middle brother, the Salt River chief of police. "Let me get this straight, you have a brother named Jesse James and a sister named Cassidy?"

His low, rueful laugh sent the hairs on the back of her neck prickling. "Our dad was what I guess you'd call a history buff. One of his ancestors, Matt Warner, was a member of Butch Cassidy's Wild Bunch, and Dad grew up hearing stories about him handed down throughout the years. Dad was always fascinated by outlaws and lawmen of the Old West. The romanticism and the adventure and the history of it, I guess."

"So you're named after this scofflaw of an ancestor?"

"Yeah." His voice sounded rueful again. "Matthew Warner Harte. When the others came along, I guess he just decided to stick with the same theme."

A Wild West outlaw. Why didn't it surprise her that he had that blood churning through his veins? "And how did your mother handle having her own little wild bunch?"

His shrug brushed his shoulder into hers, and the subtle movement sent a shiver rippling down her spine. "My parents adored each other," he answered. "Mom probably wouldn't have complained even if Dad wanted to name us Larry, Moe and Curly."

He sent her another lopsided grin, and she was helpless to prevent herself from returning it. They gazed at each other for a moment, side by side across shoulders, both smiling. Suddenly everything seemed louder, more intense—the slurp and burble of the gravy in the pan, the chink of the knife hitting the cutting board, the slow whir of the ceiling fan overhead.

His gaze dropped to her mouth for an instant, just enough for heat to flare there as if he'd touched her, then his eyes flashed to hers once more before he turned abruptly, guiltily, back to the vegetables.

Now *that* was interesting.

She was still trying to come up with something to say in the midst of the sudden tension—not to mention trying to remind her lungs what they were there for—when their daughters burst into the kitchen in mid-giggle.

They both stopped short in the doorway when they saw their parents working side-by-side. Ellie opened her mouth to greet them but shut it again when two pairs of eyes shifted rapidly between her and Matt, then widened.

The girls looked at each other with small, secretive smiles that sent the fear of God into her. They were definitely up to something. And she was very much afraid she was beginning to suspect what it might be.

Chapter 6

"So tell us what brings a pretty California beach girl like yourself to our desolate Wyoming wilderness."

Matt sat forward so he could hear Ellie's answer across the table. If *he* had asked that question, he grumped to himself, she probably would have snapped at him to mind his own business. But it didn't seem to bother her at all that his brother wanted to nose around through her past.

Instead, she smiled at Jesse, seated to her left. "I'm afraid there weren't too many beaches around Bakersfield."

"Bakersfield? Is that where you're from?" Cassie asked.

If he hadn't been watching her so intently, Matt would have missed the way her smile slid away and the barest shadow of old pain flickered in her green eyes for just a moment before she shifted her gaze to the full plate in front of her. "Until I was seven. After that, I moved around a lot."

What happened when she was seven? He wondered. And why did she phrase it that way? *I moved around a lot,* not *My family moved around a lot?*

Before he could ask, Jesse spoke. "Even if you're not a

beach girl, you're still the best-looking thing to share our Thanksgiving dinner since I can remember."

She laughed, rolling her eyes a little at the compliment, while Matt battled a powerful urge to casually reach over and shove his brother's face into his mashed potatoes.

He didn't want to admit it bugged the hell out of him the way Jesse flirted with her all through dinner, hanging on her every word and making sure her glass was always full.

Ellie didn't seem to mind. She teased him right back, smiling and laughing at him like she'd never done with Matt.

Not that he cared. He was just worried about her getting a broken heart, that's all. Maybe somebody ought to warn her about Jesse. His little brother wasn't a bad sort. Not really. In fact, for being such a wild, out-of-control son of a gun after their parents died, Jess turned out pretty okay.

Matt would be the first one to admit the kid did a fine job protecting the good people of Salt River as the chief of police, a whole hell of a lot better than the last chief, who'd spent more time lining his own pockets than he did fighting crime.

But Jess still had a well-earned reputation with the ladies as a love 'em and leave 'em type. He rarely dated a woman longer than a few weeks, and when he did, she was usually the kind of girl their mother would have described as "faster than she ought to be."

'Course, it was none of his business if Ellie Webster wanted to make a fool of herself over a charmer like Jesse James Harte, he reminded himself.

"So what brought you out here?" the charmer in question asked her again.

"My mom always wanted to move to the mountains and be a cowgirl," Ellie's daughter offered, helping herself to more candied yams.

A delicate pink tinged the doc's cheeks. "Thanks for sharing that, sweetheart."

"What?" Dylan asked, all innocence. "That's what you said, isn't it?"

She laughed ruefully. "You're right. I did. The truth is, I've always wanted to live and work in the Rockies. I met Ben Nichols when I was giving a lecture a few years ago. Afterward, when he told me about Star Valley and his practice here, I told him how much I envied him and casually mentioned I had always dreamed of living out here. I never imagined he would offer to sell his practice to me when he retired."

So that explained what brought her to Wyoming. What interested him was why a tiny little thing like her would choose such a physically demanding job as a large-animal vet in the first place. If she wanted to be a vet, she would have been better off with little things like dogs and cats instead of having to muscle a half-ton of steer into a chute.

He didn't think she'd appreciate the question, so he asked another one. "Where were you working before?"

She shifted her gaze across the table to him as if she'd forgotten he was sitting there. "I worked at a clinic in the Monterey area. That's on the central coast of California—so I guess you were right, Jesse. Technically I suppose you could call me a beach girl, although I rarely had a chance to see it."

"I've heard that's a beautiful area," Cassie said.

"It is. Pebble Beach is just south of it, and Carmel-by-the-Sea."

"How many cattle operations did you find in the middle of all those golf courses and tourist traps?" he asked abruptly, earning a curious look from Cassie.

"Not many, although there are a few farther inland. My clients were mostly horses—thoroughbreds and jumpers and pleasure horses."

The conversation turned then to the physical differences between working horses and riding horses and then, with much prompting by Dylan, onto the best choice for a pleasure horse for a nine-year-old girl. Matt contented himself listening to the conversation and watching Ellie interact with his family.

Even after three years of marriage, Melanie had never fit in half as well. He felt vaguely guilty for the thought, but it was nothing less than the truth. She and Cassie had fought like cats and dogs from the beginning, and Jess had despised her.

So much for his grand plan to give his younger siblings more of a stable home environment by bringing home a wife.

He should have known from the first night he brought her home after their whirlwind courtship and marriage at the national stock show in Denver that he had made a disastrous mistake. She spent the entire evening bickering with Cassie and completely ignoring Jess.

But by then it was too late, they were already married. It took him three more years of the situation going from bad to worse for him to admit to himself how very stupid he had been.

He wouldn't make that mistake again.

He hated thinking about it, about what a fool he had been, so he yanked his mind off the topic. "Everything tastes great, as usual," he said instead to Cassie.

She grinned suddenly. "Remember that first year after Mom and Daddy died when you tried to cook Thanksgiving dinner?"

Jess turned his attention long enough from Ellie to shudder and add his own jab. "I remember it. My stomach still hasn't forgiven me. The turkey was tougher than roasted armadillo."

"And the yams could have been used to tar the barn roof."

He rolled his eyes as the girls giggled. Jess and Cassie

teased him mercilessly about that dinner. Usually it didn't bother him—but then again, usually he didn't have Ellie Webster sitting across from him listening to the conversation with that intrigued look in her green eyes.

"Give me a break," he muttered. "I did my best. You're lucky you got anything but cold cereal and frozen pizza."

He'd been twenty-two when their parents died in a rollover on a slippery mountain road. That first year had been the toughest time of his life. Grieving for his parents and their sudden death, trying to comfort Cassie, who had been a lost and frightened thirteen-year-old, doing his damnedest to keep Jess out of juvenile detention.

Trying to keep the ranch and the family together when he didn't know what the hell he was doing.

It had been a rough few years, but they had survived and were closer for it.

"At least we had to only go through Matt's attempts to poison us for a while." Jess grinned. "Then Cassie decided to save us all and learned to cook."

"I had no choice," she retorted. "It was a matter of survival. I figured one of us had to learn unless we wanted to die of food poisoning or starve to death. Matt was too busy with the ranch and you were too busy raising hell. That left me."

Jesse immediately bristled, gearing up for a sharp retort, and Matt gave a resigned sigh. Cassie always knew how to punch his buttons. Jesse's wild, hard-drinking days after their parents died were still a sore point with him, but that never stopped Cass from rubbing his nose in it.

Before he could step in to head trouble off, Ellie did it for him. "Well, you learned to cook very well," she assured Cassie, with an anxious look toward Jess's glare. "You'll have to give me the recipe for your stuffing. I tend to overcook it. Is that sausage I taste in there?"

She prattled on in a way that seemed completely unlike her, and it was only after she had successfully turned the conversation completely away from any trouble spots that he realized she had stepped in to play peacemaker as smoothly as if she'd been doing it all her life.

Had she done it on purpose? He wondered again about her background. She hadn't mentioned brothers or sisters, but that didn't mean she had none. What had happened when she was seven, the year after which she said she'd moved around so much?

He wanted badly to know, just as he was discovering he wanted to know everything about her.

"Come on, Ellie. It's our turn to watch football."

She looked at the dishes scattered across the table. "I can help clean up...."

"No way. The men get to do it—it's tradition. That's why I try to make the kitchen extra messy for them." She smiled sweetly at her brothers. "I think I used just about every single dish in the house."

Matt and Jesse groaned in unison. Unmoved, Cassie stood up. "Have fun, boys."

With guilt tweaking her, Ellie let Matt's sister drag her from the dining room, Dylan and Lucy following behind.

Cassie led her into a huge great room dominated by a towering river-rock fireplace. A big-screen TV and a pair of couches took up one corner, and a pool table and a couple of video games jostled for space in the other. As large as the room was, though, it was comfortable. Lived in, with warm-toned furniture and shelves full of books.

The girls immediately rushed to the pool table, and Cassidy plopped down on one of the plump, tweedy couches. "Boy, it feels good to sit down. I had to get up at four to put the turkey in, and I haven't stopped since."

"I'm sorry if I made extra work for you."

"Are you kidding? I didn't do anything I wouldn't have done anyway, and it's wonderful to have somebody else with a Y chromosome at the table besides Lucy!"

Cassie picked up the remote. "So which game do you want to watch? We have blue against red—" she flipped the channel "—or black against silver."

"I'm not crazy about football," she confessed.

The other woman sent her a conspiratorial grin. "Me, neither. I hate it, actually. When you spend your whole life around macho men, you don't really need to waste your time watching them on TV. Let's see if we can find something better until the boys come in and start growling at us to change it back."

She flipped the remote, making funny comments about every station she passed until stumbling on an old Alfred Hitchcock film with Jimmy Stewart.

"Here we go. *Rear Window.* This is what I call real entertainment. Could Grace Kelly dress or what?"

Ellie settled on the couch, the seductive warmth from the fireplace combining with the turkey put her into a pleasant haze.

She couldn't remember enjoying a meal more. The food had been delicious. And with the exception of the strange tension between her and Matt, the company had been great, too.

Their banter and teasing and memories of other holidays had been a revelation. This was what a family was all about, and if she closed her eyes, she could almost pretend she was a part of it.

One strange thing, though. For all their reminiscing, they hadn't brought up Lucy's mother one single time. It was almost as if the woman had never existed. Come to think of it, nobody had ever mentioned the mystery woman to Ellie.

"What happened to Lucy's mother?"

She didn't realize she had asked the blunt question out loud until Cassidy's relaxed smile froze, and she shot a quick glance at her niece. Ellie winced, appalled at herself. When would she ever learn to think before she opened her big mouth? At least neither of the girls was paying any attention to them, Ellie saw with relief.

"I'm so sorry," she said quickly. "That was terribly rude of me. It just slipped out. It's none of my business, really. You don't have to answer."

"No. It's just a…a raw subject." She looked at her niece again, and Ellie thought she saw guilt flicker in her blue eyes, then she flashed a bitter smile. She lowered her voice so the girls couldn't hear. "Melanie ran off with my…with one of our ranch hands. Lucy wasn't even three months old."

Ellie's jaw dropped. She tried to picture Matt in the role of abandoned husband and couldn't. Her heart twisted with sympathy when she imagined him taking care of a newborn on his own—late-night feedings, teething and all.

What kind of woman could simply abandon her own child like that? She thought of those first few months after Dylan was born, when she had been on her own and so very frightened about what the future might hold for the two of them.

Despite her fear, she had been completely in awe of the precious gift she'd been handed. Some nights she would lie awake in that grimy two-room apartment, just staring at Dylan's tiny, squishy features, listening to her breathe and wondering what she had done to deserve such a miracle.

She couldn't even comprehend a woman who would walk away from something so amazing.

Or from a man like Matt Harte.

"I'm so sorry," she said, knowing the words were terribly inadequate.

Cassidy shrugged and looked toward the girls. From the raw emotion exposed on her features like a winter-bare tree branch, Ellie had the odd suspicion there was more to the story than losing a sister-in-law.

"It was a long time ago," Cassie said quietly. "Anyway, Matt's much better off without her. He'd be the first to tell you that. Melanie hated it here. She hated the ranch, she hated Wyoming, she hated being a mother. I was amazed she stuck around as long as she did."

Why on earth would he marry a woman who hated ranch life? Ellie wondered. For a man like Matt who so obviously belonged here—on this land he loved so much—it must have been a bitter rejection seeing it scorned by the woman he married.

She must have been very beautiful for him to marry her in the first place and bring her here. Ellie didn't even want to think about why the thought depressed her so much.

Cassie quickly turned the conversation to the Hitchcock movie, but even after Ellie tried to shift her attention to the television, her mind refused to leave thoughts of Matt and the wife who had deserted him with a tiny daughter.

As much as she hated bringing up such an obviously painful topic, she had to admit she was grateful for the insight it provided into a man she was discovering she wanted to understand.

No wonder he sometimes seemed so gruff, so cold. Had he always been that way or had his wife's desertion hardened him? Had he once been like Jesse, all charm and flirtatiousness? She couldn't imagine it. Good grief, the man was devastating enough with his habitual scowl!

After a moment, Cassie turned the tables. "What about

Dylan's father?" she asked suddenly. "Is he still in the picture?"

"He was never *in* the picture. Not really," Ellie answered calmly. After so many years the scab over her heart had completely healed. "Our relationship ended when Kurt saw that plus sign on the pregnancy test."

He had been so furious at her for being stupid enough to get pregnant, as if it were entirely her fault the protection they used had failed. He could lose his job over this, he had hissed at her, that handsome, intelligent face dark with anger. Professors who impregnated their star students tended to be passed over when tenures were being tossed around. Didn't she understand what this could do to him?

It had always been about him. Always. She had only come to understand that immutable fact through the filter of time and experience. In the midst of their relationship, she had been so amazed that someone of Kurt's charisma—not to mention professional standing—would deign to take her under his wing, first as a mentor and adviser, then as a friend, then as a lover during her final year of undergraduate work.

She might have seen him more clearly had she not been seduced by the one thing she had needed so desperately those days—approbation. He had told her she had talent, that she would be a brilliant, dedicated doctor of veterinary medicine one day.

No one else had believed in her. She had fought so hard every step of the way, and he was the only one who seemed to think she could do it. She had lapped up his carefully doled-out praise like a puppy starving for attention.

She thought she had loved him passionately and had given him everything she had, while to him she had been one more in a long string of silly, awestruck students.

It was a hard lesson, but her hurt and betrayal had lasted

only until Dylan was born. As she held her child in her arms—hers alone—she realized she didn't care anymore what had led her to that moment; she was only amazed at the unconditional love she felt for her baby.

"So you raised Dylan completely on your own while you were finishing vet school?" Cassie asked.

She nodded. "I took her to class half the time because I couldn't find a sitter, but somehow we did it."

Cassie shook her head in sympathetic disgust. "Men are pigs, aren't they?" she muttered, just as Jesse entered the great room.

He plopped next to Ellie on the couch, scowling at his sister. "Hey, I resent that. Especially since it just took two of us the better part of an hour to clean up the mess *you* made in the kitchen."

"I meant that figuratively," she retorted. "When it comes to knowing what a woman needs and wants out of a relationship, most of you have about as much sense as a bucket of spit."

"Don't listen to her, Doc. My baby sister has always been far too cynical for her own good."

Jesse grabbed Ellie's hand, and for one horrified second she thought he was going to bring it to his lips. To her vast relief, he just squeezed it, looking deep into her eyes. "Not all men are pigs. I, for one, always give a woman exactly what she wants. And what she needs."

His knowing smile fell just a few inches short of a leer, and she felt hot color crawl across her cheekbones at finding herself on the receiving end of it, especially from a man as dangerously attractive as Jesse James Harte.

Before she could come up with a reply, his little sister gave an inelegant snort. "See? What did I tell you? A bucket of spit."

Ellie smiled, charmed beyond words by both of them

and their easy acceptance of her. Before she could answer, she felt the heat of someone's gaze on her. She turned around and found Matt standing in the doorway, arms crossed and shoulder propped against the jamb as he watched his brother's flirting with an unreadable look in those vivid blue eyes.

The heated blush Jesse had sparked spread even higher, until she thought her face must look as bright as the autumn leaves in his sister's centerpiece.

What was it about that single look that sent her nerves lurching and tumbling to her stomach, that affected her a thousand times more intensely than Jesse's teasing?

His daughter spotted him at almost the same time she did. "Daddy, come play with us," she demanded from the pool table.

He shifted his gaze from Ellie to the girls, his mouth twisting into a soft smile that did funny, twirly things to her insides. "I will in a bit, Lucy Goose. I have to go out and check on Mystic first, okay?"

"Mystic?" Ellie's question came out as a squeak that nobody but her seemed to notice.

"One of our mares," Matt answered.

"Mystic Mountain Moon," Lucy said. "That's her full name."

"She's pregnant with her first foal and she's tried to lose it a couple times," Matt said.

"She's a real beauty." Cassie joined in. "Moon Ranger out of Mystic Diamond Lil. One heck of a great cutting horse. Matt tried her out in a few local rodeos last summer, and she blew everybody away."

"Her foal's going to be a winner, too," Matt said. "If she can hang on to it for a few more months, anyway."

He paused and looked at Ellie again. "You, uh, wouldn't want to come out and check on her with me, would you?"

She stared at him, astonished at the awkward invitation, an offer she sensed surprised him as much as it had her. She opened her mouth to answer just as he shook his head. "I guess you're not really dressed to go mucking around in the barn. Forget it."

"No," she said quickly. "These boots are sturdier than they look. I would love to." She suddenly discovered she wanted fiercely to go with him, to see more of the Diamond Harte and his beauty of a mare.

"Let me just grab my coat." She jumped up before he could rescind the invitation. Whatever impulse had prompted him to ask her to accompany him, she sensed he was offering her more than just a visit to his barn. He was inviting her into this part of his life, lowering at least some of the walls between them.

She wasn't about to blow it.

"Okay then." He cast his eyes around the room for a moment as if trying to figure out what to do next, then his gaze stopped on his daughter, pool cue in her hand.

"We shouldn't be long," he said. "I promise I'll be back in just a little while to whup both of your behinds."

The girls barely heard him, Ellie saw, too busy sharing another one of those conspiratorial looks that were really beginning to make her nervous. "You two take your time, Dad," Lucy said in an exaggerated voice. "Really, we can use all the practice we can get."

He looked vaguely startled by her insistence, then gave her another one of those soft smiles before turning to Ellie. "I'll go get your coat."

A few moments later, he returned wearing that black Stetson and a heavy ranch jacket and holding out her coat. He helped her into it and then led the way into the snow that still fluttered down halfheartedly.

Though it was still technically afternoon, she had discovered night came early this time of year in Wyoming. The sun had already begun to sink behind the Salt River mountains, and the dying light was the same color as lilac blossoms in the spring.

Her chest ached at the loveliness of it, at the play of light on the skiff of snow and the rosy glow of his outbuildings in the twilight. There was a quiet reverence here as night descended on the mountains. As if no one else existed but the two of them and the snow and the night.

He seemed as reluctant as she to break the hushed beauty of the scene. They walked in silence toward the huge red barn a few hundred yards from the house. When he finally spoke, it was in a low voice to match the magic of the evening. "Mystic likes to be outside, even as cold as it's been. I'll check to see if she's still in the pasture before we go inside the barn. You can wait here if you want."

"No. I'll come with you," she said in that same hushed voice.

They crunched through snow to the other side, with Matt just a few steps ahead of her. She was looking at her feet so she didn't fall in the slick snow when he growled a harsh oath.

She jerked her gaze up. "What is it? What's wrong?"

He pointed to the pasture. For a moment, she couldn't figure out what had upset him, then her gaze sharpened and she saw it.

Bright red bloodstains speckled the snow in a vivid, ugly trail leading to the barn.

Chapter 7

Dread clutched at her stomach. "Do you think it was a coyote?"

"I doubt it," he said tersely. "Not this close to the house and not in the middle of the day. They tend to stay away from the horses, anyway."

"What, then?"

"Mystic, I'd guess. She's probably lost the foal. Damn."

If the mare was hemorrhaging already, it was probably too late to save the foal, and Matt obviously knew it as well as she did. He jumped the fence easily and followed the trail of blood. Without a moment's hesitation, she hiked her skirt above her knees and climbed over the snow-slicked rails as well, then quickly caught up with him.

With that frown and his jaw set, he looked hard and dangerous, like the Wild West outlaw he was named after.

"I'm sorry," she offered softly.

He blew out a breath. "It happens. Probably nothing we can do at this point. I had high hopes for Mystic's foal, though. The sire is one hell of a cutter, just like—"

Before he could finish the sentence, they heard a high, distressed whinny from inside the barn, and both picked up their pace to a run. He beat her inside, but she followed just a few seconds later. She had a quick impression of a clean, well-lit stall, then her attention immediately shifted to the misty-gray quarter horse pacing restlessly in the small space.

A quick visual check told her the blood they saw in the snow was from a large cut on the horse's belly, probably from kicking at herself in an attempt to rid her body of what she thought was bothering her—the foal.

It relieved her mind some, but not much. "She hasn't lost it yet," she said.

Matt looked distracted as he ran his hands over the horse. "She's going to, though, isn't she?"

"Probably. I'm sorry," she said again. She had seen the signs before. The sweat soaking the withers, the distress, the bared teeth as pain racked the mare.

All her professional instincts screamed at her to do something, not just stand here helplessly. To soothe, to heal. But Mystic wasn't hers to care for, and her owner didn't trust Ellie or her methods.

Still, she had to try. "Will you let me examine her?"

She held her breath as he studied her from across the stall, praying he would consent. The reluctance in his eyes shouldn't have hurt her. He had made no secret of his opinions. But she still had to dig her fingers into the wood rail at the deep, slicing pain.

He blew out a breath. "I don't know...."

"I'm a good vet, Matt. Please. Just let me look at her. I won't do anything against your wishes."

His hard, masculine face tense and worried, he studied Ellie for several seconds until Mystic broke away from him with another long, frantic whinny.

"Okay," Matt said finally. "Do what you can for her."

"My bag's in the pickup. It will just take me a minute to get it."

Her heart pounding, she ran as fast as she dared out of the barn and across the snow toward the house, cursing the constricting skirt as she went. This was exactly why she preferred to stick to jeans and work shirts. Of course she had to choose today, of all days, to go outside her comfort zone just for vanity's sake.

She slipped on a hidden patch of ice under the bare, spreading branches of a huge elm, and her legs almost went out from under her. At the last minute, she steadied herself on the trunk of the tree and paused for just an instant to catch her breath before hurrying on, anxious for the frightened little mare.

She hated seeing any animal in distress, always had. That was her first concern and the thought uppermost in her head. At the same time, on a smaller, purely selfish level that shamed her to admit it to herself, part of her wanted Matt to see firsthand that she knew what she was doing, that she would try anything in her power to save that foal.

At last she reached her truck, fumbled with the handle, then fought the urge to bang her head against it several times. Locked. Rats! And her keys were in her purse, inside the house.

With another oath at herself for not learning her lesson the night he had to thaw out her locks, she hurried up the porch steps and through the front door. She was rifling for her purse on the hall table, conscious that with every second of delay the foal's chances grew ever more dim, when Cassie walked out of the family room.

Matt's sister stopped short, frowning. "What is it? Is something wrong?"

"Mystic," Ellie answered grimly. "She's losing the foal. I'm just after my bag in the truck. Naturally, it's locked."

"Oh, no. What a relief that you're here, though! Can you save it?"

As she usually did before treating an animal, Ellie felt the heavy weight of responsibility settle on her shoulders. "I don't know. I'm going to try. Listen, we might be a while. Is Dylan okay in here without me?"

"Sure. She and Lucy have ganged up on Jess at the pool table. They haven't even noticed you've been gone. Is there anything I can do to help?"

Pray your stubborn brother will let me do more than look. Ellie kept the thought to herself and shook her head. "Just don't let Dylan eat too much pie."

She rushed out the door and down the steps to her truck and quickly unlocked it. Her leather backpack was behind the seat and, on impulse, she also picked up the bag with her sensors and acupuncture needles, then ran to the horse barn.

Matt had taken off his hat and ranch coat, she saw when her eyes once more adjusted to the dim light inside the barn, and he was doing his best to soothe the increasingly frantic animal.

The worry shadowing his eyes warmed her, even in the midst of her own tension. Matt Harte obviously cared deeply for the horse—all of his horses, judging by the modern, clean facilities he stabled them in—and her opinion of him went up another notch.

"Sorry it took so long." She immediately went to the sink to scrub. "Anything new happen while I was gone?"

"No. She's just as upset as she was before."

She snapped on a sterile pair of latex gloves and was pleased he had the sense to open the stall for her so she could keep them clean.

"What do you need me to do?" he asked, his voice pitched low to avoid upsetting the horse more than she already was.

"Can you hold her head for me?"

He nodded and obeyed, then scrutinized her closely as she approached the animal slowly, murmuring nonsense words as she went. Mystic, though still frantic at the tumult churning her insides, calmed enough to let Ellie examine her.

What she found heartened her. Although she could feel contractions rock the horse's belly, the foal hadn't begun to move through the birth canal. She pressed her stethoscope to the mare's side and heard the foal's heart beating loud and strong, if a little too fast.

"Can you tell what's going on?" Matt asked in that same low, soothing voice he used for the mare.

She spared a quick glance toward him. "My best guess is maybe she got into some mold or something and it's making her body try to flush itself of the fetus."

He clamped his teeth together, resignation in his eyes. "Can you give her something to ease the pain, then? Just until she delivers?"

"I could." She drew in a deep breath, her nerves kicking. "Or I can calm her down and try to save the foal."

He frowned. "How? I've been around horses all my life, certainly long enough to know there's not a damn thing you can do once a mare decides a foal has to go."

"Not with traditional Western medicine, you're right. But I've treated similar situations before, Matt. And saved several foals. I can't make any guarantees but I'd like to try."

His jaw tightened. "With your needles? No way."

She wanted to smack him for his old-school stubbornness. "I took an oath as a veterinarian. That I'll first do no harm, just like every other kind of medical doctor. I take it very seriously. It won't hurt her, I promise. And it might help save the foal's life where nothing else will."

Objections swamped his throat like spring runoff. He liked Ellie well enough as a person—too much, if he were completely honest with himself about it—but he wasn't too sure about her as a vet.

Her heart seemed to be in the right place, but the idea of her turning one of his horses into a pincushion didn't appeal to him whatsoever.

"If she's going to lose the foal anyway, what can it hurt to try?" she asked.

Across Mystic's withers, he gazed at Ellie and realized for the first time that she still wore the soft, pretty skirt she'd had on at dinner and those fancy leather boots. The boots were covered in who-knew-what, and a six-inch-wide bloodstain slashed across her skirt where she must have brushed up against Mystic's belly during the exam.

Ellie didn't seem to care a bit about her clothes, though. All her attention was focused on his mare. She genuinely thought she could save the foal—he could see the conviction blazing out of those sparkly green eyes—and that was the only thing that mattered to her right now.

Her confidence had him wavering. Like she said, what could it hurt to let her try?

A week ago he wouldn't have allowed it under any circumstances, would have still been convinced the whole acupuncture thing was a bunch of hooey. But he'd done a little reading up on the Internet lately and discovered the practice wasn't nearly as weird as he thought. Even the American Veterinary Association considered acupuncture an accepted method of care.

Mystic suddenly jerked hard against the bit and threw her head back, eyes wild with pain.

"Please, Matt. Just let me try."

What other choice did he have? The foal was going to die, and there was a chance Mystic would, too. He blew out a breath. "Be careful," he said gruffly. "She's a damn fine mare, and I don't want her hurt."

He watched carefully while she ran her hands over the animal one more time, then placed her finger at certain points, speaking quietly to both of them as she went.

"According to traditional Chinese veterinary acupuncture, each animal's body—and yours, too —has a network of meridians, with acupoints along that meridian that communicate with a specific organ," she said softly as she worked. "When a particular organ is out of balance, the related acupoints may become tender or show some other abnormality. That's what I'm looking for."

Mystic had a dozen or so needles in various places when Ellie inserted one more and gave it a little twist. Mystic jumped and shuddered.

He was just about to call the whole blasted thing off and tell Ellie to get away from his horse when the mare's straining, panting sides suddenly went completely still.

After a moment, the horse blew out a snorting breath then pulled away from him. With the needles in her flesh still quivering like porcupine quills, she calmly ambled to her water trough and indulged in a long drink of water.

He stared after her, dumbfounded at how quickly she transformed from panic-stricken to tranquil. What the hell just happened here?

Ellie didn't seem nearly as astonished. She followed the horse and began removing the needles one by one, discarding them in a special plastic container she pulled out of her bag. When they were all collected, she cleaned and dressed the self-inflicted wounds on Mystic's belly, then ran her hands over the horse one last time before joining Matt on the other side of the stall.

"Is that it?" he asked, unable to keep the shock out of his voice.

Her mouth twisted into a smile. "What did you expect?"

"I don't know." He shook his head in amazement. "I've got to tell you, Doc, that was just about the damnedest thing I've ever seen."

Despite the circumstances, her low laugh sent heat flashing to his gut. "I had the same reaction the first time I saw an animal treated with acupuncture. Some animals respond so instantly it seems nothing short of a miracle. Not all do, but the first horse I saw responded exactly like Mystic just did."

"Was she another pregnant mare?"

"No. It was a racehorse that had suddenly gone lame. For the life of me, I couldn't figure out what was wrong. I tried everything I could think of to help him and nothing worked. He just got worse and worse. Finally, as a last-ditch effort before putting him down, the owners decided against my advice to call in another vet who practiced acupuncture.

"I thought they were completely nuts, but I decided to watch. One minute the vet was sticking in the needles, the next he opened the door and Galaxy took off into the pasture like a yearling, with no sign whatsoever of the lameness that had nearly ended his life. I called up and registered for the training course the next day."

Her face glowed when she talked about her work. Somehow it seemed to light up from the inside. She looked so pretty and passionate it was all he could do to keep from reaching across the few feet that separated them and drawing her into his arms.

"How does it work?" he asked, trying to distract himself from that soft smile and those sparkling eyes and the need suddenly pulsing through him.

"The Chinese believe health and energy are like a stream flowing downhill—if something blocks that flow, upsetting the body's natural balance, energy can dam up behind the blockage, causing illness and pain. The needles help guide the energy a different way, restoring the balance and allowing healing to begin."

"And you buy all that?"

She sent him a sidelong look, smiling a little at his skeptical voice. "It worked for Mystic, didn't it?"

He couldn't argue with that. The mare was happily munching grain from her feed bag.

"I'm not a zealot, Matt. I don't use acupuncture as a treatment in every situation. Sometimes traditional Western medicine without question is the best course of action. But sometimes a situation calls for something different. Something more."

"But doesn't it conflict with what you know of regular medicine? All that talk about energy and flow?"

"Sometimes. It was hard at first for me to reconcile the two. But I've since learned it's a balance. Like life."

She smiled again. "I can't explain it. I just know acupuncture has been practiced for six thousand years—on people as well as animals— and sometimes it works beautifully. One of my instructors used to say that if the only tool in your toolbox is a hammer, the whole world looks like a nail. I want to have as many tools in my toolbox as I possibly can."

"You love being a vet, don't you?"

She nodded. "It's all I've ever wanted."

"Why?" He was surprised to find he genuinely wanted to know. "What made you become one?"

She said nothing for several moments, her face pensive

as she worked out an answer. He didn't mind, strangely content just watching her and listening to the low, soothing sounds of the barn.

Finally she broke the comfortable silence between them. "I wanted to help animals and I discovered I was good at it. Animals are uncomplicated. They give their love freely and without conditions. I was drawn to that."

Who in her life had put conditions on loving her? Dylan's father? He longed to ask but reminded himself it was none of his business.

"Did you overrun your house with pets when you were a kid?" he asked instead.

Her laugh sounded oddly hollow. "No. My mother never wanted the bother or the mess."

She was quiet for a moment, gazing at Mystic, who was resting quietly in the stall. He had the feeling Ellie was miles away, somewhere he couldn't even guess at.

"I take that back," she said slowly. "I had a dog once when I was ten. Sparky. A mongrel. Well, he wasn't really mine, he belonged to a kid at one of the…"

She looked at him suddenly, as if she'd forgotten he was there.

"At one of the foster homes I lived in," she continued stubbornly, her cheeks tinted a dusky rose. "But that didn't stop me from pretending he was mine."

Her defiant declaration broke his heart and helped a lot of things about her finally make sense. "You lived in many foster homes?"

"One is too many. And yeah, I did."

She was quiet again, and he thought for a moment she was done with the subject. And then she spoke in a quiet, unemotional voice that somehow affected him far more than tears or regrets would have.

"My dad was a long-haul trucker who took a load of

artichokes to Florida when I was five and decided to stay.
Without bothering to leave a forwarding address, of course.
My mother was devastated. She couldn't even make a decision about what shampoo to use without a man in her life,
so she climbed into a bottle and never climbed back out. I
stayed with her for about a year and then child-protective
services stepped in." She paused. "And you can stop looking at me like that."

"Like what?"

"Like you're feeling sorry for the poor little foster girl
playing make-believe with some other kid's dog." She
lifted her chin. "I did just fine."

He didn't like this fragile tenderness twisting around
inside him like a morning glory vine making itself at home
where it wasn't wanted. Did not like it one single bit.

"I never said otherwise," he said gruffly.

"You didn't have to say a word. I can see what you're
thinking clear as day in those big baby blues of yours. I've
seen pity plenty of times—that's why I generally keep my
mouth shut about my childhood. But I did just fine," she
said again, more vehemently this time. "I've got a beautiful daughter, a job I love fiercely and now I get to live in
one of the most beautiful places on earth. Not bad for a
white-trash foster kid. I turned out okay."

"Which one of us are you trying to convince?"

Her glare would have melted plastic. "Neither. I know
exactly where I've been and where I'm going. I'm very
happy with my life and I really don't care what you think
about me, Harte."

"Good. Then it won't bother you when I tell you I think
about you all the time. Or that I'm overwhelmed that you'd
be willing to wade through blood and muck in your best
clothes to save one of my horses. Or—" he finished qui-

etly "—when I tell you that I think you're just about the prettiest thing I've ever seen standing in my barn."

Somewhere in the middle of his speech her jaw sagged open and she stared at him, wide-eyed.

"Close your mouth, Doc," he murmured wryly.

She snapped it shut with a pop that echoed in the barn, and he gave a resigned sigh, knowing exactly what he was going to do.

He had a minute to think that this was about the stupidest thing he'd ever done, then his lips found hers and he stopped thinking, lost in the slick, warm welcome of her mouth.

For a moment after his mouth captured hers, Ellie could only stand motionless and stare at him, his face a breath away and those long, thick eyelashes shielding his glittering eyes from her view.

Matt Harte was kissing her! She wouldn't have been more shocked if all the horses in the stable had suddenly reared up and started singing Broadway show tunes as one.

And what a kiss it was. His mouth was hot and spicy, flavored with cinnamon and nutmeg. Pumpkin-pie sweet. He must have snuck a taste in the kitchen when he was cleaning up.

That was the last coherent thought she had before he slowly slid his mouth over hers, carefully, thoroughly, as if he didn't want to miss a single square inch.

Ellie completely forgot how to breathe. Liquid heat surged to her stomach, pooled there, then rushed through the rest of her body on a raging, storm-swollen river of desire.

Completely focused on his mouth and the incredible things the man knew what to do with it, she wasn't aware of her hands sliding to his chest until her fingers curled into the soft fabric of his sweater. Through the thick cotton, steel-hard muscles rippled and bunched beneath her hands, and she splayed them, fascinated by the leashed power there.

He groaned and pulled her more tightly against him, and his mouth shifted from leisurely exploring hers to conquering it, to searing his taste and touch on her senses.

His tongue dipped inside, and she welcomed it as his lean, muscular body pressed her against the stall. His heat warmed her, wrapped around and through her from the outside in, and she leaned against him.

How long had it been since she'd been held by a man like this, had hard male arms wrapped around her, snugging her against a broad male chest? Since she'd been made to feel small and feminine and *wanted?*

It shocked her that she couldn't remember, that every other kiss seemed to have faded into some distant corner of her mind, leaving only Matt Harte and his mouth and his hands.

Even if she *had* been able to recall any other kisses, she had a feeling they would pale into nothingness anyway compared to this. She certainly would have remembered something that made her feel as if she were riding a horse on a steep mountain trail with only air between her and heaven, as if the slightest false step would send her tumbling over the edge.

She'd been right.

The thought whispered through her dazed and jumbled mind, and she sighed. She had wondered that day in her office how Matt would go about kissing a woman and now she knew—slowly, carefully, completely absorbed in what he was doing, as if the fate of the entire world hinged on him kissing her exactly right.

Until she didn't have a thought left in her head except *more.*

She had no idea how long they stood there locked together. Time slowed to a crawl, then speeded up again in a whirling, mad rush.

She would have stayed there all night, lost in the amazing wonder of his mouth and his hands and his strength amid the rustle of hay and the low murmuring of horses—if she had her way, they would have stayed there until Christmas.

But just as she twisted her arms around the strong, tanned column of his neck to pull him even closer, her subconscious registered a sound that didn't belong. Girls' voices and high-pitched laughter outside the barn, then the rusty-hinged squeak of a door opening.

For one second they froze, still tightly entwined together, then Matt jerked away from her, his breathing ragged and harsh, just as both of their daughters rounded the corner of a stall bundled up like Eskimos against the cold.

"Hi." The girls chirped the word together.

Ellie thought she must have made some sound but she was too busy trying to grab hold of her wildly scrambled thoughts to know what it might have been.

"We came out to see if you might need any help," Lucy said.

Ellie darted a quick look at Matt and saw that he looked every bit as stunned as she felt, as if he'd just run smack up against one of those wood supports holding the roof in place.

"Is something wrong?" Dylan's brows furrowed as she studied them closely. "Did…did something happen to the foal?"

She'd forgotten all about Mystic. What kind of a veterinarian was she to completely abandon her duties while she tangled mouths with a man like Matt Harte? She jerked her gaze to the stall and was relieved to find the pregnant mare sleeping, her sides moving slowly and steadily with each breath. In a quick visual check, Ellie could see no outward sign of her earlier distress.

She rubbed her hands down her skirt—filthy beyond redemption, she feared—and forced a smile through the clutter of emotions tumbling through her. "I think she's going to be okay."

"And her foal, too?" Lucy asked, features creased with worry.

"And her foal, too."

Matt cleared his throat, looking at the girls and not at her. "Yeah, the crisis seems to be over, thanks to Doc Webster here."

"She's amazing, isn't she, Dad?" Lucy said. Awe that Ellie knew perfectly well she didn't deserve in his daughter's voice and shining in her soft powder-gray eyes.

Finally Matt met her gaze, and Ellie would have given a week's salary to know what he was thinking. The blasted man could hide his emotions better than a dog burying a soup bone. His features looked carved in granite, all blunt angles and rough planes.

After a few moments of that unnerving scrutiny, he turned to his daughter. "I'm beginning to think so," he murmured.

Nonplussed by the undercurrents of meaning in his voice, Ellie couldn't come up with an answer. She flashed him a quick look, and he returned it impassively.

"Are you sure you don't need our help?" Dylan asked.

She wavered for a moment, suddenly desperate for the buffer they provided between her and Matt. But it was cowardly to use them that way, and she knew it.

"No," she murmured. "I'd just like to stick around a little longer out here and make sure everything's all right.

Both of you should go on back to the house where you can stay warm."

"Save us a piece of pie," Matt commanded.

Lucy grinned at her father. "Which kind? I think there are about ten different pies in there."

He appeared to give the matter serious thought, then smiled at her. "How about one of each?"

"Sure." She snickered. "And then I'll bring in a wheelbarrow to cart you around in since you'll be too full to move."

"Deal. Go on, then. It's chilly out here."

Dylan sent her mother another long, searching look, and Ellie pasted on what she hoped was a reassuring smile for her daughter. "It was sweet of you both to come out and check on Mystic, but what she really needs now is quiet and rest."

"Okay."

"But—" Lucy began, then her voice faltered as Dylan sent her a meaningful look.

"Come on. Let's go back inside," she said, in that funny voice she'd been using lately. She grabbed Lucy's arm and urged her toward the door, leaving Ellie alone with Matt and the memory of the kiss that had left her feeling as if the whole world had just gone crazy.

Dylan clutched her glee to her chest only until they were outside the barn and she had carefully shut the door behind them, then she grabbed Lucy's coat, nearly toppling her into the snow. She pulled her into a tight hug and hopped them both around in wild circles. "Did you see that? Did you see it?"

"What? Mystic? She looked fine, like nothing had happened. Your mom is really something."

She gave Lucy a little shake. "No, silly! Didn't you see them? My mom and your dad?"

"Well, yeah. We just talked to them two seconds ago." Lucy looked at her as if her brain had slid out.

"Don't you get it, Lucy? This is huge. It's working! I know it's working! I think he kissed her!"

"Eww." Lucy's mouth twisted in disgust like Dylan had just made her eat an earwig.

"Come on, Luce. Grow up. They have to get mushy! It's part of the plan."

Her mouth dropped open like she'd never even considered the possibility. For a moment she stared at Dylan, then snapped her jaws shut. "How do you know? What makes you think they were kissing? They seemed just like normal."

Dylan thought of her mother's pink cheeks and the way Lucy's dad kept sneaking looks at Ellie when he didn't think any of them were watching him. "I don't know. I just think they were."

She wanted to yell and jump up and down and twirl around in circles with her arms wide until she got too dizzy and had to stop. A funny, sparkling excitement filled her chest, and she almost couldn't breathe around it. She was going to have a father, just like everybody else!

"I can't believe it. Our brilliant plan is working! Your dad likes her. I told you he would. He just needed the chance to get to know her."

She pulled Lucy toward her for another hug. "If your dad likes my mom enough to kiss her, it won't be long before he likes her enough to marry her. We're going to be sisters, Luce. I just know we are."

Lucy still couldn't seem to get over the kissing. Her face still looked all squishy and funny. "Now what?"

"I guess we keep doing what we're doing. Trying everything we can think of to push them together. Why mess with it when everything seems to be working out just like we planned?"

As soon as the girls left the barn, Ellie wished fiercely that she could slither out behind them. Or hide away among the hay bales. Or crawl into the nearest stall and bury her head in her hands.

Anything so she wouldn't have to face the tight-lipped man in front of her. Or so she wouldn't have to face herself and the weakness for soft-spoken, hard-eyed cowboys that had apparently been lurking inside her all this time without her knowledge.

And why was he glowering, anyway, like the whole bloody thing was her fault? He was the one who kissed *her*. She was an innocent victim, just standing here minding her own business.

And lusting over him, like she'd been doing for weeks.

The thought made her cringe inwardly. So she was attracted to him. So what? Who wouldn't be? The man was gorgeous. Big and masculine and gorgeous.

Anyway, it wasn't like she had begged him to kiss her. No, he'd done that all on his own. One minute they had been talking, the next thing she knew he pulled her into his arms without any advance warning and covered her mouth with his.

She shivered, remembering. The man kissed like he meant it. Her knees started to feel all wobbly again, but she sternly ordered them to behave. She had better things to do then go weak-kneed over a gruff, distrustful rancher who seemed content to remain mired in a rut of tradition.

Still, he *had* unbent enough to let her treat Mystic, despite his obvious misgivings. He deserved points for that, at least. Of course, then he had completely distracted her with a fiery kiss that washed all thoughts of her patient out of her head.

But no more. She took a deep breath. She had a job to do here. The mare wasn't out of the woods yet, and she needed to make sure Mystic didn't lose her foal. To do it, she needed to focus only on the horse and not on her owner.

"I'd better take another look at Mystic to make sure the contractions have completely stopped."

"You think she still might be in danger?"

"Like I told the girls, it's too early to say. We'll have to wait and see."

With a great deal of effort, she turned her back on him and focused on the horse again. Somehow she managed to put thoughts of that kiss out of her head enough to concentrate on what she was doing.

She was working so hard at it, centering all her energy on the horse, that she didn't hear Matt come up behind her until she turned to pick her stethoscope out of her bag and bumped into hard, immovable man.

She backed up until she butted against the horse and clutched her chest. "Oh. You startled me."

A muscle worked in his jaw. "Look, Doc. I owe you an apology. I had no business doing that."

She deliberately misconstrued his meaning. "Startling me? Don't worry about it. Just make a little more noise next time."

"No," he snapped impatiently. "You know that's not what I mean. I'm talking about before. About what happened before the girls came in."

Heat soaked her cheekbones. "You don't have to worry about that, either."

He pressed doggedly forward. "I shouldn't have kissed you. It was crazy. Completely crazy. I, uh, don't know what came over me."

Uncontrollable lust? She seriously doubted it. Still, it wasn't very flattering for him to look as astounded at his own actions as a pup did when he found out his new best friend was a porcupine.

"You shouldn't have," she said as curtly, hoping he would let the whole thing drop.

Out of the corner of her gaze, she watched that muscle twitch along his jaw again, but the blasted man plodded forward stubbornly. "I apologize," he repeated. "It won't happen again."

"Good. Then let's get back to business."

"I just don't want what happened here to affect our working relationship."

"We don't have a working relationship, Matt. Not really. We're running a school carnival together, but that will be over in a few months. Then we can go back to ignoring each other."

"I'd like us to. Have a working relationship, I mean. And not just with the stupid Valentine's carnival, either." He paused. "The thing is, I was impressed by what you did for Mystic. Hell, who wouldn't have been impressed? It was amazing."

Okay, she could forgive him for calling their kiss crazy, she decided, as warmth rushed through her at the praise.

He rubbed a hand along Mystic's withers, avoiding her gaze. "If you're interested, I'd like to contract with you to treat the rest of my horses."

She stared at him, stunned by the offer. "All of them?"

"Yeah. We generally have anywhere from twenty to thirty, depending on the time of the year. The ranch hands usually have at least a couple each in their remudas, and I usually pay for their care, too."

She was flabbergasted and couldn't seem to think straight. How could the man kiss her one minute, then calmly talk business the next while her hormones still lurched and bucked? It wasn't fair. She could barely keep a thought in her head, even ten minutes later. How was she supposed to have a coherent conversation about this?

"What about Steve?" she finally asked.

"Nichols is a competent vet." He paused, as if trying to figure out just the right words. "He's competent, but not passionate. Not like Ben. Or like you.

"Don't get me wrong," he added. "Steve does a good job with the cattle. But to be honest, I'm looking for a little more when it comes to my horses. I can't expect somebody to spend thirty thousand and up for a competition-quality cutter that's not completely healthy."

He smiled suddenly, and she felt as if she'd just been thrown off one of those champion cutters of his. "I'd like to have a veterinarian on staff who's not content with only one tool in her toolbox. What do you think?"

She blew out a breath, trying to process the twists and turns the day had taken. The chance to be the Diamond Harte's veterinarian was an opportunity she'd never even dared dream about. She couldn't pass it up, even if it meant working even more closely with Matt.

"Only your horses?" she asked warily. "Not the cattle?"

He shrugged. "Like I said, Steve seems to be handling that end of things all right."

Steve. She gave an inward wince. What would he think when she took the lucrative Diamond Harte contract from him? It would probably sting his pride, at the very least.

On the other hand, he had no qualms about doing the same thing to her countless times since she arrived in Star Valley. If she was going to run her own practice, she needed to start thinking like a businesswoman. They were friends but they were also competitors.

"Do we have a deal?" Matt asked.

How could she pass it up? This is what she wanted to do, why she'd traveled fifteen hundred miles and uprooted her daughter and risked everything she had. For chances like this. She nodded. "Sure. Sounds great. When do you want me to start?"

"Maybe you could come out sometime after the holiday weekend and get acquainted with the herd and their medical histories."

"Okay. Monday would work for me."

"We can work out the details then." He paused for a moment, then cleared his throat. "And, uh, if you're at all concerned about what happened here today, I swear it won't happen again. I was completely out of line—a line I won't be crossing again. You have my word on that."

She nodded and turned to Mystic, not wanting to dwell on all the reasons his declaration made her feel this pang of loss in her stomach.

Chapter 8

Hours later, Matt sat in his favorite leather wing chair in the darkened great room of the Diamond Harte, listening to the tired creaking of the old log walls and the crackle and hiss of the fire while he watched fat snowflakes drift lazily down outside the wide, uncurtained windows.

He loved this time of the night, when the house was quiet and he could finally have a moment to himself to think, without the phone ringing or Lucy asking for help with her math homework or Cassie hounding him about something or other.

Ellie Webster would probably call what he was doing something crazy and far-out, like meditating. He wouldn't go that far. His brain just seemed to work better when he didn't have a thousand things begging for attention.

When the weather was warm, he liked to sit on the wide front porch, breathing the evening air and watching the stars come out one by one—either that or take one of the horses for a late-night ride along the trails that wound through the thousands of acres of Forest Service land above the ranch.

Most of his problems—both with the ranch and in his personal life—had been solved on the porch, on the back of a horse or in this very chair by the fire.

And he had plenty of problems to occupy his mind tonight.

Ellie and her daughter had gone home hours ago, but he swore if he breathed deeply enough he could still smell that sweet, citrusy scent of her—like lemons and sunshine—clinging subtly to his skin.

She had tasted the same way. Like a summer morning, all fresh and sweet and intoxicating. He thought of how she had felt in his arms, of the way her mouth had softened under his and the way her body melted into him like sherbet spilled on a hot sidewalk.

He only meant to kiss her for an instant. Just a brief experiment to satisfy his curiosity, to determine if the reality of kissing her could come anywhere close to his subconscious yearnings.

So much for good intentions.

He might have been content with only a taste—as tantalizing as it had been—but then she murmured his name when he kissed her.

He didn't think she was even aware of it, but he had heard it clearly. Just that hushed whisper against his mouth had sent need exploding through his system like a match set to a keg of gunpowder, and he had been lost.

What the hell had he been thinking? He wasn't the kind of guy to go around stealing kisses from women, especially prickly city vets who made it abundantly clear they weren't interested.

He'd been just as shocked as she was when he pulled her into his arms. And even more shocked when she responded to him, when she'd kissed him back and leaned into him for more.

He sipped at his drink and gazed out the window again. What was it about Ellie Webster that turned him inside out? She was beautiful, sure, with that fiery hair and those startling green eyes rimmed with silver.

It was more than that, though. He thought of the way she had talked so calmly and without emotion about her childhood, about being abandoned by both her parents and then spending the rest of her youth in foster homes.

She was a survivor.

He thought of his own childhood, of his dad teaching him to rope and his mom welcoming him home with a kiss on his cheek after school every day and bickering with Jess and Cassie over who got the biggest cookie.

Ellie had missed all that, and his chest ached when he thought of it and when he realized how she'd still managed to make a comfortable, happy life for her and her daughter.

Despite his earlier misconceptions, he was discovering that he actually liked her.

It had been a long time since he had genuinely liked a woman who wasn't related to him. Ellie was different, and that scared the hell out of him.

But any way he looked at it, kissing her had still been a damn fool thing to do.

He must be temporarily insane. A rational man would have run like the devil himself was riding his heels after being twisted into knots like that by a woman he shouldn't want and couldn't have.

But what did he do instead? Contract with her to take care of his horses, guaranteeing he'd see plenty of her in the coming weeks, even if it hadn't been for the stupid Valentine's carnival their girls had roped them into.

It was bound to be awkward. Wondering if she was thinking about their kiss, trying to put the blasted thing out of his own mind. He was a grown man, though, wasn't he? He could handle a little awkwardness, especially if it would benefit his horses.

And it would definitely do that. He'd meant it when he told her he'd never seen anything like what she'd done to Mystic. He never would have believed it if he hadn't seen it for himself. *Something* had happened in that barn while she was working on the horse. He wasn't the sort of man who believed in magic—in his own humble opinion, magic came from sweat and hard work—but what she had done with Mystic had been nothing short of miraculous.

Maybe that was one of the reasons for this confounded attraction he had for her—her wholehearted dedication to her job, to the animals she worked with. He respected it. If not for that, he probably wouldn't have decided to go with his gut and offer her the contract to care for all of his horses.

He had given up plenty of things for the good of the ranch in the years since his folks died. It shouldn't be that hard to put aside this strange attraction for a smart-mouthed little redhead with big green eyes and a stubborn streak a mile wide.

Especially since he knew nothing could ever come of it anyway.

The room suddenly seemed colder, somehow. Darker. Lonely.

Just the fire burning itself out, he told himself. He jumped up to throw another log onto it, then stood for a moment to watch the flames curl and seethe around it. It was an intoxicating thing, a fire on a snowy night. Almost as intoxicating as Ellie Webster's mouth.

Disgusted with himself for harping on a subject better left behind, he sighed heavily.

"Uh-oh. That sounded ominous."

He turned toward his sister's voice. She stood in the

doorway, still dressed in her jeans and sweater. "You're up late," she said.

He shrugged. "Just enjoying the night. What about you? I thought you turned in hours ago."

"Forgot I left a load of towels in the washing machine this morning. I just came down to throw them in the dryer."

"I can do that for you. Go on to bed."

"I already did it. I was just on my way back upstairs."

She stood half in, half out of the room, her fingers drumming softly on the door frame. He sensed an odd restlessness in her tonight. Like a mare sniffing out greener pastures somewhere in the big wide world.

In another woman he might have called it melancholy, but Cassie had always been the calm one. The levelheaded one. The soft April rain to Jesse's wild, raging thunderstorm.

Tonight she practically radiated nervous energy, and it made him uneasy—made him want to stay out of her way until she worked out whatever was bothering her.

He couldn't do that, though. He loved her too much, owed her too much. If something was bugging her, he had an obligation to ferret it out then try to fix it.

"Why don't you come in and keep me company?" he invited.

"I don't want to bother you."

"No bother. Seems like we're always so busy I hardly ever get a chance to talk to you anymore."

She studied him for a moment, then moved into the room and took a seat on the couch, curling her long legs under her. "What were you thinking about when I came in that put that cranky look on your face?"

It wasn't tough for him to remember, since that stolen kiss in the barn with Ellie Webster had taken center stage in his brain for the last six hours. For one crazy moment, he debated telling Cassie about it. But he couldn't quite picture himself chatting about his love life—or lack thereof—with his little sister.

"Nothing important," he lied, and forced his features into a smile. Knowing how bullheaded she could be about some things—a lot like a certain redhead he didn't want to think about—he decided he'd better distract her. "What did Wade Lowry want when he called earlier?"

Cassie picked at the nubby fabric of the couch. "He wanted me to go cross-country skiing with him tomorrow into Yellowstone."

Could that be what had her so edgy? "Sounds like fun. What time are you leaving?"

He didn't miss the way her mouth pressed into a tight line or the way she avoided his gaze. "I'm not. I told him we had family plans tomorrow."

He frowned. "What plans? I don't know of any plans."

In the flickering light of the fire, he watched heat crawl up her cheekbones. "I thought I'd help you work with Gypsy Rose tomorrow," she mumbled. "Didn't you say you were going to start training her in the morning? You'll need another pair of hands."

And he could have used any one of the ranch hands, like he usually did. No, there was more to this than a desire to help him out with the horses.

"What's wrong with Lowry? He's not a bad guy. Goes to church, serves on the library board, is good with kids. The other ladies seem to like him well enough. And he seems to make a pretty good living with that guest ranch of his. He charges an arm and leg to the tourists who come to stay there, anyway. You could do a whole lot worse."

She made a face, like she used to do when Jess yanked on her hair. "Nothing's wrong with him. I just didn't feel like going with him tomorrow. Since when was it a crime to want to help your family?"

"It's not. But it's also not a crime to get out and do something fun for a change."

"I do plenty of fun things."

"Like what?"

"Cooking dinner today. That was fun. And going out on roundup with you. I love that. And taking care of Lucy. What greater joy could I find? My whole life is fun."

Every one of the things she mentioned had been for someone else. His hands curved around his glass as tension and guilt curled through him, just like they always did when it came to his baby sister and the sacrifices he had let her make. She needed more than cooking and cleaning for him and for Lucy.

"You can't give everything to us, Cass," he said quietly. "Save some part for yourself."

She sniffed. "I don't know what you're talking about."

She did, and they both knew it. They'd had this very conversation many times before. Just like always, he was left frustrated, knowing nothing he said would make her budge.

He opted for silence instead, and they sat quietly, listening to the fire and the night and the echo of words unsaid.

She was the first to break the silence. "Do you ever wonder if they're still together?" she said after several moments.

He peered at her over the rim of his glass. "If who are together?"

She made a frustrated sound. "Who do you think? Melanie and Slater."

His wife and her fiancé, who had run off together the week before Cassie's wedding. A whole host of emotions knifed through him. Betrayal. Guilt. Most of all sharp heartache for the sweet, deliriously happy girl his little sister had been before Melanie and that bastard Slater had shattered her life.

They rarely talked about that summer. About how they had both been shell-shocked for months, just going about the constant, grinding struggle to take care of the ranch and a tiny, helpless Lucy.

About how that love-struck young woman on the edge of a whole world full of possibilities had withdrawn from life, burying herself on the ranch to take care of her family.

"I don't waste energy thinking about it," he lied. "You shouldn't, either."

He didn't mean to make it sound like an order, but it must have. Cassie flashed him an angry glare. "You can't control everything, big brother, as much as you might like to. I'll think about them if I want to think about them, and there's not a damn thing you can do about it."

"Aw, Cass. Why torture yourself? It'll be ten years this summer."

She stared stonily ahead. "*Get over it.* Is that what you mean?"

Was it? Had he gotten over Melanie? Whatever love he might have once thought he felt for her had shriveled into something bitter and ugly long before she left him. But he wasn't sure he could honestly say her desertion hadn't affected him, hadn't destroyed something vital and profound inside of him.

Maybe that was why he was so appalled to find himself kissing a city girl like Ellie Webster and for craving the taste of her mouth again so powerfully he couldn't think around it.

He looked at his sister, at her pretty blue eyes and the brown hair she kept ruthlessly short now and the hands that were always busy cooking and cleaning in her brother's house. He wanted so much more for her.

"You've got to let go, Cassie. You can't spend the rest of your life poking and prodding at the part of you that son of a bitch hurt. If you keep messing at it, it will never be able to heal. Not completely."

"I don't poke and prod," she snapped. "I hardly even think about Slater anymore. But I'm not like you, Matt. I'm sorry, but I can't just shove away my feelings and act like they never existed."

He drew in a breath at the sharp jab, and Cassie immediately lifted a hand to her mouth, her eyes horrified. "Oh, Matt. I'm sorry. I shouldn't have said that. I should never have brought them up. Let's just drop it, okay?"

"Which brings us back to Wade Lowry. You need to go out more, Cass, meet more people. Give some other lucky guy a chance to steal you away from us."

She snorted. "Oh, you're a fine one to talk. When was the last time you went out on a date?"

She had him there. What would his sister say if she knew he'd stolen a kiss from the vet earlier in the barn? And that his body still churned and ached with need for her hours later? He took a sip of his drink, willing Ellie out of his mind once more.

Cassie suddenly sent him a sly look. "You know who would be really great for you? Ellie Webster."

He sputtered and coughed on his drink. "What?"

"Seriously. She's pretty, she's smart, she's funny. I really like her."

So did he, entirely too much.

"I think the two of you would be perfect together," Cassie said.

He refused to let his baser self think about exactly how

perfect they might be together at least in one area of a relationship, judging by the way she had melted into his arms.

"Thanks for the romantic advice," he said gruffly, "but I think I'll stick to what I know. The ranch and the stock and Lucy. I don't have time for anything else."

She was quiet for a moment, then she grabbed his hand. "We're a sorry pair, aren't we? You're the one who told me not to put my life on hold. If I go skiing with Wade Lowry tomorrow, will you at least think about taking Ellie out somewhere? Maybe to dinner in Jackson or something?"

"Sure," he answered. "If you'll go skiing with Wade and promise to have a good time, I'll think about taking Doc Webster to dinner."

But thinking about it was absolutely the only thing he would do about it.

"So I'm off. I'll see you in the morning."

Ellie glanced up from her computer and found SueAnn in the doorway bundled into her coat and hat with that big, slouchy bag that was roomy enough to hide a heifer slung over her shoulder.

She blinked, trying to force her eyes to focus. "Is it six already?"

"Quarter past. Aren't you supposed to be heading out to the Diamond Harte pretty soon?"

"The carnival committee meeting doesn't start until seven. I should still have a little more time before I have to leave. I'm taking advantage of the quiet without Dylan to try to finish as much as I can of this journal article."

"She's with Lucy again?"

"Where else?"

Dylan had begged to ride the school bus home with her friend again. And since Ellie knew she would be able to pick her up when she went out to the ranch later in the evening, she gave in.

"I've got to turn this in by the end of the week if I want to have it considered for the next issue, and I'm way behind."

"I imagine you haven't had much time these last few weeks for much of anything but your patients, have you?"

Ellie knew her grin could have lit up the whole town of Salt River. "Isn't it something?"

"Amazing. We haven't had a spare second around here since Thanksgiving."

Christmas was only a few weeks away. The towns scattered throughout Star Valley gleamed and glittered. Everybody seemed to get into the spirit of the holiday—just about every ranch had some kind of decorations, from stars of Bethlehem on barn roofs to crèches in hay sheds to fir wreaths gracing barbed-wire fences. The other night she had even seen a tractor decorated with flashing lights.

With her heavy workload, Ellie hadn't had much time to enjoy it. She hadn't even gone Christmas shopping for Dylan. If she didn't hurry, there would be nothing left in any of the stores.

Still, she couldn't regret the last-minute rush. For the first time since she and Dylan had moved to Wyoming, she was beginning to feel like she had a chance at succeeding here, at making a life for the two of them.

Word had spread quickly after Thanksgiving about how she had saved Mystic's unborn foal and how Matt Harte had hired her to treat the rest of his champion horses.

She wasn't exactly sure how everyone had learned about it. She hadn't said a word to anyone, and Matt certainly didn't seem the type to blab his business all over town. But somehow the news had leaked out.

The Monday after the holiday, she'd barely been in the

office ten minutes before her phone started ringing with other horse owners interested in knowing more about her methods and scheduling appointments for their animals.

She couldn't exactly say business was booming, but she was more busy than she ever expected to be a month ago. Ellie couldn't believe how rewarding she was finding it. It was everything she had always dreamed of—doing exactly what she loved.

"So how are the carnival plans going?"

She jerked her attention to SueAnn. "Good. We've got a really great crew working with us now. Barb Smith, Sandy Nielson, Terry McKay and Marni Clawson."

"That *is* a good committee. They'll take care of all the dirty work for you. And how's our favorite sexy rancher?"

She frowned at SueAnn's sly grin. "If you're talking about Matt Harte, I wouldn't know," she said brusquely. "I haven't seen much of him."

She wasn't disappointed, she told herself. Honestly, she wasn't. "He missed the last meeting, and every time I've gone out to treat his horses, he's had one of his ranch hands help me."

She'd only caught fleeting glimpses of him out at the Diamond Harte. If she didn't know better, she'd think he was avoiding her after their heated kiss in the barn. But he didn't strike her as the kind of man to run away from a little awkwardness.

"Well, you'll see him tonight. He can't very well miss a meeting when it's at his own house."

Ellie didn't even want to think about this wary anticipation curling through her at the thought.

After SueAnn left, Ellie tried to concentrate once more, but the words on the computer screen in front of her blurred together.

It was all SueAnn's fault for bringing up Matt. Ellie had

tried for two weeks to keep him out of her mind, but the blasted man just kept popping in at all hours. She couldn't seem to stop thinking about his smile or his blue eyes or the way he teased Lucy and Dylan.

Boy, she had it bad. One kiss and she completely lost all perspective. It had become increasingly difficult to re- member all the reasons that kiss was a lousy idea and why it would never happen again.

She blew out a breath. No sense wasting her time sitting here when she wasn't accomplishing anything. She might as well head out early to the ranch. Maybe she could have a few minutes to talk to Matt and work this crazy longing out of her system.

After putting on her coat and locking up the clinic, she walked to her beat-up old truck, relishing the cold, invig- orating air. With the winter solstice just around the cor- ner, night came early to this corner of the world. Already, dozens of stars peppered the night sky like spangles on blue velvet. She paused for a moment, hands curled into her pockets against the cold and her breath puffing out in clouds as she craned her neck at the vast, glittering ex- panse above her.

The moon was full, pearly and bright. It glowed on the snowy landscape, turning everything pale.

She loved it here. The quiet pace, the wild mountains, the decent, hardworking people. Moving here had been just what she and Dylan had needed.

Humming off-key to the Garth Brooks Christmas CD SueAnn had been playing before she left, Ellie reached her truck. She didn't bother fishing for her keys, confident she'd left it unlocked. It had taken a while to break herself of the habit of locking the battered truck, but now she felt just like one of the locals.

Next thing she knew, she'd be calling everyone darlin' and wearing pearl-button shirts.

Laughing at herself, she swung open the door, then froze, her hand on the cracked vinyl of the handle.

Something was different. Very, very wrong.

Through the moonlight and the dim glow from the overhead dome, she saw something odd on the passenger seat, something that didn't quite belong here.

It took her a moment to realize what it was—the carcass of a cat, head lolled back in a death grimace and legs stiff with rigor mortis.

Icy cold knifed through her, and her pulse sounded loud and scattered in her ears. As if that wasn't horrifying enough to find in the cab of her truck, she could see a note stuck to the poor animal's side—fastened firmly into place with one of her acupuncture needles.

Her hands trembled like leaves in a hard wind as she reached for the slip of white paper and pulled it carefully away, needle and all, so she could hold it up to the dome light.

It was printed on plain computer paper and contained only five words in block capital letters, but they were enough to snatch away her breath and send shock and fear coiling through her stomach.

WE DON'T WANT YOU HERE.

Chapter 9

If somebody told him a month ago he would be hosting a gaggle of women chattering about decorations and refreshments and publicity, he probably would have decked them.

Matt sat in the corner of his dining room, afraid his eyes were going to glaze over any minute now. The only streamers he even wanted to *think* about were on the end of a fly rod.

The things he did for his kid! He only hoped when she was stretching her wings in rebellious teenagedom and thinking her dad was the most uncool person on the planet, she would look back on this whole carnival thing and appreciate the depth of his sacrifice for her.

At the far end of the big table, Ellie reached for her water glass, sipped at it quickly, then set it down hard enough that water sloshed over the top and splattered the legal pad in front of her.

For a moment, she didn't react, just stared at the spreading water stain. Finally he cleared his throat and handed down one of the napkins Cassie had set out to go with her walnut brownies before she took off to see a movie in town.

Ellie jolted when Terry McKay passed her the napkin. Her gaze flew up and collided with his. Heat soaked her cheeks, then she quickly turned her attention to sopping up the spill.

The only consolation Matt could find in the whole evening was that she seemed to feel just as out of place as he did, at least judging by her jumpy, distracted mood.

He supposed it was pretty petty of him to feel such glee at her obvious discomfort. But he liked knowing he wasn't the only one who didn't want to be stuck here.

Only half-listening to the conversation—centering on the crucial question of whether to sell tickets at the door or at each booth—he finally allowed himself the guilty pleasure of really looking at Ellie for the first time all evening.

She looked bright and pretty with her hair in some kind of a twisty style and a subtle shade of lipstick defining her mouth.

That mouth. Full and lush and enticing. He hadn't been able to stop thinking about it for two frustrating weeks. The way it had softened under his. The way those lips had opened for him, welcoming him into the hot, slick depths of her mouth. The way her tongue had ventured out tentatively to greet his.

Today it had been worse, much worse, knowing she would be coming to the ranch for this meeting. His concentration had been shot all to hell. In the middle of stringing a fence line, he'd let go of the barbed wire and ended up taking a nasty gash out of his cheek.

Tonight wasn't much better. He couldn't concentrate on the meeting for the life of him. All he could think about was how she had felt in his arms. With an inward, resigned sigh, he tried to turn his attention to the conversation.

"I hope I have this kid before the carnival so I can help,"

Marni Clawson, wife of one of his high school buddies, was saying. "I would really hate to miss it."

"How much longer?" Sandy Nielson asked her with that goggly-eyed look women get when the talk centers on babies.

Marni smiled softly. "Three weeks. I'll tell you, I'm ready right now. I just want to get this over with. Speaking of which, you're all going to have to excuse me for a minute. These days my bladder's about the size of a teaspoon. I think I need to pee about every half hour."

Information he didn't need to know, thanks very much. All the women except Ellie laughed in sympathy. As heat crawled over his face, Matt felt as out of place as the town drunk in the middle of a church picnic.

Marni must have spotted his discomfort. She gave him an apologetic look. "Sorry, Matt."

"No problem," he said gruffly, praying the night would end soon.

As Marni slid back her chair, it squeaked loudly along the wood floor. Ellie jumped as if the sound had been a gunshot. She clutched the napkin in her hand so tightly her knuckles whitened.

He straightened in his chair, his gaze sharpening. What the hell? He could see that what he had mistaken for simple restlessness was something more. Something edgier, darker.

She looked frightened.

Sensing his scrutiny again, she lifted her eyes from the papers in front of her. They stared at each other across the table for several seconds, his gaze probing and hers rimmed with more vulnerability than he'd ever seen there, then her lashes fluttered down and she veiled her green eyes from his view once more.

What happened? Who hurt you?

He almost blurted out the questions, then reined in the words. Not now, not here. He would wait until everyone else left, then force her to tell him what was going on.

He spent the rest of the evening tense and worried, amazed and more disconcerted than he wanted to admit at the powerful need coursing through him to protect her. To take care of her.

He didn't like the feeling. Not one bit. It reminded him painfully of all the emotions Melanie had stirred up in him the first time he met her, when they'd bumped into each other at a dingy little diner.

She'd had a black eye and had been running scared from a nasty boyfriend who had followed her to Denver from L.A. She'd needed rescuing and for some reason decided the hick cowboy from Wyoming was just the man to save her.

Matt flinched when he thought about how eagerly he'd stepped forward to do it, sucked under by a beautiful woman with a hard-luck story and helplessness in her eyes.

He didn't know if there really had been a nasty boyfriend at all or if it had been another of her lies. But Melanie had needed rescuing anyway, from herself more than anything.

Unfortunately, he'd failed, and his marriage had failed, too.

He pushed the thought away and focused on Ellie and that stark fear in her eyes.

Finally, when he wasn't sure he could stand the tension another moment, the meeting began to wrap up, and one by one the committee members walked into the cold, clear night, leaving him and Ellie alone in the dining room.

She rose and began clearing the napkins and glasses from the table with quick, jerky movements. "We've made a lot of headway tonight, don't you agree? I don't think we should have to meet again until February, right before the carnival."

She continued chattering about the meeting until he finally reached out and grabbed her arm. "Doc, stop."

She froze, and her gaze flashed to his once more. The raw emotions there made him swear.

"What's going on?"

She looked at the table, but not before he saw her mouth wobble, then she compressed it into a tight, uncompromising line. "I don't know what you're talking about."

"Come on, Ellie. Something's wrong. I can see it in your eyes."

"It's nothing. I'm just tired, that's all. It's been a hectic couple of weeks." She pasted on a smile that fell miles short of being genuine. "Thank you, by the way. I don't know how you did it, but you've single-handedly managed to convince people to give me a chance around here. I appreciate it, more than I can tell you."

"I didn't do anything other than let a few people know I'm now using you to treat my horses."

"You obviously have enough influence to make people think that what's okay for the Diamond Harte is okay for them."

He was arrogant enough to know what she said was true. That's why he'd tried to spread the word, whenever he had the chance, that he had contracted for Ellie's veterinary services, so business would pick up for her. It sounded like it had worked.

She picked up the dishes and headed for the kitchen with them, and he followed a moment after her.

"Shall I wash these?" she asked.

"No. I'll throw them in the dishwasher in a while."

"Okay. In that case, I'd better grab Dylan and head

home." She looked about as thrilled by the idea as a calf on its way to be castrated.

"You could stay." His offer seemed to shock her as much as it did him. On reflection, though, he warmed to the idea. He didn't like thinking about her going home to her empty house, especially not when she was so obviously upset about something.

"It's late and bound to be icy out there," he said gruffly. "We have plenty of room—you and Dylan could both stay the night in one of the guest rooms and go home in the morning."

How could he have known that the idea of walking into her dark, empty house had been filling her with dread all night? What if she found another charming little warning there, as well? It would be so much worse with Dylan along when she discovered it.

Matt couldn't possibly know what was going on. He was picking up on her nervousness, on the anxiety she knew she had been unable to conceal.

For a moment she was tempted to confide in him. He knew the valley and its inhabitants far better than she did. Maybe he would know who might be capable of delivering such a macabre message.

It would be such a relief to share the burden with someone else, especially someone solid and reassuring like Matt, to let those strong shoulders take the weight of her worry....

She reined in the thought. She wasn't her mother. She wasn't the kind of woman to fall apart at the first hint of crisis, to act helpless and weak so that everyone else would have to take care of her. This was her problem, and she would deal with it.

"I appreciate the offer," she said abruptly, "but we'll be fine. My truck has four-wheel drive."

"Are you sure?"

"Positive."

He sighed heavily. "You are one stubborn woman. Did anybody ever tell you that?"

"A few times." She forced a smile.

"More than a few, I'd bet," he grumbled under his breath. "Since you're not going to budge, I guess we'd better round up Dylan so you two can hit the road."

He led the way up the stairs, then rapped softly on the door of Lucy's bedroom. Ellie couldn't hear any sound from inside. After a moment, Matt swung open the door. They found both girls tucked under a quilt at opposite ends of Lucy's ruffly pink bed, with their eyes closed and their breathing slow and even, apparently sound asleep.

It was oddly intimate standing shoulder-to-shoulder in the doorway watching over their respective children. She'd never done this with a man before and she found it enormously disconcerting.

She could feel the heat emanating from him and smell the leathery scent of his aftershave, and it made her more nervous than a hundred threatening letters.

"Do you think they're faking it?" Matt whispered.

"I wouldn't put it past them," she whispered back, trying to ignore the way his low voice set her stomach quivering. "I think they'd try anything for an extra sleepover."

She stepped forward, grateful for even that foot of space between them. "Dylan?" she called softly. "Come on, bug. Time to go home."

Neither girl so much as twitched an eyelid.

"At least let Dylan stay the night," Matt murmured. "It seems like a pretty dirty trick to wake the kid out of a good sleep just to drag her out in the cold."

"She's always sleeping over. I swear, she spends more time here than she does in her own bed."

"We don't mind. She's good for Lucy. I've got to run into town in the morning, and it would be no big deal for me to drop her back home on the way."

If she hadn't been so nervous about Dylan stumbling on to another grisly discovery like the one she had found in the truck earlier, she would have argued with him. She was dreading the idea of going home alone, but at least this way she wouldn't have to worry about Dylan, too.

"Are you sure?"

"Don't worry about it, Doc. She'll be fine."

With one more suspicious look to see if any fingers twitched or eyelids peeked open, Ellie backed out of the room and joined him in the hall.

"I can't shake the feeling that we're being conned," she said.

"So what? If this is an act, they're pretty good at it and deserve a reward. Wouldn't hurt them to have a sleepover."

"So you want to encourage your daughter's fraudulence?"

He smiled. "I'm just glad to see her doing normal kid things for a change. Lucy's always been too serious for her own good. Dylan's done wonders for her. She's a great kid."

She smiled, genuinely this time. "What mother doesn't want to hear that her child is great? I think she's pretty cool, too."

Their gazes locked, and suddenly his eyes kindled with something deeper that she didn't dare analyze. She dropped her gaze and felt her cheeks heat as she vividly remembered those stolen moments in his horse barn.

"I should be going," she said, her voice hoarse.

"I'll walk you out."

"That's not necessary," she began.

"I know. But I'm going to do it anyway."

How did a woman go up against a man who was about

as intractable as the Salt River Range? With a sigh, she followed him down the stairs and to the great room for her coat.

"Here. Let me carry that for you," he said gruffly, and pointed to her bulky leather backpack that held everything from her planner to basic medical supplies.

She opened her mouth to argue that she carried it around by herself all the time, but she closed it at the defiant look on his face, like he was daring her to say something about it.

"Thank you," she murmured instead, handing it to him. She had to admit she found it kind of sweet, actually. Like when Joey Spiloza offered to carry her books home from school in the first grade.

She hadn't let him, of course, completely panicked at the idea of anyone at school knowing what a trash heap she lived in. Or worse, what if her mom wandered out to the sagging porch in her bathrobe, bleary-eyed and stinking like gin?

She pushed the memory away and walked into the cold, clear Wyoming night with Matt. He was silent and seemed distracted as they crunched through the snow, even after his little brindle Australian shepherd sidled up to him for some attention.

At her truck, he opened the door and she climbed inside.

"Well, thanks for everything," she said. "I guess I'll see you tomorrow when you drop off Dylan."

"Right. Be careful on the roads." He stood at the open truck door studying her out of those blue eyes that seemed to glow in the moonlight. His shoulders leaned forward slightly, and for one crazy moment, she thought he would kiss her again.

At the last moment, he jerked back. "Oh. Don't forget your bag."

She stopped breathing completely when he reached across her to set the backpack on the passenger side, and his arm brushed the curve of her breast. He probably didn't realize it since she was swaddled in a thick winter coat, but she did, in every single cell. To her horror, she could feel her hormones immediately snap to attention and her nipple bud to life.

Even leaning back until her spine pressed against the seat wasn't enough to escape him or the first physical contact between them since that heated kiss on Thanksgiving.

She could vaguely hear the crackling of paper under the backpack as he set it down on the seat. "Sorry. I set it on something." He shoved the pack toward the other door, leaning into her even more. "Is it important?"

She blinked, feeling slightly feverish. "What?"

"Whatever I tossed this onto. Here. Let me see."

She looked down and saw what he was reaching for, that damned note with the needle still stuck through it.

"What's this?"

"It's nothing." She made a futile grab for it, but he held it out of her reach and up to the dome light. When he lowered the note, his expression burned with anger.

"Where did you find this?"

"I told you, it's nothing."

"Dammit, Doc. Where did this come from?"

She took one more look at his face, then blew out a breath. Somehow she didn't think he was going to rest until he bullied the truth out of her. "Someone left it in my truck. I found it when I left the office before driving out here tonight. It was, um, impaled in the carcass of a cat."

His expression darkened even more, and he let out a long string of swearwords. "Who would do such a thing?"

"Obviously not the Salt River Welcome Wagon."

"Did you call Jess to report it?"

She shook her head. "It's just a stupid prank, Matt. I didn't see the need to call in the police."

"This is more than a prank. Anybody who would leave this for you to find must have a sick and twisted mind. I'll call Jesse and have him come out to the ranch to get the details from you. There's no question now of you going home. You'll stay the night."

She bristled at his high-handedness. "That's not necessary. I appreciate your concern but I'm fine. Honestly. I was a little shaky before but now I'm just mad. I'll call the police in the morning and deal with it then."

"Doc, I'm not letting you go home alone tonight. Not after this. A person sick enough to torment you with something as warped as this could be capable of anything. Think about what's best for Dylan if you won't think about yourself."

He picked up her backpack as if the matter were settled, and Ellie pursed her lips. She had two choices, as she saw it. She could start the truck and make a run for it or she could follow him inside the house.

After his brother arrived, she would have backup. He'd have a tough time keeping her there against her will with a cop on the premises, even if the cop happened to be his brother.

Inside, he took off her coat and settled her into a chair as if she were too fragile to take care of herself.

"Tell me what happened. Could you tell if your truck had been broken into?"

She flinched. In the city this never would have happened. This is what she deserved for trying so hard to fit in. "No," she mumbled. "I left it unlocked."

"And you saw the dead cat when you opened the door?"

She nodded. "It was a little hard to miss there on the passenger's seat, with the note pinned between the third and forth ribs on the left side."

Storm clouds gathered on his features again, making him look hard and mad and dangerous. "Where's the cat now?"

"I took it inside the clinic. I'll autopsy it in the morning to try to figure out cause of death. From an initial exam, it looked like it was a feral cat that died of natural causes, but I'll know more tomorrow after I've had a chance to take a closer look."

He took a moment to digest the information, then frowned again. "Who would do this? Do you have any enemies?"

"Believe me, I've racked my brain all evening trying to figure it out. I honestly don't know."

"You been in any fights lately?"

"Yeah," she said dryly. "Didn't you hear? I went four rounds with Stone Cold Steve Austin in the produce aisle of the supermarket just last week."

"Seriously. Can't you think of anyone who might have done this?"

She shrugged. "I've had a few little disagreements with ranchers over treatment of their animals. It's part of the territory. Just business as usual for a vet."

"What kind of disagreements?"

"Well, for one thing, you'd be amazed at some of the conditions people think are perfectly okay for their animals. I'd like to see some of them try to stay healthy when they're living knee-deep in manure. And then they think it's their vet's fault if their animals don't thrive."

"How heated did these little disagreements get?"

"Not hot enough for something like this."

"Well, I still think you better come up with a few names for Jess to check out. Some of these old-timers are set in their ways and don't like an outsider coming in and telling them how to take care of their animals."

Outsider. The word stung like vinegar poured on a cut. How long would it take before she was no longer considered a foreigner in Star Valley? Would that day ever come?

She didn't bother to point out the obvious to Matt—that, for the most part, he still had the exact same attitude. Before she could come up with a nonconfrontational answer, they heard a car door slam.

"That will be Jess," Matt said, a few seconds before his brother burst into the kitchen.

"It's about damn time," Matt snapped. "Where have you been?"

The police chief snorted. "Give me a break. You couldn't have called more than ten minutes ago. What do you want from me? The department's Bronco only goes up to a hundred twenty."

Before Matt could growl out a rejoinder, Ellie rose, stepping forward in an instinctive effort to keep the peace between the brothers. "Thank you for coming out, Jesse, although it's really not necessary. I told your brother we could have done this in the morning."

Jesse immediately shifted his attention to her. To her complete shock, he reached both arms out and folded her into a comforting hug as if they'd been friends for years. "I'm so sorry you had to go through something like this. How are you holding up, sweetheart?"

She stepped away, flustered and touched at once, in time to catch Matt glare at his brother and Jesse return it with a raised eyebrow and a look she could only call speculative.

"Fine," she said quickly. "As I tried repeatedly to tell your brother, I'm really okay. He won't listen to me."

"Matt's a hardheaded son of a gun. Always has been." Jesse grinned at her, then removed his hat and coat and hung them on the rack by the door before making a detour to the fridge.

"I'm starving. Been on since noon. Anything I can eat while Ellie gives her statement?" he asked his older brother.

Matt scowled. "This is serious. Feed your face on your own time."

Jesse ignored him and pulled out a plastic-wrap-covered plate. "Here we go. Cassie's incredible fried chicken. The woman's an angel."

He set the plate on the table, straddled a chair, then nodded to Ellie. "Okay. I'm ready. Why don't you tell me what's been going on? Start at the beginning."

Her mind felt as scattered as dandelion fluff on a windy day, and for a moment she gazed at the two brothers as she tried to collect her thoughts. That didn't help at all. The two of them together in such close proximity were nothing short of breathtaking.

She'd never considered herself a particularly giddy kind of female, but any woman who said her pulse didn't beat a little harder around the Harte brothers—with their dark good looks and those dangerous eyes—would have to be lying.

Matt was definitely the more solemn of the two. There was a hardness about him his younger brother lacked. Jess certainly smiled more often, but she thought she had seen old pain flash a few times in his eyes, like at the dinner table the other day when the talk had turned to their parents.

"Anytime here, Doc."

She pursed her lips at Matt's impatience, but quickly filled the police chief in on what had happened, only pausing a few times to glare at his brother for interrupting.

"I still think it's a prank, nothing more," she finished. "Just a really ghoulish one."

"Hmm. I don't know." Jesse wiped his mouth with a napkin. "The only thing I can do at this point is check out these names you've given me and maybe something will shake out. In the meantime—"

The radio clipped to his belt suddenly squawked static. With an oath, Jesse pulled it out and pressed a button. Then Ellie heard a disembodied voice advising of a rollover accident on U.S. 89 with multiple injuries.

Jesse rose with surprising speed from the chair. "Shoot. I've got to run out to that. We're shorthanded, and the only other officer on patrol is J. B. Nesmith. He won't be able to handle this one on his own. Sorry, Ellie. I was going to tell you to be extra cautious at home and at the clinic. I'll try to have my officers keep an eye on both places whenever they can while the investigation is ongoing."

He shrugged into his coat and shoved on his hat. "Promise you'll call right away if anything else unusual happens. Anything at all." He gave her another quick hug, then rushed out, snagging a leftover brownie as he went.

Chapter 10

The subtle tension simmering between her and Matt had eased somewhat while Jesse was there. After he walked out of the kitchen and left them alone once more, her nerves started humming again like power lines in the wind.

She blew out a quick breath and picked up her backpack from the table. "I think I'll just head home now, too."

Matt's frown creased the weathered corners of his mouth. "I thought we agreed it would be best for you to stay here tonight."

"*We* didn't agree on anything." She stared him down. "You made a proclamation and expected me to simply abide by your word."

He gave her a disgusted look. "I swear, you are the stubbornest damn woman I have ever met."

"That's why you like me so much." She smiled sweetly.

For one sizzling moment he studied her, a strange, glittery light in his eyes. "Oh, is that why?" he finally murmured.

Heat skimmed through her, and she gripped her bag more tightly. She found it completely unfair that he could disarm her with a look, that he could make her insides go all soft and gooey without even trying.

"Please stay, Doc. Just for tonight. You know, if you went home I'd spend the whole night worrying about you, and I've got a horse to train in the morning. You wouldn't want me to make some dumb mistake and ruin her just because I didn't get any sleep, would you?"

"Nice try, cowboy."

He flashed a quick smile that sent her heartbeat into overdrive. "Humor me. It would make me feel a whole lot better knowing you're not at that house by yourself after what happened tonight."

She gave a disgruntled sigh. How could she continue to argue with him when he was being so sweet and protective?

On the other hand, she thoroughly despised this insidious need curling through her to crawl right into his arms and let him take all her worry and stress onto those wide, powerful shoulders.

She could take care of herself. Hadn't she spent most of her life proving it? She wasn't her mother. She didn't need a man to make her feel whole, to smooth the jagged edges of her life.

She could do that all by herself.

"Come on." He rose and headed for the door. "I'll show you to one of the guest rooms."

She looked at the stubborn set of his jaw and sighed. Like water on sandstone, he wasn't going to give up until he totally wore her down. Either that or he would probably insist on following her home and inspecting every single inch of her house for imaginary bogeymen before he could be satisfied it was safe.

The idea of him invading her home—her personal space—with all that masculine intensity was far more disturbing to her peace of mind than spending the night in his guest room.

"This isn't necessary," she grumbled.

"It is for me." He didn't bother to turn around.

She huffed out a disgruntled breath. She would spend this one night in his guest room and then she was going to do her best to stay as far away from Matt Harte as she possibly could, given the facts that Salt River had only five thousand residents, that she was contracted to treat his animals and that they had to plan a carnival together.

He was as dangerous to her heart as his outlaw namesake to an unprotected pile of gold.

The blasted woman wouldn't leave him alone.

Matt jerked the chute up with much more force than necessary. No matter how much he tried to stay away from her, to thrust her from his mind, she somehow managed to work herself right into his thoughts anyway. He couldn't shake her loose to save his life.

Ever since the week before when she had stayed at the ranch, his mind had been filled with the scent of her and the way she had looked in the morning at the kitchen table eating breakfast and laughing with Cassie and the girls. Fresh and clean and so pretty he had stood in the doorway staring at her for what felt like hours.

She haunted his thoughts all day long—and the nights were worse. Try as he might, he couldn't stop thinking about the taste of her mouth and the way she had melted in his arms.

This, though. This was getting ridiculous. He damn well ought to be able to find a little peace from the woman while he was in the middle of checking the prenatal conditions of his pregnant cows.

But here was Steve Nichols bringing her up while he

had one hand inside a bawling heifer. "You hear what happened to Ellie last week?" he asked over his shoulder.

Matt scowled at her name and at the reminder of the grisly offering left in her truck. "Yeah. I heard."

Nichols's blond mustache twitched with his frown. "Your brother have any leads?"

"Not yet. Ellie thinks it's just a prank."

The vet looked at him. "But you don't?"

He shrugged. "I think whoever is capable of doing something like that is one sick son of a bitch."

But a canny one, Matt acknowledged. One who knew how to lay low. Nothing out of the ordinary had happened in the week since she'd found the dead cat in her truck—a stray that, she learned during an autopsy, had indeed died of a natural cause, feline leukemia.

To be cautious, Ellie had installed an extra lock at her house and had hired Junior Zabrinzki's security company to check on the clinic during the night. So far, everything had been quiet, although she still claimed that she sometimes had the eerie feeling someone was watching over her shoulder.

He didn't know any of this firsthand. He'd only seen Ellie once since she had stayed at the ranch, the day before, when she'd come out to treat some of his horses. Despite his best efforts to pry information out of her, somehow the contrary woman managed to steer every single conversation back to his animals.

Good thing his little brother was the chief of police. If he hadn't forced Jesse to give him regular progress reports on the investigation, he would have been a whole lot more annoyed at Ellie.

Progress was far too optimistic a word, though, from the reports he'd been getting. Jess was still as stumped by the threat as he'd been that first night, and Matt was getting pretty impatient about it.

"You talk to a lot of ranchers around here," he said suddenly to Nichols. "You have any ideas who might be angry enough at Ellie to threaten her like that?"

Steve shook his head, regret in his eyes. "I wish I did, but I'm as baffled as anybody else. I know she's had a rough time of it with some of the old-timers. Ellie's not exactly afraid to speak her mind when she sees things she doesn't like and, I have to admit, some of her ideas are a little out there. But I really thought things had been better for her in the last month or so."

He had to give Nichols credit for not showing any sign that he minded Ellie's presence in Star Valley. He wasn't sure he would have been so gracious in the same circumstances if a rival suddenly moved in to his business turf.

"I'd sure like to find out who it is, though," Steve said, his voice tight and his movements jerky. "It kills me to think about her finding something as sick as that. Of being so frightened. Ellie's a good vet and a wonderful person. She didn't deserve that."

Matt sent the other man a swift look, surprised by his vehemence. Maybe it was just professional respect, but somehow he didn't think so. Nichols acted more like a man with a personal stake in her business.

Did the two of them have a thing going? The thought left a taste in his mouth about as pleasant as rotten crab apples, and he had a sudden, savage urge to pound something.

But what business was it of his if she was seeing Steve? He had no claim on her, none at all. They were friends, nothing more. And not even very good friends at that.

Did she kiss Nichols with the same fiery passion she'd shown him? he wondered, then instantly regretted it.

"The investigation is still open," he said tersely. "Sooner or later Jess will get to the bottom of it."

"I hope so. I really hope so."

They turned to the cows and were running the last heifer through the chute when Hector Aguella hurried into the pens, his dark, weathered face taut with worry. "Boss, I think we got a problem."

"What's up?"

"Some of the horses, they're acting real strange. Like they got into some bad feed or something. I don't know. They're all shaking and got ugly stuff coming out their noses."

"How many?"

"Six, maybe. You better take a look."

"I'll come with you," Nichols said.

The noonday sun glared off the snow as he and Steve headed toward the horse pasture. When they were close enough to see what was happening, Matt growled an oath.

Even from here, it was obvious the horses were sick. They stood in listless little groups, noses running and tremors shaking their bodies.

"Call Doc Webster and get her out here fast," he ordered Hector, breaking in to a run. "And send Jim and Monte over to help me separate the healthy animals from the sick ones. If this is some kind of epidemic, I don't want to lose the whole damn herd."

"Do you want me to examine them?" Nichols called after him.

He hesitated for only a moment. Technically, the horses were Ellie's territory, but it seemed idiotic to refuse the other vet's offer of help when it could be an hour or more before she arrived at the ranch. "Yeah. Thanks."

With the help of the ranch hands, they quickly moved the animals who weren't showing any sign of sickness to a different pasture, then Steve began taking temperatures and doing quick physical exams.

"What do you think they've got?" Matt asked after the vet had looked at the last sick horse.

Steve scratched his head where thinning hair met scalp. "I've never seen anything like this. It looks like some kind of staph infection. They've all got the same big, oozing abscess."

"What kind?"

"I don't know. Whatever it is, it's hit them all the same. They've all got fevers, runny noses and chills. We'll have to run a culture to find out for sure. Whatever it is, it's damn scary if it can cause these symptoms to come on so fast. You said they were fine yesterday, right?"

"Yeah. I didn't notice anything unusual. So you're thinking a bacterial infection? Not something they ate?"

"That's what it looks like. I'm concerned about the abscess."

"How could something like that have hit them all at the same time?"

"I don't know." Steve paused. "When I was in vet school I heard about a herd getting something similar to this. Same symptoms, anyway."

"What was the cause there?"

"If I remember right, it was traced to unsanitary syringes used for vaccinations. Ellie hasn't given them any shots lately, has she?"

"She was out yesterday, but all she did was that acupuncture stuff on some of the mares to ease some of their pregnancy discomfort." He stopped, an ugly suspicion taking root.

Yesterday. Ellie had been here yesterday with her needles. Could she have done something that caused the animals to become deathly ill? Could she have used bad needles or something?

He couldn't believe it—didn't *want* to believe it. But it was one hell of a coincidence. He pushed the thought away. Now wasn't the time for accusations and blame. Not when his horses needed treatment. "So what can we do?"

"Push high dosages of penicillin and wait and see. That's about all we can do for the time being."

"You got any antibiotics with you?"

"Not much but enough, I think. It's in my truck over by the chutes. Let's hope it's the right one. I'll run a culture as soon as I can so we'll know better what we're dealing with."

He was only gone a few moments when Ellie's rattle-trap of a pickup pulled up, and she emerged from it flushed and breathless.

"What's happening? Hector said you've got an emergency but he didn't say what. Is it Mystic? Is she threatening to lose the foal again?"

Before he could answer, her gaze landed on the horses, still shuddering with chills, and all color leached from her face. "Holy cow. What happened to them?"

"You tell me," Matt growled.

She sent him a startled look. "I…I can't know that without a thorough examination. How long have they been like this?"

Faster than a wildfire consuming dry brush, anger scorched through him—at her and at himself. He should have known better, dammit, than to let a pretty face convince him to go against his own judgment.

He should never have let her touch his stock with her wacky California ideas. He wouldn't have, except she had somehow beguiled him with her soft eyes and her stubborn chin and her hair that smelled like spring.

And now his horses were going to pay the price for his gullibility.

"What did you do to them?" He bit the words out.

She paled at the fury in his voice and stepped back half a pace. "What do you mean?"

"They were fine yesterday until you came out messing around with your New Age Chinese bull. What did you do?"

"Nothing I haven't done before. Just what you hired me to do, treat your horses."

She narrowed her green eyes at him suddenly. "Wait a minute. Are you blaming me for this? You think *I* caused whatever is making them sick?"

"Nichols says he thinks it's some kind of virulent bacterial infection. Maybe even—"

She interrupted him. "What does Steve have to do with this?"

"We were giving prenatal exams to the cows," he said impatiently. "He was with me when Hector came to tell us about the horses."

"And he thinks *I* infected these horses?"

"He said he's seen a similar case caused by infected syringes. The only needles these animals have seen in a month have been yours, Doc. You and your acupuncture baloney."

He refused to let himself be affected by the way her face paled and her eyes suddenly looked haunted. "You… you can't believe that's what caused this."

"You have any other ideas? Because from where I'm sitting, you're the most logical source."

She looked bewildered and lost and hurt, and he had to turn away to keep from reaching for her, to fold her into his arms and tell her everything would be okay.

"You can leave now," he said harshly, angry at himself for the impulse. "Steve is handling things from now on."

He had to hand it to her. She didn't back down, just

tilted that chin of hers, all ready to take another one on the jaw. "We have a contract for another two months."

"Consider it void. You'll get your money, every penny of it, but I don't want you touching my horses again."

He drew a deep breath, trying to contain the fury prowling through him like a caged beast. It wasn't just the horses. He could deal with her making a mistake, especially since the tiny corner of his brain that could still think rationally was convinced she would never willfully hurt his animals.

But he had trusted her. Had let himself begin to care for her. He had given her a chance despite his instincts to the contrary, and she had violated that trust by passing on a potentially deadly illness to six of his animals.

He refused to look at her, knowing he would weaken when he saw the hurt in her eyes. He was a fool when it came to women. An absolute idiot. First Melanie with her needy eyes and her lying tongue and now Ellie with her sweet-faced innocence.

She had suckered him into completely forgetting his responsibilities—that the ranch came first, not pretty red-haired veterinarians. He was thirty-six years old and he damn well should have known better.

"That's your decision, of course," she said quietly after a moment, her voice as thin and brittle as old glass. "I certainly understand. You have to do what you think is right for your animals. Goodbye, Matt."

She walked out of the barn, her shoulders stiff with dignity. He watched her go for only a moment, then turned to his horses.

What was she doing?

Hours later, Ellie navigated the winding road to the Diamond Harte while the wipers struggled to keep the windshield clear of the thick, wet snow sloshing steadily down.

She should be home in bed on a snowy night like tonight, curled into herself and weeping for the loss of a reputation she had spent five months trying to establish in Salt River. A reputation that had crumbled like dry leaves in one miserable afternoon.

That's what she wanted to be doing, wallowing in a good, old-fashioned pity party. Instead, here she was at nearly midnight, her stomach a ball of nerves and the steering wheel slipping through her sweat-slicked hands.

Matt would be furious if he found her sneaking onto the Diamond Harte in the middle of the night. The way he had spoken to her earlier, she wouldn't be surprised if he called his brother to haul her off to jail.

But despite his order to stay away, she knew she needed to do this. Cassie had tried to reassure her that the horses' conditions had improved when Ellie called earlier in the evening, but it wasn't good enough. She would never be able to sleep until she could be sure the animals would pull through.

She couldn't believe this was happening, that in a single afternoon her whole world could shatter apart like a rickety fence in a strong wind.

Matt's horses had only been the first to fall ill. By midafternoon, she'd received calls from the three other ranches she'd visited the day before reporting that all the horses she had seen in the last forty-eight hours had come down with the same mysterious symptoms.

She'd done her best for the afflicted animals, treating them with high dosages of penicillin while she struggled exhaustively to convince the ranchers to continue allowing her to treat their stock.

And to convince herself this couldn't be her fault.

The evidence was mounting, though. And damning. It did indeed look like staph infection, centered near the entry marks where she had treated each horse with acupuncture the day before.

How could this be happening? She was so careful. Washing her hands twice as long as recommended, using only sterile needles from a reputable supplier.

Maybe she'd gotten a bad batch somehow, but she couldn't imagine how that was possible. Each needle came wrapped in a sterile package and was used only once.

The same questions had been racing themselves around and around in her head until she was dizzy from them, but she was no closer to figuring out how such a nightmare could have occurred.

Hard to believe the day before she'd felt on top of the world, had finally begun to think she had actually found a place she could belong here in Salt River.

All her dreams of making a stable, safe, fulfilling life for Dylan and for herself were falling apart. When this was over, she was very much afraid she would be lucky to find a job selling dog food, let alone continue practicing veterinary medicine anywhere in western Wyoming.

Every time she thought about the future, all she could focus on was this sick, greasy fear that she would have to sell the practice at a huge loss and go back to California and face all the smug people who would be so ready with I-told-you-so's.

She would have to leave the people she had come to care about here. SueAnn. Sarah McKenzie. Cassie Harte. Matt.

Her chest hurt whenever she thought about him, about the way he had looked at her earlier in the day. With contempt and repugnance, like she was something messy and disgusting stuck to the heel of his boot.

He shouldn't have had the power to wound her so deeply with only a look, and it scared her to death that he could. How had she come to care for him—for his opinion of her—so much?

He should mean nothing more to her than the rest of her clients. Only another rancher paying her to keep his horses healthy, that's all. So why couldn't she convince her heart?

The pickup's old tires slid suddenly on a patch of black ice hidden beneath the few inches of snow covering the road, and panic skittered through her for the few seconds it took the truck to find traction again. When it did, she blew out a breath and pushed away thoughts of Matt Harte and his chilling contempt for her. She needed to concentrate on the road, not on the disaster her life had turned into.

At the ranch, she pulled to the back of the horse barn, grateful it was far enough from the house that she could sneak in undetected. She climbed out of the truck on bones that felt brittle and achy and crunched through the ankle-deep snow to the door.

Inside, the horse barn was dark except for a low light burning near the far end where, she supposed, the sick mares were being kept. She made her way down the long row of stalls and was about halfway there when a broad-shouldered figure stepped out of the darkness and into the small circle of light.

Chapter 11

Matt.

Her heart stuttered in her chest, and for a moment she forgot to breathe, caught between a wild urge to turn around and run for the door in disgrace and a stubborn determination to stand her ground.

His little brindle-colored cow dog gave one sharp bark, then jumped up to greet her, tail wagging cheerfully. Ellie reached down and gave her a little pat, grateful at least somebody was happy to see her.

"Zoe, heel," he ordered.

With a sympathetic look in her brown eyes, the dog obeyed, slinking back to curl up at his feet once more.

"What are you doing here?" he asked.

Maybe it was wishful thinking on her part, but she could almost believe he sounded more resigned than angry to find her sneaking into his barn. At least he didn't sound quite ready to call the cops on her. That gave her enough courage to creep a few steps closer to that welcoming circle of light.

Behind him, she caught sight of a canvas cot and a rumpled sleeping bag. Matt had surrendered the comfort of his warm bed to stay the night in a musty old barn where he could be near his ailing horses.

The hard, painful casing around her heart began to crack a little, and she pressed a hand to her chest, inexplicably moved by this further evidence of what a good, caring man he was.

"Doc?" he prompted. "What are you doing here?"

She drew in a shaky breath. "I know you told me to stay away, but I couldn't. I…I just wanted to check on them."

"Cass said you called. Didn't you believe her when she told you the antibiotics seemed to be working?"

Heat crawled up her cheeks despite the chill of the barn. "I did. I just had to see for myself. I'm sorry. I know I have no right to be here. Not anymore. I won't touch them, I swear. Just look."

His jaw flexed but he didn't say anything and she took that as tacit permission. Turning her back on him, she slowly walked the way she had come, down the long line of stalls, giving each animal a visual exam.

As Cassie had reported, the infection seemed to have run its course. At least their symptoms seemed to have improved. Relief gushed over her, and she had to swallow hard against the choking tears that threatened.

"Delilah seems to have been hit worst," Matt said just behind her, so close his breath rippled across her cheek. "She's still running a fever but it's dropped quite a bit from earlier."

Trying fiercely to ignore the prickles of awareness as he invaded her space, she followed the direction of his gaze to the dappled gray. "What are you putting on that abscess on her flank?"

He told her and she nodded. "Good. That should take care of it."

"Now that you mention it, it's probably time for another application." He picked up a small container of salve from the top rail of the fence and entered the stall.

Speaking softly to the horse, he rubbed the mixture on to the painful-looking sore, and Ellie watched, feeling useless. She hated this, being sidelined into the role of observer instead of being able to *do* something. It went against her nature to simply stand here and watch.

He finished quickly and crossed to the sink to wash his hands. An awkward silence descended between them, broken only by the soft rustling of hay. Matt was the first to break it. "How are all the other horses faring?" he asked.

"You know about the others?" Why did she feel this deep, ugly shame when she knew in her heart none of this could be her fault?

He nodded. "Nichols told me. Three other ranches, a dozen horses in all including my six."

She had to fight the urge to press her hand against her roiling stomach at the stark statistics. "Just call me Typhoid Mary."

To her surprise, instead of the disdain she expected to see, his eyes darkened with sympathy. "So how are they?" he asked.

"I lost one." Her voice strained as she tried to sound brisk and unaffected. "One of Bob Meyers's quarter horses. She was old and sickly anyway from an upper respiratory illness and just wasn't strong enough to fight off the infection, even after antibiotics."

Despite her best efforts, she could feel her chin wobble a little and she tightened her lips together to make it stop.

The blasted man never did as she expected. Instead of showing her scorn, he reached a hand out to give her shoulder a comforting squeeze, making her chin quiver even more.

"I'm sorry," he murmured.

She let herself lean in to his strength for just a moment then subtly eased away. "I don't know what happened, Matt. I am so careful. Obsessively so. I always double scrub. Maybe I got a bad shipment of needles or something. I just don't know."

"It's eating you up inside, isn't it?"

"I became a vet to heal. And look what I've done!"

His fingers brushed her shoulder again. "You can't beat yourself up about it for the rest of your life."

He was silent for a moment, then sent her a sidelong glance. "I said some pretty nasty things to you earlier. Treated you a lot worse than you deserved. I'm sorry for that."

His brusquely worded apology fired straight to her heart. "You were worried about your horses."

"I was, but I still shouldn't have lashed out at you like that. I apologize."

"You have nothing to be sorry about. You had every right to be upset—I would have been if they were my horses. I understand completely that you want to bring Steve back on-board. He seems to have handled the situation exactly right."

He shrugged. "Well, they all seem to be doing okay now. Mystic was the one I was most worried about, but she was eating fine tonight, and neither she or her foal seem to be suffering any ill effects."

Something in what he said briefly caught her attention, like a wrong note in a piano concerto. Before she could isolate it, he continued. "As for the others, I think we're out of the danger zone."

"But you decided to stay the night out here anyway."

He shrugged. It might have been a trick of the low lighting, but she could swear she saw color climbing up his cheeks. "It seemed like a good idea, just to be on the safe side."

"Well, I'm sorry I woke you."

"You didn't. I was just reading."

She looked over his shoulder and saw a well-worn copy of Owen Wister's *The Virginian* lying spine up on the army-green blanket covering the cot. "Apparently your father was not the only one interested in the Old West."

A wry smile touched his lips. "It's a classic, what can I say? The father of all Westerns."

She could drown in that smile, the way it creased at the edges of his mouth and softened his eyes and made him look years younger. She could stay here forever, just gazing at it....

"Wait a minute." The jarring note from before pounded louder in her head. "Wait a minute. Did you say Mystic was sick, too?"

He nodded and pointed to the stall behind them. Dust motes floated on the air, tiny gold flakes in the low light. Through them she could see the little mare asleep in the stall.

The implications exploded through her, and she rushed to the stall for a better look. "I didn't treat her yesterday!" she exclaimed. "Don't you remember? I was going to. She was on my schedule. But I ran out of time and planned to come back later when I could spend more time with her."

"What does that have to do with anything?"

"Don't you get it? If Mystic came down with the same thing the others had, it can't be because of me, because of any staph infection I might have introduced through unsanitary needles, like Steve implied. I didn't even touch her yesterday!"

He frowned. "You did a few weeks ago."

"So why didn't she show symptoms of illness much earlier than yesterday, when all the other horses became sick?"

"Maybe it was some delayed reaction on her part. Just took it longer to hit her."

"No. That doesn't make sense. I've been through at least two boxes of needles since then. They couldn't have all been bad, or every single one of my patients would have the same illness. Don't you see? Something else caused this, not me!"

She wasn't thinking, caught up only in the exhilaration—this vast, consuming relief to realize she hadn't unknowingly released some deadly plague on her patients. If her brain had been functioning like it should have been, she certainly would never have thrown her arms around Matt in jubilation.

She only hugged him for a moment. As soon as reality intruded—when she felt the soft caress of his chamois shirt against her cheek and smelled the clean, male scent of him—she froze, mortified at her impulsiveness. Awareness began as a flutter in her stomach, a hitch in her breathing.

"Sorry," she mumbled and pulled away.

He stood awkwardly, arms still stiff at his sides, then moved to rest his elbows on the top rail of Mystic's stall to keep from reaching for her again. "We've still got twelve sick animals here, then. Any ideas why?"

"No. Nothing." She frowned. "Steve's right, it has all the signs of a bacterial infection, but it's like no other I've ever seen before. And how could it spread from your ranch to the rest that have been hit, unless by something I did? I seem to be the only common link."

"Maybe you tracked something on your boots somehow."

"I don't know of anything that could be this virulent in that kind of trace amount. And what about the abscesses?"

He had no more answers than she did, so he remained silent. After a long moment, she sighed. "The grim reality is, we might never know. I'll get some bloodwork done and send the rest of the needles from the same box to the lab and see what turns up. Who knows. We might get lucky and they can identify something we haven't even thought about. Something that's not even related to me."

"I hope so," he said gruffly.

He wasn't sure when the anger that had driven him all afternoon had begun to mellow, but eventually his common sense had won out. Even if she had spread the infection, he had no doubt it was accidental, something beyond her control.

She was a good vet who cared about her patients. She would never knowingly cause them harm.

"I really hope for your sake everything turns up clean," he said quietly.

She flashed him another one of those watery smiles that hid a wealth of emotions. This had to be killing her. It would be tough on any vet, but especially for one as passionate and dedicated as Ellie.

"Thanks." After a moment, she let out a deep breath. "It's late. I should go so you can get back to your book."

She didn't look very thrilled at the idea. Truth be told, she didn't look at all eager to walk out into the mucky snow. She looked lonely.

"Where's Dylan tonight?" he asked.

"At SueAnn's. I was afraid I'd get called out in the middle of the night to one of the other ranches and would have to leave her home alone. I really hate doing that, so Sue offered to take her for the night."

"You have no reason to rush off, then?"

She blinked. "No. Why?"

"You could stay. Keep me company."

Where the hell did that come from? He wanted to swallow the words as soon as they left his mouth, but it was too late now. She was already looking at him, as astounded as if he'd just offered to give her a makeover or something.

"You…you really want my company after today?"

The doubt in her voice just about did him in. He was such a pushover for a woman in distress. She only had to look at him out of those big, wounded eyes and he was lost, consumed with the need to take care of her—to relieve that tension from her shoulders, to tease a laugh or two out of her, to make her forget her troubles for a moment.

"Yeah," he said gruffly. "Come on. Sit down."

Still looking as wary as if she had just crawled in to a wolverine's den, she unzipped her coat and shrugged out of it. Underneath, she wore a daisy-yellow turtleneck covered by a fluffy navy polar fleece vest.

She looked young and fresh and sweet, and he suddenly realized what a disastrous error in judgment he had just committed. Why hadn't he shoved her out the door when he had the chance?

His control around her was shaky at the best of times. Here, alone in a dimly lit barn with only the soft murmur of animals and rustling of hay surrounding them, he hoped like hell he would be able to keep his hands off her.

She perched on the edge of his cot while he rounded up the old slat-backed wooden chair that probably dated back to his grandfather's day. He finally found it near the sink under a pile of old cattle magazines and carried it to the circle of light near the cot.

She was leafing through *The Virginian,* he saw after he sat down. Her smile was slow, almost shy. "I read this in high school English class. I remember how it made me want to cry. I think that's when I first decided I wanted to move to Wyoming. I'll have to see if the library in town has a copy I could read again."

"You can borrow that one when I'm finished if you want."

This time her smile came more quickly. "Thanks."

"It was one of my dad's favorites. He loved them all. Louis L'Amour, Zane Grey, Max Brand. All the good ones. During roundup when we were kids, he always kept a book tucked in his saddlebags to read to us by the glow of the campfire. We ate it up."

"You miss him, don't you?"

He thought of the gaping hole his parents' deaths had left in his life. "Yeah," he finally said. "We didn't always get along but he was a good man. Always willing to do anything for anyone. I'd be happy if I could die with people thinking I was half the man he was."

"Why didn't you get along?"

Zoe shoved her nose against his knee, and he gave her an obligatory pat, trying to form his answer. "Mom always said we were so much alike we brought out the worst in each other. I don't know. I thought he should have done more with the ranch. Expanded the operation, bid on more grazing rights so we could take on a bigger herd. I thought he didn't have any ambition. Took me a long time to realize he might not have seemed ambitious to his cocky eighteen-year-old son, but only because he didn't have to be. He didn't see the need to strive for more when he already had everything he wanted from life."

"Do you?"

His hand stilled on Zoe's ruff. "What?"

"Have everything you want?"

He used to think so. A month ago he would have said yes without hesitating. He had the ranch and Lucy and his family, and it should have been enough for him. Lately, though, he'd been restless for more. Hungry. He prowled around the house at night, edgy inside his skin.

A month ago he had kissed her just a few feet from here.

He pushed the memory away. That had nothing to do with it. Absolutely nothing.

"I'd like somebody to invent a horse that never needs shoes. But other than that, yeah. I guess I'm content."

It wasn't really a lie. Right now, at least, he was more relaxed than he'd been in a long time. He refused to dwell on exactly why that might be the case and whether it had anything to do with Ellie.

"I'd still like to expand the operation a little more, especially the cutting horse side of it. I guess you could say that's where my heart is, in training the horses. The cattle are the lifeblood for the ranch but for me, nothing compares to turning a green-broke horse into a savvy, competition-quality cutter."

He paused, waiting for her to respond. When she didn't, he peered through the dim light and realized he'd been baring his soul to the horses. Ellie was asleep, her head propped against the rough plank wall and her sable-tipped lashes fanned out over her cheeks.

He watched her sleep for several moments, struck again by how beautiful she was. In sleep, she couldn't hang on to that tough, take-it-on-the-chin facade she tried to show the world. Instead, she looked small and fragile, all luminous skin and delicate bones.

For just a moment, he had a wild, fierce wish that things could be different. That he was free to slide beside her on the cot and press his mouth to that fluttering pulse at the base of her neck. That he could waken her with slow, languid kisses then spend the rest of the night making love to her in the hushed secrecy of the barn.

As tempting as the idea was—and it had him shifting in the hard slat chair as blood surged to his groin— he knew it was impossible. In the first place, she likely wouldn't be too thrilled to wake up and find him slobbering all over her.

In the second, even if she didn't push him away, even if

by some miracle she opened her arms to him, welcomed him with her mouth and her hands and her body, what the hell good would it do? It wouldn't change anything.

Now that she was asleep, he could admit to himself that she was the cause of this restlessness prowling inside his skin. But even if he were free to kiss her again, it couldn't change the indisputable fact that he had nothing to give her but a few heated moments of pleasure.

For a woman like Ellie, that would never be enough. He knew it instinctively, just as he suddenly feared making love with her once would only whet his hunger, leave him starving for more. Like a little kid who was only allowed one quick lick of a delectable ice-cream cone.

She was soft and gutsy and spirited, and if he wasn't damn careful, he could lose his heart to her. The thought scared him worse than being in the rodeo ring with a dozen angry bulls.

He'd been in that position once. He had loved Melanie in the beginning—or thought he did, anyway—and it had nearly destroyed him.

Here in the silent barn, he could see his ex-wife as clearly as if she were sitting beside him. Dark, curling hair, haunted gray eyes, features delicate as a porcelain doll.

She had been so unhappy from the very beginning. Nothing he did had been enough for her. If he brought her roses, she wanted orchids. If he took her to dinner, she would make some small, wistful comment about how much she enjoyed quiet evenings at home.

Everything had always been hot or cold with her. Either she was on fire for him and couldn't get enough or she wouldn't let him touch her, would screech at him to keep his rough, working hands to himself.

In retrospect, he could see all the signs of manic depression, but he'd been too young and too damn stubborn to admit then that she needed professional help. It had taken him years to realize he couldn't have saved her, that her unhappiness had been as much a part of her as her gray eyes.

When he couldn't fill the empty spot inside her, when he finally gave up trying, she had turned to other men, throwing her many conquests in his face at every opportunity. The first one had eaten him up inside, and he'd gone to the Renegade to beat the hell out of the unlucky cowhand. By the fourth or fifth affair, he told himself he didn't care.

He could still remember his cold fury when he found out she was pregnant, the bitter, hateful words they had flung at each other like sharp heavy stones.

At first he'd been afraid Lucy had been the product of one of her other relationships. The first time he held her, though, it had ceased to matter. He'd completely lost his heart to the chubby little girl with the big gray eyes, and he would have fought to the death if someone tried to take her from him.

But now, as Lucy grew into her looks, it became obvious she was a Harte through and through, from that dimple in her chin to her high cheekbones to her cupid's bow of a mouth. She looked exactly like pictures of his mother at that age.

Something snapped inside Melanie after Lucy was born. It might have been postpartum depression, he didn't know, but everything she did had taken on a desperate edge. She'd spent every night haunting the Renegade in town, looking for trouble, trying to find some way out of Salt River, Wyoming. She'd found both in Zack Slater.

He blew out a breath. Why was he even thinking about this, about her? Maybe because Melanie was the reason he could never let another woman inside him. Why he would always be quick to fury and start throwing blame around, like he'd done with Ellie earlier that day.

He was afraid the wounds Melanie had carved in his soul would always make doubt and suspicion lurk just below the surface.

Ellie didn't deserve that. She deserved a man who could give her everything, especially the safe, secure home she'd never had as a kid. A man who could love her completely with a heart still whole and unscarred.

Whoa. Where did love fit in the picture? He didn't love her. No way. He was attracted to her and he admired certain qualities about her. Her resilience, her stubborn determination to succeed in the face of overwhelming adversity, her passion for her work. The same qualities that most irritated him, he admitted ruefully.

And he was fiercely attracted to her, no doubt about that. But love? No way.

He shifted, trying to find a more comfortable spot on the unforgiving wood chair. He didn't want to think about this. He couldn't give her what she deserved so he had to settle for giving her nothing.

He knew it, had known it since he met her. So why did the realization make him so damned miserable?

He pushed away the thoughts. They weren't doing him any good. Instead, he turned his mind to the puzzle of the sick horses. What was the connection between them?

Ellie.

He wished he could be as convinced as she appeared to be that she had nothing to do with the sick horses. But what other link could there be? Like she'd said, the ranches that had been hit were miles apart and didn't appear to share anything else in common but their veterinarian.

Or at least they *had* shared Ellie. He had a feeling she would have a hard time keeping any clients unless she could prove without a doubt she wasn't to blame for the epidemic.

He would contract with her again to treat his horses. He had to. She would be devastated if she lost the practice. That and her kid were everything to her.

If someone wanted to destroy her practice, they had hit on the perfect method—shattering her reputation.

The thought had him sitting up straighter as he remembered the grisly message left in her truck. Someone out there didn't want her in Star Valley. If he was twisted enough to leave a dead cat in her truck, wouldn't he be capable of anything? Even something as sick and warped as harming a dozen innocent animals in order to implicate Ellie? To force her to leave by driving away her patients?

No. He couldn't believe it. Who would do such a thing? And how would anyone possibly manage it? Some of the animals might have been pastured near enough to roads or in distant enough corrals for someone to slip them something—maybe give them a shot without anyone noticing—but sneaking onto the Diamond Harte would be damn near impossible.

Still, it wouldn't hurt to mention the theory to Jess. If there was a connection between the sick horses and the warning note, his little brother would find it.

Ellie made a little sound in her sleep, drawing his attention again. She'd be a whole lot more comfortable under the blanket with her head on his pillow instead of sitting up like that.

Of course, then he'd be forced to find another place to sleep for the night.

He sighed and rose to his feet, then gently eased her to the cot, knowing he didn't have a choice. She didn't stir at all when he drew the heavy blanket over her shoulders and tucked it under her chin.

He returned to the hard wooden chair, leaned his head against the rough plank wall and watched her sleep for a long time.

Chapter 12

Ellie wasn't sure what awakened her. One moment she was dreaming of lying beside Matt Harte on a white-sand beach somewhere while a trade wind rustled the leaves on the palm trees around her and water lapped against the shore, and the next her senses were filled with the musty-sweet smell of hay and the soft, furtive rustling of the horses in their stalls.

She blinked for a moment, stuck in that hazy world between sleep and consciousness, and tried to remember why she wearing her clothes and curled up on a hard cot in someone's barn. Her back was stiff, her neck ached from sleeping in an odd position and she felt rumpled and uncomfortable in her ropers and jeans.

She sat up, running a hand through tangled hair. As she did, her gaze landed on Matt across the dim, dusty barn, and the events of the night before came rushing back like the tide.

This was *his* barn. She was curled up in *his* makeshift bed.

Ellie winced and hit the light on her watch. Four a.m. She must have been sleeping for hours. The last time she remembered checking her watch had been midnight, when Matt had been talking about his horses.

Embarrassed guilt flooded through her. Not only had she been rude enough to drift off in the middle of their conversation, but she had fallen asleep in the man's bed, forcing him to sleep in that torturous hard-backed chair.

He couldn't possibly be comfortable, with his neck twisted and his head propped against the wall like that. But he was definitely asleep. His eyes didn't so much as flutter, and his chest moved evenly with each slow, deep breath.

She watched for a moment, hypnotized by the cotton rippling over his hard chest with the soft rise and fall of his breathing, then her gaze climbed higher, over the tanned column of his neck to roam across the rugged planes and angles of his face. The strong blade of a nose, the full, sensuous lips, the spike of his dark eyelashes.

He was sinfully gorgeous and completely one in his surroundings, like something out of a Charles Russell painting.

Had he watched *her* this way after she drifted off? The thought unnerved her, made her insides feel hot and liquid, but wasn't enough to compel her to turn away. Even though it was probably an invasion of his privacy, watching him like this was a temptation she couldn't resist.

In sleep, Matt lost the hard edges that made him seem so tough and formidable. He looked younger, more relaxed, as if only in sleep was he free to shake the mantle of responsibility that had settled on his strong, capable shoulders so young.

What must it have been like for him after his parents died? She tried to imagine and couldn't. He had been twenty-two and suddenly responsible for a huge ranch and two troublesome, grieving younger siblings.

No wonder he seemed so remote and detached sometimes. He had grown up and become an adult at a time when many other young men were still having fraternity parties and taking trips to Fort Lauderdale for spring break. Instead of raising hell, Matt had raised his younger brother and sister.

And yet he had another side. She thought of the teasing grin he reserved for his daughter, the soft, soothing voice he used to calm a fractious horse, the woofs of a contented cow dog being stroked by his gentle hands.

He was so different from the perceptions she had formed about him that first day in Ms. McKenzie's classroom. Before then, even. She had thought him narrow-minded and humorless. Stuffy and set in his ways. But in the weeks since, she'd come to appreciate the many layers beneath that tough exterior. Hardworking rancher, devoted family man. Honest and well-respected member of the community. He was all those things and more.

It wouldn't take much for her to fall headlong in love with him.

The thought bulleted into her brain and completely staggered her. She paled, reaching for the edge of the cot to steady herself as a grim realization settled in her heart.

She was already more than halfway there.

She shivered, suddenly chilled to the bone despite the blanket he must have thrown across her knees.

How had she let things go so far? After her disastrous relationship with Kurt, she had been so diligent. So fiercely careful not to let anyone into her heart.

She didn't need anyone else—she and Dylan managed just fine, dammit.

Emotions like love were messy and complicated. They made a woman needy and vulnerable and stupid. Like her mother had been, like she had been with Kurt.

Besides, she had enough on her plate right now, trying

to keep the practice alive and food in her daughter's mouth. She didn't have room in her life for a man, especially one like Matt Harte who would demand everything and more from her. He wasn't the kind of man who would be content to stay put in a neat little compartment of her life until she had time for him. He would want it all.

She could try to convince herself until she was blue in the face but it wouldn't change the fact that he had somehow managed to sneak in to her heart when she wasn't looking.

Was it possible to be only a little in love with someone? If so, maybe she could stop things right now before she sunk completely over her head. It would be hard but not impossible to rebuild the protective walls around her heart, especially if she kept her distance for a while.

She could do it. She had to try. The alternative was just too awful to contemplate.

She would start by leaving this cozy little corner of the barn and going back to her own house where she belonged. Soundlessly, she pushed away the blanket and planted her boots on the ground, wincing a little as stiff muscles complained at being treated so callously. If she was this sore, she imagined Matt would be much worse when he awoke.

She thought about waking him up so he could take the cot and even went so far as to reach a hand out to shake him from his slumber, then yanked it back. No. Better to sneak out and avoid any more awkwardness between them.

She shrugged into her coat and headed for the door. As she passed Mystic's stall, the little mare nickered softly in greeting, and Ellie stopped, jerking her head around to see if Matt woke up. He was still propped against the wall like one of those old-time wooden dime-store Indians, and she let her breath out in relief.

It wouldn't hurt to take a look at the horse while she

was here, she decided. She could do it quietly enough that it didn't disturb Matt. Straw whispered underfoot as she made her way to the little mare's stall. The door squeaked when she opened it, but Matt slept on.

"You're a pretty girl, aren't you?" She pitched her voice low, running her hands over the horse's abdomen to feel for the foal's position. "Yes, you are. And you'll be a wonderful mama in just a few more months. The time will go so fast and before you know it your little one will be dancing circles around you and tumbling into trouble."

The mare made a noise that sounded remarkably like a resigned sigh, and Ellie laughed softly again. "Don't start complaining now. It's your own fault. You should have thought about what you might be in for when you cuddled up to that big handsome stud who got you this way. You had your fun and now you have to pay the piper."

Mystic blew out a disgusted puff of air through her nose and lipped at her shoulder, and Ellie nodded in agreement. "I know. Men. But what's a girl to do? They look at you out of those gorgeous blue eyes and it's all you can do to remember to breathe, let alone keep your heart out of harm's way."

"You carry on heart-to-heart chats with all your patients?"

She jerked her head up at the rough, amused voice behind her and found Matt leaning his forearms on the top rail of the stall, his hair mussed a little from sleep and a day's growth stubbling his cheeks.

As predictable as the sunrise, she forgot to breathe again. "Hi," she said after a moment, her voice high and strained.

"Going somewhere?" He gestured to her coat.

"Home. I've stayed long enough. I only wanted to check Mystic one more time before I go. I hope that's okay."

He didn't answer, just continued watching her out of

solemn blue eyes, and her stomach started a long, slow tremble.

"I'm sorry I took your bed. I didn't mean to. I must have just drifted off. Yesterday was a pretty rough day all around, and I guess all that stress took its toll on me." She was babbling but couldn't seem to help herself. "Anyway, you should have booted me out and sent me home. You must be one big bundle of aches right now."

"I ache," he finally said, his low voice vibrating in the cool predawn air. "I definitely ache."

She was suddenly positive he wasn't talking about a stiff neck. The trembling in her stomach rippled to her knees, to her shoulders, to her fingers. She shoved her hands into the deep pockets of the fleece vest, praying he wouldn't notice, but she couldn't do anything about the rest except take a shaky breath and hope her knees would wait to collapse until she made it out of the barn.

"Well, I, um, I should be going," she mumbled.

Nerves scrambling, she patted Mystic one last time, then walked out of the stall. She managed to avoid looking at him until she had carefully closed the door behind her.

When she did—when she finally lifted her gaze to his— she was stunned by the raw hunger blazing in his eyes.

She must have made some sound—his name, maybe— and then he ate up the distance between them in two huge strides, and she was in his arms.

His mouth descended to hers, hot and hungry and needy.

He devoured her, like he'd just spent days in the saddle crossing the Forty-Mile Desert and she was a long, cool drink of water on the other side. His hands yanked her against him, held her fast.

Not that she was complaining. She was too busy kissing him back, meeting him nip for nip, taste for taste.

Somewhere in a dim and dusty corner of her mind,

her subconscious warned her this was a lousy idea. If her grand plan was to stay away from him until she had her unruly emotions under control, she could probably do a better job than this.

She didn't care. Not now, when her senses spun with the taste and scent and feel of this man she was coming to care for entirely too much.

With a groan, he framed her face with his work-rough hands and pressed her back against the wood stall as he had the first time he'd kissed her. She felt his arousal press against her hip, and her body responded instantly, leaning in to him, desperate to be closer.

She almost cried out in protest when he slid his mouth away, but the sound swelling in her throat shifted to something different, something earthy and aroused, when his lips trailed across the curve of her cheekbone to nip at her ear. His ragged breathing sent liquid heat bubbling through her.

"I think about you all the time," he growled softly into her ear, and her heart gave a couple of good, hard kicks in her chest.

"No matter what I'm doing, you're there with me. I hate it," he went on in that same disgruntled tone. "Why won't you get out of my head?"

"Sorry." Her voice was breathless, aroused. "I'll try harder."

His low, strained laugh vibrated along her nerve endings. "You do that, Doc. You do that."

He dipped his head and captured her mouth again in another of those mind-bending kisses. She wasn't aware they had moved from Mystic's stall until the edge of the cot pressed behind her knees, and then he lowered her onto it, the hard length of him burning into her everywhere their bodies touched.

"I hope this thing holds both of us," he murmured against her mouth, and she laughed softly, a quick mental picture flitting through her mind of them tumbling to the ground.

Before she could answer, his mouth swept over hers, his tongue slipping inside her parted lips. She lost track of time, lost in the wonder of Matt, of being in his arms again. She wanted to hold him close and never let go, to cradle that dark head against her breast, to share a thousand moments like this with him.

She wanted him.

The knowledge terrified her. She wanted Matt Harte the way she'd never wanted anyone—never *allowed* herself to want anyone.

She was supposed to be so independent. So strong and self-sufficient. How could she know she had this powerful need inside her to be held like this, to feel fragile and feminine and *cherished?*

There it was, though, scaring the hell out of her.

But not scaring her enough to make her pull away. She needed more. She needed to feel his skin under her fingertips. He must have untucked his shirt before he fell asleep, and she found it an easy matter to slip her hands underneath, to glide across the smooth, hot skin of his back, loving the play of hard muscle bunching under her hands.

She was so enthralled with his steely strength that she was only vaguely aware of his busy, clever fingers unzipping her fleece vest until he caressed the curve of one breast through the knit of her shirt. Desire flooded through her, and she felt as if she were swimming through some wildly colorful coral reef without nearly enough air in her lungs.

She went completely under when his fingers slipped beneath her shirt and began to slowly trace the skin just below her bra. For once, she was impatient with his careful, measured movements. *All right, already,* she wanted to shout, suddenly sure she would die if he didn't put those hands on her.

Finally, when she didn't know if she could stand the sensual torture another instant, she felt his hands working the front clasp of her bra, then the raw shock of his fingers skimming over her breasts.

She closed her eyes against the overwhelming sensations pouring through her one after another.

"You are so beautiful," he murmured, his voice rough with desire. "The first time I saw you, you made me think of a sunset on a stormy August evening, all fire and color and glory."

To a woman who had spent her whole life feeling like an ugly, scrawny red-haired duckling, his words caressed her more intimately than his fingers. No one had ever called her beautiful before, and she had no defenses against his soft words.

This time she kissed him, lost to everything but this man, this hard, gorgeous cowboy. She arched against his fingers, begging for more of those slow, sensuous touches. He pulled away from her mouth, but before she could protest he slid down her body, pushing her shirt aside so his mouth could close over one taut nipple.

A wild yearning clawed to life inside her, and she closed her eyes and clasped him to her, her fingers tangled in his silky dark hair. He shoved one of his muscled legs between her thighs, and the hard pressure was unbearably arousing. While his mouth teased and tasted her, she arched against him, desperate for more.

He slid a hand between their bodies, working the snaps of her jeans, and her breath caught in her throat as she waited for him to touch her, to caress her *there*. Just before he reached the last snap of her jeans, though, he froze, his breathing ragged.

He pressed his forehead to hers and groaned softly. "Stop. Dammit. We have to stop."

She didn't want to listen to him, lost to everything but this wild, urgent need pouring through her. With her hands still tangled in his hair, it was an easy matter to angle his mouth so she could kiss him again in another of those long, drugging kisses.

He cooperated for a moment, his tongue dancing with hers, then he groaned again. "Ellie, I mean it. We have to stop."

"Why?"

He pulled away from her, and she shivered as cold air rushed to fill the space he had been in, to dance across her exposed skin with icy fingers.

Matt raked a hand through his hair. "A hundred reasons. Hell, a thousand. The most urgent one being I don't have any protection."

Her mind still felt fuzzy, and for a moment she didn't know what he was talking about. "You...you don't?"

"Sorry," he said wryly. "It's not something I generally stock in my barn." She flushed, suddenly jerked to reality, to the grim fact that she was less than a scruple away from making love to Matt Harte on a hard canvas cot. In his barn, no less, with a dozen horses as witnesses, where any of his ranch hands could stumble upon them any minute.

Dear heavens. What had she been *thinking?*

She hadn't been. She had been so desperately hungry for him that she hadn't been thinking at all, had completely ignored the warning voice yelling in her head.

What had she done? This was absolutely *not* the right way to go about yanking him out of her heart. She was supposed to be grabbing hold of a branch to keep herself from falling any further in love with him, doing her best to hoist herself to safe ground, to sanity. She wasn't supposed to gleefully fling herself over the edge like this.

She was too late.

The realization shuddered through her. She had been so stupid to think she could stop things in mid-step. She was already in love with him.

"I have to go. I really have to go." She stood up and frantically began putting her clothes in order, snapping and tucking and zipping.

He saw her fingers tremble as she tried to set to rights what his hands had undone, and he had to shove his fingers into his pockets to keep from reaching for her again.

She was mortified.

He could see it in her eyes, even though she wouldn't look directly at him, just around and over him as if he didn't exist, as if he weren't standing here in front of her, frustrated and aroused.

He didn't know what to say to make it right, to ease her awkwardness. There was probably nothing he *could* say.

All he knew was that he still wanted her, that his blood pulsed thick and heavy through his veins just looking at her, all tousled and sexy from his hands and his mouth.

As awkward as things were, he had to stop it. He had no choice. They would make love—he suddenly knew that without a doubt—but this wasn't the right time, the right place. She deserved better than a quick tussle in a dusty old horse barn. She deserved flowers and candles and romance, things he suddenly wanted fiercely to give her.

She jerked on her coat and started for the door, but he reached a hand out to stop her. "Ellie—"

"I hope everything turns out all right with your horses," she said quickly. "As soon as I hear from the lab on the test results, I'll let you know."

He sighed. He was still hard enough to split bricks, and she was going on about test results. A vast, terrifying tenderness welled inside him. As much as it scared him, he knew he couldn't walk away from it. And he couldn't let her walk away, either.

She was in his system and had been since she'd first blown into town. Trying to ignore it had only heightened his attraction for her, made him more hungry than ever. It was the mystery of her, he told himself. The fact that she was off-limits. Like that kid he was thinking about before who had been denied a scrumptious ice-cream cone, suddenly that was the only thing he could think about.

Maybe giving in to it, spending more time with her, might help work her out of his system so he could have things back the way they were before she whirled into his life.

"Are you busy tonight?"

In the process of slipping on her boots, she blinked at him suspiciously. "What?"

"Have dinner with me. I know this great place in Jackson Hole that's not usually too overrun with tourists this time of year. I'm sure I could arrange it with Cassidy to watch the girls. Or we could take them with us, if you'd rather."

"Dinner?"

"Yeah. Or we could go to a movie, if that appeals to you more. If you don't want to go to the show in town, there are a couple of theaters in Jackson or we could drive over to Idaho Falls. I'm sure we could find something we'd both enjoy."

She narrowed her gaze suspiciously. "Are you asking me out on a date, Harte?"

"I think so. At least that's the way things used to be done. I'm a little rusty at the whole dating thing."

"Why?" she asked, her voice blunt.

He shrugged. "I just haven't done it in a while. But don't worry, I'm sure it will all come back to me."

She gave him an impatient glare. "No. I meant, why are you asking me out?"

"The usual reasons people go out on a date." He cleared his throat and looked away. "I'm, uh, attracted to you. I guess you probably figured that out. And I'm not a real good judge of these things, but I think you'd be lying if you said you were immune to me. I think we should get to know each other, since it's pretty clear where we're heading with this thing between us."

Everything about her seemed to freeze. Even the vein pulsing in her neck seemed to stop. "To bed? Is that where you think we're heading?"

He shifted, suddenly feeling as if he were walking barefoot across a pasture full of cow pies. "Uh, it sure looked that way five minutes ago."

"Yeah? Well, that was five minutes ago. Things change." She started toward the door again.

He plodded valiantly forward. "So you're saying no to dinner?"

"Right. No to dinner or to a movie or to any friendly little roll in the hay."

By the time she reached the door, his temper had flared, and he stalked after her. "What the hell did I do that's got you acting like a wet hen all of a sudden? All I did was ask you out on a date, for crying out loud."

She stopped at the door, her back to him, then she turned slowly, green eyes shadowed. "You're right. I'm sorry, Matt. You didn't do anything. This is just a bad idea for me right now. Yes, I'm attracted to you, but I don't want to be."

"Yeah, well, join the club," he growled. "I'm not too thrilled about it, either."

"Exactly my point. Neither of us wants this. I can't be interested in any relationship with you right now beyond vet and client, and now we don't even have that."

"I already told you last night I was sorry for the way I jumped down your throat yesterday. I'd still like to keep you on as my equine vet."

"Despite everything that's happened?"

"Yeah. Despite all of it. Mistakes happen. Whatever you did to the horses, it wasn't intentional. Consider yourself rehired."

She went stiff all over again, and he knew he'd screwed up. Before he could figure out how—let alone do anything to make it right—she drew in a deep breath and shielded her eyes from his view with her lashes, studying the tips of her ropers. "You don't get it, do you?"

"What?"

"Never mind." Her voice sounded sad suddenly. Like she'd just lost something precious. "I think you'd be better off with Steve as your vet. You don't have time to constantly stand over my shoulder to make sure I don't mess up again. And I don't think I could work that way."

"What about the rest of it? About what happened a few minutes ago?"

She swung open the door and stood framed in the pearly predawn light. "I'm sure if we try really hard, we can both forget that ever happened."

Without another look at him, she walked out into the cold.

Chapter 13

"I don't understand," Dylan moaned into the phone. "Why isn't this working?"

"Maybe they just don't like each other as much as we thought they would." Lucy sounded as discouraged as Dylan, her voice wobbling like she wanted to cry

Dylan lay on her bed and stared out the window at the black night, thoughts whizzing around in her head like angry bees. It was two days after Christmas, and she should have been happy. She didn't have to go back to school for another week, she got the new CD player and cross-country skis she'd been hinting about for Christmas, and she and Lucy were going to be having a mini New Year's Eve sleepover at the ranch in just a few days.

But the one thing she wanted more than anything else—having a dad and a sister and living happily ever after on the Diamond Harte—seemed as distant as those stars out there.

Things were not going right. Her mom and Mr. Harte didn't seem any closer to falling in love than they had when she and Lucy first came up with the plan.

In fact, they didn't seem to be getting along at all. Every time she brought up his name, her mom's face went all squishy and funny like she just stepped on a bug.

Right before Christmas she asked her mom to drive her out to the ranch so she could take Lucy her present. It had all been carefully arranged for a time when Lucy's dad would be at the ranch house, but then her mom ruined everything. She wouldn't go into the house, just said she'd rather stay out in the truck while Dylan dropped her gift off. She wouldn't even go in to say hello.

She knew her mom was really worried about work ever since a bunch of animals got sick, and Dylan felt a little selfish worrying about herself and what she wanted when her mom had so much big stuff on her mind.

But she just wanted her to be happy. She and Lucy's dad were perfect for each other. Even though he was old, he was super nice and treated his animals well and he always gave Lucy a big, squeezy hug whenever he saw her.

Why couldn't her mom just cooperate and fall in love with him?

"Dylan? Are you still there?"

She cleared the lump out of her throat so Lucy wouldn't hear how upset she was. How small and jealous those squeezy hugs always made her feel. "Yeah. I'm still here. I was just thinking."

"Do you have any ideas?"

She sighed. "I know they like each other. We just have to make them admit it to each other."

"How?"

"I think we're going to have to do something drastic."

"Like what?" Lucy sounded nervous.

"I read a book once about a girl whose parents were in the middle of a big divorce. She was all mad at them and ran away from home and while they were out looking for her, her mom and dad realized they still loved each other and didn't want to get a divorce after all. It was really mushy and kind of stupid, but maybe we could try that."

Lucy was quiet for a moment. "I don't *want* to run away, do you?" she finally asked. "It's almost January and it's cold outside. We'll freeze to death."

"We could just pretend to run away and hide out somewhere on the ranch or something. Or we don't even have to pretend to run away. We could just pretend we got lost. They'd still have to look for us."

"It doesn't seem very nice to trick them like that. Wouldn't they be awfully mad when they figured it out?"

"I'm doing the best I can," Dylan snapped. "I don't see you coming up with any great ideas." Frustration sharpened her voice, made her sound mean. "I'm starting to think maybe you don't want this to work. Maybe you don't really want to be sisters as much as I do."

Lucy's gasp sounded loud and outraged in her ear. For a minute, Dylan thought she was going to cry. "That's not fair," Lucy said in a low, hurt voice. "I've worked just as hard as you to push them together. It's not my fault nothing has worked."

The hot ball of emotions in her stomach expanded to include shame. "You're right. I'm really sorry, Luce. I'm just worried. I heard Mom on the phone to SueAnn tonight, and she sounded really depressed. I'm afraid if we don't come up with something fast to bring them together, we're going to end up having to move back to California."

"Your mom's having a tough time, isn't she?" Lucy asked quietly.

"Yeah," Dylan said, her voice glum. "I think things are really bad at work. Nobody wants her to treat their animals after what happened to your dad's horses and the others."

Lucy was quiet for a moment. "If you want to run away,

I'll do it with you. We can pack warm clothes and even saddle a couple of horses if you want. It will be okay."

"No. I think you're right. I don't think it would work. It was a dumb idea. When they found us, they'd both be really mad."

"What else can we do, then?"

"I don't know. You think about it and I'll think about it and maybe we can come up with something brilliant between now and Friday, when I'm staying over."

After she finally said goodbye and hung up the phone, Dylan lay on her horse-print quilt for a long time, staring out the window at the stars and worrying.

"Okay. Stand back and watch the master at work." With his greased fingers held up like a surgeon's sterile gloves on the way to the operating table, Matt approached the ball of pizza dough on the counter.

"This is so cool," Lucy said to Dylan. "He twirls it around just like you see guys do on TV." The two of them sat on the edge of the kitchen table, eyes wide with expectation.

"That's right." He lowered his voice dramatically. "You're about to witness a sight many have attempted but few have perfected."

"You're about to see a big show-off." Cassie rolled her eyes from across the kitchen, where she was chopping, slicing and shredding toppings for the annual Diamond Harte New Year's Eve Pizza Extravaganza.

"You're just jealous because this is one thing in the kitchen I can do better than you."

"The only thing," she muttered, and he grinned.

He picked up the dough and started tossing it back and forth between his hands, working the ball until it was round and flat. He finished off with a crowd-pleasing toss in the air that earned him two wide-eyed gasps, then caught it handily and transferred it to the pizza peel Cass had sprinkled with cornmeal.

He presented it to the girls with a flourish. "Here you go. Put whatever you want on it."

"That was awesome," Dylan said. "Do it again!"

"Sure thing, after we get that one in the oven."

The girls took the peel to the other counter where Cass had laid out a whole buffet of toppings from sausage to olives to the artichoke hearts he loved.

With them out of earshot, he finally had a chance to corner his sister. "So why didn't you go to the mayor's party?" he asked sternly. "I thought that was the plan."

She pressed her lips together. "I decided I wasn't in the mood for a big, noisy party after all. I'd much rather be here with the girls."

"I can handle the girls. It's not too late. You've still got time to get all dressed up and drive over to the Garretts'. A couple of the ranch hands are going, and they said there'd be a live band and champagne and crab cakes flown in all the way from Seattle."

"I'd rather stay here and have pizza and root beer and watch the ball drop in Times Square." She smiled, but there was that restless edge to it again that filled him with worry.

She was so distant lately. Distracted, somber. No matter how hard he tried to find out why, she kept assuring him everything was fine.

He sighed, knowing he had to try again.

"Cass—" he began, but she cut him off.

"Don't start with me, Matt. I didn't want to go, okay? I enjoy a good party as much as anyone, but I just wasn't in the mood tonight."

"That's just what my mom said. She didn't want to go anywhere, either." Dylan spoke from behind them.

He turned at the mention of the woman who was always at the edge of his brain. He hadn't seen Ellie since that morning in the barn three weeks earlier, but he hadn't stopped thinking about her, wondering about her. Brooding about her.

Questions raced through his mind. How was she? What had she been doing since he saw her last? Why wouldn't she answer his calls? Did she have a date for New Year's Eve? He almost asked, then clamped his teeth together so hard they clicked.

As much as he wanted to know, it wasn't right to interrogate her kid. To his vast relief, Cassie did it for him.

"What's your mom doing tonight?" his sister asked, and he wanted to kiss her.

"Nothing. She said she was just going to stay home and have a quiet night to herself."

Cass frowned. "That's too bad. I wish I'd known. We could have invited her to have pizza with us."

"I'm not sure if she would have come." Dylan paused, giving him a weird look under her lashes. "She's pretty sad lately."

He stiffened. No way would she have told her kid what went on between them in the barn. So why was Dylan looking at him like the news should mean something to him? Was Ellie upset because of him?

"Why is she sad?" he asked, trying to pretend he wasn't desperate to hear the answer.

Dylan cast another one of those weird looks to Lucy, who quickly looked at the pizza. "I think it's because we're moving back to California," she finally said.

"You're *what?*"

Dylan winced. "Don't tell my mom I told you. I don't think she wants anybody else to know."

He felt as if he'd been punched in the stomach. As

if the whole damn world had suddenly gone crazy. "When?"

"I don't know. Nothing's definite yet. Anyway, I don't think she's in the mood for a party, either. That's why she told the mayor's wife she wouldn't be able to go to their house tonight."

It was none of his business, he reminded himself. She'd made that crystal clear the other week in the barn. If she wanted to pack up her kid and head for Timbuktu, he didn't have a damn thing to say about it.

Still, that didn't stop him from pounding his frustration on the second hapless ball of pizza dough. By the time he was done, anger had begun to replace the shock.

Finally he couldn't stand it anymore. He whipped off the apron Lucy gave him for Father's Day the year before and turned to Cassie.

"Can you handle the girls on your own for a while?"

"Sure." She looked at him curiously. "Where are you going?"

The last thing he wanted to do was tell his little sister he planned to go have a few hard words with Ellie Webster. He could just imagine the speculative look she'd give him. "I just need to, uh, run an errand."

She studied him for a moment, then smiled broadly. "Sure. No problem. And while you're there, why don't you ask Ellie if she wants to come out for pizza? I'm sure there'll be plenty left."

"Who said anything about Ellie?" he asked stiffly.

Cass grinned. "Nobody. Nobody at all. What was I thinking? Wherever you're going, drive carefully. You know what kind of idiots take to the road on New Year's Eve."

Still grumbling to himself about little sisters who

thought they knew everything—and usually did—Matt bundled into his coat and cowboy hat and went out into the cold.

Well, this was a fine New Year's Eve, sitting alone and eating a frozen dinner. How pathetic could she get?

Quit complaining, Ellie chided herself. *You had offers.* Several of them, in fact. SueAnn wanted her to go to Idaho Falls to dinner and a show with her and Jerry. Ginny Garrett, whose pet collie she'd fixed a few months ago, had invited her to what she deduced was the big social gala of the year in Salt River, the party she and her husband were throwing. And Lucy and Dylan had invited her out to the ranch to share homemade pizza and a video.

Of the three, the girls' party sounded like the most fun. Unfortunately, it was also the invitation she was least likely to accept. She couldn't imagine anything more grueling than spending the evening with Matt, trying to pretend they were only casual friends, that she hadn't come a heartbeat away from making love with him just a few weeks ago.

Despite putting plenty of energy into it, she hadn't been able to stop thinking about him since that morning. About the way his eyes had darkened with desire, the way his rough hands caressed her skin, the soft words that had completely demolished her defenses.

The way his lack of faith in her had broken her heart.

She'd been right to turn him down, to put this distance between them. She wasn't having much luck falling out of love with him, but at least she couldn't go down any deeper when she didn't have anything to do with him.

Anyway, spending New Year's Eve alone wasn't so bad. With the exception of the frozen dinner, the evening looked promising. She had already taken a nice long soak in the tub using the new strawberry-scented bath beads Dylan had given her for Christmas and put on the comfortable new thermal silk pajamas she'd treated herself to. She'd been lucky enough to find a station on the radio playing sultry jazz and big band music, she was going to pop a big batch of buttered popcorn later, and she had a good mystery to curl up with.

What else did a woman need?

She turned up the gas fireplace so that flames licked and danced cozily, then watched the fake logs for a moment with only a little regret for the real thing. Although she might have preferred a cheery little applewood blaze, with the crackle and hiss and heavenly aroma, she certainly didn't mind forgoing the mess and work of chopping, splitting and hauling wood.

After a moment, she settled onto the couch, tucking her feet under her. She'd just turned the page when the doorbell rang right in the middle of Glenn Miller's "Moonlight Serenade."

Marking her place, she went to the door, then felt her jaw sag at the man she found on the front porch.

"Matt! What are you doing here? Shouldn't you be digging in to a big slab of pizza right about now?"

"I came to talk some sense into you," he growled.

She stared at him, noting for the first time the firm set of his jaw and the steely glitter in his eyes. "Excuse me?"

"You heard me. Can we do this inside? It's freezing out here."

Without waiting for her answer—or for her to ask what it was, exactly, he wanted to *do* inside—he thrust past her into the house, where he loomed in the small living room like a tomcat trapped in a dollhouse, getting ready to pounce.

She closed the door carefully behind him, shutting out

the icy blast of air, then turned to face him. He was obviously furious about something, but she couldn't for the life of her figure out what she might have done this time to set him off.

His glower deepened. "I can't believe you're just going to run away. I thought you had more grit than that."

She opened her mouth, but he didn't wait for her answer. "Isn't that just like a city girl?" he went on angrily. "At the first sign of trouble, you take off running and leave the mess behind for everybody else to clean up. Dammit, you can't leave. You've got obligations here. A life. Your kid deserves better than to be shuttled around like some kind of Gypsy just because you don't have the gumption to see things through."

She stiffened and returned his glare. "In the first place, don't you tell me what my daughter deserves. In the second, do you mind telling me what in blazes you're talking about?"

For the first time since he'd stomped into her house, he looked a little unsure. "About you leaving. Dylan said you're moving back to California."

"Dylan has a big mouth," she muttered.

"Are you?"

"I don't know. Maybe."

She was seriously considering it. Not that she wanted to—the very idea made her stomach hurt, her heart weep. But she couldn't keep her practice open without any patients. "I haven't made a firm decision yet and I probably won't for a few months yet. But even if I were leaving tomorrow, what business would it be of yours?"

He shifted his weight. "I just don't want you to make a big mistake. I know how much your practice means to you," he went on. "It wouldn't be right for you to give it up without a fight."

"Without a fight?" She hissed out a breath. "I feel as if I've been doing nothing *but* fighting for six months. Each time I treat an animal I wonder if it's the last one. Every time I pay a bill, I wonder if I'll be able to pay it the next month. At some point, I have to face the fact that I can't keep waging a losing battle."

"Things will get better. You've just had a few setbacks."

"Right. I believe that's what Custer said to his men halfway through the battle of Little Big Horn."

"Is this because of the outbreak?"

"Partly. Funny thing," she said pointedly, "but the rest of the ranchers around here don't seem as convinced as I am that I wasn't responsible."

He looked uncomfortable, and she regretted sounding so bitchy. "As I said," she went on before he could respond, "although I'm considering leaving, I haven't made any final decision yet. I don't know why Dylan would have told you otherwise."

"I think she's worried about you. She said you were sad."

A child shouldn't have to worry about anything more earthshaking than whether she'd finished her homework. She hated that Dylan had spent even a moment fretting about her mother, about the future.

For that reason, if nothing else, maybe she needed to give up this selfish desire for autonomy and take her daughter back to California, where she could make a safe and secure living, even if she found it suffocating.

She also hated that Dylan had blabbed to Matt about her melancholy. She didn't want to talk about any of it, so she turned the subject to him.

"I can't figure you out."

"What's to figure out?"

"Why would you pass up homemade pizza on New

Year's Eve to come give me a lecture about perseverance? You don't even like me."

"That's not true. I like you plenty. Too much," he muttered under his breath.

Before she could figure out how to answer that growled admission, he went on. "I care about you. When Dylan told me you were moving to California, I was furious."

His gaze locked with hers, his blue eyes burning with emotions she couldn't even begin to decipher, and he reached for her fingers. "All I could think about was how much I would miss you if you left."

She drew in a shaky breath. "Matt—"

"I know, it's crazy. I don't understand it myself. But I haven't been able to think about anything else except how right, how completely *perfect,* you felt in my arms. And how I want you there again."

She closed her eyes, helpless against the tumble of emotions cascading through her. Listening to this big, gruff man speak words of such sweetness, words she knew would not come easily for him, affected her more than a hundred love songs, a thousand poems.

How could she ever have been stupid enough to think she could lock her heart against him? She had no defenses against a man like Matt Harte. He might seem arrogant and authoritative most of the time, but he cared enough about her to drive out on a snowy night to try to prevent her from making what he considered a grave mistake.

Why was she still fighting against him when she ached to be with him more than she had ever wanted anything in her life?

She loved him.

The sweetness of it seeped through her like hard rain on thirsty earth, collecting in all the crevasses life had carved into her soul. She loved this man, with his rough hands and his slow smile and his soft heart.

When she opened her eyes, she found him watching her warily, as if he expected her to kick him out of her house any minute.

"I've thought of it, too," she answered, barely above a whisper.

"So what are we going to do about it?"

"What else can we do?"

With a deep breath for courage, she stepped forward, wrapped her arms around his neck and lifted her mouth for his kiss.

For just a moment after she stepped forward and lifted her mouth to his, Matt couldn't move, frozen with shock and a fast, thorny spike of desire.

He never expected this. Never. She made it pretty damn clear the other day that she didn't want any kind of relationship with him. He hadn't liked it, but what could he do when she wouldn't give him much room for any kind of argument?

If he'd been thinking at all when he rushed over here after Dylan's little announcement—if he'd been able to focus on anything but his anger that she planned to leave Star Valley—he might have expected Ellie to throw him out the door after he finished giving her a piece of his mind.

Not this. He definitely wouldn't have predicted this soft, searching kiss that was curling through his insides like grapevines on a fence or her arms wrapping around his neck to hold him close.

Just when he was beginning to wonder if he'd ever be able to move again, he felt the whisper-soft touch of her tongue at the corner of his mouth. That's all it took, one tiny lick, and he was lost.

Need exploded through him like a shotgun blast. With a ragged groan, he yanked her against him and devoured her mouth. She smelled like strawberry shortcake and tasted like heaven, and he couldn't get enough.

He'd missed her these few weeks. Missed her laugh and her sweet smile and her smart mouth. He'd wanted to call her a hundred times and had even dialed the number a few times, but had always hung up before the call could go through.

She told him she didn't want a relationship and had obviously been going out of her way to avoid him. And he had too much bitter experience with rejection to push her.

He should have, though. Should have pushed them both. If he'd known she would greet him like this, that she would welcome him into her arms so eagerly, he damn well would have been knocking down her door to get here.

In the background, Miles Davis played some kind of sexy muted trumpet solo. Matt's subconscious registered it with appreciation, but all he could focus on was Ellie and her sweet mouth.

Her hands were busy pulling off his coat, which she tossed on the floor. His hat went sailing after it, then she raked her fingers through his hair, playing at the sensitive spot at the nape of his neck.

He wanted to have her right now, to tangle his fingers in her silky clothes and rip them away, then thrust himself inside her until neither one of them could move.

"I'm not stopping this time," he warned. He would somehow find the strength to walk away if she asked it of him, but he wasn't about to tell her that.

To his vast relief, she didn't argue. "Good," she breathed against his mouth. "I don't want you to stop. In fact, I'd be really disappointed if you did."

He had to close his eyes, awed at the gift she was offering him. On the heels of his amazement came niggling worry. He hadn't done this in a while, and his body wasn't in any kind of mood to take things slow. It throbbed and ached, eager for hot, steamy passion. Writhing bodies. Heated explorations. Feverish, sloppy kisses that lasted forever.

But Ellie deserved to be wooed, and woo her he would, even if it killed him.

"You smell divine," he murmured, trying fiercely to get a little control over himself.

"Strawberry bath beads." She sounded breathless, aroused. "I just got out of the tub right before you showed up."

He had a quick mental picture of her lithe little body slipping naked into hot, bubbly water—and then climbing back out—and groaned as his hard-fought control slipped another notch.

She would smell like strawberries everywhere, and he suddenly wanted to taste every single inch.

While she was busy working the buttons of his shirt, he trailed his mouth down the elegant line of her throat to whisper kisses just under the silky neckline of her shirt. Her hands stilled, and she arched her throat, unknowingly exposing a tiny amount of cleavage.

He took ruthless advantage of it and pressed his mouth to the sweetly scented hollow, licking and tasting while his hands worked their way under her shirt. She had nothing on under her thermal silk, he realized, and heat scorched him as his fingers encountered soft, unbound curves.

Her breath hissed in sharply when his thumb danced over a tight nipple, and she seemed to sag bonelessly against him. He lowered her to the soft, thick carpet in front of the fireplace, and she responded by tightening her arms around him, by pressing her soft curves against him.

She had somehow managed to unbutton his shirt, and her hands splayed across his abdomen, branding him with her heat. His stomach muscles contracted, and she smiled and shoved his shirt down over his shoulders.

While the music on the stereo shifted to a honey-voiced woman singing about old lovers and new chances, they undressed each other, stopping only for more of those slow, drugging kisses.

As he removed the last of their clothes, he leaned back on an elbow and stared at her, her skin burnished by flickering firelight. She looked like some kind of wild-haired goddess, and his heartbeat pulsed as equal parts desire and that terrifying tenderness surged over him.

He hadn't wanted this in his life, had done his best to push her away and pretend he wasn't coming to care for her. The scars Melanie had left him with still ached sometimes, made him leery to risk anything of himself.

But Ellie wasn't anything like his ex-wife. He knew it, had known it from the beginning. He just hadn't wanted to face the truth. It was much easier to focus on the few inconsequential things the two women had in common than the hundred of important things separating them. That way he could use the ugliness of his past as a shield against Ellie and her courage and her generous spirit.

Somehow this woman had sneaked in to his heart. Now that she was firmly entrenched there, he wondered how he'd ever survived so long without her.

He wanted to take care of her. It sounded macho and stupid, and he knew his fiercely independent Ellie would probably smack him upside the head if he said it aloud, so he tucked the words into his heart along with her.

He wouldn't say them. He would just do everything he could to show her she needed him.

* * *

Why was he looking at her like that? Ellie squirmed, wishing his expression wasn't so hard to read sometimes. She felt vulnerable and exposed lying before him with her hair curling wildly around her. At the same time, she had to admit she found it oddly erotic having him watch her with those blue eyes blazing.

Finally she couldn't stand the conflicting emotions any more. She reached out and pulled him to her, nearly shuddering apart as his hard, taut muscles met her softness.

This was right. Any lingering doubts she might have been harboring floated away into the night as his body covered hers, as his callused hands skimmed over her, as his mouth devoured her.

She wanted to curl up against him, wanted to let his strength surround her.

"I've thought about this since that first time we kissed in the barn." His voice was low, throaty. "Why have we both been fighting this so hard?"

"Because we're crazy." She smiled a little and pressed a kiss to the throbbing pulse at the base of his throat.

"If I'm crazy, I know exactly who to blame. I haven't had a coherent thought in my head since a certain unnamed little red-haired vet moved in to town."

He tugged gently on the hair in question so their gazes could meet. His words and the undisguised hunger in his eyes made her feel fragile and powerful at the same time, beautiful and feminine and *wanted*.

Fresh desire pulsed through her, liquid heat, and she drew in a ragged breath and reached for him.

Their kisses became more urgent, their caresses more demanding. The jazz on the stereo shifted to something haunting, sultry, as he teased her breasts, as his fingers slid across her stomach to the aching heat centered between her thighs, and she shuddered, lost to his touch, to the music weaving sinuously around them.

He pushed one long finger inside her, readying her for him, and she gasped his name and arched against him eagerly.

"You're killing me, Ellie," he growled. "I can't handle much more of this."

"You're the one taking his dear sweet time."

His low laugh sounded raw, strained. "I was trying to go slow for you."

She shivered again as his finger touched on a particularly sensitive spot, and she thought she would die if he didn't come inside her. "Don't do me any favors, Harte," she gasped.

His low laugh slid over her like a caress. "Wouldn't dream of it, Doc."

He reached for something in his jeans—his wallet, she realized—then pulled out a foil-wrapped package. A moment later, he knelt between her thighs. His gaze met hers, and the fierce emotion there settled right into her heart, and then an instant later his mouth tangled with hers again as he entered her.

Love for this man—this strong, wonderful man—expanded in her heart then flowed out, seeping through every cell. She wrapped her arms tightly around him, wishing she had the words to tell him her feelings for him—or that she had the courage to give him the words, even if she managed to find them.

His movements started out slow, but she wasn't having any of it. She arched against him, begging for more, for fire and thunder and out-of-her-head passion.

He drew back, his breathing ragged. "Slow down. I don't want to hurt you," he growled.

"You won't. I'm not fragile, Matt."

With a harsh groan he drove into her, deep and powerful and demanding, and she shivered even as she met him thrust for thrust. He must have held himself under amazing control, she thought. Now that she'd given him permission to treat her like a woman instead of a china doll, he devoured her, kissing and stroking and inflaming her senses.

He reached for her hands and yanked their entwined fingers above her head so that only their bodies touched, skin to skin, heat to heat.

She never would have expected this wildness from him, the fierce desire that blazed out of him in wave after hot wave until she thought she would scorch away into cinders from it.

A wild, answering need spiraled up inside her, climbing higher and higher with each passing second. She had never known anything like this, this frantic ache. She gasped his name, suddenly frightened by how close she was to losing control, to losing herself.

He groaned in answer and kissed her deeply, tongue tangling with hers, demanding everything from her, then reached between their bodies to touch her intimately. Just that small caress, the heat of his fingers on the place where she already burned, and she shattered into a thousand quivering pieces.

"I can't get enough of you," he growled before she could come back together again.

He kissed her fiercely, branding her as his, then with one more powerful thrust, he found his own release.

Afterward, she trembled more from reaction than the cold, but Matt reached up to the couch behind them and pulled down the knit throw there. He spread it over them both and pulled her against him.

She snuggled close. "And here I thought I was in for another boring New Year's Eve."

His low laugh tickled the skin at the back of her neck. "Boring is not a word I would ever dare use in the same sentence as you, Doc."

She lifted her gaze to his. "Are you complaining?"

"Hell, no. Even if I had any strength left to complain, I wouldn't dare."

She smiled and settled against his hard chest. He held her tightly with one hand while the other stroked through her hair.

"I used to tell myself I was happy with boring," he said after a few moments. "That's what I thought I wanted. A nice, safe, uneventful life. Then you blew into my life, and I discovered I'd been fooling myself all these years. Safe and uneventful are just other words for lonely."

His low words slid over her, stirring up all kinds of terrifying emotions, and she tensed. Not knowing how to answer—and not at all comfortable with this yearning inside her to stay curled up against him forever—she chose to change the subject. "Cassie and the girls will be wondering where you ran off to."

He studied her, and she had the awful suspicion he knew exactly how uneasy his words made her, then he shrugged. "I doubt it. At least Cass won't. Apparently my little sister knows a lot more about me than I'd like to think she does. More than I know myself. She asked me to invite you out to the ranch for the rest of the pizza party, if the girls haven't eaten it all by now."

"Oh. That was very kind of her."

"You could stay over in the guest room."

She thought about spending the evening not being able to touch him and she sighed. "I'd better pass."

"Why?"

"We have to tread carefully here, Matt. Really carefully. Think about the girls."

"What about them?"

"They can't know about…about any of this. How would they react?"

She saw understanding dawn in his eyes, and he winced. "Right."

"This can't affect them. I don't want either of them hurt."

Dylan would build this into a happily-ever-after kind of thing, something Ellie knew was impossible. She knew perfectly well that her daughter pined for a father, and she'd be over the moon imagining Matt in that role. Ellie didn't want to see her heart get broken.

"What are you suggesting?" he asked quietly. "If you're going to tell me some bull about how you think this was a mistake that won't happen again, I might have to get mean."

If she were stronger, that's exactly what she *would* say. Letting this go any further would only end in heartache. For all she knew, she'd be moving back to California in the next few months. How much worse was it going to be to say goodbye now that she knew the wonder of being in his arms?

Still, she couldn't seem to find the words to push him away. "We just have to be careful," she said instead. "That's all I'm saying."

They stayed that way together on the floor for a long time, wrapped around each other while the soft music flowed around them. She couldn't touch him enough. His rough hands, his hard chest, the ridged muscles of his stomach. Eventually their caresses grew bold again, and she gasped when he picked her up as if she were no heavier than a runty calf and carried her to her bedroom.

There he made love to her again—slower this time, as if he planned to spend the whole new year touching her just so, kissing her exactly right, then he entered her and each slow, deep thrust seemed to steal a little more of her soul.

Afterward, she lay limp and boneless in his arms, content to listen to his heart and feel his arms around her. If the house caught fire just then, she wasn't sure she could summon the energy to crawl out of bed.

"I don't want you to leave," he said against her hair.

"This is my house." She was wonderfully, sinfully exhausted. "If anyone leaves, I'm guessing it will be you."

"You know what I mean. I'm talking about you going back to California." He was quiet for a moment, then he pressed another kiss to her hair. "You know, if your practice is really struggling that much, I could give you the money to keep it going."

In an instant, the world seemed to grind to a halt, like an amusement park ride that had abruptly lost power. The sleepy, satisfied glow surrounding her popped, leaving her feeling chilled to the bone.

She wrenched away from him and sat up, clutching the quilt to her breasts. "You what?"

"I could give you the money. Just to tide you over until things start looking up."

The roaring in her ears sounded exactly like the sea during a violent storm. "Let me get this straight. You want to ride in like some kind of knight in shining armor and give me the money to save my practice."

He shrugged, looking faintly embarrassed. "Something like that."

Fury and hurt and shame vied for the upper hand as she jumped from the bed and yanked on her robe.

"What's the matter?"

She didn't even spare him a glance. "Your timing stinks, Harte."

"What?" He sounded genuinely befuddled.

He didn't have a clue. She drew in a deep breath. "Let me give you a little advice. Next time, don't offer a woman money when her body is still warm from having you inside her unless the two of you have agreed on a price beforehand."

She thought of her mother, of the faceless, nameless strangers who had skulked in and out of her bed after her father left. The squeak of the rusty screen door as another of Sheila's "friends" dropped by, the low, suggestive laughter in the kitchen, the heavy footsteps down the hall toward her mother's filthy bedroom.

Hiding in her room with a pillow over her head so she wouldn't have to hear what came after.

Even then, at seven years old, she'd known what they were doing, had felt sick, dirty. And she'd known that in the morning, Sheila would have enough money for another bottle of oblivion.

That Matt would offer this, would put her in the same category as her mother, brought all those feelings rushing back.

"You know that's not what I meant." Anger roughened his voice. "I can't believe that kind of cheap thought would ever enter your head. It's demeaning to me and to you. Dammit, Ellie. I care about you. I want to help you. And why shouldn't I, when I have the means? What's wrong with that?"

"I don't want your help. I never asked for it."

"You'd rather have to give up the practice you love? The life you love? You'd rather go back to California and leave everything here behind?"

"If I have to, yes."

She stormed out of the bedroom, desperate to put space between them, but of course he stalked after her, fastening the buttons of his jeans and shrugging in to his shirt as he followed.

"That's the stupidest thing I've ever heard you say. Why are you so upset about this? Just call it a loan. You can pay me back when business picks up."

"What if it doesn't? How will I pay you back then? By sleeping with you? Should I start keeping a little ledger by my bed? Mark a few dollars off every time you come over? Tell me, Matt, since I don't have any idea—what's the going hourly rate for prostitutes these days?"

He went still, and she knew her jab had struck home. "That's not fair," he said quietly.

It wasn't. She knew it even as the bitter words flowed out of her like bile. He didn't deserve this, but she couldn't seem to stop, lost in the awful past.

All he did was offer his help. He couldn't be blamed because she found herself in the terrible position of needing it.

"I'm sorry," she said stiffly. "You're right. Thank you for your kind offer but I'm not quite desperate enough yet that I'd take money from you."

He glared at her. "Is that supposed to be an apology? Because it sure as hell didn't sound like one from here."

"It's whatever you want it to be."

He was quiet, his face a stony mask. "You don't want to take anything from anyone, do you?"

"Not if I can help it."

"And if you can't? What are you going to do then?"

She hated the coldness in his voice, the distance, even though she knew she'd put both things there. Regret was a heavy ache in her heart. A few moments ago they had shared amazing tenderness and intimacy, and now they were acting like angry strangers with each other. It was her fault, she knew it. This was a stupid argument, but it was also symptomatic of the greater barriers to any relationship between them.

She had been fooling herself to think they could ever have anything but this one magical night.

"I'll figure that out if that day ever comes," she finally said. "Go home, Matt. It's New Year's Eve, you should be with your family. If you hurry, you'll make it home before the clock strikes midnight."

He stood there glaring at her, looking big and gorgeous and furious, then without another word he yanked on his coat, grabbed his hat and slammed out the door.

Chapter 14

Three weeks into the new year, the temperature spiked in western Wyoming in what the locals called the annual January thaw.

Though the temperature barely hovered above forty degrees and genuinely warm weather was still months away, the mountain air smelled almost like spring. Snow melted from every building in steady drips, kids put away their sleds and took out their bikes instead, and a few overachieving range cows decided to drop their calves a few weeks early.

She was far from busy, but Ellie was grateful to at least have a few patients to occupy her time.

She'd spent most of the day trying to ease a new Guernsey calf into the world for one of her few remaining clients. She still had the warm glow of satisfaction from seeing that wobbly little calf tottering around the pasture.

In the excitement of watching new life, she had almost been able to forget the clouds hanging over her head, this terrible fear that her time here amid these mountains she had come to love so dearly was drawing to a close.

Her choices were becoming increasingly limited. Fight as she may against the truth, she knew she couldn't keep hanging on by her fingernails much longer.

She drew in a deep breath. Maybe she ought to just forget about trying to go it alone and join forces with Steve Nichols. At least then she could stay in Salt River.

He might not be willing anymore, though. He hadn't asked her about it for weeks, and lately he'd been cool and distracted every time they talked, making her wonder and worry what she had done. Maybe he, like everyone else in town, had lost all respect for her.

She could always take out a loan from Matt.

The thought, sinuous and seductive, whispered into her mind, but she pushed it away. Never. She couldn't do something that extreme, no matter what desperate straits she found herself in.

Despite her resolve, she knew she owed him an apology for her overreaction on New Year's Eve. Remorse burned in her stomach whenever she thought about how she had lashed out at him.

She hadn't seen him since the night he had come to her house. The previous evening, the committee for the Valentine's carnival had met for the last time before the big event, and she'd spent all day with her nerves in an uproar over seeing him again.

It had all been for nothing, though. He'd sent a message with Sandy Nielson that a ranch emergency came up at the last minute and he wouldn't be able to make it.

She was relieved, she tried to tell herself. The last thing she needed to deal with right now was the inevitable awkwardness between them.

She sighed as she drove through town. Who was she kidding? She missed him. Missed his sexy drawl and the way his eyes crinkled at the edges and the way he could make her toes curl with just a look.

The sun was sliding behind the mountains in a brilliant display of pink and lavender that reflected in wide puddles of melting snow as she drove into the clinic's parking lot. She pulled the truck into the slot next to SueAnn's Suburban and climbed out, determined that she would do her best not to think about the blasted man for at least the next ten minutes.

SueAnn popped up from her desk like a prairie dog out of her hole when Ellie walked in.

"How did it go?" she asked.

Ellie forced a smile. "Not bad. Mama and calf are doing well. I was afraid for a while we'd lose them both but we finally managed to pull the calf and everything turned out okay."

"I'm sure that's a big relief to Darla. She loves that little milk cow."

Ellie nodded. "She says hello, by the way, and she'll see you tomorrow night at the library board meeting. Any messages?"

SueAnn handed her a small pink pile. "None of these were urgent. Mostly carnival committee members needing your input on last-minute details. Oh, but Jeb Thacker's having trouble with Cleo again. He wondered when he could bring her in tomorrow. I told him anytime. And here's the mail. Bills, mostly."

Ellie took it, wondering what she was going to do when she left Star Valley without SueAnn to screen her mail for her.

"Oh, I almost forgot. The lab finally sent the results for that tox screen you ordered."

Ellie froze in the process of thumbing through the messages. The culture results on the animals that had fallen ill before Christmas. "Where is it?"

"Here." SueAnn handed over a thin manila envelope, and Ellie immediately ripped it open and perused the contents.

"What does it say?"

"It looks like the samples all were infected with an unusual strain of bacteria, just like Steve suspected. That's why it took so long for the results. The lab had never seen it in horses before."

"Could it have been spread by your needles?"

"Maybe." It wasn't outside the realm of possibility that the needles had been contaminated, although she would never believe that had been the cause. Damn. She had hoped for answers, for something that could definitively absolve her of responsibility.

SueAnn touched her arm. "I'm sorry it wasn't better news."

She forced a smile as the weight of failure pressed down hard on her shoulders. "Thanks."

"You have anything left for me to do today?" SueAnn asked. "It's almost six, and Jerry's got a touch of the flu. Last time he stayed home sick from work, he maxed out three credit cards on the home shopping channel."

"You'd better hurry, then, or you'll get home and find he bought a dozen cans of spray-on hair replacement."

As SueAnn switched off her computer and turned on the answering machine, Ellie unfolded from the edge of the desk. "Where's Dylan? Is she in the back doing her homework?"

SueAnn froze in the process of pulling her purse out of her bottom desk drawer. "I haven't seen her. She never came in after school." Anxiousness crept into her voice. "I...I just assumed she went home with Lucy. You didn't mention it before you went out to Darla's, but I figured it must have slipped your mind."

Unease bloomed to life inside Ellie like a noxious weed.

"I don't remember her telling me anything about riding the school bus to the ranch today."

"Maybe it was a spur of the moment thing."

"Maybe." If she went to the ranch without leaving a message, Dylan was in serious trouble. Ellie's one strict, inarguable rule was that Dylan had to leave her whereabouts with her mother or with SueAnn at all times.

A hundred terrible scenarios flashed through her mind in the space of a few seconds until she reined in her thoughts. No. This was Star Valley, Wyoming. Things like that didn't happen here.

"I'll just call the ranch. You're probably right, I'm sure that's where she is." She dialed the number then twisted the cord around her fingers while she waited for Matt or Cassie to answer. No one picked up after fifteen rings, and her stomach knotted with worry.

"I am so sorry, El." SueAnn looked sick. "I should have called you when she didn't show up just to make sure everything was cool."

"Let's not panic until we have reason. She and Lucy are probably just playing outside in this warm weather, or maybe she went home with one of her other friends."

"Do you want me to run out to the ranch and see if she's there?"

"No. You go on home to Jerry. I'll just check at the house and buzz by the school. If I don't find her at either of those places, I'll drive out to the ranch."

She would find her daughter safe and sound. She *had* to. She absolutely refused to consider any alternative.

It had been one hell of a week.

The tractor bounced and growled as Matt drove through foot-deep muck on the way to the barn after delivering the evening feed to the winter pasture. Cows had been dropping calves like crazy with all this warm weather, the ranch was a muddy mess, and to make matters worse, two of his ranch hands quit on the same day.

He hadn't had a good night's sleep in longer than he could remember, every muscle in his body ached, and his shoulder hurt where he'd been kicked by an ornery horse that caught him off guard.

Days like this, he wondered if it was all worth it. All he wanted was dinner and his bed, and at this point he was even willing to forget about the dinner.

At the barn, he switched off the tractor, making a mental note that the engine seemed a little wompy and would need to be checked before planting season. He climbed out and shut the door behind him when he saw Ellie's battered pickup pull up to the house.

Of all the people he would have expected to show up at the ranch, she would just about come in last on the list. He hadn't been able to forget the bitter words she'd flung at him, the way she had thrown his offer of help back in his face.

He could see now that she'd been right, his timing could have been a whole lot better. But his intentions had been good.

A moment later, she swung open her truck door and hopped out. She was small and compact and, despite his lingering anger, heat rushed to his groin just remembering how that lithe little body had felt under him, around him.

She walked up the porch steps to ring the doorbell, and he made a face. Cassie wasn't home, and he was a little tempted to let her stand there ringing away in vain. He immediately felt spiteful for entertaining the idea even for an instant and headed toward the house.

As soon as he was close enough to catch a glimpse of the worry in her expression, he was heartily relieved he hadn't obeyed the petty impulse.

"What's the matter, Doc?"

She whirled, and relief spread over her face when she saw him. "Matt! I was afraid nobody was home. Did Dylan come home on the bus with Lucy today?"

He frowned. "Lucy didn't take the bus today. Cass picked her up after school so they could go shopping in Idaho Falls for something to wear to the Valentine's carnival. They're not back yet. She didn't come home?"

Ellie shook her head, her green eyes murky and troubled. "I don't know where she is. She usually walks to the clinic after school. When she didn't show up today, SueAnn thought she must have come home with Lucy."

"I suppose there's a chance she might have gone with them on the shopping trip, although I think she would have cleared it with you first. She's a good kid. Just taking off like that doesn't seem like something she'd do."

"No. You're right."

She looked helpless and frightened. As he saw her mouth tremble, his remaining anger slid away. He hurried up the steps and pulled her into his arms.

"We'll go in and call Cass on the cell phone. If she's not with them, maybe Lucy will know something. It'll be okay, Ellie."

She must be out of her mind with worry or she never would have let him lead her into the house and settle her into one of the kitchen chairs while he crossed to the phone hanging on the wall. He was just dialing the number when he heard another vehicle pull up outside.

"That's probably them now."

The words were barely out of his mouth when Ellie jumped up and headed toward the door. He followed close on her heels and saw her shoulders sag with disappointment when only Cassie and Lucy climbed out of his sister's Cherokee.

Cassie's eyes widened when she saw Ellie. "Everything okay?" she asked, instantly concerned.

In the circle of light on the porch, Ellie looked small and lost, her expression bordering on panic. A mother suddenly living her worst nightmare. Sensing she was on the verge of losing control, Matt grabbed her arm and guided her up the steps to the door and into the warmth of the house.

"Come on inside," he said over his shoulder to his sister. "I'll explain everything."

By the time they made it into the kitchen, Ellie had once more gained control of her emotions, although her eyes still looked haunted.

"Lucy," she began. "Dylan didn't go to the clinic after school today. Do you know anything about where she might have gone?"

For a moment, his daughter just stared, then color leached from her face and she looked like she was choking on something. She pressed her lips together and suddenly seemed extremely interested in the green-checkered tablecloth.

"Lucy?" he said sternly. "What do you know about this?"

"Nothing." She wouldn't look him in the eye and clamped both hands over her mouth, as if she were afraid something would slip out.

"Did she say anything to you after school about where she might be going? Can you think of any other friends she might have gone home with?" Ellie asked, her voice thin, pleading.

"No," Lucy said through her fingers in barely a whisper. Her chin wobbled, and she looked like she was going to cry any minute now. Once she started, they'd never get anything out of her, he realized.

Instead of obeying his first impulse to ride her hard about it until she told them what was going on, he knelt to her level and pulled her into his arms.

"Lucy, sweetheart, this is important. Her mom is really worried about her, just like I would be if you were missing. I know Dylan is your friend and you don't want to get her in trouble, but if you know anything about where she might be, you have to tell us."

She looked at the floor for a moment, and a tear slipped out of the corner of her eye and dripped down her nose. "She said she wasn't going to do it. She said it wouldn't *work*," she wailed.

"What? What did she say wouldn't work?" Ellie asked urgently.

Lucy clamped her lips together, then expelled the words in a rush of air. "We were gonna run away."

"Run away?" Ellie again looked lost and bewildered. "Why? What was so terrible that she thought she had to run away?"

"We weren't really gonna run away. Just pretend." Lucy sniffled. "Dylan thought if the two of you had to look for us together, you guys would finally see how much you liked each other and you would get married and we could be sisters for real."

Thunderstruck, Matt looked from his daughter to Ellie. At Lucy's admission, color flooded Ellie's face, and her horrified eyes flashed to his then focused on the same tablecloth Lucy had found so interesting.

Oblivious to their reaction, his rascal of a kid plodded on. "We decided it wouldn't work and that you'd be too mad when you found out what we did. We were trying to come up with a better plan but I guess maybe she decided to do it by herself anyway. I can't believe she didn't tell me what she was going to do," she finished in a betrayed-sounding voice.

"But where would she go?" Ellie exclaimed. "It's January. It's cold and dark out there."

"I don't know." Lucy started to sniffle again. "We were gonna hide out in one of the ranch buildings."

"She wouldn't have been able to walk all the way out here." Cassie frowned. "She must have gone somewhere in town."

Matt headed for the door. "I'll send the ranch hands out looking around for her just in case. Cassie, call Jess and let him know what's going on. Meanwhile, Ellie, you and I can run back to town and see if she might have turned up at your house or at the clinic. Who knows, maybe her teacher has some clue where she might have gone."

Grateful to have a concrete plan instead of this mindless panic, she nodded and followed him out to his truck.

On the six-mile ride to town, she was silent and tense, her mind racing with terrible possibilities. While Matt drove, he compensated for her reticence by keeping up a running commentary about everything and nothing, more words than she'd ever heard from him.

He was doing it to keep her from dwelling too long on all those awful scenarios. She knew it and was touched by his effort but she still couldn't get past her worry to carry on a real conversation with him.

The trip from the ranch to town had never seemed so long. "Let's stop at your house first," Matt said when they finally passed the wooden city limit sign. "It's on the way and that seems the logical place for her to go."

When she didn't answer, he reached a hand across the seat to cover hers. "Hang in there, Doc. She's probably sitting at home waiting for you to get there and wondering if she'll still be grounded by the time she graduates from college."

She managed a shaky smile and turned her hand over to clasp his fingers. Reassured by the heat and strength there, she clung to his hand the rest of the way. When she saw her little brick bungalow was still dark and silent, her fingers tightened in his.

Matt pulled in to the driveway and turned off the pickup's rumbling engine. He gave her hand a comforting squeeze. "Okay, she's not here. But maybe she left a message for you."

Trying to keep the panic at bay, Ellie climbed from the truck and unlocked the side door leading to the kitchen. When she saw no blinking light on the answering machine, she almost sobbed. She probably would have if Matt hadn't followed her inside.

Instead, she flipped on every light in the kitchen, even the one over the stove. It seemed desperately important suddenly, as if she could fight the darkness inside her.

That done, she moved through the house urgently, only vaguely aware of Matt shadowing her while she turned on the lights in every single room until the house blazed like a Christmas tree.

The porch light. She should turn that on, too, so her little girl could find her way home.

She went to the front door and flipped the switch. Just as she turned away, something jarring, out of place, caught the edge of her vision through the small beveled window in the door.

She pushed aside the lace curtain for a better look, then felt the blood leave her face and a horrified scream well up in her throat. What came out was a pathetic little whimper like a distressed kitten's, but it was enough for Matt to grab her and shove her aside so he could look.

He bit out a string of oaths and yanked the door open. "What the hell is that?"

Her hands began to shake, and she was afraid she was going to be sick. "I...I think it's a calf fetus."

The yellow porch light sent a harsh glare on the poor little creature, still covered with the messy fluids of birth. She forced herself to walk toward it and saw at once that it was malformed and had probably been born dead.

Matt crouched beside the animal. "Dammit. Why can't Jesse find whoever is doing this to you?"

It had to be connected to the cat left in her truck. She could see that another note had been impaled to the side of the calf with an acupuncture needle.

She didn't want to look at it. She would rather shove the needle through her own tongue, would rather have a hundred needles jammed into every inch of her body than have to face the idea that there could be some link between this gory offering and her baby.

But there had to be. She knew it as sure as death.

"He's got her," she said raggedly.

Matt stared. "Who?"

"Whoever left this has Dylan. I know it."

She couldn't breathe suddenly, couldn't think. Could only watch numbly while he ripped the note away to read it, then uttered a long string of oaths.

"What does it say?"

Wordlessly, he handed her the note. Her stomach heaved after she read it, and she had to press a hand to her mouth as bile choked her throat.

"If you don't want your kid to end up like this," the note said in that same ominous black type that had been used for the note left in her truck, "you're going to have to prove it."

Chapter 15

Prove it? Prove it how?

Ellie stared at the note in her hand, afraid that if she looked away from those sinister words she would find the whole world had collapsed around her. This couldn't be happening. Salt River, Wyoming, was a slice of America. Soccer games, PTA meetings, decent, hardworking people. She would never suspect someone here could be capable of such hideous evil.

Her baby.

Someone had her little girl.

She thought of Dylan, helpless and scared and wondering where her mother was, and she felt herself sway as every drop of blood rushed from her head.

Instantly, Matt was there, folding her into his arms. "Hang on, sweetheart. Stay with me."

"I have to find her. He has her."

"Shh. I know. I'll call Jess. He'll know what to do."

The phone in the kitchen jangled suddenly, sounding obscenely loud in the quiet house. She stared at it, then her heart began to pound. It was him. She knew it without a shadow of doubt.

She raced into the other room and grabbed the phone before it could ring again. "Where is she, you sick son of a bitch?" she snarled.

An electronically disguised voice laughed roughly in her ear. "You'll find out. If you do what you're told."

"What do you want?"

"You're still here. I thought I told you to leave. You obviously didn't learn your lesson."

"I'll go. I'll leave now, tonight. Please, just bring back my little girl." She hated the pleading in her voice but she would have groveled to the devil himself if it would have kept her baby safe.

A bitter laugh rang in her ear. "I won't make it that easy on you anymore. You had your chance. Now you have to cough up a hundred grand before you kiss Star Valley goodbye."

"I don't have that kind of money!" Sheer astonishment raised her voice at least an octave.

"You'd better find it by tomorrow noon. I'll let you know the drop-off site."

Before she could answer, could beg to at least talk to her daughter and make sure she was safe, the line went dead.

For several seconds, she stood in the harsh lights of her kitchen holding the phone while the dial tone buzzed in her ear. Then she carefully replaced it onto the base, collapsed into the nearest chair and buried her face in her hands.

Matt found her there when he returned to the kitchen after hanging up the extension in the bedroom. Everything in him screamed out to comfort her, but he knew he had to deal with necessities first. He called Jesse's emergency number, then quickly and succinctly laid out for his brother what had happened.

That done, he finally could turn his attention to Ellie. He knelt by her side and pulled her trembling form into his arms. "We'll get her back, Doc. Jesse's a good man to have on your side. He'll find her."

Her breathing was fast and uneven, and she seemed as fragile as a snowflake in his arms. "Where am I going to come up with a hundred thousand dollars in cash by noon tomorrow?"

"Me."

She stared at him, eyes dazed like a shell-shocked accident victim. "You?"

"I'll call the bank right now and get started on the paperwork." The ranch had a line of credit more than twice what the kidnapper was asking—plenty of credit and enough influence that he shouldn't have any problem rushing things through.

"It's almost seven-thirty," she said numbly. "The bank closed hours ago."

"The bank manager played football with me in high school. I'll call him at home. When Rick hears the story, I know he'll want to help, even if he has to work all night putting the ransom together."

He could almost see the objections gather like storm clouds in her eyes. Damn stubborn woman was going to put up a fuss even now. Sure enough, she shook her head. "No. I can't take your money. I'll...I'll figure something else out."

"Like what? Sell a kidney?"

That little chin of hers tilted toward the ceiling. "I don't know. But this is my problem, and I'll find a way."

It took everything in him not to reach out and shake her until her teeth rattled. This was for real. Didn't she realize that? He didn't have either the time or the patience to work at wearing down that brick wall of independence she insisted on building around herself.

"Look," he snapped, "I'm going to help you, whether you want me to or not, so just deal with it."

"This is serious money, Matt."

"Chances are the bastard won't get far enough away to spend even a few dollars of it before Jess finds him. I mean it, you don't have a choice, Ellie. For once, just accept my help gracefully."

She studied him, her green eyes murky with fear and frustration, then she crossed to the phone and ripped off a piece of paper from a pad next to it, scribbled on it for a moment, then handed it to him.

"These are my terms."

He read it quickly, then scowled. "What the hell is this?"

"I'll let you help with the ransom only if I can deed over the clinic and this house to you. It's probably not binding just handwritten like that, but I'll have official papers drawn up as soon as I can. You have my word on it."

"No way. Then what will you do without a clinic?"

"I'll be leaving anyway," she said tonelessly. "I won't be needing it."

He refused to think about how the idea of her leaving sliced into him like a jagged blade. "What am I supposed to do with an animal hospital? I'm a rancher, not a vet."

"Sell it and take the profits. It won't begin to cover what you're loaning me, but it will be a start. I'll have to figure out a way to pay back the rest as soon as I can."

He wanted to crumple it up and throw it in her face, but now wasn't the time for his temper to flare. If this was the only way she would take his help, he would let her think he was agreeing to her terms. Then he would shred the blasted thing into tiny little pieces and mail them to her.

As he pocketed the paper, a bleak resignation settled in his gut.

She was leaving, and there wasn't a damn thing he could do about it.

Her mom was gonna be so mad.

Dylan tried to keep from shivering, but it was really hard, not only because it was cool and damp on the straw-covered cement floor but also from the fear that was like a big mean dog chewing away inside her.

She didn't have a clue where she was or who had put her here. But she did know she was in serious trouble.

This was all her fault for disobeying. Her mom told her she was always supposed to walk right to the clinic after school, and she usually did. Today, though, she'd decided to take the long way.

Cheyenne Ostermiller said her dad was going to sell her pony since she got a new horse for her birthday and that if Dylan wanted to buy it, she could probably get a good deal.

She wanted that pony so bad.

It was all she had been able to think about since lunch, when Cheyenne told her about it. All afternoon, during math and music and writer's workshop, she hadn't been able to do anything but daydream about having her own horse. Taking care of it, feeding it, riding anytime she wanted.

Since it didn't look like her mom was going to marry Mr. Harte any time soon, she at least ought to be able to get a horse of her very own. It was only fair.

All she planned to do was walk by Cheyenne's house and take a look at the paint in the pasture. Maybe make friends with him, if he'd let her. It was pretty far out of the way on the edge of town, but she figured if she hurried she'd only be a little late to the clinic and SueAnn wouldn't even notice.

The pony had been perfect. Sweet and well-mannered

and beautiful. She'd been standing there petting him and trying to figure out how she could convince her mom to buy him when she heard a truck pull up.

She hadn't paid much attention, thinking it was probably Cheyenne's mom or dad. Next thing she knew, somebody had grabbed her from behind and stuffed a rag that tasted like medicine into her mouth. It must have been something to put her to sleep because the next thing she knew, she woke up lying on the straw in this windowless cement room that reminded her of the quarantine room at the clinic.

She shivered again and pulled her parka closer around her. If only it were the clinic. Then she could bang on the door and bring SueAnn or her mom running.

This was newer than her mom's clinic, though. And instead of being clean and nice, this room had an icky smell, and the straw on the cement floor didn't seem very fresh.

Where could she be? And who would want to kidnap her?

If she weren't so scared, she might have been able to look on this whole thing as a big adventure, something to tell Lucy and the other kids at school about. But she couldn't help thinking about her mom and how worried she probably was and how mad she was gonna be when she found out Dylan hadn't gone straight home after school.

Tears started burning in her throat, and she sniffled a few times, but then she made herself stop. She couldn't be a crybaby. Not now. Crying didn't help anything, that's what her mom always said.

Her mom never cried. But she figured even her mom would have been a little scared a few moments later when there was a funny noise by the door then the knob started to turn.

She huddled as far into the corner as she could, her heart

pounding a mile a minute, as a man walked through the door wearing a stupid-looking clown mask with scraggly yellow hair.

"You're awake." The voice from inside the mask sounded hollow and distorted, like when you talked into a paper cup, only a whole lot spookier.

She was afraid she was gonna pee in her pants and she was breathing as hard as she did when Mrs. Anderson made them run a mile in gym class, but she tried to stay calm, just like her mom would have done.

"Keep your hands off me. I know karate," she lied. "I'll kick you so hard in the you-know-where, you'll wish you were dead."

Through the round holes for eyes in the plastic clown mask, she could see pale blue eyes widen, and the alarm in them gave her confidence to sit up a little straighter.

"No. You've got this all wrong. That's disgusting! I'm not going to touch you. Look, I just brought you a couple of blankets and a pillow. It's cold in here. I'm sorry, but I didn't have any place else to put you."

She stuck her jaw in the air defiantly. "How about my house?"

The kidnapper made a sound that might have been a laugh. "Nice try. But I'm afraid that's not possible right now. You're stuck with me for a while, kid."

He handed the blankets and a small pillow to her but she refused to reach for them, just continued watching him warily.

"Nobody's going to hurt you," he said impatiently. "Just don't make any trouble and you'll be back with your mom by lunchtime tomorrow, I promise."

"Why should I believe you?"

"Believe what you want. Makes no difference to me. I have to go out for a while. Are you hungry? I can pick up some dinner for you on the way back, if you want. How about a nice hamburger and some French fries from the drive-up?"

Despite her fear, her mouth watered, since she'd been too busy talking about Cheyenne's pony to eat much of the cafeteria's chicken surprise at lunchtime. She wasn't about to tell him that, though, so she kept her lips stubbornly zipped.

The clown mask wobbled a little as the man sighed. "I'll take that as a yes. I'll be back in a little while. Maybe later, I can bring a TV in for you if that will help pass the time."

After he left, she wanted to throw a pillow at the door. What a jerk, if he really thought he could make everything all better by bringing her a hamburger and a TV.

She wanted to go home and hug her mom and tell her she was sorry. She wanted to sleep in her own bed, not in some stinky cement room with moldy straw on the floor.

There had to be some way to get out of here. But how?

She spread one blanket on the floor, then sat down and crossed her legs and wrapped the other one around her. She could figure this out. She just had to put her mind to it.

After a minute of thinking hard, a smile suddenly crept over her face, and she knew exactly what she was going to do.

See, she had this plan....

Matt stood in the doorway between Ellie's living room and kitchen feeling about as useful as a milk bucket under a bull.

His brother had taken over as soon as he arrived, and now Jess was on the couch holding both of Ellie's hands while he briefed her on what was happening. "The FBI handles kidnapping cases but they can't get agents here from Salt Lake City for at least an hour or two," Jess was saying.

"That long?" Her voice sounded small, tight, not at all like the confident, self-assured woman he'd come to care about so much.

"I'm sorry, Ellie. It takes time to mobilize a team and send them up here by chopper. In the meantime, I have every one of my officers and as many deputies as the sheriff could spare out interviewing anybody who might have seen her after school. They'll keep in constant contact and let us know if anything breaks."

She drew in a ragged-sounding breath, and Jesse squeezed her hands. "Dispatch is getting call after call from people wanting to help look for her. Your buddy Steve Nichols has offered to head up the volunteer search effort and he's getting plenty of support. Nobody in town wants to believe something like this could happen in Star Valley."

"Thank you so much for everything you're doing," she said softly.

Jess's mouth twisted into a reassuring smile. "We'll find her, El. I promise."

Given the circumstances, Matt was ashamed of himself for the powerful urge raging through him to yank his little brother off the couch and shove him out the door.

It really chapped his hide that she could sit there looking all grateful to Jess for what he was doing to help find Dylan and still go all prickly at Matt's offer to help.

She wouldn't grab Matt's hand if she were drowning, yet she seemed to think Jess hung the damn moon.

All this time, he thought she just had a hard time letting anyone help her. Now he realized it was only *him* whose help she didn't want. Why? Was it only his brother's badge that made the difference?

He cared about her a whole hell of a lot more than Jess

did. They had a relationship, as stormy as it had been. So why did she continue to push him away?

"You've been so kind," she said to his brother, and Matt decided he'd taken just about all he could.

"I'm going to call Rick about getting started on the ransom," he said abruptly, daring either of them to argue with him. Her kid was a lot more important than his hurt feelings, and he needed to keep that uppermost in his mind. "I'll use my cell phone so I don't tie up your line here."

He stalked outside and noticed the temperature had dropped. A cold wind howled out of the south, promising an end to the January thaw. He barely felt it sneaking through his coat as he made his way to his truck, ashamed of himself for letting his temper get the better of him.

Inside the truck, he quickly dialed Rick Marquez's number. The bank manager answered on the second ring, and Matt quickly filled him in on Dylan's kidnapping.

"I just heard," Rick said, his voice tight with shock. "MaryBeth just got off the phone with Janie Montgomery, whose niece works over at the police station. Any leads on what kind of an SOB would do such a terrible thing?"

"Jess is working on it."

"How's Dr. Webster holding up?"

"Pretty shook up. Who wouldn't be?"

"It's a real shame. Nice woman like that. Anything I can do?"

"Matter of fact, Rick, there is. I need to borrow some money from my line of credit." He cleared his throat. "Um, a hundred thousand dollars. Think you could round up that much cash by tomorrow morning?"

There was a long, pregnant pause on the other end of the phone. Even though he was the meanest linebacker Star Valley High had ever seen and had fooled many an opponent into thinking he was just another dumb jock, Rick was as smart as a bunkhouse rat. "You're giving Ellie the money for the ransom?"

The speculation in his friend's voice made him bristle. Would everybody in town have the same prurient reaction? Probably, if word got out. He blew out a breath, suddenly realizing at least one of the reasons Ellie objected to his help. People were going to read far more into it than just one friend helping out another.

"Yeah," he said gruffly. "Yeah, I am. You got a problem with that?"

"You sure that's a good idea, Matt?"

He had no choice. Even though she would probably choke on her own tongue rather than admit it, she needed his help. And he was damn well going to give it.

"Can you get the money or not?" he asked, impatience sharpening his tone.

"It will take a lot of wrangling tonight, but I think I should be able to get my hands on that much."

"Good. Let me know as soon as the papers are ready and I'll come sign them."

After a moment, Rick ventured into risky waters again. "Is there something going on between you and Ellie Webster I should know about?"

Other than I'm crazy in love with her? The thought rocketed into his head, and he stared out the windshield as the wind rattled the skeletal branches of her sugar maple tree.

Love? No way. He didn't love her. He couldn't. He just didn't have that in him anymore. Not after Melanie.

On the other hand, what else could he call it when he suddenly couldn't imagine a life without her?

Yeah. He had it bad. He was only shocked it took him this long to figure it out.

"Matt?" Rick's voice yanked him back to the conversation.

"We're friends," he finally said.

"Pretty darn good friends if you're willing to cough up a hundred Gs for her."

"Look, I don't need a lecture. Her kid's been kidnapped, and I'm only trying to do what I can to make sure she comes back safely. Just get the money, okay?"

"I hope you know what you're doing."

He clamped his teeth together. It would have been easier to hold up a damn train. "I'll call you later to find out how it's going," he snapped.

He was getting ready to hang up when a thought occurred to him. "Wait a minute," he said to Rick. "You have your finger on the financial pulse of the whole valley, right? You probably have a pretty good idea who might be in need of a little cash, don't you?"

"Some." Rick drew the word out slowly, warily.

"So you could maybe point out a couple of people who might have a financial incentive to do something like this."

"I could. Of course, then I'd lose my job for handing out confidential bank information. I'm sorry, but I happen to like my job, Matt."

"A couple of names. That's all I'm looking for."

"No."

"What I can't figure out is why somebody would want her to leave town so badly they'd be desperate enough to risk fifteen to life on a federal offense like kidnapping. We're talking some major time here."

"Leave town?"

"Yeah. That's one of the conditions of him returning Dylan. Seems to me that was just as important to the kidnapper as the money. More, maybe. So who would benefit with Ellie out of the picture?"

"Even if I had any ideas, I couldn't tell you. You're not even a cop!"

"I can have Jess on the line in two seconds. Or better yet, why don't I call back and tell MaryBeth all about that little blond buckle bunny who followed you clear down from Bozeman after the college rodeo finals?"

"Hey, that was way before I got married." Despite it, Matt could hear the panic in his old friend's voice.

He pushed his advantage. "As I recall, you and Mary-Beth were almost engaged. Man, that blonde was one hot little number, wasn't she?"

There was a long, drawn-out pause, then Rick sighed heavily. "I don't know what you're looking for. But I can maybe give you one name of somebody who might have a motive."

"Go ahead. I'm listening."

As soon as Rick mentioned the name, his heart started to pound. This was it. He knew it in his bones.

Chapter 16

Ellie sat at the kitchen table drinking the glass of water Jess had forced on her.

This had to be a nightmare. But if it was, it was a pretty surreal one. Matt's brother sat beside her barking orders into the phone while the doorbell rang again with yet another concerned neighbor bearing food.

The Salt River grapevine worked fast. She'd received the ransom call less than forty-five minutes ago, and already she had at least four casseroles in the fridge and a half-dozen plates of cookie bars.

How did people whip these things up so fast? And did anyone really think tuna noodle bake with crushed potato chips on top was going to make everything okay?

Food seemed to be the panacea for every trouble in Star Valley. She wondered if there was some secret cookbook spelling out the best way to handle every situation. *Betty Crocker's Crisis Cuisine?*

Your neighbor's kid gets busted for growing pot? Take over banana nut bread. Your best friend's husband walks out on her for some secretary he met over the Internet? A nice beef pie ought to do the trick.

Your veterinarian's little girl is kidnapped walking home from school? Pick your poison. Anything was apparently appropriate, from soup to nuts.

Fortunately SueAnn had rushed right over to run interference at the door. There was nothing left for Ellie to do but sit here obsessing about what kind of monster would steal a nine-year-old girl.

She couldn't think about it. If she did, she would go crazy imagining Dylan's terror. Her mind prowled with terrible possibilities. Every time she started to think about it, she wanted to fall apart, to disintegrate into a mindless heap, but somehow she managed to hold herself together.

Still, when Matt burst into the kitchen a few moments later she had to fight with everything in her not to jump up and burrow against that strong chest.

She'd been so horrible to him, it was a wonder he would even stand to be in the same room with her. She had seen the hurt in his eyes when she pushed him away, when she rejected the comfort he wanted to give. She hated herself for it, but she couldn't seem to bend on this.

The need to lean on him, to let him take this terrible burden from her, was so powerful it terrified her. She couldn't, though. This was her burden and hers alone.

She had to be strong for her little girl.

Once she started down that slippery slope and let herself need him, it would be so easy to tumble all the way to full dependence. She was afraid she would lose herself in the process. And then what good would she be for Dylan?

Matt spared her one quick glance, then turned to his brother. "I think I know where she is. Come on, let's go get her."

Jess stared at him like he'd just grown an extra couple

of appendages. "Lou, I'm gonna have to call you back," he said into the phone. "Yeah. Let me know as soon as you hear from the Feds."

He hung up the phone and frowned at his brother. "Are you completely nuts?"

"I just got a lead I think you'll be interested in. Did you know Steve Nichols is delinquent on payments to the Salt River bank to the tune of about ninety-five thou? He's up to his eyeballs in debt and is just a few weeks away from foreclosure on that fancy new clinic he just built."

Ellie stared at him, trying to process the information. "Steve? You think *Steve* took Dylan?" She wouldn't have been more shocked if he'd accused Reverend Whitaker.

"It makes sense, doesn't it? Somebody's been trying real hard to run you out of town. Who would benefit more if you left Star Valley than your main competition?"

"I hardly have a practice anymore! I'm not much of a threat to him."

"If he's only breaking even by the skin of his teeth, maybe you're what stands between survival and failure."

"But...but we're friends. He even offered to head up the search effort for Dylan."

"Think about it, Doc. Whoever left those notes for you had access to two things—dead animals and needles. Doesn't it make sense that it might be another vet?"

She couldn't believe it. Not Steve. He had welcomed her into town, had treated her as a respected colleague and a friend.

"That's not enough for an interview, let alone a search warrant," Jess snapped.

Matt stared him down. "I'm not a cop, little brother. I don't need a warrant."

Jess glared for a moment, a muscle working in his jaw,

then he picked up the phone again. "Lou, patch me through to Steve Nichols, will you?"

A minute later, he growled into the phone. "What do you mean, he's not there? I thought he was coordinating the civilian searchers."

After another pause, he hung up. "Lou says he had to take care of some business at his clinic. She said he told her he'd be back in an hour or so."

"Then that's probably where he took Dylan, to his clinic."

"You don't know that. It doesn't mean a damn thing."

Matt shoved on his Stetson. "I'm going, Jess. You can come along or you can sit here on your duff and forget we ever had this conversation. Your choice."

"I think you're crazier than a duck in a desert," Jess growled. "But I'm not about to let you head over there by yourself in this kind of mood."

"I'm going, too." Ellie jumped up from her chair.

Both of them looked at her with the exact same glower. "Forget it," Matt said. "It could be dangerous."

She glowered right back. "This is my child we're talking about. I'm going with you."

"You'll stay in the truck, then."

Not likely. She pressed her lips together, and Matt finally sighed. "Come on, then."

They took Jesse's big department Bronco so he could radio for backup if necessary, but he drove without sirens or lights.

Steve's clinic was a low-slung, modern facility on the other side of town. Ellie had always thought it looked more like some kind of fancy assisted living center than a country vet's office, with a porte cochere and that long row of high, gleaming windows.

The blinds were closed, but she could see the yellow

glow of lights inside. If Dylan wasn't there—and Ellie wasn't nearly as convinced as Matt seemed to be that she was—Steve would be hurt and outraged when they barged in and accused him of kidnapping her.

She couldn't let it bother her, she decided. In the scheme of things, when it came to her daughter, the possibility of hurting Steve's feeling didn't matter at all.

"Let me do the talking," Jesse said after he drove under the porte cochere and turned off the Bronco.

"Sure, as long as you're getting answers."

Jess rolled his eyes at his brother, and Ellie felt like doing the same thing when Matt turned to her and ordered her to stay put.

She thought about obeying for all of ten seconds, then waited until they were at the front door of the clinic before she climbed out of the vehicle and followed them.

Matt scowled when he saw her but said nothing. As they walked inside, she thought she saw just the slightest movement behind the long, low wall separating the reception desk from the waiting area.

Before she could react, the men both tensed and moved together, their shoulders touching so they created a solid, impenetrable protective barrier in front of her.

Jesse's hand went to his sidearm. "Nichols? Is that you?"

Time seemed to slow to a crawl, and the only sound in the room was their breathing. She couldn't see what was happening over their broad shoulders, so she stood on tip-toe for a better look as a small, frightened face peeked over the wall.

Ellie didn't know who moved first, her or Dylan, but an instant later she had shoved her way past the men and gathered her daughter into her arms.

Sobs of overwhelming relief welled in her throat as she held the small, warm weight. She forced them down, knowing she would have time later to give in to them. Right now her daughter needed her to be strong.

Dylan held tightly to her mother. "I'm so glad you're here! I was just calling nine-one-one when I heard a car outside. I thought maybe someone else was helping Dr. Nichols and I got really scared and tried to hide under the desk, then I heard Lucy's uncle. How did you know where I was?"

She couldn't seem to hold her daughter close enough. "It doesn't matter, honey. Are you okay? What happened? Where's Steve?"

A shudder racked her little frame. "In the back, in a quarantine room just like you have. That's where he kept me." She nibbled her bottom lip nervously. "Um, he might need an ambulance. He hit his head on the cement floor pretty hard."

Matt started to take a step toward the hallway, his face blazing with fury, but Jess reached a hand out to stop him. "No way am I letting you go back there right now. That's all I need is a murder investigation on my hands in addition to the kidnapping case. I'll handle this. You stay here with the ladies."

Despite everything, Ellie had to fight a smile when Dylan preened a little at being called a lady.

"Oh. The door's locked," she said suddenly. "I have the key."

She fished around in the pocket of her parka then pulled it out and held it out to the police chief. "Are…are you gonna shoot him?"

Jesse crouched and took her small hand, key and all, and folded it into his. "You want me to, sweetheart?"

"No," she said seriously. "He didn't hurt me. Just scared me a little."

"Sounds like you scared him right back."

Dylan gave a watery giggle then handed over the key, and Jesse disappeared down the hall.

After he was gone, Dylan's smile slid away and she looked nervously at her mother. "This is all my fault, Mom. I'm really sorry. I should have gone right to the clinic after school and I didn't. I just went to see Cheyenne's horse but I'll never do it again, I promise. Don't be mad. Please?"

"Oh, honey. I'm not mad. You're not to blame for this." She was, for not keeping her daughter safe. Just another thing she would have to deal with later. "What happened? How did you get away?"

"I tried to stay calm and use my brain, just like you always tell me to do. I didn't think he'd hurt me, but I still wanted to go home. The first time he came in, I saw he left the key in the lock and it gave me an idea. When he brought me dinner, I tripped him and he fell over and hit his head. I didn't know it was Dr. Nichols until he fell and his mask fell off but as soon as he did, I ran out and locked the door."

How on earth had she managed to raise such an amazing daughter? Ellie hugged her tightly again. "It sounds like you did exactly the right thing."

"You're about the bravest kid I've ever met." Matt's voice was rough, and he reached a hand out and squeezed Dylan's shoulders.

Dylan blushed at his approval and looked at him with an expression of such naked longing in her eyes that Ellie suddenly remembered Lucy's confession earlier in the evening, about how the two girls had connived and schemed to throw her and Matt together.

Dylan wanted a daddy, and she had obviously picked Matt for the role. *Oh, sweetheart.* Her heart ached knowing her daughter was destined for disappointment. She would give Dylan the world, but she could never give her this.

She pushed the thought away. She couldn't worry about how she would ever ease the pain of futile hopes and un-realized dreams. For now, all she could do was hold on to her daughter and whisper a prayer of gratitude that she had her back.

Hours later, Ellie sat in her darkened living room watch-ing the gas logs and their endless flame.

Dylan was finally asleep, lulled only by the grudging promise that, yes, she could go to school the next day and tell everyone of her harrowing adventure and how she had single-handedly rescued herself.

Ellie had held her hand until she'd drifted off. Even long after her daughter was lost to dreamland, she hadn't been able to make herself move, had just sat on the edge of that narrow bed feeling each small breath and thank-ing Whoever looked over mothers for delivering her baby back safely.

Eventually she'd wandered here. Hard to believe that just a short time ago, the old house had been a frenzy of activity with people coming and going, the phone ringing, all the lights blazing. Now the air was still, with only the low whir of the artificial fire to keep her company.

She didn't mind. In truth, she was grateful for the chance to finally catch hold of her fluttering thoughts and sift through the amazing events of the day.

Every time she thought of Steve and what he had done, her stomach burned and she wanted to break something. He had tried to destroy her in every conceivable way. Fi-nancially, professionally, emotionally. She'd never before been the subject of such undiluted hostility, and it fright-ened her as much as it shocked her, especially because she had been so completely blind to it.

When Steve regained consciousness and found Jess and six other officers surrounding him, he had first tried to bluff his way out of the situation. Faced with the overwhelming evidence against him, though, he'd finally blurted out everything.

He had been desperate and had come to blame all his problems on her for scheming to take his uncle's clinic away from him. It should have come to him, Steve said. He'd spent years working there, even as a kid, cleaning cages and doing miserable grunt work, all with the expectation that someday the practice would be his and he could reap the benefits of his uncle's reputation in the community.

Then Ben had ruined everything by refusing to sell the clinic to him, instead bringing in an outsider with wacky California ideas that didn't mesh at all with the conservative Star Valley mind-set.

Left with no other choice, Steve had been forced to build his own clinic and had ended up getting in over his head.

He told Jess he realized too late that the community wasn't big enough to support two veterinary clinics so he tried to persuade Ellie to go into business with him to cut down overhead. When she refused, he knew he had to find another way to make her leave, especially after she started to eat into his patient load.

He was the one who had left the warning in her truck. And, he confessed, he'd broken into her truck and read her planner. It hadn't been difficult to study her treatment log and inject specific horses with a virulent bacteria to make it look as if her shoddy care had spread disease.

When that didn't work, he knew he had to take drastic measures, so he'd come up with the twisted kidnapping plan.

She could forgive him the rest. Although it would take time and effort, she could rebuild her reputation, her practice.

But she would never be able to forgive him for terrorizing her little girl.

She'd been a fool not to see it before. No. She hadn't *wanted* to see it, the ugly bitterness he hid so well behind a veneer of friendship. It had been much easier to take Steve at face value, to see what she wanted to see.

SueAnn had seen it, had tried to warn her about him, but she hadn't listened. She had trusted him, and her daughter had ultimately paid the price for her mistake.

She wrapped her arms around her knees and gazed at the flickering flames. How had she forgotten the lessons she'd learned so early in life? Depend only on yourself and you won't ever have to know the cruel sting of disappointment.

A soft knock at the front door disturbed the silence of the house. She felt an instant's fear and then she remembered all was well. Her daughter was safe at home, where she belonged.

She pulled aside the lacy curtain at the door and felt only a small quiver of surprise to find Matt standing on the other side. He wore that shearling-lined ranch coat again, leather collar turned up against the cold night, and his chiseled features were solemn, unsmiling.

He looked strong and solid, and she wanted nothing more than to fall into his arms and weep after the emotional upheaval of the day.

She couldn't, though, and she knew it. Instead, she opened the door and ushered him inside. "Matt! What are you doing here? I thought you went back to the ranch hours ago."

"I did. But I couldn't stay away." He stood just inside the door watching her, a strange light in his blue eyes that suddenly made her as nervous as a mouse in the middle of a catfight.

She cleared her throat and seized on the only benign topic she could think of. Food. "Would you like something to eat? I've got enough here to feed most of the town. I haven't tried any of it, but SueAnn said Ginny Garrett's cinnamon sugar cookies were to die for."

To her intense relief, he shielded that strange light from her with his lashes. "Ginny does make one fine cookie," he said after a moment. "You sure you don't mind?"

"Eat as many as you want." She led the way to the kitchen, where the table practically bowed from the weight of all the plates of goodies covering it. "I've got enough stuff here to have a bake sale."

She peeled back the plastic wrap covering the plate the mayor's wife brought over, and Matt took one cookie and bit into it. "It's comfort food," he said after he'd swallowed. "Sometimes people don't know how else they can help."

"I know. Everyone has been so kind. I've just been trying to figure out how I'm going to find room in my freezer for everything. Maybe you should take some home to your ranch hands."

He leaned a hip against her counter. "Sure."

Grateful for something to do with her hands, she found some paper plates in the back of a cupboard and started loading them up with fudge and lemon bars and chocolate chip cookies.

"So how are you?" he asked solemnly while she worked.

She flashed him a quick look. "Okay. A little shaky still."

"Yeah. Me, too. I keep thinking, what if it had been Lucy? I wouldn't have handled it with nearly the guts you did."

A bitter laugh scored her throat. "I didn't handle anything. I completely fell apart."

He studied her solemnly out of those blue eyes, and for a terrible moment she feared he was going to cross the space between them and pull her into his arms. And then she really *would* fall apart, would give in to the tears of relief and hurt and remembered terror that choked her.

She turned to the table, ashamed that she couldn't control her emotions better, and after a moment of silence, he spoke again. "Almost forgot. One of the reasons I dropped by was to give you this."

Out of the corner of her gaze, she saw him hold out a wrinkled paper. It took her a few seconds to realize what it was, and then her face burned. It was the note deeding the practice over to him in exchange for the money to have her child returned.

She made no move to reach for it, mortified again that she had needed his help, that she had failed her daughter once more.

"Here. Take it. I don't want it," he growled.

As reluctantly as if it were covered in razor blades, she reached for it. A thousand unspoken words hovered between them. She would have preferred to leave them all that way—unspoken—but she knew she had to say something.

"I… Thank you for what you were going to do. I can't say I understand why you would be willing to do such a thing, but it meant a lot to me anyway."

"Did it?"

The hardness of his voice shocked her. "Yes! Of course!"

He didn't say anything, just continued to study her out of those blue eyes, and she flushed under his scrutiny.

"I said I appreciated it. I don't know what more you want from me."

"Why is it so hard for you?"

"What?"

"Accepting help from me. Admitting you're not some kind of superwoman and can't handle every rotten curve life throws at you by yourself."

She tensed. "I don't know what you're talking about." The lie burned her tongue, scorched her heart.

"No matter how hard I try, you keep pushing me away."

Better to hurt him by pushing him away than the alternative. He would leave her shattered if she let him. Would make her weak and needy and *vulnerable,* and she could never allow it, especially after tonight. She was all Dylan had, and she needed to remember that.

She said nothing, knowing there was nothing she *could* say. After a moment, he spoke again, his voice low and expressionless.

"It makes loving you pretty damn hard when you won't let anybody inside."

His words sucked the air from her lungs, every thought from her head. He didn't say he loved her. He *couldn't* have. It was a mistake. A terrible, cruel mistake.

Terror flapped through her on greasy bat wings. How could he say such a thing? Didn't he realize that she didn't want his love, that she couldn't handle it?

Her breath started coming in deep, heaving gulps. What was she going to do? She didn't want to hurt him, but she couldn't let him destroy her like her father had destroyed her mother.

"Aren't you going to say anything?" he finally asked.

I love you. Heaven help me, I love you. Even though I know you would leave me broken and bloody, I want to curl up against you, inside you, around you, and never, ever let go.

Instead, she made her voice tight, toneless, and hated herself for it. "What do you want me to say, Matt?"

He gazed at her, and she nearly sobbed at the hurt in his eyes, then those blue depths hardened. "How about the truth? That you love me, too. That you push me away because you're afraid."

He knew. Shame coursed through her. How could he say he loved her when he knew what a terrible coward she was?

"I'm sorry," she said, curling her hands into fists at her sides. "I can't tell you what you want to hear."

"You mean you won't."

"That, too." Her hands were trembling, and she didn't know if they would ever, ever stop.

"Dammit, Ellie. You don't think loving you, needing you, scares the ever-living hell out of me, too? It's the absolute last thing I ever wanted or expected."

She dared a look at him and found his eyes fierce with emotion.

"My wife walked out on me, Ellie. Before that, she screwed around with just about every guy in town. I told myself I didn't care, that I'd stopped loving her long before she took off, but Melanie still left me with deep scars covering every inch of my heart. I thought they'd be there forever, and I'd even learned to live with them."

He reached for her then, picked up one fisted hand and brought it to his lips. "But then you blew into town with your smart mouth and your compassion and your courage. And one day I realized I couldn't even feel those scars anymore. You healed them, Doc. I don't know how, but while you were treating my horses, you were working your magic on me, too."

This time a sob did escape her mouth, and she yanked her hand back to press it against her mouth so the rest didn't follow.

"I love you, Ellie," he went on. "I want you in my life, forever if you'll have me. Up until now, you've shown more courage than any woman I've ever met. Don't let your fear win now."

For one wonderful, terrible moment, she let herself believe in fairy tales. In knights on white horses and orange blossoms and a happily ever after filled with laughter and love and joy.

And then the glowing picture faded.

In its place was a ramshackle trailer and a solemn-eyed little girl watching a woman who drank too much and sold her body and sobbed every night for a man who would never come back.

"I'm sorry," she whispered, and blood sceped from her heart.

"I won't ask again." His terse warning was edged with infinite sadness.

She hitched in a ragged breath. "I know. I... Good-bye, Matt."

With one last, searching look, he shoved on his Stetson and walked out into the night.

Only after he closed the door quietly behind him did her knees buckle, and she slid to the hard linoleum floor of her kitchen and wept.

Chapter 17

He never would have believed it.

Matt stood in the gymnasium of the elementary school on Valentine's Day, completely amazed at what creativity and a little elbow grease could achieve.

Instead of a dingy old room that smelled like a cross between canned peas and dirty socks, the gym had been completely transformed into a magical place.

Thousands of little twinkling white lights had been strung across the ceiling like stars in the night sky and wrapped around the branches of a couple dozen small trees temporarily commandeered from Jerry Clayton's greenhouse in town. A city skyline painted by the elementary school art classes graced the stage, covered by even more tiny white lights so it looked as if the windows of the buildings really glowed.

With the lights dimmed and the high school's jazz band playing old dance numbers, this was the crowning jewel of the library fund-raiser—which by all accounts looked to be a smashing success.

It had been Ellie's idea to try to provide something for everyone at the fair. The little kids were still running from classroom to classroom using the tickets their parents had purchased for fishponds and beanbag tosses and cakewalks. Their older siblings were busy in the auditorium watching a PG-rated scary movie. And judging by the crowd already out on the dance floor, their parents and grandparents were obviously enjoying the romantic escape the committee had created.

He thought he would feel pretty weird about having his name listed on the program as one of the organizers, but as he watched couples dancing cheek-to-cheek under the starry lights, he had to admit to a fair amount of pride.

All evening, people had been telling him what a great job the committee had done. It seemed bitterly ironic that he'd been even a little instrumental in helping everyone else celebrate this holiday for romance, especially when things with Ellie had ended so badly.

She was here somewhere, but he hadn't caught more than a fleeting glimpse of her all night as she ran from crisis to crisis.

Even those brief, painful glimpses were better than what he had endured the last three weeks. Before today, he hadn't seen her since the terrible night he'd gone to her house, told her his feelings and had them thrown back in his face.

He wanted to be angry at her. He had been for a day or two, and the thunder and fury had been much easier to deal with than this constant, aching sadness that settled in his bones and weighed down his heart.

Why was she being so stubborn about this? He knew she loved him. She never would have given herself to him so sweetly, passionately, if she didn't. He couldn't make her admit it, though. Not when she so obviously wanted to deny her feelings, to him and to herself.

A couple of giggles sounded behind him, distracting him from the grimness of his thoughts, and he turned to find Lucy and Dylan being teased by Jess. The girls both wore dresses for a change and had put their hair up, and they looked entirely too grown up for his peace of mind.

"Hey, big brother." Jess grinned. "I think we need to escort these lovely ladies out on the dance floor. What do you say?"

The girls giggled again, and he summoned a smile for their benefit. "I think we'd be stupid not to grab the two prettiest girls here while we have the chance."

Jess had already snagged Lucy so Matt obligingly held his arm out to Dylan, who took it with a blush that reminded him painfully of her mother. Out on the dance floor, she stumbled around awkwardly for a moment then quickly lost her shyness and started jabbering away about her favorite subject, horses.

"My mom says maybe I can get a horse in the summer, when I'd have more time to take care of him and learn to ride him. That would be so cool. Then I could ride with Lucy around the ranch without anybody having to worry about us getting into trouble."

Like that day would ever come. The two of them invented the word. "I'll believe that when I see it," he teased.

Ellie's daughter giggled again. "Well, we wouldn't get into trouble because I don't know how to ride, anyway."

He smiled and twirled her around. Dylan was a great kid, despite her mischievous streak. Full of spunk and fire, just like her mother. He thought of the night she had spent frightened and alone in a concrete room because of that bastard Nichols and saw red again. Good thing the man was in the county jail awaiting sentencing after his guilty plea. Maybe by the time he was released, Matt might have cooled down enough to keep from beating the hell out of him.

"Oh, look," Dylan said suddenly. "There's my mom."

She pulled her hand from his arm and started waving vigorously to someone behind him, and he turned and found Ellie standing alone on the edge of the dance floor.

In the low, shimmering light, her green eyes looked huge. Haunted.

"Doesn't she look pretty?" Dylan asked innocently, and he dared another look. Like her daughter, Ellie wore a dress—a soft, sapphire-blue clingy thing that flared and bunched in all the right places.

He cleared his throat, but his voice still came out gruff. "Very," he said.

"I told her she'd be a lot prettier if she'd smile once in a while," Dylan said, sounding like a middle-aged, nagging mother instead of a nine-year-old, "but she hasn't been doing much of that lately."

"No?" He tried to sound casual and disinterested, even though the little scamp had his full attention, and she probably knew it.

"She's been really sad," Dylan said. "She even cries at night sometimes after I'm in bed, so I know something must be really wrong. My mom never cries."

His heart stuttered in his chest at the thought of Ellie crying alone in her house.

Damn stubborn woman. If she was hurting, it was her own fault. Didn't she know how absolutely right they were for each other? He needed her to bring lightness and laughter into his life, to keep him from taking himself too seriously.

And she needed him to show her nobody expected her to bear the whole weight of the world by herself.

"Maybe you could talk to her, or ask her to dance, even. You're friends, aren't you? That might make her feel better."

Dylan's green eyes shone with hope, and he hated to douse it, but he was pretty sure he was the last person on earth Ellie wanted to talk to right about now.

On second thought, maybe that's just what he needed

to do. He'd told her he wouldn't grovel. But just trying to talk some sense into her wasn't really the same, was it?

He had to try. Even if he looked like a lovesick fool, he had to try. Much more of this heartache was going to destroy both of them.

As soon as the dance was over, he would grab her, he decided, yank her into a dark corner and kiss her until she came to her senses.

But when the music ended and he walked Dylan back to Lucy and Jess, Ellie was nowhere to be found.

She couldn't do this.

Ellie stood outside the side door of the school breathing the February night air and praying the bitter cold would turn her heart to ice, would take away this pain.

She pressed a palm to her chest, breathing hard with the effort it took to regain control of her emotions. Seeing Matt tonight—looking so strong and gorgeous in his black dress jeans and Western-cut shirt—had been bad enough. Watching him spin around the dance floor while Dylan smiled at him like he'd just handed her the stars had been excruciating.

They looked like they belonged together—like they *all* belonged together—and she knew she had to escape.

What a fool she had been to think she could handle seeing him tonight without falling apart. She had spent three weeks trying to get through each day without thinking about him more than once every five minutes. Of course the shock of seeing him would be an assault to her senses, especially surrounded by all the trappings of the most romantic day of the year.

How was she going to get through this? They lived in a small, tight-knit community and were bound to bump in to each other occasionally. Would it get easier in time or would her heart continue to pound out of her chest and her pulse rate skyrocket every time she saw him?

What could she do? She wasn't sure she had the strength to endure seeing him every week or even every month, not if it made her feel as if her heart were being sliced open again and again.

Yet she couldn't leave. She had a job here, a business that was booming now that people in town knew how Steve had tried to blacken her reputation. She and Dylan had a life now, and she couldn't walk away from that.

She blew out another breath. She could handle this. She was a strong and capable woman who could do anything she set her mind to.

Except stop loving Matthew Harte.

The door at her back was suddenly thrust out, and for one terrible moment she was afraid he had followed her outside. To her vast relief, Sarah McKenzie peeked her pretty blond head out the door.

"Ellie! I was wondering where you ran off to."

"I just needed a little air." A vast understatement. If she'd been any more breathless watching Matt dance with her little girl, she would have needed to yank old Bessie Johnson's portable oxygen tank right out from under her and steal a few puffs.

Concern darkened the schoolteacher's brown eyes. "Everything okay?"

"Sure." Ellie managed a smile. "I've been running all night and I just needed a breather."

"That's why I came to find you. I had to tell you what a fantastic job you and Matt did organizing this evening. I've had so many comments from people telling me it's the best carnival they've ever attended, and they can't remember having such a good time."

"I'm glad people are enjoying themselves."

"And the bottom line is that we've already raised twice what we were expecting for tonight! The school library will have more books than shelf space now."

Ellie smiled. "Maybe next year you can raise enough money to build a whole new library."

"I hope you'll help us again next year. You and Matt both."

Sure. When monkeys fly out of my ears. "Let's get through tonight before we worry about next year."

"Well, I just wanted you to know how good you have been for Salt River. This town needed shaking up. I'm so glad you're staying—we would all miss you very much if you left."

After Sarah slipped inside the school, Ellie stood looking at the rugged mountains glowing in the pale moonlight and thinking about what she had said. If she had given anything to the town, she had received it all back and then some.

She thought of all the people she had come to care about in the months since she had come to Wyoming. Sarah. SueAnn. The rest of the friends she had made on the carnival committee, and the people—some perfect strangers—who had rallied around her after Dylan's kidnapping, bringing food and offers of help and comfort beyond measure.

Her life would have been so much poorer without all of them.

She stared at the mountains as the truth she had refused to see finally slammed into her.

She needed them. All of them.

How stupid she had been. She thought she was so damned independent, so self-sufficient. But she would have crumbled into nothing after Dylan was taken if not for the people of Salt River she had come to love.

She had been trying so hard to stand on her own two feet that she never realized she would have fallen over long ago if it hadn't been for the people around her providing quiet, unquestioning support.

The door pushed open behind her once more, and she thought it would be Sarah again or one of the other committee members. She turned with a teary smile that fell away instantly at the sight of Matt standing in the open doorway, looking strong and solid and wonderful.

Her heart began a painful fluttering in her chest when she thought of how she had wounded him by rejecting the incredible gift of his love.

He had been right. She had pushed him away because she was afraid of needing, of trusting. It had all been for nothing, though. She had needed him from the very beginning, his slow smile, his strength, his love. Especially his love

She had just been too stubborn to admit it.

Tears choked her again and she suddenly knew, without a shadow of a doubt, that he would never hurt her. He would protect her heart like he had tried to protect her body that day in Steve's office, by placing himself in front of anything that threatened her.

"Hi," she whispered.

He continued to study her, his beautiful, hard face as still as the mountains, and for one terrible moment she was afraid that her epiphany had come too late. That she had lost any chance she might have had.

Then she saw his eyes.

They looked at her with hurt and hunger and a vast, aching tenderness, and she forgot to breathe.

"It's frigid out here," he finally said. "Come inside. Are you crazy?"

A tear slid down her nose, and she quickly swiped at it before it could freeze there. "Yeah. Yeah, I am. Completely crazy. I must be or I wouldn't be so miserable right now."

He said nothing, just continued watching her, and she gathered up that courage he seemed to think she had in spades and took a step forward. "I'm sorry, Matt. I'm so sorry."

He stared at her for several seconds, blue eyes wide with disbelief, then she was in his arms. Her heart exploded with joy as he kissed her, his mouth fierce and demanding.

"I have to say this," she said, when she could think straight again. She pulled away and wrapped her cold hands around the warmth of his fingers. "You were right the other night. I didn't want to let you help me, to let you inside. I think I knew even from the beginning that you would have the power to destroy me if I let you."

"I never would," he murmured.

"I know. I should have realized it then, but I'm afraid I don't have much experience with this whole love thing."

His eyes turned wary suddenly, and she realized she had never given him the words. "I love you, Matt," she said softly. "I love the way you smile at your daughter and the way you take care of your horses and the way you hold me like you never want to let me go. I love you fiercely and I hate so much that I hurt you."

Emotions blazed out of his blue eyes. "I'm tough. I'll survive. Just don't do it again, okay?"

Another tear slipped down her cheek. "I won't. I swear it."

His thumb traced the pathway of that lone tear. "Dylan says you never cry."

She sniffed. "See all the bad habits you're making me develop?"

A soft laugh rumbled out of him, then his face grew serious. "I want everything, Ellie," he warned. "Marriage, kids, the whole thing. I won't settle for less. Are you ready for that?"

She thought of a future with him, of making a home together among these mountains she loved, of raising their daughters together—and maybe adding a few sons along the way with their father's eyes and his strength and his smile.

She couldn't imagine anything more wonderful. In answer, she lifted her mouth to his and wrapped her arms tightly around him.

His exultant laugh rang out through the cold February night. "Come on. Let's go inside where it's warm and tell the girls. Hell, let's tell the whole world."

She went still in his arms, suddenly horrified. "Oh, no. The girls."

He shrugged. "What's the problem? This is what they wanted all along. They figured out we belonged together months before we did."

"That's what I mean." She groaned again. "They are going to be completely insufferable when they find out how well their devious little plan worked."

He winced. "Good point. So what do we do about it?"

"I don't think there's anything we *can* do, just accept the fact that our nine-year-old daughters are smarter than either of us."

"That's a terrifying thought."

"Get used to it, Harte. I have a feeling the two of them are going to make our life extremely interesting."

His smile soaked through her, filling every empty corner of her heart with sweet, healing peace. "I can't wait," he murmured.

She smiled and took the hand he offered. "Neither can I, Matt. Neither can I."

* * * * *

CASSIDY HARTE
AND THE COMEBACK KID

To Angela Stone and her band of angels,
especially Merrilyn Lynch, Dorothy Griffiths,
Terri Crossley and Leslie Buchanan,
for nurturing my family when I couldn't.

Chapter 1

Forget bad hair days. Cassidy Harte was having a bad *everything* day.

The ancient commercial-grade oven had been giving her fits since lunch; the owner of the small grocery in town had messed up her order, as usual; and her best assistant had decided to run off to Jackson Hole with a hunky, sweet-talking cowboy.

And now this.

With a resigned sigh, she set the spoon down from her world-famous, scorching-hot chili bubbling on the stove and prepared to head off yet another crisis.

"Calm down, Greta, and tell me what's happened."

One of the high school students Jean Martineau had hired for the summer to clean rooms and wait tables at the Lost Creek Guest Ranch looked as if she was going to hyperventilate any second now. Her hair was even spikier than normal, her eyes were huge with panic behind their horn-rimmed glasses, and she was breathing harder than a bull rider at the buzzer.

"He's here. The new owner. A whole week early!" she wailed. "What are we gonna do? Jean and Kip took the guests on a trail ride before dinner, and there's no one else here but me and I don't know what to do with him," she finished on a whimper.

Is that all? From the way the girl was carrying on, Cassie would have guessed a grizzly had ambled into the office and ordered a cabin for the night. "It's okay. Calm down. We can handle this."

"But a whole week early! We're not ready."

It *was* pretty thoughtless of the Maverick Enterprises CEO to just drop in unexpectedly like this. But the man hadn't done anything in the usual way, from the moment his representative had made Jean Martineau an offer she couldn't refuse for her small guest ranch in Star Valley, Wyoming.

All of the negotiations had been handled by a third party—the few negotiations there had been, since the company hadn't so much as raised an eyebrow at Jean's seven-figure asking price.

She turned her attention back to Greta. "We'll just have to do our best. Don't worry about it. Maverick has made it clear it wants the ranch pretty badly. The company has already invested buckets of time and money into the sale. As far as I know, it's basically a done deal. Even if we tried, I don't think we can possibly blow it at this late date."

The girl still had the wide-eyed, panicky look of a calf facing a branding iron. "You know how much I need this job. If he doesn't like the service here, he could still fire every single one of us after Maverick takes over. I don't want to go back to making ice-cream cones at the drive-up."

True. And Cassie would really hate to lose her job cooking meals for the guest and staff at the ranch. Finding a well-paying job she was qualified for in rural Wyoming wasn't exactly easy. Especially one that included room and board.

She knew she could always move to a bigger town but she didn't want to leave Star Valley. This was her home.

If she had to, she knew she could *really* go home, to her family, but the idea of crawling back to the Diamond Harte appealed to her about as much as sticking one of those branding irons in her eye.

Besides that, she loved working at the Lost Creek. These last few months on her own had been so rich with experiences that she couldn't bear the idea of losing it all, just because some spoiled, inconsiderate executive decided to drop in on a whim.

She sighed. What a pain in the neck. He'd ruined her plans. With a twinge of regret she remembered the great menu she had planned for the new boss's first night at the ranch—rack of lamb, caramelized pearl onions and creamed potatoes, with raspberry tartlets for dessert.

Tonight's dinner was good, hearty fare—chili, corn bread, salad and Dutch-oven peach cobbler—but it was nothing spectacular. It would have to do, though. She didn't have time to whip up anything else.

"You have to help me," Greta pleaded. "I don't know what to do with him and I'm afraid I'll ruin everything. You know how I get."

Cassie winced at the reminder. Two weeks before, the president of a fast-food chain from back east had rented the entire ranch for a family reunion. In the midst of a severe case of nerves, Greta had ended up accidentally short-sheeting his bed, leaving out towels altogether and overcharging his credit card by a couple of extra zeros. Then at breakfast she'd topped it off by spilling hot cocoa all over his wife.

"Where is the new guy now?"

"I left him in the gathering room. I didn't even know which cabin to put him in, since that doctor and his family have the Grand Teton for another two nights."

Their best cabin. Rats. "What's left?"

"Just the Huckleberry."

One of the very smallest cabins. And the one next to hers. She blew out a breath. "That will have to do. He can't expect to drop in like this and have the whole world stop just for him. Check to make sure the cabin sparkles and then send one of the other wranglers up the trail after Jean. I'll go out and try to keep him busy until she gets back."

With a last quick stir of the chili—and a heartfelt wish that she were wearing something a little more presentable than jeans and a T-shirt with her favorite female country band on the front—she headed for the gathering room.

It didn't matter what she was wearing, she assured herself. He was probably a rich old man who only wants to play cowboy, who wouldn't notice anything but the ranch unless a stampede knocked him over. He had to be. Why else would his company go to so much effort to buy the Lost Creek Guest Ranch?

The ranch consisted of a dozen small guest cabins and the main ranch house that served as lodge and dining hall. The centerpiece of the split-log house was the huge two-story gathering room, with several Western leather couches set up in conversational groups, a huge river-rock fireplace and a wide wall of windows overlooking the beautiful Salt River Mountain Range.

At the doorway Cassie found the new owner standing with his back to her, gazing out at the mountains.

Okay, she was wrong.

This was no pudgy old cowboy-wannabe, at least judging by the rear view.

And what a view it was.

She gulped. Instead of the brand-spankin'-new Western duds she might have expected, the new owner wore faded jeans and a short-sleeved cotton shirt the same silvery green as the sagebrush covering the mountains. Dark blond hair touched with gold brushed the collar of his shirt and broad shoulders tapered down to lean hips that filled out a pair of worn jeans like nobody's business. The long length of faded denim ended in a pair of sturdy, battered boots built more for hard work than fashion.

Whoa, Nellie.

By sheer force of will she managed to rein in her wandering thoughts and douse the little fire of awareness sparking to life in her stomach. What in the world was the matter with her? She wasn't the kind of woman to go weak-kneed at a pretty, er, face. She just *wasn't.*

Standing in a hot kitchen all day must have addled her brain. Yeah, that must be it. What other excuse could there be? She couldn't remember the last time she had experienced this mouthwatering, breathless, heart-pumping reaction.

On some weird level, she supposed it was kind of comforting to know she still could. For a long time she'd been afraid that part of her had died forever.

Still, it was highly inappropriate to entertain lascivious thoughts about her new employer, tight rear end notwithstanding.

She pasted on what she hoped was a friendly, polite smile and walked toward the man. "Hello. You must be from Maverick Enterprises," she said. "I'm Cassidy Harte, the ranch cook. I'm afraid you caught us by surprise. I apologize for the delay and any inconvenience. Welcome to the Lost Creek Ranch."

Oddly enough, as soon as she started to speak, the man

completely froze, and she saw the taut bunching of muscles under the expensive cotton of his shirt.

For one horrified moment, she wondered if he was going to ignore her. When she was within a half-dozen feet of him, though, he finally began to slowly turn toward her.

"Hello, Cassie."

The world tilted abruptly, and she would have slid right off the edge if she hadn't reached blindly for the nearest piece of furniture, a Stickley end table that, lucky for her, was sturdy enough to sustain her weight.

She couldn't breathe suddenly. This must be what a heart attack felt like, this grinding pain in her chest, this roaring in her ears, this light-headedness that made the whole room spin.

Even with the sudden vertigo making her feel dazed and disoriented, she couldn't take her eyes off him. In a million years she never would have expected him to show up at the Lost Creek Guest Ranch after all this time.

"Aren't you going to say anything?" her former fiancé and the man who had destroyed her youth and her innocence asked her with that same damn lopsided smile she'd fallen in love with ten years before.

She gulped air into her lungs, ordered oxygen to saturate her brain cells once more. Still gripping the edge of the oak table, she finally forced herself to meet his gaze.

"What are you doing here, Zack?"

Zack Slater—ten years older and worlds harder than he'd been a decade ago—angled his tawny head. "Is that any way to greet me after all these years?"

What did he want from her? Did he honestly think she would embrace him with open arms, would fall on him as if he were a long-lost friend? *The prodigal fiancé?*

"You're not welcome here," she said, her voice as cold as a glacial cirque. She had ten years of rage broiling up inside her, ten years of rejection and betrayal and shame. "I don't know why you've come back but you can leave now."

Get out before I throw you out.

For just an instant she thought she saw the barest hint of a shadow creep across his hazel eyes, then it slid away and he gave her a familiar, mocking smile. "Funny thing about that, Cass. Welcome or not, I'm afraid I won't be leaving anytime soon. I own the place."

Her heart stumbled in her chest as instant denial sprang out. "No. No, you don't."

"Not yet, technically. But it's only a matter of time."

Owned the place? He couldn't. It was impossible. Fate couldn't be that cruel. She wouldn't believe it.

"I don't know what kind of game you're playing this time," she snapped, "but you're lying, something we both know you're so very good at. How stupid do you think I am? Maverick Enterprises is buying the Lost Creek."

Again he offered nothing but that hard smile. "And I'm Maverick Enterprises."

She wouldn't have been more shocked if he'd suddenly picked up the end table still supporting her weight and tossed it through the eighteen-foot window.

Zack Slater and Maverick Enterprises? It wasn't possible. Jean had done her research before she agreed to sell the ranch. She might be in her seventies but she wasn't some kind of doddering old fool. According to the papers provided by the lawyer who had brokered the deal, Maverick had more investments than Cassie's oldest brother had cattle—everything from coffeehouses to bookstores to Internet start-ups.

The one common thread among them was that each business had a reputation for fairness and integrity, things the man standing in front of her would know nothing about.

"Nice try, but that's impossible," she snapped. "Maverick is a huge operation, with its fingers in pies all over the West."

"What's the matter, Cass? You don't think a money-grubbing drifter who could barely pay for his own wedding might be the one licking the apple filling off his fingers?"

She scowled. "Not you. You never had any interest in business whatsoever."

"Sorry to shatter your illusions, sweetheart, but it's true. Do you want the number to my office so you can check it out?"

In the face of his cocky attitude, her assurance wavered. This couldn't be happening. He had to be lying, didn't he?

"Why should I believe anything you say?" she finally snapped. "You don't exactly have the best track record around here. I made the mistake of trusting you once, and look where it got me."

He shifted his gaze away, looking out at the mountains once more. After a moment he turned back, his expression shuttered and those long, dark lashes shielding his vivid eyes.

"Would it help if I said I was sorry for that?" he asked quietly.

For what? For leaving her practically at the altar...or for asking her to marry him in the first place?

She gazed at him, words choking her throat like Western virgin's bower around a cottonwood trunk. Did he honestly have the gall to stand in front of her and apologize so casually, as if he'd simply bumped shopping carts or pulled in front of her in traffic?

She thought of her oldest brother and those first days *after,* when Matt had walked around in a state of dazed disbelief. Of a tiny, frail Lucy, just a few months old, wailing shrilly for the mother who would never come back.

Of her own shock and the agonizing pain of complete

betrayal, those days and months and years when she knew the whole town looked at her with pity, when the whispers behind her back threatened to deafen her.

Sorry? Zack Slater could never be sorry enough to make right everything he and Melanie had destroyed.

"You're about ten years too late."

Zack winced inwardly at the bitterness in her voice, though it was nothing more than he expected. Or than he deserved.

He wanted to kick himself for blurting that out so bluntly. He should have slowly worked up to his apology, waited until she had time to get to know him again before he tried to explain away the decisions he'd made that summer.

But since the moment she had walked into the vast room with its cozy furniture and spectacular view, his brain seemed about as useful as a one-legged chicken and he had to fight with everything inside him not to reach for her.

And wouldn't *that* have gone over well? He could just picture her reaction if he tried to pull her into his arms. Knowing Cassie, if he tried it, she would probably scratch and claw and aim a knee at a portion of his anatomy he was fairly fond of.

She said he was too late for apologies, for explanations He hoped not. He *really* hoped not, or all his work these last few months would have been for nothing.

Before he could answer, she drew herself up with the unconsciously sensual grace that had been so much a part of her, even as an eighteen-year-old young woman just growing into her body.

Eyes glittering with fury, she faced him. "I don't know what kind of scam you're trying to pull here, Slater. But I'll warn you, Jean is not some feeble-minded old lady to sit by and just let you waltz in and swindle her out of the ranch she has loved all her life. And even if she were, you can bet, I'm not. Jean has people who love her, who look out for her. Whatever twisted scheme you've come up with, you won't get away with this."

At that, she stalked out of the room, her wildflower scent lingering behind her.

He blew out a sharp breath. So much for a warm welcome. Not that he'd expected one. But then, he'd never imagined Cassie would be the first one to greet him when he arrived, either. He'd thought he would at least have had a little more time to prepare for the shock of seeing her.

She had changed.

What had he expected in ten years? Time didn't stand still except in his entirely too-vivid imagination. There, Cassidy Harte had remained as fresh and innocent as she'd been at eighteen, when she had stolen his heart with her mischievous smile and her boundless love and her unwavering loyalty.

That Cassie—the one who had haunted his dreams for so long, through the dark months when he had nothing else—had worn her hair long, in a sleek ponytail he used to love to pull from its binding and twist his fingers through.

Sometime during the long years since, she had cut it off. He wondered when, and felt a little pang of loss he knew he had no right to.

Her hair was still as dark and luxurious as it had been ten years ago—as glossy and rich as fine sable—but now she wore it in a sexy little cap that, on any other woman he might have called boyish.

There was nothing remotely boyish about Cassidy Harte, though. From her high cheekbones to her full lips to her body's soft, welcoming curves, she was one hundred percent woman.

Her eyes were the same. Blue as the spring's first columbine, fringed by long thick lashes that didn't need any kind of makeup to enhance their natural beauty.

Ten years ago those eyes would have softened when he walked into a room, would have lit up with joy just at the sight of him. Now they were hard and angry, filled with a deep betrayal he had put there.

This had to work.

He shoved away from the couch and turned back to the mountains, looking out at the magnificent view with the same yearning he imagined was in his gaze when he looked at Cassie.

It had to work. He couldn't imagine the alternative.

He had made mistakes—he would be the first one to admit them. But he had paid for them, and paid dearly. Could he make it right with her? What were the chances that she would ever be able to find it in her heart to forgive him, after the hurt he had caused her?

Slim to none, he figured.

He rubbed a hand over the ache in his chest. He would just have to do his best. No matter how tough, how seemingly insurmountable the task might seem, he had to do everything he could to make it work.

No matter the risk, he must take this chance.

To see if somewhere inside this hard, angry woman still remained any shred of the one person in the world who had seen something in him worth loving.

Chapter 2

It was true. All of it.

To her shock and dismay, it turned out he was telling the truth this time. By some sadistic twist of fate, Zack Slater was indeed the CEO of one of the most powerful companies in the West—and the man who would be signing her paycheck from here on out.

What kind of warped sense of humor must Somebody have to mess up her life so completely? Just what, exactly, had she done to deserve this?

She tried to be a good person. She didn't lie, didn't cheat on her income taxes, didn't swear—much, anyway. She obeyed the Golden Rule, she was kind to the elderly and small children and she really made an effort to go to church as often as she could manage. And for all her effort, this is what she got?

She should have raised a little hell when she had the chance.

Jean Martineau, steel-gray hair yanked back into her usual ruthlessly tight braid, frowned at her with concern in her snapping brown eyes. "I had no idea, Cassie. I swear I didn't. The man who signed the papers went by William Z. Slater. Other than the last name bein' the same, why would I have any reason to think for one minute that he might have anything in common with Zack Slater, the no-good drifter who caused Star Valley's biggest scandal in years?"

Thank you so much for bringing that up again. Cassie pounded out more of her emotional uproar on the hapless ball of dough for the next morning's sweet rolls. At this rate, the poor things would be as tough and stringy as cowhide.

"It's not your fault," she assured her friend and employer slowly. "I'm sure he concealed his identity on purpose."

But why? That was the question that had been racing through her head all afternoon. If this whole thing wasn't a scam—and apparently it wasn't—why would Zack put himself to so much trouble to buy a small guest ranch that would probably never be more than moderately successful? It didn't seem like the kind of savvy investment a fast-track company like Maverick Enterprises would make.

The ranch was geared toward families, with plenty of activities for all ages. Jean had the philosophy that children needed to be exposed to the history of the West, to what life was like on a real working cattle ranch, in order to preserve appreciation for the old ways.

To that end she tried to keep her rates affordable, well within range of the average family's vacation budget.

Cassie would hate to see Zack come in and turn the ranch into some kind of exclusive resort for the rich and famous, like some of the other guest ranches in the area had become. It would be a shame, not to mention take a huge investment in capital.

But why else would he want it, especially when he had

to know he wouldn't be welcomed back by many of the good people of Star Valley?

And why all the secrecy?

Maybe for that very reason—if Jean knew he was the one buying the ranch, she never would have agreed to the sale.

Cassie pounded the bread one last time, wishing it were a certain man's lean, masculine, *treacherous* features.

"I can try to back out of the sale, if it's not too late." Jean didn't sound very confident. Her frown cut through her wrinkled, weather-beaten face like sagging barbed wire.

Cassie shook her head. "You won't get another offer to match the one Maverick made for the ranch."

"Well, I can get by without the money."

Maybe, but both of them knew Jean wouldn't be able to run the ranch much longer, at least not with the same hands-on approach she had always maintained. Some days her arthritis was so bad she couldn't even raise her arms to saddle a horse.

"I can't let you back out of the sale," Cassie said gently. "Not on my account. I'll find a job somewhere else. Wade Lowry is always after me to come cook for the Rendezvous Ranch."

Jean touched her shoulder. "I'd hate to lose you. I wouldn't be able to find anybody else with your gift in the kitchen."

"I'm sorry," she said helplessly. "I can't work for him. Surely you understand that."

Jean squeezed her shoulder, then stepped back to lean a bony hip against the table. "The past is past, honey. Nothing you can do to change what happened ten years ago. You got to move on."

It was so much like the lecture Matt always used to give her, she wanted to scream. "Maybe I can't change the past.

But I also don't need to have it thrown in my face every day when I go to work."

"True enough. Can't say as I blame you."

Still, the disappointment in the feisty rancher's eyes gnawed at Cassie's insides. Guilt poked at her. Leaving right now in the middle of the ranch's busiest season would create a bundle of problems. Jean would have to find someone else fast to fill her position, which meant she would have to take time from the ranch's guests for hiring and training someone new.

She wavered. Maybe she could stick it out a little longer, just for Jean's sake.

Then she thought about working for Zack, having to see him regularly. Ten years ago she had been nothing short of devastated when he jilted her. She had worked hard during the intervening years to get to this place where she had confidence again, where she could see all the good things about herself instead of constantly dwelling on what it was she had lacked that had driven the man she loved into the arms of her brother's wife.

Seeing him all the time, working for him, was bound to undermine that confidence. She couldn't do it. Not even for Jean.

"I'm sorry," she said again.

Jean shrugged and managed a weathered smile. "We'll just have to make the best of a bad situation. That's all we can do. Now, it's been a heck of a day. Why don't you go back to your cabin and I'll finish up here?"

"No. I'm almost done. You get some rest."

Jean touched her shoulder again. "Good night, then," she said, then hobbled from the kitchen.

After her boss left, Cassie quickly finished her prep work for breakfast, then turned the lights off and walked out of the kitchen toward her own cabin next to the creek.

She considered her little place the very best perk of working for the ranch. It was small, only three rooms—tiny bedroom, bathroom and a combined kitchen and living room—but all three rooms belonged to her.

For another few days, anyway.

The cabin was more than just a place to sleep. It represented independence, a chance to stand on her own without her two older brothers hovering in the wings to watch over her, as they had been doing for most of her life.

She was twenty-eight years old and this was the first time she had ever lived away from home. How pathetic was that? She had never known the giddy excitement of moving into a college dorm and meeting her roommates for the first time or the rush of being carried across the threshold of a new house by a loving husband or repainting a guest bedroom for a nursery.

She didn't like the bitter direction her thoughts had taken. Still, she couldn't help thinking that if it hadn't been for Zack Slater, her life might have turned out vastly different.

She had just graduated high school when he blew into her life. She had been young and naive and passionately in love with the gorgeous ranch hand with the stunning gold-flecked eyes and the shadows in his smile.

To her amazement he had seemed as smitten as she. The fierce joy in his face whenever he saw her had been heady stuff for a girl who had never even had a serious boyfriend before.

Right from the beginning they had talked of marriage. He had wanted her to finish college before they married, but she couldn't stand the idea of being away from him for four long years. She had worked for weeks to persuade him that she could still attend college after they were married, that he could work while she went to school since she had a scholarship. After she graduated, she would work to put him through.

Finally she had worn down his resistance. She flushed now, remembering. Maybe if she hadn't been in such a rush, had given him time to adjust to the idea of settling down, he wouldn't have felt the need to bolt.

But he did, taking her dreams—and her brother's wife—with him, and leaving Matt a single father of a tiny baby.

What else could she have done but stay and try to repair the damage she had brought down on her family? If she had the choice to do all over again, she honestly didn't think she would change anything she had done after he left.

She sighed and let herself into the cabin, comforted by the familiar furnishings--the plump couch, the rocker of her mother's, the braided rug in front of the little fireplace. She had made the cabin warm and cozy and she loved it here.

Functioning more on autopilot than through any conscious decision, she walked into the small bathroom and turned on the water in the old-fashioned clawfoot tub, as hot as she could stand. When the tub was filled almost to overflowing, she took off her clothes and slipped into the water, desperate to escape the unbelievable shock of seeing the only man she had ever loved, after all these years.

Taking a bath was a huge mistake.

She realized that almost as soon as she slid down into the peach-scented bubbles. Now that she didn't have her work in the kitchen to keep her busy, she couldn't seem to fix her mind on anything but Zack and the memories of that summer ten years ago, memories that rolled across her mind like tumbleweed in a hard wind.

The first time she had talked to him—really talked to him—was branded into her memory. He had worked at the

Diamond Harte for several months before that late spring evening, but she had been so busy finishing her senior year of high school that she had barely noticed him, except as the cute, slightly dangerous-looking ranch hand with the sunstreaked hair and that rare but devastating smile.

Matt liked him, she knew that. Her oldest brother had raved about what a way Zack had with horses and how he worked the rest of the ranch hands into the ground. And she remembered being grateful that her brother had someone else he could trust to run things, while he had so many other worries on his mind.

Melanie had been in the advanced stage of a pregnancy she obviously hadn't wanted. Never the most even-tempered of women, her sister-in-law had suddenly become prone to vicious mood swings. Deliriously happy one moment, livid the next, icy cold a few moments later. Her brother definitely had his hands full, and she was grateful to Zack for shouldering some of that burden.

Then, in late May, the week after her high school graduation when the mountain snows finally began to melt, Matt had asked Zack to take a few of the other ranch hands and drive part of the herd to higher ground to graze. Because it was an overnight trip, they would need someone to cook for them, and Cassie had volunteered, eager for the adventure of a cattle drive, even though it would be a short one.

When she closed her eyes, she could see every moment of that fateful trip in vivid detail....

She loved it up here.

With a pleasant ache in her muscles from a hard day of riding, Cassie closed her eyes and savored the cool evening air that smelled sweet and pure, heavy with the rich, intoxicating perfume of sagebrush and pine.

The twilight brushed everything with pale-rose paint,

and the setting sun glittered on the gently rippling surface of the creek. Hands wrapped around her knees, she sat on the bank and listened to the water's song and the chirp and trill of the mountain's inhabitants settling down for the evening.

She would miss this so much in the fall when she moved to Utah for college. The campus in Logan was beautiful, perched on a hill overlooking the Cache Valley, but it didn't even come close to the raw splendor of the high country.

This was home.

So many of her most pleasant memories of her parents were built on the firm foundation of these mountains. Every summer and fall on the way to and from their grazing allotment they used to camp right here where the creek bowed. Her mom would cook something delicious in a Dutch oven and after supper her dad would gather her and Matt and Jesse around the campfire and read to them out of his favorite Westerns.

She smiled softly. Her memories had begun to fade in the six years since her parents had died in a wintry rollover accident, but she could still hear Frank Harte's booming voice ring through the night and see his broad, callused hands turn the pages in the flickering firelight.

She missed them both so much sometimes. Matt did his best. Both her brothers did. She knew that and loved them fiercely for working so hard to give her a good, safe home for the past six years.

Matt had only been twenty-two, Jesse seventeen, when their parents died, and she knew a lot of men would have figured a grieving twelve-year-old girl would have been better off with relatives or in the foster care system. Their aunt Suzie over in Pinedale had offered to take her in, but Matt had been determined they would all stick together.

It must have been so hard for him. She thought of how

rotten she'd been sometimes, how often she'd snapped at him when he told her to do her homework or make her bed.

You're not my mother and you can't make me.

She owed him big-time for putting up with her. Someday she would have to find a way to repay him.

She sighed, resting her chin on her knees. She was reluctant to leave this peaceful spot, even though she knew she should probably go check on the stew and see if the ranch hands had eaten their boots yet.

When she walked away from camp a half hour earlier, Jake and Sam Lawson had been snoring in their tent in a little before-dinner nap after beating the brush all day. But they were probably awake now and wondering where she'd wandered off to.

She smiled at the thought of the two bachelor brothers, who were in their early sixties and had worked for the ranch her entire life. They treated her like a favorite spoiled niece, and she loved them both fiercely.

And then there was Slater.

A whole flock of magpies seemed to flutter around in her stomach whenever she thought of the lean, hard cowboy leading the cattle drive. This was the longest she had ever spent in his company, and she had to admit she had spent most of the day watching him out of the corner of her eyes.

The few times he'd caught her watching him, he had given her that half smile of his, and she felt like a bottle rocket had exploded inside her.

He made her so nervous she couldn't think straight. What was it about him? She'd been around cowboys all her life and most of them were simple and straightforward—interested in horses, whisky and women, not necessarily in that order.

Zack seemed different. Despite the way he joked with

the older cowhands, there was a sadness in his eyes, a deep, remote loneliness that probably made every woman he met want to cuddle him close and kiss all his pain away.

She rolled her eyes at the fanciful thought. If a woman wanted to kiss Zack Slater, it wasn't to make him feel better. He was totally, completely, gorgeously male, and a woman would have to have rocks for brains not to notice.

Well, she couldn't sit here all night mooning over Zack Slater. Not when she had work to do.

Just as she started to rise, the thick brush ten yards upstream on the other side of the creek begin to rustle with more than just the breeze. A few seconds later, a small mule deer— no more than a yearling doe, probably— walked out of the growth and picked her way delicately to the water's edge. After a careful look around, she bent her neck to drink and Cassie watched, smiling a little at the ladylike way the doe sipped the water.

The deer so entranced her that she almost missed another flicker of movement, again on the opposite side of the creek, at the halfway point between her and the deer. She narrowed her eyes, trying to figure out what other kind of animal had come to the water, then inhaled sharply. She caught just a glimpse of a tawny hide and a long swaying tail as something slunk through the brush.

A mountain lion!

And he had his sights on the pretty little doe.

Even though she knew it was all part of the rhythm of life—hunter and hunted, another link on the food chain and all that—she couldn't bear to watch the inevitable.

She squeezed her eyes shut for a moment, then changed her mind and jumped to her feet, waving her arms and hollering for all she was worth. As she'd hoped, the doe lifted her head from the water with one panicked look, then bounded back into the trees with a crash of branches.

"Ha, you big bully," she said to the cougar. "Find your dinner somewhere else."

The big cat turned toward her and she could swear there was malice in those yellow eyes. With a loud, deep growl that made the hairs on the back of her neck stand at attention, the animal turned, his long tail swaying hypnotically.

Uh, maybe drawing attention to herself with a cougar on the prowl wasn't exactly the best idea she'd ever had.

"Nice kitty," she murmured in a placating tone. "Sit. Stay."

The big cat paced the bank on the other side, staying roughly parallel to her. For the first time Cassie began to feel a real flicker of fear, suddenly not at all sure the eight-foot-wide creek would be enough of a barrier between them if the cat decided she made a better snack.

Moving slowly, she scooped up a softball-sized rock, just in case, and began backing toward camp and the men.

She had only made it a few yards when the cat tensed his muscles as if to spring back into the brush. Before she could breathe a sigh of relief, he turned at the last minute and spanned the creek in one powerful leap. With a strangled shriek, she threw the rock but it only glanced off the cougar's back before landing in the water with a huge splash.

Cassie didn't wait around to see if her missile found a target. She whirled and took off for camp, heart racing and adrenaline pumping through her in thick, hot waves. The cat was gaining on her. She knew it and braced, expecting jagged teeth to rip into her flesh at any second. This was it, then. She was going to die here in these mountains she loved, all because of her stupid soft heart.

And then, when she thought she could almost smell the predator's breath, fetid and wild, and feel it stir the hair at the back of her neck, a gunshot boomed through the twilight.

For an instant time seemed to freeze and she became aware of the total silence on the mountainside as the echo died away. A few moments earlier the evening had buzzed with activity but now nothing moved except the soft wind rustling the new leaves of the aspens.

She stopped, gratitude and relief rushing through her, then shifted her gaze to see which of the ranch hands had come to her rescue. She wasn't at all surprised to see Slater just lowering a rifle.

What did surprise her was the yowl behind her. To her shock, the cat wasn't dead, just royally teed-off. Apparently he decided he'd had enough of interfering humans. With a last angry screech exactly like one of the barn cats tangling with the wrong cow dog, the mountain lion skulked back into the trees.

She whirled back to Zack. "You missed him!"

"I shot into the air."

"Why?" she asked, incredulous.

He shrugged those broad shoulders. Despite the fierce need to pump every ounce of air to her oxygen-starved cells now that the danger had passed, her heart skipped a beat at how big and strong and wonderful he looked leaning there against a rock. "I saw you scare away his prey. You can't blame the guy for going after the consolation prize."

She stared at him. "You were going to let him take a chunk out of me just because I didn't want to watch him kill a poor, helpless deer in front of me?"

"Naw." He grinned and she began to feel a little shaky. "I probably would have gotten around to shooting him once he caught up to you."

"Well, that's comforting."

He only laughed at her snappish tone. "You okay?"

"Swell. Thanks so much for your help." The panic of the moment, coupled with the fact that she hadn't had time to eat anything since breakfast, combined to make her feel a little light-headed.

Zack walked closer to her, then frowned. "You're shaking."

"I think I need to sit down."

To her complete chagrin, she swayed and would have fallen over if he hadn't suddenly moved as fast as the cougar had—and with exactly the same lithe grace—and reached for her.

He guided her to the soft meadow grass. "Here we go. Just sit here for a minute until you feel more like yourself."

She hissed in fast breaths between her teeth, thinking again of that terrible moment when she thought her number was up. Remembering it wasn't helping calm her down, any more than having Zack Slater crouching so close.

She knew she was trying to distract herself from her scare but she couldn't help noticing his hard mouth, just inches from hers. A little wildly, she wondered what it would be like to have those lips on hers, how he would go about kissing a woman.

"Deep and slow." His voice broke through her thoughts, and she stared at him, suddenly terrified he'd read her mind.

"Wha-what?"

"You're going to hyperventilate if you keep breathing so fast. Slow down a little."

Wrenching her mind away from any thoughts of the man's kisses, she focused once more on the cougar. "Do you think he'll be back? We should watch the calves."

"I think between the two of us, we've probably scared him clear to Cody by now."

They sat there for a moment longer until she felt she had enough control of herself to return to camp.

To her amazement Zack had stuck close to her all evening, as if afraid she might have some delayed reaction to almost becoming cat bait. He was sweetly protective, even insisting on going with her to bury the remains of their food from any wandering bears.

Later they sat around the campfire long after the Lawson brothers had gone to bed, talking softly while each glittering star came out and the wind mourned through the tops of the pines and the fire hissed and sputtered.

She told him of her parents and her grief and how tough it had been after their deaths. He shared snippets of his own childhood, of moving from town to town with a saddle bum for a father and of being on his own since he was fifteen.

And then, when the campfire burned down to embers, he walked her to her tent, pushed her hair away from her face with a work-hardened hand and softly kissed her.

It had been worlds better than anything she could have imagined. Sweet and tender and passionate all at once. Just one kiss and he had completely stolen her heart.

That had been the beginning. They were inseparable after that and had tumbled hard and fast into love. It had been the most incredible three months of her life, filled with laughter and heady excitement and slow, sexy kisses when her brothers weren't looking.

Until it ended so horribly....

Cassie came back to the present to several depressing realizations. The water in the tub was now lukewarm, bordering on cool, and any bubbles had long since fizzled away.

And, much worse, silent tears were coursing down her cheeks as she relived the past.

Oh, cripes. Hadn't she cried enough tears over Zack Slater? It was a waste of good salt. The man wasn't worth it ten years ago, and he certainly wasn't worth it now.

She climbed from the tub, wrapping herself in a thick towel, then splashed her face with cold water to cool her aching, puffy eyes. She hadn't indulged in a good, old-fashioned pity party for a long time, and she figured she must have been long overdue. But enough was enough. Now that it was all out of her system, she could move on.

She put on her robe and decided on a glass of milk before bed. Just as she was opening the refrigerator and reaching for the carton, she heard a knock at the front door.

Rats. It was probably Jean coming to check on her one more time. The last thing she wanted was to have company, with the mood she was in tonight. She thought about ignoring it, but the knocks only grew louder and more insistent. Gritting her teeth, she looked out the small window at the cabin next to her, thinking of the man who now stayed there.

The man who now owned the whole blasted place.

What if he decided to venture outside to investigate the commotion? She didn't need another encounter with him today. Swearing under her breath, she went to the door and swung it open, then her breath seemed to tangle in her lungs.

Well, she didn't have to worry about Zack coming out to see who was banging on her door, since he was the one standing there, fist raised to knock one more time.

Chapter 3

As he'd expected, she didn't look exactly thrilled to see him. Her eyes turned wintry, her mouth went as tight as a shriveled-up prune, and her spine stiffened, vertebrae by vertebrae.

Even so, she looked so beautiful he had to shove his hands into his pockets to keep from reaching for her.

She must have only just climbed out of the bath. Her still-damp hair, a few shades darker than normal, clung to her head, and she had wrapped herself in a silky robe of the palest yellow. The delectable smell of peaches wafted to him on the cool, early-summer breeze, and his mouth watered.

Framed in the light from inside her cabin, she looked warm and soft and welcoming, just as he had imagined her a thousand times over the years.

Her voice, though, was as cold as her eyes. "What do you want?"

Just to see you. To hear your voice again. He shifted his weight, alarmed at the need instantly pulsing through him just at the sight of her. He would have to do a much better job of controlling himself if he wanted this plan to work.

"I just spoke with Jean." Despite his best intentions, his voice came out a little ragged. "She said you tendered your resignation."

He didn't think it was possible, but that prune-mouth tightened even more. "What else did you expect?"

"I expected you to show a little more backbone."

She stared at him for several seconds. In the porch light her eyes looked huge, those dark lashes wide with disbelief, and then she laughed harshly. "Oh that's a good one, coming from you. Really good. Thanks. I needed a good joke tonight."

Okay. He deserved that. He had no right to lecture her about staying power when he had been the one who walked away just days before their wedding. Still, that was a different situation altogether.

He plodded gamely forward. "So you're just going to walk out and turn your back on Mrs. Martineau when she needs you?"

Her gaze shifted to some spot over his shoulder. "Jean has nothing to do with this. You're the new owner. That means I'm turning my back on *you*."

"We need to talk about this."

"No, *we* don't." She started to close the door, but his instincts kicked in and he managed to think fast enough to shove a boot in the space. Still, she pushed the door hard enough to make him wince.

"We don't have anything to say to each other," she snapped.

"I think we do. Come on, Cass. Let me in."

After a long pause where she continued to shove the door painfully against his foot, she finally shrugged and stepped back. He followed before she had a chance to change her mind.

Inside, he saw the cabin's floor plan matched his. Here, though, it was obvious Cassie had decorated it to suit her

personality. It was warm and comforting, with richly tex-
tured rugs and pillows and Native American artwork covering the walls.

Cassie was a nurturer. She always had been, even as a
girl just barely out of high school. She used to talk about
her brothers raising her, but he had spent enough time with
the family to know she took as much care of them as they
did her. The Hartes looked out for each other.

The cabin reflected that nesting instinct of hers.

He smiled a little at an assortment of whimsical, ugly,
carved trolls filling an entire shelf above her mother's
rocking chair. She'd been collecting them since she was a
girl and he recognized several new ones since he had last
seen her collection.

He narrowed his gaze, looking closer. Where were the
little kissing trolls he'd given her as a gift during their first
month together? He couldn't see the piece here with the
rest of the figurines.

He almost asked her what she'd done with it—why she
hadn't set it out, too—but then clamped his teeth against
the question. He had no right to ask her. Even if she burned
it and flushed the ashes down the toilet, nobody would
have blamed her.

"This is nice," he murmured instead.

"You must live in some grand mansion somewhere, now
that you've hit the big time."

He thought of his cold, impersonal apartment in Denver,
with its elegant furniture he was never quite comfortable
using. Her little cabin held far more appeal.

"Not really," he answered. "It's a place to sleep and
that's about it."

There was an awkward pause between them, and he
thought about the little trailer home they'd planned to buy
in Logan while she finished school. She had decorated it in

her head a hundred times, talking endlessly about curtains and furniture and wallpaper. He had even gotten into the spirit of things, something that still amazed him. Neither of them had cared how cramped the little trailer would be. They were too excited about starting their lives together.

She finally broke the silence, her expression stony and cold. "Can we skip the small talk? I've had a long day and need to be up at five to start breakfast over at the lodge."

He pushed away his memories. If he wanted this to work, he had to focus on the present. "Okay. Let's get down to business. I don't want you to quit."

"What you want hasn't mattered to me for a long time, Zack."

He ignored her clipped tone. "From all the research my people did before we made the offer, we know that the food at the Lost Creek is one of the main draws of the ranch. In just a few months you've developed quite a reputation for delicious, healthy meals."

He paused, waiting for her to respond, but she remained stubbornly silent. After a moment he went on. "I want to build on that reputation. Use it as a selling point. That's been one of my goals for the ranch from the beginning."

She rolled her eyes. "Come on, Zack. You didn't really think I would stay here and work for you, did you?"

At his continued silence she gazed at him for a moment, then her jaw sagged. "You did! I can't believe this!"

He had hoped. Now he realized how completely foolish that had been. "You used to be the kind of woman who would never back down from a good fight."

Her mouth hardened again. "I used to be a lot of things. Ten years is a long time. I'm not the same person I was then. I've become much more choosy about the things I'm willing to fight for."

"And your job isn't one of them?"

"I won't lie to you. I like working for the Lost Creek. Jean is a sweetheart and gives me all the freedom I could ever want to create my own menus. But I would rather take a job cleaning truck-stop toilets than stay here and work for you."

He deserved everything she dished out and more. He knew it, but her words still stung.

"Is there anything I can say to change your mind?"

She shook her head firmly and he chewed the inside of his cheek. He hadn't wanted to play this card but she was the one folding way too early in the game. "Fine," he said, his voice cool and detached. "I'll let Jean know in the morning that Maverick will have to pass on the ranch."

Her eyes widened, and that stubborn little jaw threatened to sag again. "You can't! You've already signed papers. Jean already has a check."

"Earnest money, that's all." He refused to let the shocked outrage in her voice deter him. "We had thirty days to reach a final decision on the sale. I'll just tell Jean I've changed my mind."

"You're willing to walk away from the whole deal just because I refuse to work for you?"

"I'm a businessman, Cassie, as unbelievable as you seem to find that. The food you provide is an important component of the ranch's appeal to its guests. Who knows what kind of an impact your resignation will have? I don't want to take that risk."

"You can't be serious."

"Do I look serious?" He brushed an imaginary piece of lint off the sleeve of his shirt while she continued to gape at him.

"This is blackmail," she hissed.

"Call it what you want." He smiled as if his whole world wasn't riding on this moment.

"You bastard." Her voice quivered with fury.

Her reaction cut deep, but he only smirked. "You think I've never been called that before?"

"I'll just bet you have."

"I never would have made it this far without a thick skin."

"Just like every other snake in the world, right?"

Her eyes were bright with anger, and hot color flared high on her cheekbones. He wanted to reach across the distance between them and kiss away her anger, wanted it so badly his bones ached with it. He clamped down hard on the need for some kind of contact—any kind—between them.

"Think what you want about me—"

"Oh, I do. You can bet I do."

He went on as if she hadn't interrupted him. "But as far as I'm concerned, you're part of the package deal." He paused. "However, I can understand your reluctance, given our unfortunate history."

She snorted. "Unfortunate, my eye. The day you ran out on me was the luckiest day of my life."

A muscle in his jaw twitched. "I'm trying to be reasonable here, Cassie, but you're not making it very easy."

She remained stubbornly silent.

"As I was saying," he said, "I understand why you might want to find a new position. So I'm willing to make a deal with you."

"What kind of deal?" Suspicion coated her voice like a thin sheet of ice on a puddle.

"You stay the thirty days until the sale is finalized, and Maverick won't back out. In the meantime you can hire someone as your replacement, someone who can learn your menus and build on your success."

"And what do I get in return, besides the oh-so-appealing pleasure of your company?"

The Boy Scouts probably would have laughed themselves silly if he'd ever tried to join up, but he certainly believed heartily in their motto about being prepared.

Through a little casual conversation with Jean during the negotiations for the guest ranch, his lawyer had learned Cassie's job at the ranch was always considered temporary between the two women, that she was saving for a down payment on the diner in town.

Why she didn't use some of the vast Diamond Harte resources was beyond him, but in this case her typical dogged determination worked to his advantage.

"Stick it out for thirty days, and I'll give you a bonus of five thousand dollars."

Only the slightest flicker in her gaze betrayed that she had even heard him. "I don't want your money."

He shrugged. "Then stay for Jean's sake. I'm sure I don't have to tell you it will probably be a long time before she'll see another offer as good as the one we've made."

Not just a long time. Never. Cassie drew in a breath, trying to gather the thoughts he seemed to scatter so easily. Maverick had offered far more than the appraised value for the ranch. And who knew when Jean would even get another offer? The ranch had been on the market for a year already with little to show for it but a few nibbles.

He had her backed against the wall, and he damn well knew it. Would he be ruthless enough to make good on his threat to renege on the deal, even knowing he would hurt a sweet, feisty woman like Jean Martineau in the process?

Yes. She didn't doubt it for a second.

She wasn't stupid enough to buy his argument that the ranch's reputation would suffer without her. She was a good cook but there were plenty of others who could pick up right where she left off. No, he wanted her here for his own sinister reasons. She couldn't begin to guess what they might be. Just thinking about his motives made her stomach flip around like a trout on the end of a line.

On the other hand, Jean was her friend. She had been kind to her and given Cassie a chance to prove herself, when all she had for experience was ten years spent cooking for her family's cattle ranch.

How would she be able to live with herself if the deal fell through because of her?

Anyway, what did it matter who signed her paycheck? She probably wouldn't even see him during that thirty days. The president and CEO of Maverick Enterprises most likely didn't have a spare second to spend hanging around supervising a dude ranch in western Wyoming. He would probably be here for a few days and then crawl back under whatever rock he'd been hiding under.

The realization cheered her immensely. She could handle a few days. She was a strong and capable woman. Besides, he didn't mean anything to her anymore. Any feelings she might have had for him so long ago had shriveled up and blown away in the endless Wyoming wind.

"Ten thousand dollars," she said promptly. With that much, she'd have all she needed to make the down payment Murphy wanted.

"You really think you're worth that much?"

She refused to let him see her flinch at his words. "At least."

"Okay. Fine. Ten it is."

She had never expected him to agree. The very fact that he did left her as wary as a kitten in the middle of a dogfight. "One month, then. For Jean's sake."

At least he didn't spin her platitudes about how she wouldn't regret it. Instead his dazzling smile sent a chill of premonition scuttling down her spine. She ignored it and held the door open for him to leave in a blatant message even Zack Slater couldn't disregard.

After a pause he sent her another one of those blasted smiles and obediently trotted for the door. As he walked out into the cool June night toward his own cabin next door, she couldn't help wondering if she had just made the second biggest mistake of her life.

* * *

He was already up and dressed when he heard her leave her cabin an hour before sunrise.

From his comfortable spot in the old wooden rocker, Zack listened to the squeak of her screen door, her footsteps on the wooden planks of her porch, then her sleepy, muffled curse as she stumbled over something in the predawn darkness.

He grinned into the hidden shadows of his own front porch. His Cassidy Jane had never been much of a morning person. Apparently, she hadn't changed much in the past decade.

His smile slid away. Wrong, he reminded himself again. Maybe she still wasn't crazy about getting up early, but she was no longer the same girl he had loved ten years ago. Everyone changed. He couldn't come back after so long and expect her to have waited for him in suspended animation like some kind of moth trapped in glossy amber.

She was a different woman, just as he had changed drastically from that wild, edgy ranch hand. The only thing they shared was a bittersweet past ten years old.

But last night in her house he had seen glimpses of the girl she had been, like some kind of ghostly reflection shimmering under deep, clear water. The way she tucked her hair behind her ear. The stubborn jut of her chin as she had argued with him. Those luminous blue eyes that showed every emotion.

She was the same but different, and he wanted to find out all the ways she had changed over the years.

He would see this through. He had come too damn far to back down now. If nothing else, he could at least explain to her why he had left. He owed her that much.

On impulse, he rose from the comfortable old rocker and followed her on the gravel pathway toward the lodge, maintaining a discreet distance between them.

The early-morning air was cool, sharp and sweet with pine pitch and sagebrush. He inhaled it deeply into his lungs, listening to the quiet. He had missed this place. More than he realized, until the day before when he returned.

He bought his own ranch in the San Juans a few years ago and he escaped to it as often as he could manage, but it wasn't the same. Western Colorado had never felt as comfortable to him as Star Valley.

As right.

The months he spent working the Diamond Harte were the best of his life. Not just because of Cassie, although he had watched her and wanted her for a long time before that fateful trip into the high country when he had kissed her for the first time.

Cassie was a big part of his bond to this place, but there was more. Her brother Matt had treated him well, far better than any other man he'd worked for over the years.

Wandering ranch hands without their own spreads generally had a social status roughly equivalent to a good cow dog. He'd become accustomed to it as a boy following his father from ranch to ranch across the West. He didn't like it but he accepted it.

At the Diamond Harte, everything had been different. Zack had been given more responsibility than he'd ever had before. He'd been treated as an equal, as a trusted friend.

And he had repaid that trust by abandoning the boss's sister a week before their wedding.

He frowned and pushed the thought away, concentrating instead on moving quietly several yards behind her. By now they had reached the lodge. Instead of going in the main door, Cassie slipped around the back of the big log structure and unlocked a door on the side, going straight into the kitchen, he assumed.

After a moment's debate as to the wisdom of another

confrontation with her so early in the game, he gave a mental shrug, twisted the knob and walked inside.

He found her standing across the large, comfortable kitchen with her back to him, her arms reaching behind her as she tied on a crisp white apron.

She didn't bother looking up at his entrance. "I'm glad you're on time this morning, Greta. We've got a lot of work ahead of us for breakfast if we're going to do this right today. As much as I would love to serve a steaming bucket of slop to Zack Slater, I can't do that to Jean."

He paused several seconds, then couldn't resist. "I appreciate that," he drawled. "How about we save the bucket of slop for tomorrow? I think I'd prefer bacon and eggs this morning."

She whirled around at his voice, her blue eyes going wide. Color soaked her high cheekbones but she didn't apologize, just tilted her chin a little higher as her cool beauty punched him hard in the gut. "You're up early."

He leaned a hip against one of the wide counters. "I spent too many years as a ranch hand. Old habits, you know. It's tough for me to sleep past six these days."

"It's only half past five," she pointed out. "You have another half hour to laze around in bed."

"Must be all this fresh, invigorating mountain air." Or something.

"Well, I'm afraid you're too early for breakfast." Her voice was sharp as she reached for a metal pan on a shelf. "We don't start serving until seven."

"I can wait."

She studied him for a moment, then pursed her lips together. "If you're starving, there might be a few muffins left over from yesterday. And the coffee will be ready in a few moments."

Despite the grudging tone of voice, her words still

reached in and tugged at his heart and he saw another ghostly reflection of the woman he had loved, the soft-hearted nurturer who hated to see anybody go hungry on her watch. Even him.

"I'm fine," he assured her. Better than fine. He thoroughly enjoyed watching her bustle around the kitchen, even though her movements were jerky and abrupt, without her customary elegant grace.

His presence unnerved her. He could see it in the way she fumbled through drawers and rummaged blindly in the huge refrigerator.

Under ordinary circumstances she probably knew this kitchen like she knew her own name, but you'd never be able to tell by her movements this morning.

He found it very enlightening to see her composure slip. Enlightening and entertaining.

Somewhat ashamed of himself for finding secret pleasure in the knowledge that he could fluster her so much just by invading her space, he straightened from the counter. "Can I help you do something?"

She peered around the chrome door of the refrigerator to stare at him. "You mean like cook?"

He shrugged. "I have been known to rattle a few pots from time to time."

Her gaze narrowed. "Why would the CEO of Maverick Enterprises volunteer to cook breakfast for ten hungry families?"

Because the CEO of Maverick Enterprises has spent ten years mooning over the chef. "Maybe I'm bored."

"Don't you have some kind of leveraged buyout or hostile takeover to mastermind somewhere?"

"I'm all leveraged out this morning. And I've found takeovers to be generally much less hostile once I've had my morning coffee."

She didn't return his smile, just watched him with that suspicion brimming out of her blue eyes. Finally he decided not to argue with her. Instead, he picked up a knife and went to work cutting up the green peppers she'd pulled from the refrigerator.

"Am I doing this right?"

She watched him for a moment, a baffled look on her features, then she shrugged. "You're the boss. If you want to play *souschef,* don't let me stop you. Dice the pieces a little smaller, though."

She returned to rifling through the refrigerator, and they worked in silence for a few moments, the only sounds in the kitchen the thud of the knife on the wooden cutting board and the delicate shattering of eggshells from across the room.

He had a quick memory of other meals they had cooked together, when he had been free to sneak up behind her if the mood struck him. When he could wrap his arms around her and lift her long, thick hair to plant kisses on the spot right at the base of her neck that drove her crazy, until she would turn breathlessly into his arms, the meal forgotten.

They had ruined more than one meal at the Diamond Harte together. He smiled at the mental picture, and of the slit-eyed look her older brother would give him when he would come in and find something burning on the stove and the two of them flushed and out of breath.

Not caring for the direction of his thoughts or the awkward silence between them, he looked for a distraction, finally settling on what he thought would be a benign topic of conversation.

"So how's your family these days?" he asked.

The egg she had just picked up slid out of her fingers and landed on the floor. She made no move to clean it up, just stood across the kitchen staring at him with her eyes murky and dark.

He only meant to make a casual inquiry. What had he said? "Was that the wrong question?"

"Coming from you, yeah, I'd say it's the wrong question." With color again high on her cheekbones, she snapped a handful of paper towels off a roll and bent to clean up the egg mess.

He set the knife down carefully on the cutting board and frowned at her. "What's that supposed to mean? I'm not allowed to ask how your brothers are doing these days?"

She rose, her eyes hard, angry. "I will not let you do this to me, Slater. I can't believe you have the gall to show up here after all these years and act like nothing happened."

While he was still trying to figure out how to answer that fierce statement, she shoved the paper towel in the garbage, then returned to cracking eggs with far more force than necessary.

"My brothers are fine." Her voice was as clipped as her movements. "Great. Jess is the police chief in Salt River. He and his fiancée are planning a late July wedding. Matt remarried a few months ago, and he and his new wife are deliriously happy together. She's a vet in town and she's absolutely perfect for him."

He wondered about the defiant lift to her chin as she said this, as if daring him to say something about it. "So he and—what was her name? Melanie, wasn't it?—aren't together anymore?"

She didn't say anything for several moments. At her continued silence, he looked up from the cutting board and saw with some shock that she was livid. Not just angry, but quaking with fury.

The woman he'd known a decade ago rarely lost her temper, but when she did, it was a fierce and terrible thing. He only had a second to wonder what had sparked this sudden firestorm when she turned on him.

"No, they're not together anymore." Her voice sounded as if it was coated with ground glass. "They haven't been *together* since you ran off with her."

He blinked at the cold fury in her eyes. "Since I *what?*"

She turned away from him. "I'm really not in the mood for this, Slater. I have too much to do this morning if I'm going to feed your guests."

His own temper began to spiral. "The hell with the guests. I want to know what you're talking about. Why would you say I ran off with Melanie?"

"Hmm. Let me think. Maybe because you did?"

"The hell I did!"

"Drop the innocent act, Zack. People saw you. *Jesse* saw you. The two of you were making out in the parking lot of the Renegade. There are variations on the story but from what numerous people told me, she was climbing all over you like the bitch in heat that she was, and you weren't doing much to fight her off. Before Jess could beat the living daylights out of you, you and my darling ex-sister-in-law climbed into your truck and drove off into the sunset, never to be seen in Star Valley again."

His mind reeling, he scrambled to come up with something to say to that stunning accusation.

Before he could think past the shock, the side door swung open and the teenager who had greeted him the day before with such dumbstruck inadequacy whirled in, tucking a T-shirt into her jeans as she came.

"Sorry I'm late, Cassie. I slept through my alarm again."

The kitchen simmered with tension, with the fading echoes of her ridiculous claims. The idea that he would take up with that she-devil Melanie Harte was so ludicrous he didn't know where to start defending himself.

"No problem, Greta. You can take over for Mr. Slater.

He was just leaving. Isn't that right?" she challenged him, her lush mouth set into hard lines.

He wanted to stay and have this out, to assure her he would rather have been hog-tied and dragged behind a pickup truck for a couple hundred miles than go anywhere with Melanie. He didn't want to do it in front of an audience, though. And since he couldn't figure out a polite way to order the poor girl out of the kitchen, he decided their shoot-out could wait.

"This isn't over," he growled.

Her eyes were still hot and angry. "Yes, it is, Zack. It was over ten years ago. You made sure of that."

He studied her for a few moments, then set the knife down carefully on the cutting board and walked out of the room before he said something he knew he would regret.

As Cassie watched him leave, a vague unease settled on her shoulders like a sudden summer downpour.

Why did he seem so astonished when she told him she knew he left with Melanie? Was he honestly dense enough to think they could both disappear on the same night and nobody would be smart enough to put two and two together and come up with four?

He had definitely been shocked, though. That much was obvious. He couldn't have been faking that dazed, dismayed expression.

She shrugged off the unease. She had too much work waiting for her, to sit here trying to figure out what was going through the mind of a man who was a virtual stranger to her now.

"Do you want more green peppers?" Greta asked.

She saw that Slater had diced a half dozen, far more than

she really needed for the *huevos rancheros.* "No. That's plenty. Why don't you start putting together the fruit bowl?"

While Greta moved around the kitchen gathering bananas and strawberries and grapes, she kept sending curious little looks her way. Cassie ignored them as long as she could, then finally gave a loud sigh. "What?"

Greta yanked a grape off a cluster and popped it into the bowl. "Just wondering what that was all about. What's the story with you and the new boss?"

For a moment she was surprised at the question, then she realized the teenager would have been only a child a decade ago, too young to hear about the biggest scandal in town. "Nothing. No story."

Greta raised her eyebrows doubtfully. "What were you saying has been over for ten years, then?"

She didn't want to talk about this. Especially not with someone who had a reputation for garbling stories until they had no resemblance whatsoever to the original.

On the other hand, Slater's return was a rock-solid guarantee that the whole ugly business was going to be dredged up all over town, anyway. She might as well get used to answering questions about him. "It was a long time ago," she said tersely. "We were engaged, but it didn't work out."

There. That was a nice, succinct—if wildly understated version. It seemed enough for Greta. "You were engaged to the CEO of Maverick Enterprises?"

"Like I said. A long time ago."

"Wow! That's so romantic. Maybe he came back to try to win your heart again."

When pigs fly.

"I strongly doubt it," she murmured, then tried desperately to change the subject. "When you're done there, you can start squeezing the orange juice."

Greta wasn't so easily distracted. "For what it's worth, I think he's gorgeous. Like some kind of movie star or something."

Gorgeous he might be. But Cassie didn't have the heart to tell the starry-eyed teenager that beyond that pretty face, Zack Slater was nothing but trouble.

She was telling the truth.

Two hours later Zack poked at a runny omelette and half-cooked hash browns with his fork, trying hard to pretend he didn't notice the sullen whispers and the not-so-subtle glares being thrown his way by the Salt River locals.

When he had lived here before, Murphy had a well-earned reputation for good, hearty meals. Either the service and the menu had drastically gone downhill or Murphy was saving all the edible food for his other customers.

He supposed he was lucky to get anything, given the overwhelmingly hostile atmosphere in the diner.

When he walked into the café—with its red vinyl booths and mismatched paneling—the breakfast conversation of the summer crowd had ground to an awkward halt like a kid cartwheeling down a hill and hitting the bottom way too fast.

At first he figured everybody focused on him only because he was a new face in town. It was a sensation he was well acquainted with after spending most of his life being the worthless drifter who would never quite belong.

By the time the waitress slammed a menu down in front of him, the tension in the diner still hadn't eased a bit, and he began to suspect the attention he was receiving had its roots in something else.

So a few people remembered him from a decade ago. Big deal.

Soon the whispers began to reach him, and it didn't take long to hear his name linked with Melanie Harte's.

Cassie hadn't been making it up. Judging by the reaction at Murphy's, everybody in town thought he had not only been chicken enough to run out on his sweet, loving bride-to-be less than a week before the wedding but that he'd stolen her brother's wife in the bargain.

The one taste of greasy eggs he'd managed to choke down churned in his gut.

Son of a gun.

He had known that leaving so abruptly a decade ago would cause a scandal, that Cassie would be hurt by it. He'd had his reasons for going, and at the time they had sure seemed like good ones.

Hell, when it came right down to it, he hadn't really been given much of a choice, had he?

At the time—and in the years since—he had tried to convince himself that leaving was the least hurtful option. He was going to break her heart eventually. He knew it, had always known it, even as they had planned their future together.

This way was best, he'd decided. Better to do it quick and sharp, like ripping off a bandage.

But he would have stayed and faced all the grim consequences if he had for one moment dreamed everybody would link his disappearance with a twisted, manipulative bitch like Melanie Harte.

What the hell were the odds that they both had decided to run off on the same night?

Cassie would never believe it was only a coincidence. He couldn't blame her. He had a hard time believing it himself.

Giving up on the eggs, he sipped at his coffee, which was at least hot and halfway decent. Of course, Murphy and his glowering minions probably hadn't had time to whip up a new pot of dregs just for him.

What was he supposed to do now? Going into this whole thing, he'd been prepared for a tough, uphill climb convincing Cassie to give him another chance.

To forgive him for walking out on her.

Tough was one thing. He could handle tough, had been doing it his whole life.

But he'd never expected he would have to take on Mount Everest.

Maybe he ought to just cut his losses and leave. He had plenty of other projects to occupy his mind and attention. Too many to waste his time on this harebrained idea.

This little hiatus from company headquarters was playing havoc with his schedule. Maybe it would be best for everyone involved if he just handed the Lost Creek over to one of the many competent people who worked for him and return to what he did best.

Making money.

He sipped at his coffee again. Why did the idea of returning to Denver now seem so repugnant? He had a good life there. He'd worked damn hard to make sure of it. He had a penthouse apartment in town and a condo in Aspen and his ranch outside of Durango.

He had a company jet at his disposal and a garage full of expensive toys. Everything a man should need to be happy. Yet he wasn't. He hadn't been truly happy since the night he drove out of Star Valley.

"You want anything else?" The waitress stood by the table with a coffeepot in her hand and surliness on her face.

Yeah. He wanted something else. He wanted a woman he couldn't have. Was there anything more pathetic?

"No. I'm finished here."

"Fine. Here's your tab. You can pay the cashier." She

yanked the ticket from the pocket of her apron and slapped it down on the table, then turned away without an ounce of warmth in her demeanor.

Okay. So this little junket into town had established he wasn't going to be welcomed back to Star Valley with open arms by anyone. He fingered the tab for a moment, tempted to climb into his Range Rover parked outside and just keep on driving.

No. That's what he had done a decade ago, and look where it had gotten him. He wouldn't give up. Not yet.

He could show Cassidy Harte—and everybody else in town, for that matter—that his stubborn streak would beat hers any day.

With new determination he slid out of the booth, reached into his wallet and pulled out a hundred, just because he could. He left it neatly on top of the ticket then walked out the door, leaving the whispers and glares behind him.

The morning air was clean and fresh after the oppressive atmosphere inside the diner. It was shaping up to be a beautiful summer day in the Rockies, clear and warm.

He nodded to a man in uniform walking through the parking lot toward him, then did a double take.

Hell.

Cassie's middle brother, Jess, was walking toward him, fury on his features. Great. Just what he needed to make the morning a complete success.

Chapter 4

Uncomfortably aware of the patrons inside the café craning their necks out the window to watch the impending scene, Zack straightened his shoulders and nodded to the other man.

Hard blue eyes exactly like his sister's narrowed menacingly at him, and Jesse folded his arms across his chest, a motion which only emphasized the badge pinned there. "Slater."

"Chief," he answered, remembering that Cassie had told him her brother now headed the Salt River PD.

The other man stood between him and his vehicle and showed no inclination to move out of the way as he stood glowering at Zack. Yet one more person who wasn't exactly overjoyed to see him turning up in Star Valley again.

Zack couldn't say he was surprised. For while he hadn't known Jesse as well as Matt, Jesse had at least tolerated him.

Even so, neither brother had been exactly thrilled at the developing relationship between their baby sister and the hired help—a penniless drifter without much to his name but a battered pickup and a leather saddle handed down from his father.

Although they hadn't come right out and forbidden the marriage, they hadn't been bubbling over with enthusiasm about it, either. He hated to admit their attitude had rubbed off on him, making him feel inadequate and inferior.

He'd gotten their unspoken message loud and clear. Their baby sister deserved better.

Jesse had been a wild hell-raiser back then. Hard drinking, hard fighting. In a hundred years Zack never would have expected the troublemaker he knew ten years ago to straighten up enough for the good people of Salt River to make him their police chief.

Of course, the fact that Jesse was a cop didn't mean a damn thing. Not around here. Zack knew more than most that a Salt River PD uniform could never completely cover up the kind of scum who sometimes wore it.

He shifted, wary at Jesse Harte's continued silence. Either he was gearing up to beat his face in or he was going to order him out of town like a sheriff in an old Western.

The irony of history repeating itself might have made him smile under other circumstances.

And while he was definitely in the mood for a good, rough fight, he had a feeling Cassie wouldn't appreciate him brawling with her cop of a brother on Main Street.

If he had learned anything after ten years of building a successful business from nothing, he'd learned that sometimes diversion was the best course of action. "I understand congratulations are in order," he finally murmured, stretching his lips into what he hoped resembled a polite smile. "When's the big day?"

Jesse continued watching him with that stony expression. "Next month."

"Lovely time of year for a wedding."

The other man had apparently contributed all he planned to in the conversation because he didn't respond. Zack finally gave up. "Nice talking to you," he murmured coolly, prepared to walk through him if he had to.

Jesse stepped forward, shoulders taut and his face dark. "You're not welcome here, Slater."

Big surprise there. He felt about as wanted in Salt River as lice at a hair party.

Jesse took another step forward, until they were almost nose to nose. "Now, why don't you make this easy on yourself and everybody else? Just go on back wherever you came from and forget about whatever game you're playing."

He tensed. "Who says I'm playing a game?" he asked, even though he was. It was all just a risky, terribly important game.

"I don't care what you're doing here. I just want you to leave. No way in hell will I stand by and let you hurt my family again."

The hands he hadn't even realized he had clenched into fists went slack as he remembered what people thought of him. What Cassie thought of him. That he had run away with Melanie, destroying her own dreams as well as her brother's marriage.

What a mess. Damn it, Melanie had left a new baby, no more than a few months old. He remembered a sweet little thing with dark curly hair and big gray eyes who had immediately stolen her aunt Cassie's heart.

Melanie had abandoned her husband, her baby daughter, her whole life here in Wyoming. And everybody thought she did it because of him.

No wonder the whole town despised him.

"I'll be keeping an eye on you," Jesse muttered. "You screw up one time—drive one damn mile over the speed limit—and I'll be on you like flies on stink. I'll tie you up in so much trouble you'll be begging me to let you leave town."

He didn't doubt it for a minute. "Good to know where we stand." He offered a bland smile but wisely refrained from holding out his hand. "Nice seeing you again."

Since the police chief still showed no inclination to step aside and let him pass, he finally moved around him and headed for his Range Rover.

Leaving would be the easy thing, he thought as he pulled out of the parking lot and headed on the road back to the Lost Creek. The smart thing, even. But he'd taken that route once and lived with the guilt and self-doubt for a decade. He wasn't ready to do it again.

Not yet, anyway.

Cassie hung up the phone in her small office off the main kitchen of the ranch and fought the urge to slam her forehead against her messy desk three or four dozen times. If she received one more call about the scene in front of Murphy's between Slater and Jesse that morning, she was afraid she couldn't be held responsible for the consequences of her actions.

She had a whole afternoon of work ahead of her, planning menus and ordering supplies, and she didn't have the time—or, heaven knew, the inclination—to sit there listening to salacious gossip.

What had Jesse been thinking to confront Zack in front of the most popular hangout in Salt River, where he could have optimum visibility? As if all the busybodies in town needed a little more fuel to add to the fire. She was sure the grapevine was just about buzzing out of control over Zack Slater's triumphant return.

It all made her so furious she wanted to punch something. She had spent ten years trying to live down the past, hoping people were starting to forget the scandal.

Hoping *she* was starting to forget.

And now here he was again, stirring them all up like a boy poking at a beehive with a stick.

Still, Jess had no business pulling his protective, big-bad-cop act in front of Murphy's. She could just picture him scowling and threatening, trying to intimidate Slater into leaving town.

As if he could. She leaned her head back in her chair with a grimace. Two of the most stubborn men she had ever known going at it like a couple of bull moose tangling racks.

And Slater. She blamed him even more. None of this would have happened if he had stayed clear of town.

Why did he have to go into Murphy's for breakfast, anyway? Didn't he think the food at the Lost Creek was good enough for him? He was sure willing to pay a heck of a lot of money for it.

With a stern reminder, she caught herself just before she could build up a good huff. She didn't really give a flying fig what Zack Slater thought of her food. He could eat at Murphy's three meals a day if the mood struck him. It was none of her business. She ought to be grateful to him for staying out of her way.

She forced her mind back to her work and dialed the number to the small grocery store in town. Alvin Jeppson, the owner and produce manager, was a good man. She'd gone to school with one of his five daughters and Al had coached her ponytail softball team several years running. Maybe it was all that cheering he did back then—or maybe just the din created by five daughters—but over the years he had become a little hard-of-hearing.

In typical stubborn Western male fashion, he refused

to turn his hearing aid up loud enough, which resulted in some interesting twists whenever she tried to purchase supplies from him.

When he picked up the phone, she automatically raised her voice several decibels. "Mr. Jeppson, this is Cassie Harte at the Lost Creek. I need to check on my order."

She smiled while Alvin greeted her with warmth and affection. The smile faded to a grimace when he immediately launched into a diatribe against that "no-good cowboy who done her wrong" daring to show his face in town again.

"If he turns up in my store, he'll wish he hadn't. I can tell you that much for darn sure."

She had a quick, undeniably gratifying mental picture of old, deaf Mr. Jeppson whacking Slater with a can of cream of mushroom soup. "Like it or not, it looks like he's going to be the new owner of the Lost Creek," she said loudly. "You're going to have to do business with him."

"What's that? You say I'm going to have to learn to swim? What does that have to do with anything."

"No! I said you'll have to do business with him when he takes over the ranch," she repeated in a near-shout.

"I won't do it. Not after the way he treated you and your kin. He can buy what he needs over in Idaho Falls and that's that."

Even though she was touched by his loyalty, she knew Jeppson's couldn't afford to give up the guest-ranch account. She was about to tell him so when her shoulders began to itch and she sensed someone standing behind her in the doorway. She swiveled slightly and spied a pair of worn jeans covering long, muscled legs.

They ended in a pair of scuffed boots that had definitely seen better days. She knew before her gaze traveled up the rest of that frame who was standing in her doorway leaning against the jamb.

How long had he been there? She felt hot color climb up her cheeks, grateful he couldn't hear Alvin Jeppson's diatribe against him. "Mr. Jeppson, I'm going to have to go. I just wanted to let you know there was a mistake on our order. I need two hundred pounds of potatoes, not tomatoes. Potatoes," she enunciated carefully. "Idaho russets. Yeah. That's right. I'll send someone to pick them up this afternoon. Okay. Bye-bye."

She hung up while he was still ranting about the injustice done to her by the man standing in front of her. It would probably take Alvin at least five minutes to realize she was no longer on the line.

She swallowed hard and turned toward Slater, cursing her pulse for jumping at the sight of those hard, masculine features. "If you're looking for something to eat, there are box lunches in the refrigerator," she said curtly. "We never fix a formal meal for lunch since most of our guests are busy with sight-seeing or riding around the ranch."

He continued watching her out of those gold-flecked eyes like a cat ready to pounce on a helpless mouse. "Thanks, but I'm not hungry right now."

"No. I imagine you had your fill at Murphy's, didn't you?" She couldn't resist the gibe any more than she could keep the bitterness out of her voice.

He didn't respond other than to raise an eyebrow. "News travels fast."

"This is Salt River, Zack. What else did you expect? I imagine phones started ringing the moment you passed the city limits sign yesterday, and they haven't stopped since."

"So you've probably heard I had a little chat with big brother number two."

"Yes, I heard. Repeatedly." She glared at him. "Congratulations. The two of you and your little contest have now replaced Peggy Carmichael and her hernia operation as the biggest news in town."

"Well, *that's* something," he murmured, his voice dryly amused.

She wanted to ask what they had talked about, since none of her informants had been close enough to hear the conversation, but she figured she could guess. "It's a good thing Jesse wears a badge now, or you'd be smiling with a few less teeth from now on."

He demonstrated his still-intact dentistry by flashing her a devastating grin. "I think it's fair to say he was still sorely tempted to take a swing or two at me, badge or not."

The smile faded as suddenly as it appeared. He was silent for a moment, his face solemn, then his gaze met hers. "And I would have deserved it."

Before she could answer that startling admission, the phone rang again. She gazed at it with loathing, wishing fiercely that she could ignore it. The last thing she wanted to do was try to appease someone else's prurient curiosity about Zack Slater in the presence of the man himself.

It might be important, though. Maybe Alvin needed to double-check something. Something that couldn't wait.

She glared at the phone for a few more seconds but finally picked up the handset after the fourth ring. "Yes?" she asked, her voice sharp enough to slice through concrete.

"Cassie? Is that you?" a deep voice asked, and she barely managed to choke down her groan.

She definitely wasn't in the mood for this. She almost thought she would prefer talking to the worst gossip in town rather than Wade Lowry right now.

"Yes, Wade," she murmured, her voice as stiffly polite as an army cadet. "How are you?"

Out of the corner of her gaze, she saw Slater stiffen suddenly, but she didn't have a chance to figure out why.

"You'll never believe what I heard at the bank this morning," he exclaimed, shock and dismay in his voice.

"Oh, I'm sure I will," she murmured.

He went on as if he hadn't caught her sarcasm, which was probably exactly the case. "I heard Zack Slater is back in town. Is it true? Have you seen him?"

"Yes. And yes." She'd seen way too much of him in the last twenty-four hours for her sanity's sake.

"How does he have the nerve to show up around here again after everything he's done?"

"That's something I'm sure you'll have to ask him," she murmured, surprised by the depth of his outrage. She and Wade were friends and had dated on and off for the past few years, but she would never have expected the bitter fury in his voice when he talked about Slater.

"You can be sure I'm going to do exactly that if I see him," her would-be champion answered.

He continued in the same vein for a few more moments, apparently expecting little more than monosyllabic responses from her. Good thing, since she couldn't come up with anything more intelligent to offer. Not when Zack stood in the doorway, arms crossed over his muscled chest as he blatantly eavesdropped.

She was more than a little annoyed with herself for finding the conversation so awkward and for the low, subtle tension that always seemed to draw her shoulders back whenever she talked to Wade.

He was a very nice man. Considerate, decent, hardworking. The very antithesis of Zack Slater.

He had made it clear several months earlier that he wanted more from their casual relationship, and she was furious with herself that she couldn't manage to drum up more feelings than friendship for him, no matter how hard she tried.

Wade would be perfect for her. They shared common interests, common background, common goals in life. He was good-looking and even owned his own very successful guest ranch just a mile or so from the Lost Creek.

If she married him, she could have his entire modern kitchen at her disposal. Could probably have free rein doing what she loved for the rest of her life.

But the no-good-cowboy-who-done-her-wrong currently standing behind her, listening to every word, had left a gaping hole in her heart that no one else had ever been able to fill.

Wade began to wind down, and she forced herself to pay attention as he reached what she discovered was the real reason for his call. "One of the repertory companies in Jackson Hole is doing a production of *Shenandoah*. It's getting fairly good reviews for a small theater, and I've got tickets for Sunday night. Would you be interested?"

His voice was tinged with a faint hesitation that only intensified her self-disgust. These days Wade offered each invitation with the wariness of a child whose fingers had been slapped one too many times, but who still couldn't help hoping this time he might be able to reach the cookie jar.

What was worse? she wondered. Continuing to turn down his tenaciousness in the hope that he would eventually give up? Or dating him when she knew she would never be able to feel anything more than friendship for him?

She opened her mouth to decline once more, then she caught sight of Zack leaning against the door frame, looking lean and tawny and gorgeous. The heartless, cheating son of a gun.

She jerked her gaze back to her desk and winced as she heard her next words tumble out. "Sure," she told Wade. "Sounds like fun."

An awkward pause simmered across the line and she

knew he was taken aback that she had agreed but he quickly recovered. "Great. Show starts at eight. I'll pick you up at six and we can have dinner first. Will that work?"

"Yes. Oh, no. Wait a minute." Her Sunday commitments jostled through her memory. "I'll be having dinner at the Diamond Harte on Sunday with my brothers. We always do."

"Oh." The disappointment in his voice was painful to hear.

She caught sight of Zack again and swallowed her resigned sigh, trying to inject enthusiasm in her voice. "We can eat early and finish up by six-thirty. Why don't we skip dinner together and just go to the show? You can pick me up at the ranch."

The polite thing would be to invite him to dinner with her family but she didn't want anybody—especially not Wade—getting the wrong idea.

"That would be great. I'll spend the rest of the week looking forward to it."

"Me, too," she lied. "I'll see you then."

As soon as she hung up the phone, Zack uncoiled from the wall to loom over her. "Big plans?"

"A show in Jackson." She busied herself pretending to tidy up her desk, just to give her hands something to do.

Zack was quiet for a moment, then his mouth tightened. "I don't want you going anywhere with Lowry. Call him back and tell him to forget your plans."

It took several moments for the sheer audacity of his words to pierce her brain. When it did, she could do nothing but stare at him. "Excuse me?" she finally managed to exclaim.

"He's trouble. Stay away from him."

"Trouble? You're warning me that *Wade Lowry* is trouble?" She didn't know whether to laugh or scream. She thought she had been as angry as she'd ever been that morning in the kitchen, but when it came to Slater she was discovering all her emotions were on a short fuse, just looking for any excuse to come brimming to the surface.

"I'm serious, Cass. I don't want you going out with him."

"And I don't want to be the topic of dinner conversation at every house in Star Valley tonight because you showed up again," she snapped. "Here's a little life truth for you, Slater. One I learned the hard way. We don't always get what we want."

A muscle in his jaw flexed. "What would you think if I told you Lowry is one of the reasons I left town?"

She eyed him skeptically. "If I believed you —which I absolutely don't— I would probably think I should just run over to the Rendezvous right this minute and give Wade a big, sloppy, wet kiss for doing me the biggest favor of my life."

His face went completely still, and she thought she saw a glimmer of hurt in his gold-green eyes. For one terrible moment she had to fight the urge to apologize to him. As if she had anything to be sorry about in this whole awful mess!

"Stay away from him," Zack finally growled. "I don't trust the man. You shouldn't, either."

He turned on his heels and walked out of her office, taking with him any soft feelings toward him she might have been crazy enough to entertain for even a second.

Furious with the blasted man and with herself for being such an idiot about him, she picked up the paperweight shaped like a chef's hat that Lucy had given her for Christmas. With all the strength and technique Alvin Jeppson had tried to drum into her head through those years of coaching, she threw it as hard as she could at the door frame where Slater had just been leaning.

It bounced off with a loud thud, leaving a big, ugly nick in the wood, then clattered to the floor.

She'd chipped it, she saw when she went to pick it up. Just a little on one side, barely noticeable, but still, tears pricked behind her eyelids. She blinked them back. She refused to cry over a silly little paperweight, even though it had been a gift from her beloved niece.

And, damn it, she wouldn't cry for Zack Slater, either.

He had no business here.

In Star Valley, at the Lost Creek, and especially not camped out on the front porch of Cassie's cabin. The porch swing chains rattled as he shifted position, watching moonlight gleam like mother-of-pearl across the gravel pathway leading to the main lodge.

Why wasn't she home? The dining room had closed more than an hour ago and all the guests at the ranch were either taking an evening ride around the lake or playing board games at the main lodge or relaxing in their cabins.

So where was Cassie? If these were the kind of hours she kept, he was going to have to do something about it. It wasn't healthy, physically or mentally, no matter how much she loved her work.

He heard his own thoughts and grimaced at the irony. He was a fine one to talk. He'd spent just about every moment of the past ten years pouring his blood and sweat and soul into Maverick, trying to make it a success.

The magnitude of what he had accomplished still sometimes made him sit back in wonder. The kid of a dirt-poor drunk had no business wheeling and dealing with the big boys.

While he listened to the night seethe and stir around

him, he thought of the strange, twisting journey that had begun when he left Salt River a decade earlier. He had wandered aimlessly for a while, then had joined up on the rodeo circuit, looking for a bit of quick cash.

Amazingly enough, right out of the gate he'd won a couple of fairly decent bronc busting purses, fueled more by reckless despair than any real skill on his part. He wasn't aware of any kind of conscious plan at the time, but some instinct had led him to plow the money into investments that had paid off.

He had turned around and invested those dividends again, then again and again, hitting big on just about everything he turned his hand to. Much to his surprise, he discovered he had an uncanny knack for predicting market trends. Through that knack, a lot of hard work and a few mistakes along the way, he had built Maverick into a huge, highly successful company.

By all rights, he should be deliriously happy. He had just about everything a man could want. Everything he'd ever dreamed about.

Hell, more than that. A decade ago, he hadn't had any dreams. Whenever he pictured the future—something he didn't like to do much back then—he figured he would turn out just like his father, a penniless drifter always looking to see what was over the next hill.

Cassie had given him the rare and precious gift of faith. She had believed in him, had seen potential he'd never even suspected lurked inside him. Even after he left her, he had cherished that gift. Without it, he probably would have lived out that prophesy and become just like his old man.

Yeah, he had just about everything he'd ever wanted.

Except Cassidy Harte.

He gazed out at the moonlight, remembering the silk of her skin and the slick, incredible heat of her mouth under his. Even after a decade, the memory of her enthusiastic, wholehearted response to his touch was still as strong and as vivid as it had been the day he drove out of town with his heart shredding into little pieces.

The way things were going, he had a fairly strong feeling he would never again taste her mouth or feel those small, competent hands caress him. He blew out a breath, cursing again the tangled whims of fate.

Why the hell did Melanie have to leave the same night he did? It would have been hard enough trying to explain everything to Cassie, trying to make things right again, without the onus of trying to explain away the unbelievable coincidence.

Maybe he should give this whole thing up. Just go on back to his life in Denver and get on with things, forget about trying to repair the damage of his decisions.

He fiddled with a loose link on the swing's chains. He didn't want to give up. Not yet. He needed to talk to her, at least. He owed her an explanation that was ten years overdue.

He had tried to tell her earlier in the afternoon. That's why he had gone in search of her after his dismal trip into Murphy's, to set the record straight. He'd gotten a little sidetracked, though, when he had overheard her on the phone with Lowry.

Fierce jealousy hadn't been the only emotion curling through him when he pictured the two of them together. He didn't like the idea that Cassie could ever be mixed up with scum like Lowry.

He sighed and shifted in the swing again. Jealousy hadn't been the only emotion but it had been by far the strongest. Even though logic told him he had no right to be jealous—absolutely no claim over her—he had about as much control over it as he did that moon up there.

He leaned his head back, watching the path for some sign of her and listening to the chirp of crickets, the tumble of the creek behind the cabins, the far-off whinny of a horse....

He must have dozed off. He wasn't sure how long he slept but he awoke to find her propped against the porch rail watching him, her arms folded across her chest and her face in shadows.

"Hi." He heard the sheepishness in his voice at being caught in a vulnerable moment and tried to clear it away. "You're late."

The moon slid from behind a cloud, and he saw her raise an eyebrow. "I didn't realize I had a curfew."

"You put in long hours. Too long. Is it like this every day?"

"No. Not usually. Claire Dustin, one of the wranglers' wives, usually helps out with breakfast but she's in Bozeman catering her sister's wedding this week." She paused. "I'm thinking she'll make a good replacement for me. I'll talk to her about it when she gets back Monday. If she's agreeable, I can start training her right away."

"That eager to be gone, are you?"

She said nothing for several moments, then straightened from the porch railing. "I'm tired, Slater. As you said, it's been a long day. To be perfectly honest, I'm not sure I have enough energy left to tangle with you again tonight."

"I don't want to fight. I just want to talk to you. Explain a few things."

"I don't think I have the energy for that, either."

He should just let her go inside and sleep. But he didn't want this ugliness between them any longer. Not if he had any chance of clearing it away. "Please. Sit down."

She was quiet for a long time watching him across the width of the porch with only the night sounds between them—the cool sigh of the wind, the crickets' chatter, the creek tumbling along behind the trees.

Just when he began to fear she would ignore him and march into her cabin, she blew out a breath and slid onto the swing next to him.

Now that she was there, he didn't know where to begin.

"Gorgeous view from here," he finally said, which wasn't at all what he wanted to talk to her about. Still, it was the truth. He could see the Salt River Range behind them. Even in mid-June, the mountains still wore snow-caps that gleamed bluish white in the moonlight.

The Lost Creek had a prime location on a foothill bordering national forest land. From here he could see small glowing settlements strung along the Star Valley like Christmas lights.

"I like it," she finally murmured.

"I would have to say it's almost as nice as the view from the Diamond Harte."

"Almost. Not quite."

The pride in her voice for her family ranch made him smile. Although he knew she wouldn't be able to see much in the darkness, he could feel the heat of her gaze on him. What she could see apparently displeased her because her voice was curt when she spoke. "I'm tired, Zack. What did you want to talk about?"

This wasn't the way he wanted to do this, with her already testy and abrupt. But it didn't look as if she was going to give him much of a choice.

"I'm sorry about this afternoon. About Lowry."

"You should be."

He winced at the residual anger in her voice. He wasn't sorry for warning her about the bastard, just that he had gone about it the wrong way.

She didn't give him a chance to explain. "I find it unbelievably arrogant that you think you can blow back into town like nothing happened and start ordering me around," she snapped.

"I don't think that."

"Don't you?"

"No!"

"Let's see." She ticked off his shortcomings on her fingers. "In the thirty-six hours since you showed up again, you have blackmailed me to keep me from quitting my job, you have once more dredged up old, painful gossip about me all over town and you have commanded me not to go out with a man I've known most of my life. Seems to me you're working pretty hard to control me."

Put so bluntly, he could understand why she would be more than a little annoyed with him. Maybe he *had* been a little heavy-handed since he'd seen her. What other choice did he have, though?

"I didn't come to fight with you, Cass. We need to talk. I'd like to clear the air between us."

"I really don't think that's possible." Her voice was small and maybe a little sad, which gave him some hope.

"Will you let me at least try?"

She remained silent, which he took as assent. Where to start? he wondered, gazing out at the mountains. At the crux of the matter, he figured.

"I didn't leave town with Melanie."

She froze, stopping the swing's motion mid-rhythm. "We went over this earlier. I don't want to hear it again."

She started to rise but he held a hand out to keep her in place, brushing the denim of her jeans as his hand covered her leg. She jerked away from his touch but stayed in the swing beside him, which he took as a good sign.

"Please. Listen to me. I know you're going to find this

an amazing coincidence—hell, I have a hard time believing it myself—but I left alone. I swear it."

"So how did Melanie leave town? Teleportation?" A thin shear of skepticism coated her voice. "Her car was left in the parking lot of the Renegade. She was last seen climbing into your pickup truck, then the two of you were observed going at it inside the cab like a couple of minks. Are you saying everybody else who saw you two drive off together was lying?"

"No. They weren't lying. We did drive off together."

She made a *hmmph* kind of sound and folded her arms across her chest. He sighed. This was going to be much harder than he expected.

"You know what Melanie was like. She was wild. Out of control. That night she was drinking like a sailor with a three-day pass and throwing herself at anybody in sight. I offered to give her a ride home because I knew she was too drunk to be safe behind the wheel of a car. When she climbed into my truck, she attacked me."

"Oh, you poor helpless man. I'm sure that was just terrible for you."

"It was, dammit! I couldn't stand her. I was engaged to marry the woman I loved and didn't want to have anything to do with someone like Melanie Harte."

Cassie remained stubbornly silent, her arms folded tightly, and he knew with grim certainty that she didn't believe a word he was saying.

"She kissed me," he tried again. "Started grabbing me as soon as she climbed into the truck. I told her to stop. I thought she was going to behave herself but as soon as we pulled out of the parking lot, she started all over again. Eventually I told her I would just leave her on the side of the road if she didn't cut it out. She laughed and said I wouldn't dare, that if I did, she would tell you I put the moves on her."

His memory of this was hazy because of what had happened later that night but he tried his best to reconstruct it. "I laughed at her. I told her you'd never believe it. She was crazy that night, though, and wouldn't stop. About the third or fourth time she tried to grab my crotch, I pulled over just outside the city limits, yanked her out of the truck and drove away, to hell with being a gentleman. That's the last time I ever saw her. I swear."

She didn't answer for several moments. When she spoke, her voice was subdued. "And somehow in the middle of all that, you just decided to keep on driving, right? Tell me, Zack. When did you decide you weren't really in love with me? When did you realize you couldn't stomach the idea of being married to me and decided running was a better option?"

Was that what she thought all these years? *Of course,* he answered his own question, his heart aching. What else could she have thought?

"It wasn't like that, Cass," he murmured, wondering how much to tell her about the other events that had unfolded that night. Ten years later it all sounded so inconceivable, even to him.

Who would she be more willing to believe the worst about? People she has known and cared about all her life or the man she had spent years believing had betrayed her in the worst way possible?

He didn't want to make her have to choose. Truth was, he was afraid where he would stack up. But he had to give her some kind of explanation. If he didn't, the past would remain an insurmountable wall between them and she would never let him through.

"After I dropped Melanie off, I drove back to the Diamond Harte, then started to feel a little guilty about dumping her out like that in the middle of nowhere. Once I cooled off, I realized I couldn't leave her alone in the dark to find her own way home. I imagined her falling into the river or something else terrible happening to her, so I turned around to go look for her."

"And did you find her?"

"No. I just figured somebody else must have given her a ride. But while I was looking for her, I stumbled onto something else. Something illegal."

"What?" She sounded every bit as skeptical as he expected.

"When I didn't find her on the main road, I thought she might have wandered off in the wrong direction so I decided to look along this gravel road near where I dropped her off. I was feeling pretty guilty by then, when I saw a little puddle-jumper Cessna landing in a field a mile or so down the road. I figured they must have had to make some kind of emergency landing so I went to investigate."

"And?"

"It wasn't an emergency. It was a planned drop site. The plane was delivering a large shipment of cocaine. I was in the wrong place at the wrong time and stumbled on a crew transferring it from the Cessna to a truck."

She was silent for a moment then she began to laugh, low and rich and full of disbelief. "Okay. You might have had me going there for a moment but this is too much. What kind of idiot do you take me for? This is Star Valley, Slater. I'll admit, I'm not naive enough to think we don't have any illegal narcotic use in the valley but certainly not enough to make it some drug smuggling hub."

"Maybe not here. But I imagine there are plenty of tourists and movie stars just over the mountains in Jackson Hole who wouldn't care how their drugs arrived as long as they had a ready supply."

"Assuming I believe you—which I don't—it still doesn't

explain why you just decided to take off. Why not go to the police? Someone would have helped you."

Oh, yeah. Salt River's finest would have helped him, all right. Helped him right into a five-to-life prison sentence for drug smuggling. He doubted Cassie would believe the depth of corruption in the small-town police department. Hell, he still had a hard time believing it and he had witnessed it firsthand.

Trying to figure out the best way to answer, he gazed out at that sliver of moonlight on gravel and the shadows beyond.

She wasn't ready for the whole truth, he thought, so he slipped her something a little more palatable. "Back then I didn't trust a man in uniform the way you did. Call it cynicism or whatever you want. I suppose I could have gone to someone, but I really didn't think anyone would believe me."

"Why not?"

"I knew what people said about me. What everybody in town was saying. That I was some kind of gold digger after your share of the ranch."

"Nobody really thought that."

He studied his fist resting on the armrest of the swing, not willing to shatter that last illusion of hers. She had been a sweet, loyal eighteen-year-old girl in love who hadn't wanted to see what everyone was saying behind her back.

He suddenly missed that girl fiercely.

"Maybe not. Maybe that's only how I interpreted things. Like I said, I guess I was too cynical. I thought I would end up in jail if I came forward. That I would take the fall."

Not that such a conclusion had just sprung into his head out of the blue. After he'd been beaten so badly he could hardly move by four masked police officers wielding billy clubs and pistol butts, he'd been given the message loud and clear. Leave town or go to prison for drug smuggling.

What else could he have done?

"So you decided it would be easier to just leave, to hell with me and all our plans." Her voice was low, bitter, and ripped through his heart like a ricocheting bullet.

"Either way you would have despised me, whether I walked out or whether I stayed and ended up in jail. I figured leaving would be the best thing I could ever do for you."

"How thoughtful of you."

This time her bitterness made him wince. "Cassie—"

"Let me ask you one question. Why on earth would you want to marry a woman you thought so little of?"

"I thought the world of you! I loved you!"

She was the one shining light in a life that had been gray and colorless before their paths collided.

"You couldn't have loved me. You didn't even know the first thing about me."

"Sure I did."

"If what you say is true—if you really did stumble onto some drug ring and were afraid of taking the fall for it—you should have known that you didn't have to run. I would have stood by you, no matter what happened. No matter what anybody said about you."

He tried to see her expression in the dim porch but her face was just a pale blur in the moonlight. "I thought I did the right thing. I didn't want you to have to endure the shame of having your fiancé arrested the week before the wedding."

"What do you think would have been worse for me?" Her voice was just barely audible above the sighing wind. "The shame of you being arrested on some trumped-up charge that any good lawyer could have beaten? Or the shame I've lived with for ten years, of believing you preferred my brother's wife to me?"

Aw, hell. He closed his eyes against the pain lodging thick and heavy in his chest.

"If I'd had any idea everyone thought I jilted you to run off with Melanie, I would have come back and faced any consequence. I'm so sorry you had to deal with that."

"And that's supposed to mean something to me now, after all this time?"

"I don't know. I hope so."

She rose from the rocking chair and stood over him, a slender shadow in the night. "You still left, Zack. Whether you left with Melanie or not. You still left without a note or a phone call or anything. You owed me that much, at least."

She was right. He had wanted to call her a thousand times that first year but had always stopped before dialing the number. A clean break would be best for her, he had rationalized. She would move on with her life and forget about him.

Find someone better.

It sounded good in the abstract. Noble and selfless, even. But he had faced some fairly ugly truths about himself a long time ago. He hadn't refrained from making contact with her out of some high-minded desire for her to heal. He'd been a coward. Pure and simple. Afraid that the moment he heard her soft voice, he would turn around and head back to the Diamond Harte like a compass finding north.

"I'm tired, Zack," she finally said into the silence. "As I told you, it's been a long, hard day."

She moved past him for the door, and he felt his last chance with her slipping through his fingers. He stood and reached out to grab on to something—anything—and found the soft, bare skin of her forearm.

"I'm sorry I hurt you, Cass," he murmured. "I never wanted to do that. I thought I was protecting you."

Now that they were face-to-face, he could see the fatigue on her face, the purplish circles under her eyes. He wanted to smooth a hand over that tousled cap of hair. To hold her on his lap and tuck her head close to his chest and listen to her breathe against him while she slept.

His gaze locked with hers, and he realized some of what he was feeling must have shown in his expression. Her mouth opened just a little, and a breathy little sound escaped.

He could no more keep from bending toward that mouth than he could yank the moon from the sky.

If he'd been thinking at all, he would have expected her to jerk away when his mouth met hers. Knowing Cassie, he might have expected at least a slap or a knee to the groin. Heaven knows, he deserved all that and more.

She didn't lash out at him, though. Instead she whispered another of those little sighs and her lips softened under his.

He kept the kiss gentle. Slow and tender. Nonthreatening. A shadowy remembrance of other kisses.

She leaned into him just for a moment—just enough for his blood to begin singing and his body stir to life—and then she wrenched away from him so abruptly her elbow caught the door frame with a hard whack.

Chapter 5

She wasn't sure exactly when awareness slipped over her like a chilling mist.

One moment she wanted to weep from the tenderness of his kiss, from the unbelievable wonder of being in his arms once more. Of tasting his lips and feeling his skin and absorbing the taste and smell of him that had haunted her dreams for so long after he left.

The next, her spine stiffened, her muscles tensed, and she wrenched away. The impact of her elbow hitting wood jarred her completely back into reality.

Damn him for kissing her like that.

And damn her right along with him for allowing it.

"Don't touch me again." She meant to sound strong and determined, but she heard the quaver in her voice and cursed herself for her weakness.

"Cassie —"

"I'm serious, Slater. You want me to stay and work here, fine. I'll stay. We made a deal, and I, for one, always try to keep my word. But I don't want you near me."

She didn't wait for him to answer, just opened the door to the cabin and hurried inside before she did anything else stupid. Inside she slammed the door and stood for a moment, then slumped to the floor, one trembling hand covering her mouth that still burned from his kiss.

She felt stunned, immobilized by shock. As if every illusion she had ever had about herself had just disintegrated into a fine, chalky dust.

What just happened here?

Had she really just let Zack Slater kiss her? Not just let him, she corrected herself with dawning horror. She had been a willing participant, had wanted to dissolve in his arms like sugar in warm water.

She closed her eyes, remembering the heat of his mouth, the strength of his arms around her. The overwhelming sense of rightness, of belonging, that had seeped through her skin—through her bones—like spring sunshine.

As if she were home again after a long and treacherous journey.

What the bloody blazes had come over her? She blew out a shuddering breath. There was nothing *right* about kissing Zack Slater. It was wrong in every single definition of the word.

Her hands trembled as she pressed them over her face. Where was her pride? Her self-respect? Her sense of self-preservation, at least?

She meant what she said. She couldn't allow him to touch her again. Especially now that she realized her body still responded to him with all the enthusiasm of dry tinder to a match.

She wouldn't let him do this to her again. She had worked too hard the last ten years to become someone she could like and respect again. Now, when she finally felt as if she could hold her head high again, that she was a strong and capable woman—not that needy, trusting girl who had given her heart so completely—Slater had to turn up again.

She thought of the unbelievable story he had told her, sick to realize how desperately she wanted to believe him. It would still sting to know he chose to leave her rather than give her the opportunity to prove to him she loved him enough to stand behind him, no matter what happened.

It would still hurt, yes. But at least she wouldn't have to live with the constant, deep, burning shame of knowing he had preferred a woman like Melanie to her.

She let her hands drop and shuddered out a breath. She wanted to believe him, but she couldn't. The story was too outlandish. Too contrived. He and Melanie must have been carrying on a sordid affair, just as everyone had said. Melanie made no secret of her desire to leave Star Valley, and she had finally found someone willing to take her.

Cassie leaned her head back against the door. She couldn't believe him. She had to stand strong and solid as the mountains she loved. Ten years ago Zack Slater had left her bruised and broken, had nearly destroyed her and her family and had turned her into the laughingstock of Star Valley. She couldn't forget all that just because of a few self-serving words of explanation and a soft, tender kiss that left her yearning for something she could never regain.

She wouldn't let her heart be vulnerable to him.

This time she might not survive.

"So are you going to tell us how you're really dealing with all of this?"

In the big, comfortable kitchen of the Diamond Harte, Cassie looked up from the potato salad she was throwing together. Though her sister-in-law, Ellie, had been the one who asked the question, she and Jesse's fiancée Sarah were both watching her with identical expressions of concern on their faces.

She knew exactly what they were talking about but she wasn't at all in the mood to get into it right now, so she pretended ignorance, even though she knew it wouldn't fly with them for long. "Dealing with what?"

"Come on, Cass," Ellie muttered. "You know what I mean. With that man showing up again after all these years!"

Here it comes. She sighed. She should have known she couldn't get through the regular Sunday afternoon Harte family gathering without Zack Slater starring as the main topic of conversation.

Trying to avoid the question as long as possible, she looked out the window where her brothers, beer bottles in hand, went through the strictly male ritual of manning the steaks on the grill. She almost wished she were out there with them.

But whose inquisition was she more willing to face? Her stubborn brothers' or that of their equally persistent women?

Finally she turned back to the table, pasting a smile on her face that probably fooled nobody. "I'm fine. Really. I can't say I'm thrilled Slater has the gall to come back and I'm not crazy about everything being dredged up again, but I'm coping."

Sarah's green eyes darkened with sympathy. "This must be so difficult for you. I can't even imagine it."

A quick image of their soft, late-night kiss of earlier in the week flickered through her mind. *Difficult* didn't even come close to describing the tumult shaking around her psyche since Zack Slater had shown up at the Lost Creek Ranch, rich and self-assured and as gorgeous as ever.

"I'm coping," she repeated, as blatant a falsehood as she had ever uttered.

She was fairly certain her friends saw through it, but they loved her too much to call her a liar to her face.

Instead Ellie stuck her chin out with a pugnacious tilt. "I know I, for one, would love to spend an hour or two locked in a room with the man, giving him a piece of my mind. Turning up again after all these years as if nothing had happened! How does he dare show his face around here?"

She remembered the regret she thought she'd seen in those eyes that night on her porch as he had told her his version of events. If he were telling the truth—that he hadn't left with Melanie—he had been judged unfairly.

It was one thing for a man to get cold feet about his wedding and decide to bolt. Better before the wedding than after, most people would say.

It was quite another if he took off with someone else's wife in the process.

But he couldn't have been telling the truth. Where else would Melanie have gone?

She looked out the window again at her brothers. Matt stood at the grill ready to turn the steaks, smiling at something Jesse must have said.

She adored both of her brothers, but she and Matt shared a special bond. After their parents' death when she was twelve, he had been the only authority figure in her life and she loved him deeply for taking on the responsibility of a young girl when he could easily have handed it off to someone else.

Deep in her heart she had always suspected he'd married Melanie in the first place to provide Cassie with a more normal home life than just that of an impressionable girl living with her two young bachelor brothers, one of them a wild hell-raiser.

He had never said as much—and he never would, she

knew—but deep down she had always feared she was the one responsible for his disaster of a marriage.

Guilt washed through her as she realized she had given very little thought to Matt and how *he* must feel to have Slater back in town.

His marriage to Melanie had been over a long time before Zack Slater entered the picture—that much had been glaringly obvious—but it still couldn't be easy for Matt to live in the same town with the man everyone believed had run off with her.

No, she corrected herself again, angry at the part of her still clinging to that wild, foolish hope. The man who *had* run off with her brother's wife. She couldn't forget that. She wasn't ready to give up ten years of betrayal just because Zack claimed their mutual disappearance on the same night had been strictly coincidental.

"What has Matt said about Slater coming back?" she asked Ellie, her voice subdued.

Her sister-in-law shrugged. "Not much. He's upset about it of course, but mainly I think he's worried about you."

"Still, it must sting his pride a little bit to have all those old, ugly bones dug up."

Ellie's mouth tightened. "I don't think he had much pride left when it came to Melanie."

She couldn't dispute that. Cassie knew there were plenty of folks around Salt River who thought Slater did them all a big favor by taking away Matt's wild, troubled wife.

The silence in the kitchen was broken by Sarah ripping open a bag of chips and pouring them into a serving bowl. "What puzzles me," she said with a thoughtful frown, "is why the man would come back to Salt River at all. I would think anyone with a kernel of sense would stay as far away from here as possible. He had to know he wouldn't exactly be Mr. Popular. Not with all the lives he hurt when he left. He must have a very good reason to come back. Either that or he's crazy."

"Maybe that's it," Ellie said, crunching on a chip. "Maybe he's bonkers. Or maybe he's just a heartless bastard who doesn't care about who he's hurting by coming back."

Cassie remembered that flash of vulnerability she thought she'd seen as he had kissed her, and had the sudden, insane urge to defend him. He wasn't crazy or heartless. She opened her mouth to say so, then clapped her lips shut again.

She wouldn't defend him. Anything she said was bound to be misinterpreted by her family.

Why *had* he come back, though? It was a darn good question. One she was ashamed to realize she didn't have the courage to explore.

"Can we change the subject?" she finally asked. "Those steaks out there smell delicious, but I'm afraid I won't have much of an appetite if we keep talking about Zack Slater."

Sarah was quick to apologize. "Don't mind us," she said softly. "We're just a couple of nosy old busybodies."

"Speak for yourself," Ellie said with a teasing grin. "I'm not old."

The conversation quickly drifted to other subjects, especially Sarah and Jesse's upcoming nuptials. But even while Sarah described the dress she had finally picked out and the shower Cassie and Ellie were throwing her in a few weeks, Cassie couldn't shake the memory of that breathless moment on the porch right before Slater had kissed her.

They were discussing the menu Cassie planned to serve at the wedding dinner when her nieces burst into the kitchen, dusty and sunburned from their favorite activity, horseback riding.

The girls were a contrast in appearance—Dylan red-haired like her mother, with freckles and a snub nose, and Lucy with curly dark hair and big gray eyes. But they were partners in crime in just about everything. They'd been best friends since Ellie and Dylan moved to town the summer before and had connived and schemed to bring their parents together.

Cassie had a feeling they also secretly took credit for bringing their fourth-grade teacher, Sarah, together with Jesse.

She shuddered to think what would happen if they ever decided to turn their fledgling matchmaking skills in her direction.

"We're starving," Dylan moaned dramatically. "When are we gonna eat?"

"Yeah," Lucy chimed in. "I'm so hungry I could eat my boots."

"From the looks of it, those boots have been in places I don't even want to think about," Ellie said. "Why don't you take them off in the mudroom and then scrub all that barn grime off your hands and faces?"

They groaned but quickly obeyed, then both reached for the potato chip bowl at the same time. Before they could reach it, Cassie whipped the bowl behind her back with a grin. "Nope. Neither one of you is getting anything to eat until you give me my hug."

This time they obeyed without the groaning. She put the bowl back on the table and gathered them close. Dylan was quick to return to the chips, but Lucy lingered in her arms and Cassie planted a kiss on the top of her dark curls, smelling shampoo and sunshine.

All too soon Lucy pulled away and Ellie stepped into the breach. "Why don't you girls help carry some of this food out to the picnic table and tell your dad and uncle to hustle with those steaks?"

Cassie watched the girls obey, trying hard to ignore the sharp little niggle in her heart.

It shouldn't still bother her. Not after all these months. Everything had changed now that Matt had married Ellie. Lucy had a different family now—a stepmother and a sister. The four of them had forged a loving family and she couldn't be happier for them.

But she still couldn't help an aching sense of loss that pinched her heart every time she was around her niece now.

After Melanie left, she had taken over caring for Lucy. What else could she have done? There was no way Matt could handle a three-month old infant by himself and run the ranch, too.

And giving up her college plans and devoting herself to her niece hadn't been completely unselfish on her part. She had needed the distraction, a firm purpose, something to help restore her shattered self-esteem. She found it in mothering the poor lost little baby.

For nearly ten years she had been Lucy's mother in everything but name. She had held her chubby little hands when Lucy took her first fledgling steps, she had cuddled her at night and read her bedtime stories, she had nurtured her when she was sick. She had given the little girl all the love in her heart and had it returned a thousandfold, with sticky kisses and tight hugs and whispered secrets.

Everything was different now. She had moved away to give Matt and Ellie space to build their new life together. It was the right thing to do, she knew. But a part of her still grieved to know Ellie was the one who now heard those secrets of Lucy's, who now received those sticky kisses and tight hugs, while she was relegated to the role of maiden aunt.

Now Jesse and Sarah were getting married, and she

knew it probably wouldn't be long before they added their own little branches to the Harte family tree.

She would love their children, just as she did Lucy and Dylan. She would spoil them with presents and take them to the movies and baby-sit so their parents could have a night on the town.

And she would always be on the outside looking in.

She ground her teeth, angry at the direction of her thoughts. She was childish to think such things, even for a moment. Her family loved her. She had absolutely no doubt about that. Lucy loved her. Their hearts would always be knit together by those ten years she had nurtured her niece. Nothing could change that.

"Are you sure you're all right?" Sarah asked in her quiet voice while Ellie was occupied loading the girls up with plates and silverware.

Cassie pushed away her thoughts and summoned a smile. "Sure. I'm fine. Just hungry."

Sarah didn't look convinced, but to her relief, her future sister-in-law was too tactful to push her on it as they finished preparations for dinner.

As usual, the meal was noisy and rambunctious, full of heated debates, good food and plenty of laughter. Cassie joined in, but a part of her sat back, watching her brothers with the women they loved.

Matt and Ellie never seemed to stop touching each other. Ellie's hand on Matt's arm as she made a point. Matt's quick caress of his wife's shoulder as she leaned back in her chair. A soft kiss when they thought no one was looking.

It still amazed her to see her big, gruff oldest brother teasing and smiling at his spunky little wife.

Jesse and Sarah were the same, and she whispered a quick prayer of gratitude that her middle brother had finally realized he deserved better than the wild, bubble-headed party girls he usually dated, that he had been wise enough to latch on to someone as soft and good as Sarah.

She was jealous of them for their happiness. All of them. For a few brief months she had known that same deep connection with Slater, but she was terribly afraid she would never find it with someone else. The knowledge had her picking at her steak and barely touching the homemade ice cream Dylan and Lucy had churned.

She had a good life, she reminded herself. Thanks to Slater, in just a few weeks she would have enough money to put the down payment on Murphy's and finally realize her dream of running her own restaurant. She would have purpose in her life again. Direction.

"You gonna eat the rest of that?" Jesse asked, gesturing with his spoon toward her melting ice cream.

She grinned at her bottomless pit of a brother. And wasn't it just like a man that for all he ate, he never gained an ounce of fat, just hard muscle? "What will you give me if I let you finish it off?"

"How about a ride in my police Bronco with all the lights and sirens blaring?"

"Ohh. As tempting as that sounds, I just don't think my poor heart could stand so much excitement."

Jesse pondered for a moment. "How about I let you keep Daisy while we're in Vancouver for our honeymoon?"

She laughed, looking toward the shade of the sycamore where his big golden retriever lounged with Dylan and Lucy. "Again, a very enticing offer. But I think your baby would be happier here on the ranch where she can chase the cats and play with the cow dogs. Is that the best you can do?"

"Come on, Cass. Your ice cream is just sitting there going to waste, melting all over the place. Why don't you just tell me what you want?"

She hadn't want to bring this up in front of the rest of the family but she couldn't pass up the chance. "Promise you won't make any more scenes in town like the one in front of Murphy's this week with Slater, and it's all yours."

Jesse glowered, all teasing forgotten. "I can't make a promise like that. I should have pounded the bastard's pretty-boy face in."

She glowered right back. "It's not your battle to fight, Jess."

"The hell it isn't."

"All you did with your little chest-pounding demonstration was stir up more gossip. You're not helping anything."

"I'm not about to sit by and let him hurt you again."

"I can take care of myself," she snapped, even though she wasn't at all sure of that, as evidenced by her response to that slow, sexy late-night kiss.

Before Jesse could argue, Matt broke in. "Neutral corners, you two. Looks like we have company."

From here she could see the long, curving driveway into the ranch and she recognized Wade's truck kicking up dirt as he roared toward the house.

"Who could that be?" Ellie wondered.

Color climbed up her cheekbones. "Um, that would be my date."

"Who?" Jesse asked suspiciously, and she fought the urge to dump the rest of her melting ice cream in his lap.

"Wade Lowry. We're going to a show in Jackson. You have a problem with that?"

Jesse made a face but didn't say anything. She knew he and Wade didn't get along, something to do with the days when Wade worked for the police department.

"That's great!" Ellie interjected, with just enough enthusiasm to make Cassie wonder if her family thought she had zero social life. Which was basically the truth. "You should have invited him to dinner."

She made a noncommittal sound, heartily glad she hadn't. "I'm sorry I can't stay to help clean up."

"Don't worry about it," Ellie said. "Just go have a great time."

She rose from the picnic table and plopped her bowl of what was now plain vanilla cream without the ice in front of Jesse. "Here you go. Enjoy."

And that's just what she would do, she thought as she walked out front to meet Wade. She would do her best to enjoy their date and try to summon more than just friendly feelings for him.

She wanted to grab for happiness where she could find it, not spend the rest of her life pining for something she could never have again.

Chapter 6

This was getting to be a bad habit.

Zack sat on the little front porch of his cabin, uncomfortably aware he was lurking in the corner like some kind of peeping Tom. He had pushed the comfy rocking chair as close to the wall as he could without the rockers hitting it. Nobody could see him, he assured himself as he watched the small driveway for any sign of Lowry's pickup truck.

He wasn't spying on her.

He *wasn't*.

He was simply savoring the quiet of the night, enjoying a beautiful cool summer evening in the mountains, with the fresh, intoxicating smell of sage mixed with pine, and the stars twinkling overhead in a vast glittering blanket. He was only enjoying the soothing sounds of the crickets and the creek and the soft wind tinkling the wind chimes Cassie had hung on her porch.

Right. Who was he kidding? He had been sitting out here all evening trying to convince himself his motives were pure, even while one part of him kept watch like a nervous father for Cassie to return from her night out.

He had maintained his solitary vigil while the ranch guests returned in pairs or small family groups to their own cabins after a hard day of recreating. Now, just past midnight, the ranch was mostly quiet. Peaceful.

Even with this edginess that forced his gaze toward the driveway a dozen times a minute, he still found himself enjoying it.

A barn owl hooted somewhere in the night, a low, mournful call, and a few seconds later it was answered from one of the big cottonwood trees near the creek.

At least somebody wouldn't be alone tonight.

He found himself smiling at the whimsical thought but sobered quickly. He, on the other hand, was still alone. Always alone, just as he'd been from the age of fifteen, except for that brief, magical time when his life had merged with Cassie's.

Before he could dwell on that grim reminder he saw headlights flash into the driveway and shifted a little deeper into the shadows.

Lowry drove a late-model pickup truck with a fresh wax job that gleamed in the pale moonlight.

Zack watched him climb out and hurry toward the passenger side to open the door for Cassie, ever the gentleman, and Zack had to clench his hands into fists to keep from marching down the steps and slugging the bastard.

Cassie hopped out of the truck with what he thought might be just a little too much eagerness, as if all she wanted was to be home.

Or maybe that was just wishful thinking on his part.

No. Everything about her body language spoke of a woman who wasn't eager for any post-date clutch. She shoved her hands in the pockets of her sweater and walked briskly up the walk toward her cabin.

"I had a great time, Wade," she murmured when they reached the steps to her porch. "Thank you for inviting me."

Lowry edged a little closer, and Zack went completely still so he could hear his next words.

"We need to do this more often," Lowry murmured, and Zack didn't realize he was holding his breath until he heard her make a little noncommittal sound in response.

"Well, good night," she said, somewhat breathlessly. "And thanks again."

Zack couldn't help his smirk as she hurried up the steps of her cabin as if she wanted to put as much distance as possible between them. His smirk faded quickly when Lowry bounded after her to the door.

In the gleam of the porch light she had left burning, Zack could see her unease. Her shoulders were tight, and she was already reaching to unlock her front door.

She might have made it through the door unscathed. He would never know. At that moment he leaned forward slightly for a better view, and the rocker squeaked on a loose floorboard under his feet.

It was just a tiny sound in the night, no louder than the wind rubbing two limbs together, but she whirled her head toward his cabin. Though the lighting was dim, he was fairly certain her eyes narrowed suspiciously at the corner of darkness where he lurked.

When she turned back to Lowry, her smile was unnaturally bright, with none of the hesitation that had been there before. "I really did have a wonderful time, Wade. I know the Applewood Players in Jackson are performing a melodrama this summer. I've heard good things about it. Maybe we could go sometime."

Wade looked slightly dazzled. "I'd like that."

After an awkward pause he angled his head and Zack held his breath, knowing with grim certainty what was going to happen next. Sure enough, the bastard leaned down and brushed his lips against Cassie's.

It wasn't a long kiss, only a few heartbeats, but it went on long enough that Zack was forced to curl his hands into fists on the armrests to keep from throttling both of them.

He wasn't sure through the haze of green over his eyes which of them broke it off. The next thing he knew, Cassie had unlocked her door slicker than spit on a griddle.

"Have dinner with me this week."

"I don't know," she answered, and he wondered if that breathy note in her voice stemmed from reaction or nervousness. "My schedule's pretty full for a while. Jean wants everything to be perfect for…for the new owner, plus I'm going to be busy training my replacement."

"When is your next day off? I'm flexible. We can work around your schedule."

"I'll have to let you know. Good night, Wade," she finally said with firmness, then slipped inside her house, leaving her clean wildflower scent floating in the air, torturing him even across the distance between their cabins.

Lowry stood on the porch for just a moment, then bounded down the porch steps, whistling cheerfully as he climbed into his pickup. He revved the engine a little too much, then drove away.

Zack stayed in his dark corner a few moments longer, wondering when he could safely get up and go inside without her hearing him. He was still mulling it over when her door opened again and she peeked her head out.

"You can come out now. He's gone," Zack called softly. He only meant to tease her a little, but he immediately realized he had made a severe miscalculation in judgment

His old man always warned him not to yank a barn cat's tail unless he was in the mood for some damn good scratches.

With both hands, she shoved open her screen door the rest of the way then marched down her steps and up his until she loomed over him, angry tension in every tight line of her body.

"How was the show?" she snapped. "See anything interesting while you were lurking out here in the dark?"

He leaned back in the rocking chair with a grin. "To be honest, it didn't look real thrilling from here. But then, I wasn't the one with Lowry's tongue down my throat, either."

The sound she made was somewhere between a growl and a cussword. "What are you doing out here, Slater?"

He shrugged. "Can't a man sit out on a warm summer evening and just enjoy the night?"

"You have no right to spy on me."

He assumed an injured tone. "Spy? Why would I want to do that?"

"Beats me. Why do you do anything? Why come back to Star Valley in the first place? Why go to so much trouble to buy the Lost Creek? Why force me to stay and work for you?"

Because I'm still crazy about you, after ten years. He heard the words in his head and shifted in the rocking chair, swallowing them back.

"I like it here," he muttered. "I've always liked it here."

"No. It's more than that. You're up to something. Why not just admit it and tell me what it is you want?"

What would she say if he told her what he wanted was to pull her into his lap right now and show her a real kiss, not that thing Lowry gave her?

Since he was pretty sure she wouldn't appreciate it,

he opted to change the subject. "How was your date?" he asked instead.

She was quiet for a moment, her eyes narrowed as she studied him. "Fine. The musical was good."

"And the company?" he couldn't resist asking.

"None of your business, Slater."

Every instinct in him warned him to hold his tongue, but his next words slipped out, anyway. "I thought I told you it wasn't a good idea to go out with him."

"And I thought I told you I don't give a damn what you want. Good night, Slater."

She whirled to go, but he reached out and grabbed her arm before she could march back down the steps. "Just be careful around him, okay? I don't think he's the nice guy everybody seems to think."

She slid her hand from his loose grasp. "You've been gone for ten years, Zack. You don't know Wade at all. And you don't know me, either."

He watched her walk back into her cabin then purposefully move about the place yanking every curtain closed.

That barn owl hooted again but this time there was no answering call.

The silence made him feel more alone than ever.

She was cutting radishes into flowery garnishes the next afternoon when Jean walked into the kitchen, her gray hair yanked into its regular braid and a smile on her weathered face.

"Hear you went into Jackson with Wade Lowry last night to see a show. Have a good time?"

She sighed. She had answered that very question half a dozen times already that day. Why was it she couldn't even buy a new toothbrush without everybody hearing about it?

"They have a talented group this year, even though

those college kids seem to get younger and younger every year."

"Time marches on, whether we want it to or not."

True enough. Just that morning she had ruthlessly yanked a solitary gray hair from among her short dark cap like a gardener after weeds. Maybe that's why she couldn't seem to shake this black mood. It surely didn't have anything to do with her snoopy next-door neighbor or the insane urge that had come over her the night before to kiss that smirk right off his face.

"Anyway, it was very professionally done," she said, hastily dragging her mind from those dangerous waters. "I was thinking maybe some of the guests might enjoy an outing into town one of these nights. You could probably get a good rate on tickets for a large group."

"Good idea. Maybe I'll try to set something up next week." With a long sigh, Jean settled into a chair and plucked one of the radishes from the tray, then popped it into her mouth.

It was so rare to see the Lost Creek owner—well, the lame duck owner, anyway—sit down for any length of time that Cassie set down her knife and studied her boss carefully.

"Everything okay?" she asked.

Jean shrugged. "Sure. Just fine."

"How are you feeling, really?"

The older woman was quiet for a moment and Cassie ached for the weary frustration flickering through those steely gray eyes. "I won't lie to you. Some days are better than others. Without this damned arthritis I'd feel half my age."

No matter what she might think about Zack Slater, she couldn't forget that Jean really didn't have a choice about selling the ranch to his company. She wasn't sure if he would be ruthless enough to make good on his threat to back out of the sale if she didn't stick it out for a few short weeks, but she couldn't take that chance.

"Just think." She summoned a smile for her friend. "In a few months you'll be in San Diego with your daughter and can take it easy just soaking in the ocean breezes."

A spasm of worry tightened the older woman's features. "I suppose. If everything goes through with Maverick and young Slater."

"Has there been a problem?" Cassie asked carefully.

"Don't know. He's a man who plays his cards pretty close to his chest. Hard to know what he's thinking."

Wasn't that the truth? There was a time she thought she knew him as well as she knew herself. She could see now exactly how foolish and young she'd been. Age had taught her that people could be married for years and still keep a large chunk of their souls to themselves.

"You know," Jean went on pensively, "I couldn't figure out at first why he wanted the ranch, but the more I see him around the place, I think I'm beginning to see it."

Cassie hated the curiosity prowling through her. At the same time she couldn't quite manage to control it. "What have you figured out?"

"I don't think it's about money at all. I think he loves it here. I think maybe he feels he belongs."

Cassie chopped so hard she mangled the pretty little radish flower under her hands. Zack Slater would never belong. Not at the Lost Creek, not in Salt River, not in the entire Star Valley. He couldn't.

Jean was wrong. It had to be the money. He was a greedy opportunist who knew a good deal when he saw it. And if he could find a way to hurt her in the bargain, so much the better.

She opened her mouth to say so but shut it again. She

had no call to hurt Jean's feelings. If the woman wanted to believe Zack's motives for buying the guest ranch were so pure, Cassie didn't have the heart—or the cruelty—to disillusion her.

Besides, after their agreement ended in just three more weeks, he would have no more hold on her than their shared past. What he did wouldn't concern her at all.

"Anyway, the reason I stopped by is to ask how you'd feel about going up with the cattle drive tomorrow. I was planning to go as camp cook but I'm just not sure I can manage it, the way I've been feeling the past two or three days."

The idea held instant appeal. She hadn't gone on an overnight ride into the mountains since the previous fall's roundup at the Diamond Harte. The thought of a night spent breathing clear, high-altitude air seemed exactly what she needed to make some order of her chaotic thoughts.

She could have Matt bring her favorite mare over from the ranch and her pack tent and camping supplies.

"What about the meals here while I'm gone?" she asked, warming quickly to the idea.

"Claire can cover for you. Most all the guests have signed up for the roundup, anyway. I know it's short notice, but it would really help me out."

"No problem." She was already running through possible menus in her head. "I can easily put together all the supplies this afternoon."

Since the roundup would leave before first light in the morning, she spent the rest of the afternoon planning the four meals she would need to fix, then carefully loading the necessary ingredients into large panniers to be carried by two packhorses.

While she worked, eager anticipation curled through

her like black-eyed Susans on a fence, lifting their cheerful faces to the sun.

If nothing else, a trip into the mountains would help put some distance between her and Slater. And maybe a little physical distance would be all she needed to keep the blasted man from invading her thoughts every fifteen seconds.

Cassie stepped back and surveyed her handiwork in the pale early-morning light while the sturdy pack-horses nickered softly to each other and to the other mounts being saddled for the trip.

"Does the load look even to you?" she asked Marty Mitchell, one of the oldest of the Lost Creek wranglers. A horse that wasn't loaded right would tire too quickly on the climb into the mountains.

He spat a wad of chew on the ground. "Far as I can tell. You sure you remembered everythin'?"

"I think so." She did a quick mental inventory. She was probably forgetting something—she usually did on the Diamond Harte cattle drives, anyway—but she had double-checked her list as carefully as possible the night before.

"The dudes are rarin' to go." Marty spat another wad of chew to the ground. She followed his gaze and saw that Jean had been right the night before. While she'd been finishing with the packhorses, most of the Lost Creek guests had shown up and were being matched by one of the other wranglers with appropriate mounts for their riding skills.

"Those two are gonna be trouble," Marty said, pointing to a pair of towheaded twins, a boy and a girl a few years younger than Lucy and Dylan. The twins wore matching Western regalia—vests, chaps and jaunty little red cowboy hats—and looked as if they were ready to come to blows over a pretty black-and-white speckled pinto pony.

As Cassie watched, ready to step in as peacemaker, the girl took matters into her own hands by shoving her foot into the stirrup of the pony they both obviously wanted, gripping the saddle pommel and mounting up before her brother had a chance to blink.

Cassie grinned.

"You would appreciate such a dirty trick," a low voice murmured in her ear. In an instant her blood turned to ice and then just as quickly to molten fire.

She whipped her head around, and dread clutched her stomach when she saw Slater leading one of the Lost Creek geldings, a big, muscular blood bay. Zack wore jeans, a denim jacket and a battered Stetson, and the horse he led was outfitted just like the others, with a bedroll, tent and all the supplies a person would need for an overnight stay in the mountains.

She found herself made speechless by the implications.

He *couldn't* be going on the cattle drive. Fate wouldn't be that cruel to send the two of them into the same circumstances that had brought them together in the first place a decade ago.

How could she possibly spend two days with him in the mountains? She couldn't. Her mind raced around in circles trying to figure out a way to escape the inevitable.

Even as she wildly examined her options, she knew she had no way to get out of it. She was trapped, just as surely as a wildcat treed by a pack of hounds. She had promised Jean she would do it and she couldn't back out now. Her assistant couldn't handle the trip on such short notice, and she had seen by the trembling exhaustion on her friend's face the day before that Jean simply wasn't up to it.

It was far too late in the game to find anyone else.

Had Jean known Slater planned to ride along? Or had he only decided to join the expedition when he found out she was going, as part of his general plan to torment her?

"What's the matter? You look surprised to see me."

Surprised was far too mild a word. *Horrified* fit much better. "Doesn't the owner and CEO of Maverick Enterprises have far more important things to do with his time than go with a bunch of greenhorns on a mock cattle drive?"

"I can't think of a one," he answered with a small smile and a funny look in those hazel eyes.

He held her gaze for just a moment longer than necessary, until heat soaked her cheeks and she had to look away. Her gaze landed on his mouth, and for one crazy instant she could remember nothing but their brief kiss the week before on her porch.

Not just that kiss, but a hundred others. Slow, drugging kisses that sent her blood churning through her veins. Quick ones that made her heart flutter like a trapped bird in her chest.

Once she had known that mouth as well as her own, had tasted every inch and savored every curve and hollow.

Her insides trembled in remembered heat. She closed her eyes, willing him to disappear. When she opened them, he was—to her everlasting regret—still standing beside her, reins held loosely in his hands and looking as gorgeous as ever.

"If you need some suggestions for what to do with yourself, I can come up with plenty," she snapped.

His grin only added to his looks, she was disgusted to admit. "I'm sure you could, sweetheart," he answered, then swung into the saddle with a power and grace that left her a little light-headed.

It was going to be a very long two days.

* * *

She tried her best to pretend Zack Slater didn't exist throughout most of the day.

It wasn't easy, especially since she and her string of packhorses brought up the rear of the haphazard group that stretched along the wide trail like worry beads.

From back here, she had an excellent rear view of him riding ahead of her. Not that she was paying the least bit of attention. She most certainly was not. But if she *had* been, she might have had a hard time not observing how the blasted man still sat in the saddle as if he had been born there, loose and easy and natural.

She didn't notice, though. Any more than she saw the way the bright summer sun gleamed off that tawny hair under his hat like August wheat or the way his smile flashed at something one of the Carlson twins said to him or the way her breath seemed to catch in her chest every time he turned around and speared her with a hot look from those murky gold-flecked eyes.

He didn't exist, she reminded herself. Instead of focusing on him, she tried to turn her attention to the thrill of a cattle drive—even a light version like this one, where there were almost more drivers than cattle.

The Lost Creek guests loved this, living out their own version of the movie *City Slickers.* Jean didn't keep a big herd at the Lost Creek, maybe one hundred and fifty head. Not like the Diamond Harte, with its herd four times that size.

Jean moved her Herefords only about twenty at a time. Half the summer was spent moving them up to higher ground, the other half bringing them back to the ranch in small groups so that guests throughout the season had the opportunity to participate in a cattle drive.

The formula seemed to work, to the exhilaration of all—except maybe the somewhat bewildered-looking cattle.

It was exciting, Cassie had to admit. Even though she had always participated in the Diamond Harte roundup on a much more massive scale, this was still fun—the bawling of the cattle, the creak of saddles and jangle of tack, the barking of the three low-slung cattle dogs who did most of the actual work.

What was there not to enjoy? They were on a wide trail—a Forest Service fire road, really—surrounded by spectacular scenery: fringy Douglas firs, white-trunked aspens with their pale-green leaves fluttering in the breeze, and wild carpets of wildflowers spreading out in every direction.

She breathed in the scent—of horse and sagebrush and mountains. It was a smell so evocative of summer she had to smile. Oh, she had missed this. She wasn't going to let Slater ruin her delight in something she had always loved.

She was so busy trying not to pay attention to him that she didn't notice that he'd pulled away from the rest of the group until he was coming toward her.

She stiffened in the saddle enough that Solidad grew fractious, both at Cassie's sudden tension on the reins and at the presence of the big bay Slater rode.

"Easy, girl," she murmured, but she wasn't sure if it was a message aimed more at herself or at her mare.

Now beside her, Zack gestured toward the ranch guests whooping and hollering and yippy-cay-aying. "Not quite like a Diamond Harte cattle drive, is it?"

She looked for derision in his eyes, in his voice. To her surprise, she found none, just genuine enjoyment. It reminded her of what Jean had said the day before about his motives for acquiring the ranch.

"It's what keeps people paying the big money to stay at the Lost Creek and all the other dude ranches like it. Traditions like this and the romance of the Old West."

"It's not hard to understand why the ranch is such a success. Who wouldn't enjoy this?"

How in the heck was she supposed to ignore him when he flashed that smile in her direction?

She tried not to acknowledge the heat sizzling through her or the way her legs suddenly trembled in the stirrups.

"I figured the kind of slick, high-dollar guests Maverick Enterprises is planning to bring in probably won't have time to bother with something as noisy and smelly as an old-fashioned cattle drive. What with all those facials and massages, right?"

She heard her words, snippy and childish, and wanted to yank them back, but they lay between them like the rocks strewn across the trail.

He tipped his Stetson back and speared her with a glittering look. "Is that what you think? That I'm going to turn the place into some kind of ritzy spa?"

"How should I know? It's not my business, anyway. A few more weeks and I'm gone."

That funny look appeared in his eyes again. He opened his mouth, but she had the feeling he changed his mind about whatever he was going to say and chose another topic instead.

"I like the Lost Creek just the way it is," he said after an awkward moment. "I wouldn't have decided to buy it otherwise. Once my company takes over, I don't expect we'll make many changes."

She pondered that surprising snippet of information while they rode abreast through the dust kicked up by the small herd a hundred yards ahead of them now.

She wanted to study him, to gauge his sincerity, but she wasn't exactly sure she trusted herself to spend too much time looking at him.

Riding so easily in the saddle in his battered Stetson

and Western clothes, this man seemed to have appeared right out of her memories. It was too easy to forget old heartaches and pretend she was riding once more beside the lean, hungry cowboy she had loved so fiercely.

No. She wasn't going to think about that. Casting about for another topic of conversation, she remembered what Jean had said the day before. "What made you decide to buy the ranch?" she asked, before she'd really had time to think the question through.

He frowned as if disconcerted by the question. "What do you mean?"

"There are probably a dozen other guest ranches for sale across the West. Why the Lost Creek? Why come back to Star Valley after all this time?"

He was quiet for a moment, then tilted his head and studied her, his eyes as bright as jade under the shade of his hat. "You haven't figured it out yet?"

She blinked at him, suddenly wary. "Figured what out?"

The power of his smile snatched the breath right out of her lungs. "I came back for you, Cassidy Jane."

Before she could absorb the sheer stunning force of his words, a confused dogie broke away from the main herd and headed into the sagebrush. Zack spurred the big bay and took off after it.

She watched him go, not sure whether she should be furious at his shocking admission.

Or scared to death.

Okay, he'd screwed up. Big-time.

At their campsite on the shore of a small mountain lake rimmed by sharp, white-capped peaks, Zack split his time between helping the Lost Creek wranglers as they set up camp and sneaking little looks at Cassie preparing the evening meal.

He knew he was staring at her but couldn't seem to help himself. She moved like water—graceful and smooth and fluid.

And every time she caught him looking at her, she flushed brighter than the red-hot embers of the campfire.

He had made a tactical error of major proportions. He never should have opened his big mouth about his true reasons for coming back. He should have just bided his time, let her get to know him again. See if, by some miracle, she might be able to trust him again.

Now she was jumpier than a grasshopper on a hot sidewalk.

He hadn't meant to tell her so bluntly, but the truth had just slipped out when she'd asked him why he returned to Star Valley.

Well, part of the truth, anyway.

How could he tell her he had never stopped loving her? How the memory of those few months he'd spent with her had been burned into his mind and had set the course for his entire life?

By the world's standards he was a successful man. He had money, he had power, he had influence. The dirty, white-trash kid in hand-me-downs had yanked himself up by the proverbial bootstraps and made something of himself.

Ten years ago he was nothing. Or that's what he felt like, anyway. Now when he walked into a room, people sat up and took notice.

But it wasn't enough. Nothing he did had ever seemed enough since he'd left Star Valley and Cassidy Harte.

She didn't want to hear that from him. He had seen the shock in her eyes. Hell, it went beyond shock. Her pupils had widened with something close to horror.

Could he blame her? A decade ago he had left her heart shattered, the subject of gossip and speculation.

Zack knew what small towns could be like; his father had carted him through enough towns from Montana to Texas. He knew damn well how the scandalmongers had probably circled around her like a howling pack of wolves, just waiting their turn to gnaw at her.

She had every reason to be bitter.

He was crazy to think he could make right in just a few precious weeks what he'd done to her. How could he make her see past his desertion and the terrible wrong he had unwittingly done her by leaving the same night as Melanie?

He might have had a chance if people thought he'd just taken off, gotten cold feet and wandered off to greener pastures. After all, he was the son of a drifter, a rambling man.

But there was Melanie. It was a far different matter for everyone to believe he'd taken her along for the ride.

Where *was* the blasted woman? he wondered again. He had already contacted the discreet team of private investigators he used to see if they could get a lock on her current whereabouts.

If he could find her, she could corroborate his story—that they hadn't run off together and it was just lousy timing that they'd both decided to leave Salt River on the same night.

So far the investigators had come up dry. They couldn't seem to find any trace of her after she left the Star Valley.

Anyway, even if he managed to locate her and somehow drag her here, what reason would Cassie have for believing Melanie, anyway, when she obviously had no inclination to think *he* was telling the truth?

With a sigh he finished hammering the final tent stake and stood back while two of the Lost Creek wranglers quickly shoved in the poles and erected the structure.

"Thanks for your help, Mr. Slater. I think we can handle it from here." Like everybody else, Kip Dustin, the lead wrangler, couldn't seem to look him in the eye as he offered the words.

Zack ground his teeth at the "Mr." business. All the wranglers—hell, all the employees of the Lost Creek—teetered on an awkward, precarious line, torn between loyalty to Cassie and showing proper respect for their new boss.

"Call me Zack," he ordered.

"Yes, sir," the wrangler mumbled, his big ears going red under his slouchy felt Stetson.

He didn't want to make the man uncomfortable. He only wanted to be clear that he didn't expect to be treated any differently from the rest of the guests on the trip.

One of the other wranglers called out a question to Dustin about a couple of the horses, and the man escaped with alacrity to answer it.

With most of the work setting camp finished, Zack was left with little else to do. While they waited for the evening meal, some ranch guests had headed down to the small mountain lake to fish with tackle supplied by the ranch. Since he hadn't brought along waders or his own custom-built fly rod, the idea of drowning a worm didn't hold much appeal.

Others were holed up in their tents, probably stretched out on their sleeping bags as they tried to relax sore muscles unused to spending a hard day's work in the saddle.

He knew if he retired to his tent, he wouldn't be able to think of anything but the woman twenty feet away who was bustling about cooking. He'd rather sit here and watch her, he decided, and settled back against a tree trunk.

He loved looking at her.

With her face a little rosy from the sun and her short cap

of dark hair tousled from the breeze, she looked sexy and mussed, like she'd just come from a lover's arms.

He closed his eyes while memories haunted him of watching her sleep tucked against him, her breathing deep and even and a soft smile on her face as she nestled closer.

She had loved him so generously, without reservation, throwing her whole heart and soul into it. The first time he had kissed her, in the hushed silence of the night on that other long-ago cattle drive, she had looked at him with dazed delight in her eyes.

"Wow!" she had said in a breathless voice. "So that's what all the fuss is about."

He remembered laughing roughly and giving her another light kiss on the tip of her nose. After she had gone inside her tent, he had stood outside for a long time under the moonlight studying the vivid red marks on his palms where his nails had dug into skin to keep from devouring her.

He opened his eyes, chagrined to realize he had clenched his hands into fists again just at the memory.

He jerked his mind from the past and saw that the Carlson twins, Maddie and Max, were now pestering her at the camp cookstove, apparently bored with fishing.

Their parents were among those resting in their tent. He suspected it had more to do with taking a short break from the twins' incessant chatter than with aching muscles.

He sympathized with them. The twins were two ferocious bundles of energy. Their blond curls that had looked so shiny and clean that morning were now coated with dust, and they each had pink cheeks that would probably be a full-fledged sunburn in the morning.

They looked hot and dusty and cranky. He rose with some vague idea of rescuing Cassie from their clutches, though he didn't have the first clue where to begin.

As he drew closer he could hear them bickering about who would be able to eat more peach cobbler. Cassie stepped in before the argument could get more heated. "I could use a couple of strong hands to bring me more water from the spring to purify. There might be a cookie reward in it. Anybody interested?"

They both jumped at the chance, bickering now about who could carry more water without spilling it. She handed them each a blue-speckled enamelware coffeepot, and they rushed eagerly down the trail toward the cold spring at one end of the lake.

"That ought to keep them occupied for fifteen minutes or so," he murmured.

Her shoulders stiffened and she looked up at his approach. "I can only hope."

"You're good at that."

She raised an eyebrow. "Cooking Dutch-oven potatoes? I've had plenty of practice."

"I meant with the kids. You're a natural."

"I've had plenty of practice with that, too."

He was confused for a moment, then remembered. "That's right. You helped your brother with his little girl. Lucy, right?"

"Yes." For a moment he thought she might have forgotten his presence. Her mouth curved into a wistful little smile while she peeled and sliced potatoes in a steady rhythm. She was so preoccupied that she didn't seem to notice when he picked up another knife and began doing the same.

"Is she as much of a handful as those two?" he asked after a moment of working beside her.

The smile became more pronounced. "She was always the sweetest little girl. So loving and eager to help. She still is, but now that she has Dylan for a stepsister and partner in crime, I have a feeling Matt and Ellie are in for one heck of a wild ride."

"You miss her, don't you?" he asked quietly.

Her hands went still. "Why would I miss her? I see her all the time. Every Sunday at least, when we all get together for dinner."

Though she spoke with casual acceptance, he thought he saw a deep ache in her eyes. This was boggy, tricky ground, made even more treacherous by her stubborn refusal to listen to him about Melanie. Still, he longed to comfort her. Or at least to acknowledge her pain.

"It's not the same, is it?"

"No. It's not the same." She was quiet for a moment, the only noise the solid thunk of the knife slicing through a potato. Her expression softened, her columbine-blue eyes turned thoughtful. "For nine years she was my child in everything but name. I taught her to read and to do cartwheels and to always tell the truth. I suppose in some ways she'll always be the daughter of my heart."

The softness vanished as suddenly as it appeared and her movements became brisk, even though he thought he saw just the faintest sheen of moisture in her eyes. "Anyway, now she has Ellie and Dylan. The four of them are a family. A wonderful family. And Ellie couldn't be a better mother to both girls."

His heart twisted for her, for those tears she wouldn't shed. Despite her brave talk, it couldn't have been easy to leave the Diamond Harte. To leave the child she had nurtured and loved for ten years into another's care.

He knew all about walking away and how it could eat away at a person's soul.

He almost reached out and pulled her into his arms, but he knew she wouldn't welcome the sympathy or the gesture. "She was lucky to have you," he murmured.

The sloshy ground he'd been worried about suddenly gave way. Her gaze narrowed as she seemed to remember who, exactly, she was talking to. "I didn't have much choice. Thanks to you and Melanie, there was no one else, was there?"

The fragile moment of shared intimacy shattered like a bird's egg toppling from a high tree, and he mourned its loss.

"I didn't leave with her, Cassie. What is it going to take to convince you?" He set down the knife and sighed, more defeated than angry. "I couldn't look at any other woman but you. I still can't."

She hitched in a sharp breath, and for a moment their gazes locked. Awareness bloomed in those blue depths like the carpets of wildflowers they had ridden past earlier in the day.

He wanted to kiss her.

He *had* to kiss her.

The urge to step forward and take her in his arms trampled over him with more force than a hundred bawling Herefords. Before he drew breath enough to move, though, two bickering voices heralded the return of the Energizer Bunny twins.

"We brought your water, Miss Harte," Maddie reported, arms straining to carry the full coffeepot.

Cassie jerked her gaze away from his, her color high. "Thanks," she said to the twins. "I really appreciate your help."

"Max spilled some on the trail but I didn't. I didn't spill a drop."

"Did so," her brother argued.

"Did not! I was way more careful than you."

Because she looked about ready to pour the rest of her water all over her brother—and because he had a feeling Cassie would prefer to dump the other pot on *his* head—

Zack intervened. "I was just going to see how the fish are biting at the lake. Anybody want to come with me and help put the worms on my hook?"

"That's so easy!" Max exclaimed, showing off a couple of empty holes in his grin where a tooth used to be. "My dad showed me when I was just a little kid."

He swallowed his smile at that. "All right. The job is yours, then. Fifty cents for every worm you put on the hook for me."

"Wait!" Maddie exclaimed, not to be outdone by her brother. "I know how to put worms on hooks, too!"

He pretended to consider. "I don't know I think one fishing guide is probably enough."

She looked so disappointed he had to relent. "All right. You can each take turns. And then when we come back, Cassie, here, will fry up all our trout for us, right?"

She sniffed, but he thought he detected just a hint of a smile wrinkling the corners of her eyes. "I'm fixing barbecued chicken and potatoes tonight. If you're in the mood for fish, you can fry them yourself."

He whistled as he walked down to the lake followed by two little chattering shadows. He was making progress with her, he knew it, despite the occasional bumps along the way.

Chapter 7

Hours later Cassie sat on a fallen log at the lakeshore, listening to the darkness stir around her.

Night creatures peeped and chirped, small waves licked at the pebble-strewn shore in a steady, comforting rhythm, and a cold wind whistled in the tops of the pines. All of it was punctuated by the occasional soft slap of a fish leaping to the surface for a midnight snack.

She huddled in her denim jacket, unwilling to face the warm comfort of her sleeping bag just yet even though she knew she was crazy to linger out here in the cold.

The rest of the Lost Creek guests and wranglers had turned in long ago. She had watched the last flashlight flicker out inside a tent at least fifteen minutes ago.

And still here she sat.

A gust of wind whistled down the mountain toward her, and she shivered. If she wanted to sit up all night, she could at least stir the glowing embers of the campfire back to life and enjoy its warmth a little instead of lurking down here at the water's edge alone.

But there was something restful about watching that pale spear of moonlight gleam across the rippled surface of the lake. Something soothing, calming.

Heaven knows, she needed anything peaceful she could find.

She wouldn't be able to sleep. Even as tired as she was after a long day on the trail, she recognized her own restlessness far too well to think she might even have a chance, not with all these thoughts chasing each other through her mind.

And every single one of them centered on the lean, dangerous man sleeping a hundred feet away.

Damn him. Damn him straight to the burning hell he deserved for shaking her up like this. He had no right to say what he had earlier in the day. To mention so coolly that he had come back for her—as casually as if he were talking about the low-pressure system building over the intermountain West or how his favorite baseball team would fare in the conference championships this year.

What did he expect from her? That she could just blink her eyes and make the past disappear, all the heartache and loss and disillusionment she had suffered because of him?

She drew a ragged breath. Why was she letting the blasted man tangle up her thoughts like fishing line jumbled into a pile? Zack Slater could say anything he wanted. He could say he came back to Salt River to plant palm trees down Main Street for all she cared. She felt nothing for him. Nothing but anger and the echo of a long-ago hurt.

She closed her eyes to the night and huddled lower in her jacket. Who was she kidding? A part of her wanted to do exactly that—snap her fingers and make the past disappear. To recapture that magical summer when the world stretched out in front of them, full of joy and promise.

There were invisible ties between them. She had felt them tug at her even over the ten years since she'd seen him last.

Since his return, they wound tighter and tighter, until she was beginning to fear she would never be able to break free.

Maybe it was because he was the only man she had ever slept with. The only one she had ever wanted to be with.

How pathetic was that? She had remained faithful to a man who had deserted her.

Not that she'd ever dreamed he would come back. She had dated in those ten years. Not a lot—she'd been busy with Lucy, after all—but she had been out more than a few times over the years.

But nothing serious. Nothing lasting. She had never made love with any man but Zack Slater.

Her first and her only.

Back then he had been as cautious about intimacy as he was about everything else, wanting to take things slowly. Finally, with the single-minded purpose only an eighteen-year-old girl in love can claim, she had decided to take matters into her own hands.

On her suggestion, they had taken his pickup up the network of dirt roads crisscrossing the foothills overlooking Salt River, looking for the perfect spot to watch the town's annual July Fourth fireworks display. She had packed a picnic of sorts. Fresh strawberries. Crusty French bread. A bottle of wine she had been forced to ask the clerk at the store to pick out for her.

All carefully designed with seduction in mind.

She felt ridiculous that it had come to that, to seducing her own fiancé. They were getting married in less than a month. She had her dress picked out, the flowers had been ordered and she was in the middle of addressing all the invitations.

But while they had done just about everything else together, from sweet, tender kisses to long makeout sessions in his pickup that left them both trembling with need, Zack had stubbornly refused to take things all the way.

He wanted to wait, he said. She had to be sure.

"You're so young," he had said with those rough, callused hands tracing bare skin just above her hip. "I don't want your brothers or anybody else saying you rushed into this just because of this…heat between us."

In those miserable weeks and months after he left, she finally realized that even then he must have been having doubts that he would be able to go through with the wedding. His feet must have already been chilling in his boots even as she set out to remedy her lack of experience.

At the time, though, she had known only the frustration of thwarted desire and had finally convinced herself to take matters into her own hands.

She had loved Zack Slater. Completely and forever. They were going to spend the rest of their lives together and she wanted to take this natural step with him more than anything. So she had packed a thick blanket and her seductive food and suggested they drive above the town lights, where they could watch the fireworks away from the noisy, boisterous crowd.

She closed her eyes now and could see it as vividly as that morning's trail ride.

The evening sky was streaked with purples and reds as the sun began to set in a blaze of glory. After driving around for a while, Zack had finally parked his battered old pickup on a plateau high above the valley.

She sat next to him, her nerves dancing. She wanted to do this. Wanted it more than she wanted her next breath. But she had to admit she was also scared to death.

"Does this look like a good spot?" he asked.

"Yes," she mumbled through a mouth that suddenly felt full of dusty rocks. "I think so."

He spread the thick blanket in the bed of the truck, then

lifted her up easily with those powerful hands that could touch her with such breathtaking tenderness.

He seemed a little distant at first, maybe picking up on her own nervousness, but as the sky began to darken and the stars came out one by one, they both began to relax. They laughed and talked and fed each other strawberries.

When she produced the wine and the plastic cups the clerk at the liquor store had graciously provided, he raised an eyebrow but didn't say anything.

He must see right through her, she thought, a blush scorching her cheeks. All this time she thought she was being so clever, he knew exactly what she was planning.

She knew they would get around to kissing eventually—they couldn't seem to be within a few feet of each other without their mouths connecting. Still, the stubborn man let her set the pace.

She laughed and chatted the way she had every other time they'd been together, even while her insides shivered every time she looked at those hard, chiseled features and felt the heat of his gold-flecked eyes on her.

She was right in the middle of a breathless story about the time she'd been caught skinny-dipping with her friends in the mayor's pond by the mayor and his wife, who had obviously come down to the pond with the same idea, when Zack suddenly yanked her into his lap.

"I can't take any more," he murmured against her mouth, and she tasted wine and the sweetness of the berries. "I've got to kiss you."

"Who's stopping you?" she murmured back, and was rewarded with a fierce, possessive kiss. The shivers in her insides turned to devastating earthquakes of awareness.

That kiss had led to more. And more.

She could remember every second of that night. Every gliding touch, every drugging kiss. Before long, the buttons of her lacy shirt slipped free, and those wonderful hard hands found her unbound breasts.

"No bra tonight?" he murmured against her neck with a surprised laugh.

"It's the Fourth of July," she said on a gasp as his fingers danced across a nipple. "My own little celebration of freedom."

"I'm not sure this is quite what the Founding Fathers had in mind, but hey, I'm as patriotic as the next guy."

Her laugh turned into a gasp when he slid down her body and drew the nipple into his mouth, sending shock waves rippling through her. He had never gone this far and she knew this was it.

While he licked and tasted her skin, desire exploded inside her, building and building until she was afraid she would shatter. Finally she couldn't stand this aching tension. She reached down and cupped his hardness through the thick material of his jeans, her fingers fumbling with the button fly so she could really reach him.

He groaned and shoved against her hand for a moment, then eased away, flopping back on the blanket to stare up at the sky. "Stop. Slow down."

She sat up, her shirt still unbuttoned and her long hair flying loosely around her face. "Why? I'm so tired of slowing down! I love you, Zack. We're going to spend the rest of our lives together. This is right. Why do we have to wait?"

She leaned over him, and this time she kissed him with all the fierce love in her heart. "I love you, Zack Slater," she murmured. "I will never stop loving you."

With a groan, he fisted his hands in her hair and devoured her mouth. Lit by only the moonlight and the last glowing rim of sun streaking the mountains, he quickly removed the rest of her clothing.

Though July, it was chilly at this higher elevation, and she shivered a little as a cool wind kissed her bare skin. But only for a moment. Then he covered her with his hard, muscled body and the shocking, incredible sensation of his naked flesh against hers warmed her completely.

She clutched him to her tightly and kissed him while a thousand sensations burned themselves into her brain. He had been so careful. So gentle. Even though she could feel the need trembling through him, feel the strength of his arousal against her, he still moved slowly.

She was far from naive about what went on between a man and a woman but she wasn't prepared for Zack Slater and that dogged determination of his. He took his dear, sweet time, touching every inch of her skin, until she was ready to weep from frustration.

Finally his hand slid between her thighs, to the slick, aching center of her need. She shattered apart instantly, crying out his name.

While her body still pulsed and trembled, he knelt over her. "Are you absolutely sure, Cass? We can still wait."

She groaned and bit his shoulder hard enough to leave two little crescent-shaped marks. "Yes! I'm positive! Will you just do it?"

With his glittering hazel gaze locked with hers and his hands crushing her fingers, he entered her slowly, carefully, just as the first booming fireworks exploded far below them in town.

They spent the next three weeks finding every opportunity they could to be alone together. Each time they made love was more incredible than the last, and those invisible bonds tightened even more.

And then he'd left.

Something stirred behind her in the brush, and Cassie jolted back to the present, horrified to feel the wet burn of tears in her eyes. She swiped at them with the sleeve of her denim jacket, furious at herself for dredging that all up again and for the low thrum of remembered heat that had burrowed under her skin while she relived those moments in his arms.

With the instincts of one of the small, scurrying creatures of the night, she sensed who was coming long before she saw him. Maybe it was his scent of cedar and sage carried by the breeze. Or maybe it was just the hum and twang of those bonds between them.

Whatever the reason, by the time he broke through the brush to her spot by the lake, all her defenses were firmly in place.

"You should be in bed, Cassie. Aren't you freezing out here?"

"It's not so bad," she answered, relieved that her voice only trembled a little.

The wind whistled through the pines as he stood looking at her. "May I join you?" he finally asked.

No. Go away and leave me in peace. "I was just about ready to turn in."

He reached out as if to touch her arm, then checked the movement. "Stay a moment with me. Please?"

She studied his features, wishing the moon were full so she could see him a little more clearly. Every instinct warned her that lingering here would be dangerous, especially when her thoughts were filled with the remembered passion between them and the feel of his hands upon her skin.

But she couldn't walk away.

Oh, sweet mercy. She couldn't leave. What was wrong with her? She hated Zack all over again for the ache in her throat, the heaviness in her chest. For breaking her heart into tiny jagged pieces, which she still couldn't seem to make fit back together completely.

He sat beside her on the wide log, sending out an ambient heat that seemed to seep through her jacket. She wanted to burrow closer to that warmth, but she knew it wouldn't be enough to thaw the cold that had been inside her for ten years.

They sat in silence for several moments, lost in the night and the past. He was the first to break it.

"I thought I could forget you," he murmured.

She stiffened at his quiet words. She didn't want to hear this. The urge to run back to the safety of her tent was overwhelming, but pride and something else—an unwilling compulsion to know—kept her glued to the log.

"I *wanted* to forget you," he went on. "That was my plan. Move on to the next town, bury myself in hard work and forget all about the Diamond Harte and Star Valley and the pretty blue-eyed girl with the long brown hair and the smile that could make me feel a hundred feet tall."

"Why?"

The word was wrenched out of her, and she hated herself for asking it and hated him more for forcing her to ask. Why did he want to forget her? Why had he left in the first place?

"Survival," he answered, his voice grim. "It was sheer torture remembering those nights I held you in my arms. Remembering all the dreams we made together and the future we planned. Somehow I ended up on the rodeo circuit. Those first few months after I left, I think I probably spent more time in the bottle than sober."

She pictured him ten years younger, desperate and drunk. "If you were so miserable, why didn't you just come back?"

"I almost did a hundred times. But I knew nothing had changed. I was still the wrong man for you."

She bit her tongue to hold back the bitter words that wanted to flow out like vinegar from a spilled bottle.

"I tried my damnedest to forget you. But I couldn't. For ten years I remembered the way you always smelled like wildflowers. The way you tucked your hair behind your ear when you were concentrating on something. The way your mouth would soften like warm caramel when I kissed you."

He finished on a murmur, his voice just a hush, barely audible above the wind. The low timbre of it reached deep inside her, plucking at those strings only he had ever found.

She shivered, not from the cold this time but from a slow, achy heat she didn't want to face.

"Is that supposed to matter to me?" she snapped, to cover her reaction. "That once in a while you spared a thought for the stupid, naive girl you left behind?"

"Not only once in a while. Much more often than that."

She drew in a shaky breath. "Slater, you could have tattooed my name across your forehead for all I care. It still wouldn't change the basic fact that you left."

His mouth tightened. "I had reasons. I told you that. At the time it seemed like the best decision all around."

"Oh, right. I almost forgot. Salt River's evil drug cartel that was going to arrange things so you were thrown in jail."

"Damn it, Cassie. I'm telling the truth. I was threatened with exactly that. Ask yourself this. How would you have faced your friends, your brothers, if the man you planned to marry went to prison?"

"We'll never know, will we?"

He opened his mouth as if to say something, then snapped it shut again. An uneasy silence descended between them again, and he picked up a stone and skipped it into the lake, where it bounced five times, one more than her own personal best. Where the stone hit water, ripples spread out in ever-widening circles that shimmered in the moonlight.

"I figured you'd be long married by now to some prosperous rancher," he finally said. "Even though that was what I wanted for you, I hated picturing you with a house and a husband and a pack of kids."

She had to close her eyes at the raw note in his voice. She wouldn't let him get to her. She couldn't.

"When I found out you never married, that you were working at the Lost Creek, I realized I had to come back to find out why."

Why had she never married? Because no one else had ever asked her. Maybe someone might have if she hadn't always constructed an invisible wall of protection around her wounded heart that no man had ever been able to breach.

"Wait a minute." Her attention finally caught on his words. "How did you find out I never married?"

In the moonlight she thought she saw his color change slightly, and he refused to meet her gaze, looking out at the water instead.

Finally he shrugged. "I sent out private investigators. You weren't very hard to find."

Of course she wasn't hard to find. She had never gone anywhere. All her life, the only time she had been beyond a hundred-mile radius of Star Valley was the time she and Lucy spent a week with Matt at a stock show in Denver.

She hadn't been anywhere, hadn't done anything, hadn't lived beyond the insular world she had known all her life. The world had marched on in the last ten years—just look at how much Slater had changed while she had stayed behind, forever frozen in ice.

Waiting for him.

No. No she wasn't. She denied it vehemently. She had

done what she had to do, stayed and raised her niece and helped her brother. She couldn't regret that.

She loved it here. She had a good life. Good friends, her family. Once she bought Murphy's in town, she would have everything she had ever needed.

Still, her face burned and she wanted to press a hand to the sudden slippery self-disgust flipping around in her stomach like one of those trout.

It was far easier to focus her anger at him. "You sent hired dogs after me?"

He grew still, his eyes suddenly cautious over her tone. "Cassie—"

"Am I supposed to be flattered by that?"

"You're not supposed to be anything."

"So that's why Maverick decided to buy the Lost Creek. You found out the ranch was for sale and figured maybe I was, too."

"No. Of course not."

"I don't care how much money you have, Slater, and I never did. You're the only one who cared about that. If you bought the ranch with some crazy, misguided idea that I would fall back into your arms, you've wasted your money."

Now she wasn't cold anymore. She was burning up, an angry inferno, and she embraced the heat. She only prayed it would blaze hot enough that the little part of her still clinging to the past would burn away into cinders.

She rose and glared at him. "I was stupid enough to fall for you once, Slater. You can be damn sure I won't make the same mistake again."

She whirled and marched away, leaving him sitting by the small mountain lake, watching after her.

Chapter 8

Zack lay in his sleeping bag, watching his breath puff out in little clouds in the cold predawn air.

He hadn't slept more than an hour or two all night, and those had been restless, tortured with dreams of her. In one, she had been standing above him on a high glassy tower flanked by hundreds of giant steps, each taller than he was. Every time he tried to hoist himself up and managed to make it within a few steps from her, she moved a little higher up the tower.

Forever out of reach.

The dream's symbolism didn't escape him. He huffed out a breath, grimly aware that he'd messed this whole thing up from the day he came back. What had seemed like such a great idea in Denver—doing everything he could to persuade her to give him another chance—now seemed quixotic in the extreme.

How could he undo the past? Even if he had the power to do so, she wouldn't let him close enough to try healing the wounds his desertion had inflicted on her spirit.

His presence here was torture for both of them. He was beginning to see that. She wanted him to leave so she could get back to the life she had made for herself.

And he wanted to stay so badly he ached with it.

He should just give up. Cut his losses and go on back to Denver. Every time he considered it, though, he remembered the way she had responded to his kiss earlier in the week. The way she shivered if they accidentally touched. The color that climbed her cheeks whenever she caught him looking at her, as he knew he did far too often.

She wasn't immune to him. She'd be lying if she said she was. Even if her mind and her heart couldn't see beyond his past sins, her body was more than willing to forgive and forget.

If only he could manage to convince the rest of her that he deserved that forgiveness.

Or convince himself.

He sighed and rolled over just as he heard the zip and rustle of someone climbing out of a tent nearby.

Cassie.

It had to be. As camp cook she was probably trying to get a head start on breakfast before the rest of the guests and wranglers woke up.

Without stopping to debate the wisdom of confronting her again so soon after their encounter the night before, he moved quietly. He slipped his jeans on over the thermals he'd been wise enough to pack, grateful once more that he had remembered how cold it could get in the Wyoming mountains, even in June.

He shoved his boots on quietly, then grabbed his denim jacket and Stetson.

Outside in the frosty mountain air, he saw her crouched at the fire ring, busy trying to coax the embers back to life She wore a forest-green ranch coat but her head was bar her short-cropped dark hair tousled and sexy from sleep. He imagined it would probably look exactly like that after making love all night.

A low groan rumbled in his chest as his unruly body stirred at the mental image. After a moment of fierce concentration, he managed to force it away and offered what he hoped was a harmless smile.

If he expected a smile in return—or any sign at all that she was happy to see him—he was doomed to disappointment. She glowered but went back to work trying to kindle a blaze.

Undeterred, he stepped closer. "Need help?"

For a moment he thought she was going to refuse his offer, then she shrugged and rose to her feet. "Knock yourself out. I need to get some water for coffee."

He took her place, then watched as she grabbed a small bag from inside her tent, then picked up one of the coffeepots. She flipped on a flashlight against the early-morning darkness, then disappeared through the trees toward the lake.

She hadn't left matches for him, he noted with a wry grin. And the embers were as cold as her heart.

Little brat. Did she expect him to rub a couple of sticks together? Joke's on you, sweetheart, he thought, and dug into the pocket of his jacket for his lighter. A few moments later he had a nice little fire snapping to ward off the chill.

A slightly ridiculous sense of pride glowed in him as brightly as the flames while he warmed his hands in the heat emanating from the fire.

When she returned a few moments later carrying the coffeepot filled with water, her hair was wet and under control, her face damp and clean.

A memory flashed through his mind of that first cattle 'rive they went on, the one that had started everything between them. He had been amazed and intrigued that she had somehow managed to stay fresh and clean and pretty even when trail dust covered everyone else in a fine layer.

He had noticed the boss's younger sister long before then—how could he not?—but he had kept those very facts uppermost in his mind. She was the boss's sister. And she was young.

He was far too wise a man to mess up a good job over a girl, no matter how pretty and fresh she might be. Besides that, she was far too young and innocent for a rough man like him.

Still, on the trip he had seen another side of her. She had been funny and gutsy and mature beyond her years. And she had looked at him with a wary attraction in her blue eyes that he had been helpless to resist.

She still looked at him that way, whether she was conscious of it or not. That, more than anything else, kept him in Star Valley when he knew damn well he should have given up and gone back to Denver days ago. As soon as he found out about Melanie.

He shoved his hands in his pockets and approached her at the big four-burner propane camp stove, with its prep counter and griddle. "What else can I do to help?"

"Nothing. Everything's under control here."

Except me, he thought. "Can I get you more wood for the fire?"

She shrugged, which he took as assent. He spent the next few moments gathering a few more armfuls of wood. By the time he returned, the enticing aroma of coffee and sizzling bacon reached him.

None of the other guests or wranglers had ventured out yet, he saw. Cassie still stood at the camp stove, mixing together ingredients for flapjacks, and she barely looked up when he returned to camp. He set the wood atop the dwindling pile and joined her.

He longed to kiss that pink, sunburned nose but he didn't want a spatula covered in batter across his face so he contented himself by just leaning back against a tree trunk and watching her graceful movements.

"Do you remember that first cattle drive we went on together?" he finally asked. "You and your cougar friend?"

She paused for just a fraction of an instant in stirring the pancake mix. "I remember."

"I think that's the moment I fell in love with you," he murmured. "When you faced an angry mountain lion with your chin out and that smart mouth of yours going a mile a minute."

When she returned to the batter, her movements were brisk, almost agitated. "Shut up, Slater."

He moved closer, until he was only a few feet away. She edged away as far as she could without her post at the stove. He was making her nervous, but he didn't care.

He was desperate, fighting for his life here.

"That's when I fell in love with you," he repeated. "On that trip. But I knew even that first time I kissed you by your tent that there wasn't a chance for us. Not then."

"And not now," she snapped.

"I had nothing to offer you. No money, no prospects. Nothing to provide you the future you deserved."

Her eyes were hard blue flames in an angry face. "And just because you're Mr. Big Shot Businessman now, because you have enough money to buy whatever you want, you think that's going to make a difference to me? That I'm shallow enough to care? Are you honestly arrogant enough to think I'll just fall into your arms now that you've so magnanimously decided to return like some kind of damn conquering hero?"

He couldn't keep his hands away from her another second. He reached out and curved a finger along the silky skin under her high cheekbones, aware he was taking the biggest chance of a life filled with risky choices.

"Not because of the money," he said quietly, his heart beating a mile a minute. "Because you never stopped loving me. Any more than I ever stopped loving you."

She froze at his words and stared at him, her eyes huge and stunned. A small, distressed sound escaped her mouth, and he moved faster than that mountain cat she'd confronted to catch it.

He kissed her tenderly, gently, trying to show her the fierce emotions in his heart. At first she remained motionless under the slow assault, then, just when he was beginning to feel a little light-headed from holding his breath, her hands crept around his neck like tiny, wary creatures coaxed out of hiding.

With a hushed sigh, she settled against him, and her mouth softened under his. He wanted to shout in triumph. Wanted to grab her tightly against him and mold her body to his, to devour that soft, sweet mouth.

He didn't want to send her running back for cover, though, so he forced himself to keep the kiss slow and easy while his blood sang urgently through his veins.

She wanted to weep from the tenderness in his kiss and from his words. She wanted the soft, devastating kiss to go on forever while the sun burst above the mountains, bathing them in its warmth. She wanted to stay right there for the rest of her life with his hands cupping her face and his mouth soft and gentle on hers.

When he eased away, both of their breathing came in shallow gasps. "Don't lie to me, Cassidy Jane." His voice was low, compelling, and his hazel eyes gleamed with an emotion she didn't want to acknowledge. "No matter what happened ten years ago, you still have feelings for me, don't you?"

She blinked at him as reality came crashing back. Dear heavens. He was right. She did. Part of her had never stopped loving him, even when she hated him.

Heat soaked her skin, and she wanted desperately to escape, to hide away until she could come to grips with this horrifying realization. Before she could, she heard two high-pitched voices already bickering, then the zip of a tent flap. An instant later the Carlson twins burst out into the clearing.

She barely had time to step away from Zack before their mother crawled out of the tent after them.

"Is that bacon? We're starving! When will it be ready? Can we have some?" The twins punched questions at her in rapid succession.

The jarring shift from the sensuous, dreamlike encounter with Zack to the very real demands of two nine-year-olds left her disoriented. She blinked at them for a moment, then quickly composed herself.

She had long practice with hiding her feelings, after all. Even from herself.

"Yes, it's bacon. And if you each wash your hands with one of those wet wipes, I might let you snitch a few pieces now, before breakfast."

The next hour passed in a rush as she prepared pancakes and hash browns and pound after pound of bacon to feed sixteen people. She welcomed the hard work, grateful for something to keep her mind away from Zack and the stunning truth he had forced her to finally admit to herself.

While she was occupied with cooking and cleaning up breakfast and then reloading the food supplies, the Lost Creek wranglers broke camp. The sun was still low in the east when the group began the trail ride back to the ranch.

Without the excitement of the cattle to prod along, the

guests were far more subdued during the ride back. Even the dogs plodded along without much energy.

Cassie didn't mind. She had far too many thoughts chasing themselves through her mind to concentrate on anything but a slow, easy ride down the wide trail.

After that cataclysmic kiss, Zack's low words had unleashed a flood of emotions that still whirled and cascaded through her. She thought she had been able to exorcise him from her heart after he'd left. But with just a few words, he had shown her how foolish and naive she was for clinging to that notion.

She still loved him. Had never stopped. Now what was she supposed to do about it?

Absolutely nothing, the cautious side of her warned. She couldn't afford to do anything about it.

"You know who he is, don't you?"

Cassie hadn't noticed Amy Carlson, the twins' pretty, frazzled-looking mother, had fallen behind the rest of the riders and was riding abreast of her. The twins were up closer to the line, being closely monitored by their father and a couple of the wranglers.

She followed the woman's gaze right back to Zack riding ahead of them in that loose-limbed way of his and felt a blush climb her cheeks as she realized she must have been staring at him.

"Who?" she asked, pretending ignorance.

Amy made a fluttery gesture with her hand. "Mr. Gorgeous. Zack Slater. I just about died when I recognized him at the ranch the first night we arrived, eating in the dining hall just like the rest of us mortals."

"I know who he is."

"Besides being every woman's secret fantasy, the man is close to a legend in Denver," Amy went on. "Every single thing he touches seems to turn to gold. I read a piece on him in the business section of the *Post*. It was fascinating stuff."

She had always thought him fascinating, even when he'd been a rough-edged ranch hand. Though she suddenly discovered she desperately wanted to hear about the life he had made for himself, she didn't want to appear too obvious. "Really?" she asked blandly.

Amy didn't appear to need much encouragement. "He keeps to himself for the most part. Reclusive, almost. I never see his picture on the society pages. But he has this really gorgeous apartment in Denver and a big ranch in western Colorado. According to the reporter at the *Post*, although he keeps it a secret, he's also a big-time philanthropist who gives huge amounts of money to all kinds of pet projects. A couple of alcohol rehab centers. The children's hospital in Denver. A mentoring program for kids living in abusive situations."

Alcohol rehab centers? Abused children? The little crack in her heart widened even further.

Zack had never wanted to talk much about his childhood, even when they were engaged. He had no family left, she knew that. His mother had died of cancer when he was six and his father hadn't taken her death well. From what she had pieced together, Zack's father had packed up his little boy and carted him from ranch to ranch across the West, never staying long in one place.

Zack had finally struck out on his own when he was just fifteen, although he had never told her why he dropped out of high school or left his father somewhere in Montana.

He had mentioned one time, almost in passing, that his father used to drink too much. She wondered now if his father had been a mean drunk. If he had taken his frustrations with life out on his son.

Was that the reason Zack had preferred the hardscrabble life of a rambling cowboy to staying with his father?

She wanted to rub a hand at the sudden ache in her chest for that young boy. He had passed a high school equivalency test before she met him, she knew, but it had still bothered him that he hadn't graduated in the traditional way or gone on to college.

He had considered himself uneducated, rough.

She thought of what he had said the night before, that he hadn't been the kind of man she deserved a decade ago.

She hadn't cared a thing about his education level or his bank balance. She had loved his solid core of decency, his honor and his sense of humor. His inherent kindness. The way she always felt cherished and protected in his arms.

A hundred things about him were far more important than what he had or had not accomplished with his life.

But with stunning clarity she finally realized that the things she had considered inconsequential had been anything but to Zack.

She jerked her attention back to Amy Carlson and her recital of his success.

"But why am I telling you this?" Amy said with a rueful smile. "You probably know all about the mysterious Zack Slater."

Ten years ago she thought she knew him. Now she wasn't so sure. "Why would you say that?"

Amy sent her a knowing look. "The two of you have something going, right?"

More heat soaked her cheeks. "What do you mean?"

The other woman grinned. "I have the two eyes God gave me, sugar. I saw the way you two were looking at each other this morning before breakfast. You were both putting out enough heat, I was afraid for a minute there you were going to start a forest fire. Besides that, the man hasn't stopped watching you for longer than a few minutes this entire trip. I'll tell you, there are plenty of days

I'd trade both my twins plus my left arm to have a man like Zack Slater looking at me like that."

Cassie barely resisted the compelling urge to see if he was watching her now. "You're mistaken. We don't have a relationship. We…knew each other a long time ago. That's all."

"Well, if I'd had half a chance with a man like him before I met my Paul, you can bet I would have grabbed hold with both hands and not let go for all the pine needles in Wyoming."

That's exactly what she wanted to do, she realized with sudden panic. He was asking for another chance. And, heaven help her, she wanted desperately to give it to him.

But how could she? She wasn't that heedless, optimistic eighteen-year-old anymore—that girl who was confident that everything would work out exactly as she wanted.

Ten years ago she had gone after what she wanted with single-minded purpose. She'd decided she wanted Zack Slater, and she hadn't been about to let anything stand in her way.

Not even him.

She had pushed them both into a relationship, then into an engagement. Maybe if she hadn't been in such a headlong rush—maybe if they had taken more of a chance to build a stronger foundation—he wouldn't have run.

She had been a different person then. What had happened to that reckless, spirited girl who took chances, who embraced every day with boundless excitement and joy?

A few weeks ago she might have said Zack Slater destroyed her when he left.

Now, as she rode along the trail lined with towering spruce and ghostly pale aspen, she faced some grim facts about herself. She had let that girl wither away, until she had become a cold shell of a woman afraid to take any chances for fear of something going wrong.

So terrified of being hurt again that she never let herself dream.

That's why she hadn't made an offer on the café in town yet. Heaven knows, she had enough money from her share of the Diamond Harte revenue over the years that she could have paid cash for the café the day she moved away from the ranch.

Taking the job at the Lost Creek had just been a stall tactic.

She sat a little straighter in the saddle, stunned by the realization. She forgot about the raw beauty of the mountains around her as the cold truth settled in her chest. She had been too afraid of failure, of taking chances. Zack hadn't done that to her. She had done it to herself.

No more. She wasn't going to hide behind the past anymore. Excitement began to churn through her like the creek still swollen with runoff. She was obligated to stay at the ranch for another few weeks, but after that she would start negotiations with Murphy. By the end of the summer she would have her own restaurant.

After her brother's wedding in a month, the cute little rental Sarah lived in would be available. Maybe she could take over Sarah's lease—or even make Bob Jimenez an offer to buy it.

Suddenly the day seemed brighter, the air more fresh. She could do this. She wanted to be that fearless girl again.

And Zack. Did she dare take a chance with him, too?

With her heart pounding hard, she thought of the sweetness of his kiss that morning, the thick emotion in those green eyes. He hadn't been lying when he said he still cared about her.

Trying again with him would take a huge leap of faith. Could she trust him to catch her on the other side?

Zack sat on his favorite chair on the porch watching the stars come out one by one and trying like hell not to spend too much time watching the windows of the cabin next door for an occasional shadow to move past the closed curtains.

What was the matter with him? He was turning into some kind of sick and twisted voyeur, hoping to catch even a glimpse of her. Where was his pride? His dignity?

He didn't have much of either left when it came to Cassidy Jane Harte.

Going along on the cattle drive the day before had turned out to be a complete bust. He was no closer to regaining her trust today than he'd been a week ago when he first arrived at the ranch.

He sighed into the darkness and thought of the stacks of messages Jean Martineau had handed him as soon as they rode back to the ranch. Claudia, his very competent assistant, was frantic to have him back in Denver, with a dozen projects needing his urgent attention. He couldn't keep putting off his return to real life.

He hated to admit defeat at anything, but he was beginning to think this was a battle he couldn't win.

The thought left an acid taste in his mouth. The future stretched out ahead of him, stark and lonely and colorless, but he didn't know what else he could do to change it.

If only he could find Melanie. But one of the messages from Claudia contained another worthless report from his P.I. So far it looked as if the woman had either changed her name and moved out of the country or had been abducted by aliens.

He was betting on the aliens at this point.

Either way, he figured he was damned. If he couldn't find her, Cassie would have to take his story on blind faith. He couldn't see that happening anytime soon.

The only bright spot about the cattle drive had been the way she'd responded to his kiss that morning. He had seen awareness and some deeper emotion flicker in her eyes before she had shielded them with her lashes and surrendered to him.

He shifted in the chair, remembering the sweetness of her mouth and the fluttering of her hands against his chest. She hadn't been exactly bubbling over with enthusiasm during the kiss—hadn't participated much at all, really—but she hadn't poured hot coffee on him, either. That had to count for something, right?

And a few times on the ride down the trail, their gazes had met and he thought he saw something else there besides anger and disdain. A different light. Softer, somehow.

No. That was probably only wishful thinking on his part. He hadn't seen her since they arrived back at the ranch several hours earlier, when she had treated him with the same cool reserve.

Her porch light suddenly flickered off, leaving only a soft glow through the window. Damn. Now she was going to bed before he had a chance to come up with any kind of half-rational excuse to knock on her door in the middle of the night.

He should do the same. He hadn't slept much all week, and his muscles ached from two days in the saddle. Still, something kept him planted here, watching the stars and regretting the past.

With a sigh he planted his hands on the armrest of the old rocker and prepared to rise, when he suddenly heard the squeak of hinges. An instant later his breath caught and held somewhere in the vicinity of his throat as she stepped out onto the porch.

Though her porch light and his were both out, he could see her clearly from the soft light still on inside her cabin. Her hair was damp around the edges as if she had just stepped out of the tub, and she was wearing a loose, flowing white cotton robe that glowed iridescent in the moonlight.

He opened his mouth to greet her, then paused for just a moment, struck by the stunning picture she made. Sensual and sweet at once. Wistful and wanton. As he watched her move to the porch railing, he couldn't seem to remember how his voice worked. All he could do was stare, his throat dry, as she leaned out and gazed up at the vast glittering night sky, her attention fixed on the same stars he had watched appear.

What was she wishing for? he wondered. He would give anything to know, to be the man she shared her secrets with.

He couldn't sit here like this, lurking in the corner and watching her in such a solitary moment. Remaining silent was an unconscionable invasion of her privacy.

"Hey," he finally called out, his voice sounding rough and ragged to his ears.

She froze for an instant, then turned toward him with something like resignation in her eyes. "Zack. Isn't it past your bedtime?"

"Probably. The night was too gorgeous to ignore." And so are you, he thought, and unfolded his length from the rocker to go to her. When he joined her at the railing, he was heartened considerably when she moved aside to make room for him.

For a moment they were silent, both contemplating the mysteries of the heavens, then she sent him a sidelong look. "Why do we always keep meeting in darkness?" she murmured.

He was going to say something flip, but stopped and gave her question a little deeper consideration. "Maybe it's easier facing each other and ourselves at night than in the harsh glare of daylight."

She lifted one slim, dark eyebrow. "That's very philosophical, Slater. And surprisingly insightful."

He shrugged. "I'm just chock-full of surprises, Cassidy Jane."

"Yes. I'm beginning to see that," she murmured.

Just what did she mean by that? he wondered. Before he could ask, she spoke again.

"I heard quite an earful about you today from Amy Carlson on the ride down the mountain. She read all about you in the business section of one of the Denver papers, apparently."

"Oh, no." His oath was low and heartfelt.

Her soft laugh drifted over him like imported silk. "It was very educational, I must admit. I never would have pegged you for such a philanthropist."

"Have I just been insulted?" he asked, with an inward curse at the business reporter at the *Post* for being so damned good at his job and ferreting out that closely held secret.

She laughed again. "I don't know. Maybe. Sorry. You know, in all these years, I just never pictured you as a pillar of the community, giving bundles of money away like some modern-day Robin Hood."

He couldn't control the sudden tension rippling through him. He hated talking about this. What the hell was the point of giving anonymous donations if they weren't going to stay that way?

So what if he contributed to a few causes he cared about? That didn't make him any kind of hero. Just a man with astonishing good luck in a lot of ways that seemed hollow and unimportant unless he could share that luck.

He blew out a breath, turning away the conversation before it became any more uncomfortable. "How did you picture me?"

"Oh, plenty of ways. All of them very creative, you can be sure. I believe staked out naked on an anthill some where with buzzards circling around your head was always a personal favorite."

He heard the humor in her voice. But he also heard the thin thread of pain woven through it, like a pale, out-of-place color on a rich tapestry. Regret washed over him again, bitter guilt that he had been the cause of that pain.

He shifted to face her, leaning a hip on the railing. A wild yearning to reach out and caress that face, to touch her soft skin, welled up inside him. He almost did it but checked himself at the last moment, afraid she would shy away from him like an unbroken colt.

"I never meant to hurt you, Cassie. I should have high-tailed it out of Star Valley the minute things started to get serious between us. Before everything went so far."

She didn't answer him, just watched him out of those solemn blue eyes that had always seen deep inside his soul.

"I thought about leaving a hundred times but I couldn't do it. For once in my godforsaken life, something right had happened to me. Something real and beautiful. I was too selfish to give that up—to give you up—even though I knew I would end up hurting you in the end."

"But you did give it up. You left and you never looked back."

"I left," he allowed. "But I've spent every day of the last ten years looking back, Cassie. Knowing I made the biggest mistake of my life walking away from the only woman I have ever loved. And wondering how I could ever make it right with her again."

After he finished speaking, her eyes turned murky and dark. A second later one fat tear slipped out. Dismayed, he stared as it caught the moonlight, wanting to call back whatever he'd done to make it appear.

His Cassie hardly ever cried. He couldn't bear this, the heavy, unforgiving weight of knowing he had hurt her.

Not just once, but a thousand times over the past ten years. Self-disgust filled his chest, his throat, even as he had to force himself not to reach for her.

She didn't want him here. He was only hurting her more every day by his stubbornness.

"Don't cry, sweetheart. Please. I'm sorry. I should never have come back. I'll leave in the morning, I promise. I won't bother you again."

She swiped at the tear and glared at him. "Don't you dare walk away from me again, Zack Slater. Not when I was just trying to gather the courage to give you another chance."

He froze, afraid to believe what he thought he just heard her say. It took every ounce of energy within him to remember to breathe. "You mean that?"

"I must. Why else would my legs be shaking?"

A shocked joy exploded inside of him, fierce and bright and buoyant. He drank in her tousled beauty, wanting to burn every second of this into his brain.

Her smile trembled just a little, like a small, tender wildflower in a mountain breeze. With a groan, he reached out and clasped her face in both hands and lowered his mouth to hers.

He kissed her slowly, reverently, savoring every inch of her mouth. She kissed him back, this time with no hesitation or wariness. Her lips moved under, opened for him.

Welcomed him home.

He wanted to weep from the torrent of emotions gushing through him. This was where he belonged. Right here, with her arms around him and her mouth soft and giving beneath his.

This was where he had always belonged.

Entwining his hands in her sexy little cap of hair, he deepened the kiss. Her breathy sigh of response acted on his already inflamed body like a rush of hot wind on a grass fire.

Her arms pulled him closer, then closer still, until he could feel her soft curves through the thin cotton of her robe. He folded her against him, marveling again at how perfectly they fit together.

Gradually, through the haze of joy and desire engulfing him like coastal fog, he realized she was shivering against him, ever so subtly but enough to make him draw away. "Is that from the cold or from nerves?"

She blinked at him. "What?"

"Your legs aren't the only thing shaking, sweetheart." He looked closer and realized she had come outside with no shoes. The wooden porch slats must be freezing beneath her bare feet.

"No wonder you're trembling. Here, let's get you inside."

He picked her up and opened her door. The soft glow inside came from a trio of slim candles she had left burning on the mantel.

"You didn't have to do that. I'm not helpless."

"I know. You've always been so strong and determined. It's one of the things I love most about you."

Strong? He must have her mixed up with another woman. She had been anything but strong in those days and months after he had left, when she had kept herself from shattering apart only because Matt and poor Lucy needed her.

In the intervening years she had cowered in her safe little life like a rabbit in a hole. And like that rabbit, while she might have felt free from the danger of heartache in that insular world, she had also been slowly starving to death.

Depriving herself of the very things she needed to survive.

Even knowing that—even with the vow she had made to herself that morning—she didn't feel very strong right now. A low, constant fear hummed through her but she refused to give in to it.

The simple truth was, she believed him. About Melanie. About the crime ring he stumbled onto. About how he thought he was doing the right thing for her by leaving.

She would never agree with the choice he had made. But that morning as they had ridden through the mountains where she had fallen in love with him so long ago, she had finally come to understand it.

Maybe he had to leave so that he could finally learn to see himself the way she always had—as a good, decent, honorable man who deserved whatever happiness life had in store for him.

The candles' glow burnished him in gold, catching in his hair and the gold flecks in his eyes. That beautiful, sculpted face she had loved for so long.

She smiled suddenly. She could be stronger than fear. She would be.

She wrapped her arms around his neck and kissed him fiercely. He remained still for one instant then he groaned and dragged her against him, his mouth ardent and demanding as he pressed her down to the plump cushions of her couch.

Eventually kissing wasn't enough. It had been too long and her emotions were too raw, too close to the surface. She gasped when his hand shifted from the skin at her hip until he was barely touching the curve of her breast. Heat pooled in her stomach, in her thighs, and she arched against him.

He groaned against her throat and trailed kisses along her jawline, then back to her waiting mouth while his fingers touched her.

Oh, dear heavens, she had missed him. Missed this. The fire and the closeness and the sweet churn of her blood.

Only with Zack had she ever felt so stunningly alive, and she wanted it to go on and on forever.

His fingers danced over her nipple, and the shock of it was like leaping into an icy mountain lake without testing the waters first. She couldn't seem to catch her breath, and for a moment she was afraid she was in way over her head.

"Zack, stop," she gasped.

The slow torture of his fingers stilled instantly. Wariness crept into his eyes.

"I'm just not…I don't think I'm ready for…for more. Not yet."

He gazed at her for a moment, his eyes glittering, then he drew in a ragged-sounding breath. "I can understand that. I'm sorry. I've just dreamed of touching you for so long."

He stepped back from the couch and raked a hand through his sun-streaked hair. When she saw his hand trembling slightly, she had to admit to a certain completely feminine sense of power.

"Thank you for understanding," she murmured. "We rushed into things before. I don't want to make that mistake again."

"You're right. You're absolutely right." With a lopsided smile he reached out and grabbed her hand and pulled her to her feet. "Slow and easy. I can handle that."

He kissed her forehead and wrapped his arms around her tightly. At the feel of that hard, muscled body against her, she suddenly wasn't so sure "slow and easy" would be enough.

The next week was as close to heaven as she could imagine.

The pace of life in the Lost Creek kitchen didn't slow at all just because she and Zack were busy rediscovering each other. She still put in long hours cooking for the ranch guests, ordering supplies and training Claire Dustin to take over for her.

Zack was busy, too. Although he didn't put it in so many words, she had a feeling his continued absence from his business interests in Denver was causing problems, because a few days after that momentous kiss at her house, he moved his office to one of the extra rooms in the ranch, installing computers, phone lines and a crisp, efficient, somewhat snooty assistant named Claudia.

While she devised menus and tested out recipes, his days were filled with conference calls as he ran his little empire in absentia.

And it *was* an empire, she was coming to realize. It was one thing to know in the abstract that Zack had built his own very successful business from the ground up. It was quite another to watch him in action, with his sleeves rolled up and a pair of wire reading glasses perched on the tip of his nose as he talked on the phone about capital outlays and IPOs.

She had to admit she found the contrast between the rough-edged cowboy she had known and this high-powered executive very sexy.

Even with their respective workloads, they still tried to spend every available moment together. In the past week they had managed to squeeze time to go riding together several times, to take moonlit hikes into the mountains around the ranch, and the night before they had taken a drive through the massive splendor of Grand Teton National Park to have dinner at Jenny Lake Lodge inside the park.

Although they spent long, drugging hours kissing and rediscovering each other, he always stopped before things went too far. While she was touched—and amazed—at his restraint, she was also growing increasingly frustrated.

She was falling for him again, and hard. A part of her still quaked at the thought, but the rest of her couldn't deny that she was happier than she had been since she was that fresh-faced eighteen-year-old girl head over heels in love.

Just now they were on their way to the Independence Day parade in Salt River, set to begin in just under fifteen minutes.

She had almost said no when he'd suggested it after breakfast that morning. Not because she didn't want to go—the small-town parade was usually one of the highlights of her year—but she was fairly sure gossip about poor Cassidy Harte and her long-lost fiancé was still running rampant around town. She wasn't sure if she had the fortitude to face the inevitable stares and whispers.

Small-town life definitely had certain advantages over living in a big city. But the endless buzzing grapevine—where everyone thought they had a God-given right to dabble in everybody else's business—wasn't among them.

Most people in Star Valley still believed Zack Slater had run off the week before their wedding with her brother's wife. What would they think when they saw the two of them together?

Trying not to pay attention to the butterflies step kicking in her stomach, she folded her hands tightly together. She didn't care what anyone said. She was strong. She could handle a few stares and whispers.

If she was going to show up in the middle of the Independence Day parade with Zack Slater, she wasn't going to have much of a choice.

Chapter 9

It wasn't quite as bad as she had feared.

Once they'd walked the short distance from their parking space to the parade route, her nerves had settled somewhat. They still received their share of raised eyebrows, and she could hear more than a few whispers behind their backs. But no one was outright rude to them.

Either Zack didn't notice or he didn't care. He placed a hand at the small of her back as they looked for a spot to watch the parade, both to guide her and to stake his claim, she suspected.

He looked gorgeous, as usual, in weathered boots, faded jeans and a tailored short-sleeved navy cotton shirt that stretched over the hard muscles of his chest. Her mouth watered just looking at him as he set up the folding lawn chairs they had borrowed from the Lost Creek at an empty spot in front of the grocery store.

She settled into the chair and tried to put the murmurs and prying looks out of her mind, content just to bask in the moment.

She enjoyed all of Salt River's little celebrations—from

the summer concerts in the park to the homecoming football game to the Valentine's Day carnival at the elementary school—but the Independence Day parade was always a highlight.

Folks here took their patriotism seriously. They hadn't been sitting for five minutes when one of the elderly American Legion members rushed over with a couple of small flags for them to wave along with everyone else.

Cassie smiled as she took it, scanning the crowd for some sign of her brothers. She couldn't see them and wasn't sure if that little fact relieved her or disappointed her.

Jesse would be busy directing traffic away from Main Street, she remembered. But Matt and Ellie and the girls were probably planted somewhere along the crowded parade route, Sarah watching along with them.

She hadn't seen them in a week. Guilt pinched at her as she realized how isolated she had become from them, how she had ducked out of their regular Sunday barbecue and had declined Ellie's invitation to go to the annual rodeo with them later that night.

Although she winced at the realization, she was too terrified about their reaction if they saw her with Zack. She still hadn't told her family the two of them were in the slow process of renewing their relationship. She couldn't. Not yet.

She might have forgiven Zack for walking away ten years ago but she was fairly certain her overprotective brothers wouldn't be so quick to let bygones be bygones.

Not when it came to Zack Slater.

But since they were nowhere in sight, she didn't have to worry about it right this minute. She had a parade to enjoy.

Half an hour later she was smiling at the antics of a couple of clowns who looked remarkably like Reverend Whitaker and his wife when she happened to glance at

Zack. He was watching her intently, an odd light in his hazel eyes.

Heat soaked her cheeks. "What's the matter?"

He gave her one of those soft, beautiful smiles that made her catch her breath and feel more than a little light-headed. "Nothing. I just like watching you."

What was she supposed to say to that? She could feel more heat crawl up her cheekbones and figured she was probably as red as the stripes on her little flag.

"You belong here, don't you?" he asked quietly.

"Jeppson's? Well, I do spend plenty of time inside yelling out my produce order."

He smiled, then turned serious again. "No, I mean all of it. Salt River. The whole small-town thing. You're very lucky."

"Lucky? Because I've never been anywhere in my life?"

"Because you're part of this and it's a part of you. You belong," he repeated.

She narrowed her gaze, giving him a closer look. That odd light in his eyes was envy, she realized. He was envious of *her?* A woman whose entire life had been spent within a sixty-mile radius? Who couldn't walk a block through town without having to stop and visit with at least three or four people along the way and who had to schedule at least an extra half hour for any shopping trip just because she knew she was bound to run into someone who wanted to chat?

Zack had never had any of that. She was barely aware of the high school band passing by with its enthusiastic rendition of "Stars and Stripes Forever." Instead she remembered his childhood. His drunk saddle bum of a father with the itchy feet, who had dragged his young son from ranch to ranch across the West, never content to stick long in any place.

Zack had gone to nine different elementary schools, he had told her, in six different states.

He had never experienced this. The sense of continuity, of community. Of being inextricably linked with something bigger than yourself. A wave of pity for him crashed over her, and she wanted to gather him close in her arms right there in front of everyone and cradle him against her.

"You belong in Denver now," she offered. "You have a big apartment there and your business. Oh, and your ranch in the San Juans. You belong there."

He was quiet for a moment, then he gave her another of those slow, serious smiles. "I've never felt as much at home in either of those places as I do right here in Salt River when I'm with you."

Unbearably touched, she felt the hot sting of tears welling up in her eyes. She blinked them back and reached across the width between them to place her hand on his where it rested on the arm of his lawn chair. He turned his hand over and clasped hers, and they stayed that way, fingers locked together, for the rest of the parade.

She always grew a little melancholy when the last float passed by, when people gathered up their little flags and their lawn chairs and headed home. It was the same ache that always settled in her chest as she watched the last leaf fall from the big sycamore outside her window at the Diamond Harte at the knowledge that she wouldn't see another until spring.

Where would she be a year from now when the parade again marched down Main Street? Would the man who sat beside her still be a part in her life? Or would he march on just like the parade?

Her chest felt tight and achy at the thought. She knew she was going to have to face that possibility, but right now she didn't want to think about anything beyond the moment.

"So what's next?" he asked as they packed up their own chairs and began the trek back to his Range Rover. "Do you have to hurry on back to the ranch to fix dinner?"

"No. Jean told all the guests they were on their own today. I think most of them were coming into town for the Lions Club barbecue later."

"So you're free for the rest of the day?"

She nodded. "What did you have in mind?"

His grin somehow managed to be mischievous and seductive at the same time, something only Slater could pull off. "Well, if I had a pickup truck, we could always take a picnic up in the mountains later and make out while we watch the fireworks."

An instant image of their first time together flashed through her mind and an answering heat curled through her stomach. Drat the man for stirring her up like this right on crowded Main Street!

"What's that old saying? If wishes were horses then beggars would ride?"

He laughed. "Not a horse. A pickup. I have this sudden, overwhelming compulsion to buy a truck. Where's the nearest dealership?"

"Matt always buys his ranch vehicles in Idaho Falls. It shouldn't take more than an hour to pick out a truck, right? I should think we can make it there and back before the fireworks show with time to spare."

He stopped dead and stared at her. She met his gaze squarely, wondering if he could correctly read the message in her eyes. She was ready to move forward, to take the next step with him. The sooner the better, as far as she was concerned.

"Are you sure?" he murmured, as if he could read her thoughts.

With a slow smile she nodded. An instant later he dropped the folded lawn chairs and yanked her into his arms, right in the middle of town, and lowered his head for a fiery kiss.

She would have stood there all afternoon just basking in the hot promise of that kiss—with no thought at all for where they were and who might be watching—if a carload of teenagers hadn't chosen that moment to drive past honking and catcalling.

With a flustered laugh she broke the kiss. "Whoa." That was the only coherent thought she could put into words.

Before he could answer, she saw his gaze sharpen on something behind her. Fearing one of her brothers had stumbled onto them, she turned and saw with relief that it was only Wade Lowry.

Her relief was short-lived.

Wade stepped forward, his hands clenched into fists and his handsome face twisted with anger. "I heard the rumors but I couldn't believe they were true. How can you stand to be seen with this…this son of a bitch after what he did to you?"

She blinked, stunned by his words, his animosity. A regular churchgoer, Wade hardly ever used profanity. It was so out of character that she didn't know how to answer him.

Why would he be so furious? Was it jealousy? Maybe he thought they had more of a relationship than they did. She went out with him occasionally but she had always tried to be clear that she wasn't interested in anything more serious with him. He was her friend. She hated the idea that she might have hurt him.

"Wade—" she began, but he cut her off.

"He took Melanie away! She never would have left if it hadn't been for him."

She blinked, disoriented by his words. Melanie? This was about *Melanie*? Had Wade been one of the many men ensnared in her sister-in-law's twisted, sticky web of destruction?

She couldn't believe it. The man she knew was far too decent and principled to sleep with another man's wife, no matter how alluring she might be. But the emotions in his eyes told a different story. Of betrayal and loss and something else she couldn't recognize.

"Wade, he didn't leave with Melanie," she said gently.

He turned his anger toward her, and she drew in a shaky breath at the force of it blazing at her. "Of course he did! Everybody knows that! People saw the two of them go. Your own brother saw them leave together!"

Zack stepped forward. "You know exactly why I left town ten years ago, don't you, Lowry? And it wasn't because of some imaginary tryst with Melanie Harte." Zack's voice was sharp, his eyes suddenly as hard as granite.

Wade stiffened. "I don't know what you're talking about."

"I'm sure if you put your mind to it and thought real hard, you could probably figure it out."

"You're crazy. Everybody knows you ran off with Melanie. The only mystery is why a woman like her would be willing to settle for a no-account drifter like you."

"That's what I might have been then," Zack murmured, pure ice against Wade's fiery anger. "But not anymore. Now I have money and power. And a very long memory."

Wade flexed his hands into fists, looking as though he was ready to lash out any second and turn the verbal confrontation physical.

She could just imagine Jesse's reaction as Salt River chief of police if he had to come break up a fight between the two men. She huffed out a breath, furious with both of them—Wade for starting it and Zack for tossing fuel onto the fire.

"This is ridiculous. You two are not going to brawl in the middle of Main Street. Not if I have anything to say about it. I'm sorry you're upset, Wade. I don't know what was between you and Melanie. That's your business. Just as what is between Zack and me is mine."

She didn't give him time to respond, just grabbed on tightly to Zack's arm. "Come on, Slater. If we're going to make it to Idaho Falls and back, we had better hurry."

He looked down at her as if just remembering her presence. With one last stony look at Wade, he opened the door to his glossy Range Rover for Cassie, then climbed in and drove away, leaving the other man standing in the street glaring after them.

They were almost to Tin Cup Pass before she finally lost patience with his continued silence. "Okay. Spill it. What was that all about."

He gripped the wheel. "You tell me. He's *your* boyfriend."

She barely refrained from slugging him while he was driving. "He's my friend. You want to tell me what you have against him?"

He said nothing for several moments while yellow lines passed in a blur. "I'm fairly certain he was one of the men I saw that night unloading that airplane full of drugs," he finally said.

She stared at him. "Wade? You're telling me you think *Wade Lowry* was part of some vicious criminal operation? A drug smuggler? That's impossible! You must be mistaken."

"Why?"

She could give him a hundred reasons. A thousand! Wade was a kind and gentle man. A little stuffy, maybe, but generally considered to be one of the nicest men in own.

She was struggling to put it into words when she suddenly remembered something else. "It's impossible! Ten years ago he was on the other side of the law. He was an officer with the Salt River PD."

He kept his eyes on the road but his mouth hardened. "So were the rest of them."

Her jaw sagged. "What? You're telling me the Salt River Police Department was running drugs?"

"I don't know about all of them. There were only four men there that night, all wearing masks. The only one I recognized for sure was Chief Briggs. He was the one giving the orders."

She didn't find that such a stretch of the imagination. Jesse had told her enough horror stories about his predecessor that she could certainly believe Carl Briggs would have been capable of anything. He had been completely dirty, as crooked as a snake in a cactus patch.

Briggs had been under indictment on multiple counts of corruption five years earlier when he'd dropped dead of a heart attack.

Jesse was still trying to repair the damage Briggs had done to the small police department's reputation during his tenure.

But Wade? The image of him involved in any kind of criminal enterprise just didn't fit the man she knew. "You said they were all wearing masks," she said slowly. "So you can't be sure Wade was there."

"Not one hundred percent," he admitted. Damn, he wished he could remember that night more vividly, could put faces and names to the men who had so gleefully taken turns beating him.

If he could, he would find a way to even the score now that he was no longer that no-account drifter Lowry had called him. What was the saying? Vengeance was sweeter when it was savored. He would love to be able to savor a little delayed justice.

His memories were just too hazy, though. He only had vague impressions of Briggs ordering one of the men to cuff him. Then the chief had circled around him a few times, just for intimidation's sake, before offering him three choices that were really no choices at all.

They could kill him right then and bury him deep in the mountains surrounding Star Valley where nobody would ever find him.

They could let him take the rap for the drugs.

Or he could leave Salt River and never come back.

Cocky bastard that he'd been a decade earlier, he had spat in the chief's face. Briggs had eased back on his heels, his pale blue eyes narrowed.

"Boy, you just made a big mistake," he murmured softly, then had ordered the other men to finish him off.

They had all taken turns beating on "Cassie Harte's pretty-boy boyfriend" who stuck his nose in the wrong place.

He must have passed out from one too many kicks in the head. His last thought before he had surrendered to the pain had been for Cassie.

When he regained consciousness, he'd been alone. No plane, no handcuffs, no Briggs. Only his beat-up truck and a note staked to the ground in front of him that said only five words. "Jail or bail. Your choice."

He had no doubt in the world Briggs could make a charge of drug smuggling stick against him. He wanted to stay and fight it. But then he thought of the expression he would see on Cassie's face if she saw him behind bars. The hurt and the dismay. The disillusionment.

He couldn't make her endure that kind of shame. She deserved better than to have to go through that.

She deserved better than him.

It had taken him a good fifteen minutes to make his shaky way into the driver's seat of his old truck and start it up, pain shrieking through him with every second from what he would later learn had been a half-dozen broken ribs, a concussion and a shattered elbow.

He had a vague memory of that drive out of town, how he'd decided to head south toward Utah. He had known he was leaving Cassie forever, and his heart had cracked into sharp little pieces that gouged him just as painfully as his broken ribs.

"Where did you go?"

He blinked back to the present, to the soft, beautiful woman beside him who had suffered the consequences of that decision. "What?"

"Just now. You looked like you were miles away."

"I was remembering. Regretting. I should never have left. I should have stayed and fought Briggs."

Her eyes softened and she reached across the vehicle and touched his arm. "You would have lost. He might have killed you."

"Maybe. But at least I would have known I tried."

"Small consolation that would have been to you in your grave. No. I can't believe I'm actually saying this, but I'm glad you made the choice you did."

He stared at her, taking his eyes off the road for several beats too long. When he realized he had just narrowly missed hitting a reflector pole, he yanked the Range Rover into the nearest pullout and shoved it into Park.

"How can you say that? Running out on you was unforgivable."

"No it wasn't. You broke my heart when you left, I won't lie about that. But broken hearts eventually heal, even if they never quite fit together perfectly again." She was quiet for a moment, then she grabbed his hand. "If you had been killed, Zack, I never would have recovered."

After her low admission, he didn't say anything for several moments, just gazed at her with a bemused kind of wonder in his eyes, then with a muffled groan he reached for her.

The kiss was soft and sweet and so full of tenderness she melted against him, her bones dissolving inside her skin.

They had shared dozens of kisses in this last week. Hundreds of them. But she sensed something deeper in this embrace, as if they had both crossed some invisible line.

A heavy tractor trailer passed them, and its wake rattled the windows of the Range Rover. Zack groaned and pressed his forehead against hers. "I don't deserve you."

"You deserve whatever you want out of life." She touched his cheek. "You always have."

"You're what I want. Whether I deserve you or not." He drew away suddenly and shoved the Range Rover into gear. "Come on. Let's go buy a pickup truck."

A little disoriented by the shift in the conversation, she blinked at him. "You're serious? I thought you were only teasing!"

His lopsided grin left her as breathless as his kiss. "Sweetheart, I wouldn't joke about something as important as this."

Driving with one hand, he grabbed her fingers suddenly with the other and pressed a kiss on her palm. "Seriously, Cass. I know nothing I do will bring back the last ten years. But I'd like to re-create at least one thing from that time."

"You're crazy! You can't just walk into a dealership at two in the afternoon on the Fourth of July and walk out with a new pickup truck!"

"Watch me."

She did just that. Not that she had much choice. The sales manager at the small dealership didn't quite know how to deal with an immovable force like Zack Slater with his mind set on something.

The two of them—Cassie and LeRoy Thomas, his nametag read—just stood back and watched, while Zack quickly perused the inventory on the lot.

"What's your favorite color?" he asked her at one point while he peered under the hood of one big beast.

"I don't know," she answered helplessly, unable to believe he was actually doing this. "Um, I like the sage color of this one."

She didn't think he would appreciate the observation that when he stood next to it, the color perfectly matched the green flecks in his eyes.

"Sage it is, then," he said, poking his head up. "LeRoy, my friend, let's talk."

A half hour later, after some hard-core negotiations that made her head spin, Zack was the proud owner of a hulking three-quarter-ton pickup with all the extras and a price tag that left her feeling slightly ill.

He took her to a late lunch at a pizza place in Idaho Falls. On the way out of the restaurant he offered her the choice of driving home the new truck or the sleek Range Rover.

Home. She really liked the sound of that. Pretending to consider, she cocked her head, looking at both vehicles in the parking lot. "You take the truck," she finally said. "It's your new toy."

He grinned with such boyish excitement that she fell in love with him all over again.

She loved Zack Slater. The sweetness of admitting it to herself flowed through her like pure honey.

She loved his strength and his laughter and his decency.

As certain as she was that this was right between them—that she wanted to take this next step with him—

by the time they drove under the wooden Lost Creek Ranch sign, her nerves were stretched thin, her body taut with restless anticipation.

When she parked the Range Rover next to the shiny new truck that gleamed in the late-afternoon sun, she was chagrined to realize her hands were shaking, just a little. She climbed out, then shoved them in the pockets of her jeans to hide her nerves.

"Let me just grab a couple of…of quilts." She felt herself blush furiously. "I'm afraid I, um, don't have any strawberries."

"That's okay." He smiled. "Strawberries aren't what I'm hungry for, anyway."

Her mouth went dry and she had to grab the railing of the porch steps to steady herself. He followed her up the steps, and she was almost painfully aware of him as she unlocked the door.

Inside her little cabin he seemed to take up all the available air, leaving her breathless and a little dizzy.

She cleared her throat. "I'll just grab those quilts."

She turned away and nearly jumped out of her skin when he reached out and rested a strong hand on her shoulder. The heat of his fingers scorched through the soft cotton of her shirt as he turned her to face him.

His eyes were intent, searching, and she knew all her sudden anxieties must be glaringly obvious on her far-too-transparent features.

"Do you want me to leave?"

She shook her head fiercely.

"We don't have to do anything you're not ready for. Slow and easy, remember? That's what I promised. I meant every word. We don't even have to go anywhere. We can sit right out on your porch swing and watch the fireworks from here, okay? You can always make me go jump in the cold stream out back if I start misbehaving."

While he spoke, her nerves slid away. She had nothing to be afraid about. Not with Zack. A soft smile captured her mouth at the sincerity in his eyes. He probably would march right to the stream out back if she commanded him.

"You are a very sweet man, Zack Slater," she murmured.

He snorted. "You know me better than that. I just want to do everything right this time."

"So far you're doing a pretty darn good job." She smiled again, sultry this time, and stepped forward to press a kiss to his strong jaw where a hint of late-afternoon shadow rasped against her mouth. She liked it so much she kissed him again. And once more.

He stood motionless while she tasted his skin and meandered her way to his mouth. He wanted slow and easy. She could give him slow and easy. She brushed her lips across his, then back again with leisurely attention to every centimeter of his mouth.

His eyes fluttered closed and he leaned into her. Under her hands, his heart pounded hard and fast in erotic contrast to the unhurried pace of their kiss.

He seemed content to let her take the lead in the kiss, and she reveled in the heady power of his response. As she explored his mouth, she could feel the hard jut of his arousal at her hip, feel his breathing accelerate, grow labored.

When she gripped a handful of shirt and licked at the corner of his mouth, he groaned and parted his lips slightly, just enough for her to slip her tongue inside. But still he didn't move.

She knew the exact moment when his thin hold on control snapped apart. One moment he was motionless under her sensual onslaught. The next, he shuddered and his arms whipped up, twisting in her hair as he gripped her head and ravaged her mouth.

With a sigh of surrender she wrapped her arms around his neck and pressed her body to him.

She couldn't wait another hour, another moment, another second. She wanted him now, right here.

The dying sun sent long, stretched-out shafts of light through a break in the curtains to dapple the furniture and wood floor as she grabbed his hand and pulled him into her small bedroom.

He dug his boot heels into the floor just inside the doorway, his eyes intent and searching on her face. "Are you sure, Cass? There's no going back after this."

She smiled. "I couldn't be more sure than I am right this moment. Kiss me, Slater."

His mouth quirked a little at the order but he promptly obeyed, his hands busy untucking her shirt and exploring the sensitive skin above her hips. She shivered as those hard, rough hands moved closer to her breasts, to her nipples that ached and burned for his touch.

The next few moments were a flurry of buttons and snaps and zippers yanking free.

Finally no barriers remained between them. All her nerves came fluttering back like a flock of magpies to chatter noisily at her.

No man had ever seen her naked except him, and that had been a decade ago. She was suddenly painfully aware of all her imperfections, every single extra calorie she had ever indulged in over the years.

He didn't appear to notice. At least not judging by the stunned expression on his face.

"I thought I remembered everything about you in exquisite detail," he murmured. "Every curve, every hollow. I can't believe I forgot the sheer impact of the whole package."

"Oh, stop." Hot color saturated all those curves and hollows as he gazed at her with stark longing in his eyes.

He grinned. "Get used to it, sweetheart. I'm just getting warmed up."

She decided the only way out of this was distraction. "That's too bad," she murmured. "Because I'm already very, very warm. And getting warmer by the second."

"Let's see." He stepped forward and kissed her, skimming one sneaky hand from her shoulders down her back to the curve of one rear cheek, pulling her against him. She gasped as fluttery little nerve impulses rocketed through her everywhere her skin brushed his.

"Mmm. You're right. Very warm," he murmured against her mouth.

They stood that way for a long time, wrapped together and rediscovering each other while the room darkened around them.

At last he lowered her to the bed. His hands were strong and hard and clever. He knew exactly how and where to touch her—where to linger, where to tease with fleeting caresses.

She closed her eyes, lost to the swirl of sensation and the steadily building heat he stoked so adroitly. When she opened them, she found him watching her, his eyes heavy with passion. Their gazes locked and stayed that way while his hands caressed her intimately. A restless, aching need gripped her and she curved into his fingers, nearly crying out from the tangle of emotions that bound them so tightly.

Still watching her, he lowered his mouth to hers. The kiss was fierce and possessive and demanding—and she found it every bit as arousing as his hands on her flesh.

"Please," she begged, unable to stand the slow, exquisite yearning another instant. His thumb stroked a particularly sensitive spot just then, hidden in folds of flesh, and she sobbed his name as she climaxed in a wild tumble of color and light and sensation.

He entered her while her body still seethed and shivered. She gasped as tight, unused muscles had to stretch to accommodate his size.

Muscles corded in his neck as he eased deeper. She wasn't sure if his growled words were an oath or a prayer. "You're so tight."

"I'm sorry. I just haven't done this in a…in a long time."

He froze, his hot gaze piercing the soft, satiated fog enveloping her. "How long?"

She flushed and focused on the hard blade of his collarbone. "Oh, ten years. Give or take a month or so."

He blinked but not before she saw the stunned disbelief in his eyes. "You haven't been with anyone at all?"

Did they have to talk about this right now, when she could hardly find her breath? When he was invading every inch of her soul? Apparently so. She knew that stubborn look in his eyes and knew he wouldn't let it drop.

"I've been a little busy raising my niece," she retorted. "When was I supposed to fit in any torrid sexual encounters? In between changing her diapers or before I picked her up from school? I'm sorry. It just wasn't a priority."

The stunned look in his eyes began to give way to something else. Something that looked like an awed kind of wonder. "It shouldn't matter to me. It *doesn't.* I would have understood, Cass, if you had been involved with someone else. You had every right."

"Yes, I did. I just don't view making love with someone lightly. It was…never the right situation with anyone else."

"And this is right, isn't it? Between us?"

She nodded, helpless to do anything else.

"I love you, Cassidy Jane."

The gruff words stole what little breath remained in her lungs. If she'd had any left, it wouldn't have lasted long as he surged deeply inside her, his body taut and hard.

She gasped and rose to meet him, clinging to him as the need spiraled inside her again with each deep, steady movement.

"I love you," he repeated, and the words sent her soaring over the edge once more. An instant later he followed her with a low, exultant moan.

While she floated, featherlight, back to earth, he switched their positions so she was sprawled over him, listening to his ragged breathing while his hands stroked her skin.

A few minutes later, just as she thought she might be able to think straight again, she heard a tremendous boom and saw a sparkle of red and gold through that slim spear of open curtain.

She gasped. "Oh no! We're missing the fireworks!"

His hand curved over her hipbone. "I wouldn't exactly say that."

"But your new truck. You wasted all that money for nothing!"

Hard muscles rippled against her as he shrugged. "We'll use it next year. Make it our own annual tradition."

Would they have a "next year" together? She wanted fiercely to believe it. But even here in the sanctuary of his arms, she couldn't shake the niggling voice warning her that nothing lasts forever.

She had learned that lesson all too well.

In the meantime she needed to do all she could to protect whatever tiny remnants of her heart he hadn't already snatched for his own.

It worked.

He couldn't believe she was here, in his arms. That his weeks of planning, of hoping, had paid off.

Zack watched her sleep, fascinated by the steady rise and fall of her chest under the sheet, the fluttering of her eyelids, the little half smile that played around her mouth.

She was here. And she was his.

He had to be the luckiest son of a gun who ever lived. When he arrived at Salt River three weeks ago, he figured nothing short of a miracle could have convinced her to give him another chance.

Heaven knew, he didn't deserve one.

Yet here she was, warm and soft and cuddly as she slept curled against him.

Somehow she had turned to that steely core of courage inside her and taken a huge leap of faith into his arms. He could only guess what it must have cost her. If she had left *him* a decade ago like a thief in the night—without any kind of explanation—he wasn't sure he would be so willing to let her back into his life. Especially if he believed all that time that she left with another man.

She was a far better person than he was. He had always known that. Loving and generous and sweet.

For a man who had lived most of his life in a hard, unforgiving world, was it any wonder Cassidy Harte had been irresistible?

She was still irresistible, even though the years had changed her. Now that optimistic, artless girl had become a woman. A little less optimistic, maybe. A little more wary, but still as loving and generous as she had been when he lost his heart to her.

He pressed a soft kiss to her forehead. Not to wake her, simply because he still couldn't believe she was here.

She stirred, then her eyes fluttered open. A dazed kind of smile tilted that luscious mouth a little as their gazes met, then color flared across her cheekbones.

"What time is it?" She tried to peer around him to her alarm clock.

"Early. About four-thirty."

She groaned and buried her head under the pillow. "I have to get up in an hour to make breakfast."

"Or, since you're already awake, we could find something more interesting to do for an hour."

She pulled the pillow away and squinted at him. "You're inhuman. I figured four—or was it five?—times would be enough for you."

He couldn't stop the pure, sinful smile stealing over his mouth. "No. I'm very, very human. And I don't think I will ever get enough of you."

The disgruntled look in her eyes began to fade as he reached for her. It didn't take him long to make it disappear entirely, replaced by soft, dreamy desire.

Afterward, he held her tight, her head tucked under his chin.

"Marry me, Cassie."

The words slipped out of him like horses over downed barbed wire. Why had he blurted it out like that? So much for waiting, taking the time and effort to repair the damage he had done by leaving her.

He could tell the words shocked her. She went deepwater still and slid away from him. "Wha-what?"

He couldn't go back now—it was too late for that—so he plodded gamely forward. "I love you. I never stopped loving you. I fell for you all those years ago. For ten years the memory of that time has stalked me. Haunted me. I love you. I want to marry you."

She jumped out of bed as if the sheets were ablaze and scrambled for a silky robe tossed over a chair.

Panic skittered around her, through her. "Don't do this

to me, Zack. This is not fair. You can't just blow back into town and expect everything to be the same."

"I don't. I hope we can build something even better than what we had before." He sat up, the sheets bunched at his hips and that wide, hard chest bare, looking so gorgeous her mouth watered. She jerked her gaze away, to something safe like the pale-pink dawn breaking outside her bedroom window.

How could he throw this at her? It was far too much, far too soon. She was still a little light-headed about having taken this giant step and spent the night in his arms.

"Slow and easy. Wasn't that what you said?"

"Yeah. That's what I said."

"This is not slow and easy! This is jumping straight from *hello* to picking out china patterns together. I…I need more time, Zack. I'm sorry. I'm just not ready yet."

A cold, hard knot of terror lodged in her throat at the very idea of committing to a future with him. She was being a yellow-bellied coward and she hated herself for it.

But the cruel lessons of the past were just too ingrained in her psyche.

She had a sudden memory of a pretty little blue heeler her brother Matt bought at a livestock auction a few years ago. The dog's previous owner must have been one mean son of a gun because she quailed, her belly slunk low to the ground and her tail between her legs, whenever Matt tried to work with her.

It had taken months of hard work and patience before her brother could gain the dog's trust.

She knew exactly how that poor bitch felt right now. So afraid to let down her guard. To believe this was any more than just another vicious trick—an outstretched hand that concealed a harsh stick.

"I'm sorry," she repeated. "I'm not ready."

"You still love me, though. Admit it."

She shoved her hands in the pockets of her robe to conceal their trembling. "Sometimes love is not enough. Ten years ago I might have thought it was. But I know better now."

He was silent, his expression resigned, regretful. "You think I'm going to leave you again, don't you?"

She wanted to deny his words but she couldn't. Until this moment she hadn't realized just how afraid she was that he would do exactly that.

Her silence spoke far more loudly than words. He nodded, "Okay. I won't pressure you, Cassie. I'll wait. We have the rest of our lives."

She wanted so fiercely to believe him.

But still she cowered.

Chapter 10

The nervous jitters fluttering through her before the Independence Day parade nearly a week earlier seemed like tiny rippling waves in a spring breeze compared to this tidal wave of terror.

Cassie shifted in the leather passenger seat of Zack's new truck, adjusted her seat belt, tried to find a comfortable spot for her trembling hands.

Everything's going to be fine, she assured herself, trying hard not to give in to the fierce urge to gnaw her lip to shreds.

"You okay?" Zack asked, with such calm serenity she wanted to punch him. Hard.

Just dandy. She blew out a breath. "No. No, I'm not okay."

He sent her a reassuring smile. "Relax. Everything will be fine. We'll all try to get along."

"Right. Relax. You spent maybe six months with my brothers and that was ten years ago. I've lived with them my entire life. I know exactly what they're like. Everything is *not* going to be fine."

They were on their way to Sunday dinner at the Diamond Harte, and she wouldn't have been more terrified if she were standing barefoot in a nest full of rattlers.

The whole thing had been her idea, she was chagrined to admit. She wasn't sure what kind of evil demon had planted this seed in her head, but she had blurted out the invitation a few days before when she had been lying in his arms, sated and relaxed.

They had both been spending a lot of time in that condition in the last week. Not that she had any regrets. It had been incredible, far better than her memories of before. They laughed together, they talked together, they did everything but broach the subject of the future.

Friday was supposed to have been her last day at the Lost Creek under the terms of their agreement, but neither of them had given it much thought, too wrapped up in rediscovering each other.

"Do you want to forget it?" Zack asked her now. "I could just drop you off and make myself scarce for a couple hours if you want me to."

She blew out a breath. Matt and Jesse both knew she was bringing Zack to dinner. She had called them the day before to warn them. It wouldn't have been fair to just spring it on them out of the blue.

They knew she was seeing him again, and neither was happy about it. She winced remembering their identical, very vocal reactions to the news when she had called them.

But she knew if she and Zack had any future at all—that future she didn't want to think about—they had to confront the past first.

"No," she answered firmly. "We're going to have to do this eventually. We can't keep hiding out from them like we're holed up in Robber's Roost waiting for the posse to catch up to us. One of these days my brothers are going to see that I'm all grown up and can live my own life. Make my own decisions."

"How bad can it be?" He grinned. "I'll let them each punch me around a few times—I figure I deserve at least that much for breaking their baby sister's heart—then we'll all have a beer and move on."

She slugged his shoulder, more for the cocky grin than his words. "Don't even joke about it. That's exactly what I'm afraid of. I'm fairly fond of that pretty face of yours. I'd hate to see my obstinate brothers mess it up."

He grabbed her hand. "Don't worry about your brothers, I can hold my own. Physically or otherwise." He kissed the fingers he held. "Everything is going to be fine, Cass. Just watch."

If she closed her eyes, she could almost believe him.

The Diamond Harte was exactly as he remembered it—big and sprawling and as brightly polished as a prize rodeo buckle.

Of all the ranches he'd seen in the years his father had dragged him around like a worn-out saddle, the Harte ranch stood out in his memory as one of the cleanest, most efficient operations he'd ever had the pleasure of working.

They pulled up in front of the ranch house, a massive stone-and-log structure that had always intimidated him a little. Immediately two little dynamos—a redhead and a tiny brunette with long dark hair-hopped down from a swing on the front porch and rushed to their vehicle.

Before he could play the gentleman and open the passenger door for Cassie, they did it for him, all but climbing onto her lap.

"Aunt Cassie! It's been forever since we've seen you!" the darker one exclaimed. He looked closer at her and immediately saw Melanie Harte's silvery-gray eyes looking back at him. This one must be Lucy.

"I know, sweetheart. I'm sorry I didn't make it last week for dinner. I've been really busy at work and with…with things."

"Guess what? Maisy had kittens. They're all black-and-white except one that has ginger stripes. Do you want to see them?"

She laughed. "I will later, okay." She gestured toward him. "Zack, these beautiful creatures are my nieces, Lucy and Dylan. Lucy, Dylan, this is Zack Slater. A friend of mine."

He smiled. "Hi, ladies."

Instantly the girls' enthusiasm switched off like a burned-out bulb. The happy welcome in their eyes faded, and they nodded politely to him, their faces stiff.

Obviously, they had heard about the evil Zack Slater who had blown back into town to ruin their beloved aunt's life once again.

If he couldn't win over a couple of ten-year-olds, he was in serious trouble with the rest of her family. He was racking his brain trying to come up with something harmless and friendly to say when Cassie beat him to it.

"Where is everybody?"

"Mom and Sarah are in the kitchen," Lucy said. "Dad's checking on one of the horses down at the barn, and Jesse's not here yet. He had some stuff to do at the police station and said he'd be a little late."

Cassie lifted an eyebrow. "On Sunday?"

"Sarah said he was waiting for a fax or something. She said it was something real important."

Zack pulled their contribution from behind the seat— a heavy, cast-iron Dutch oven filled with the makings for Cassie's world-famous blueberry cobbler and a huge plastic container loaded with pasta salad—then he followed her up the porch steps and into the ranch house.

Inside, he heard the low, musical murmur of women's voices as they neared the kitchen but it stopped in midnote when they walked into the big, airy room.

One woman stood at the professional stove stirring something while the other sat at the table husking corn-cobs. Their eyes turned wary, the way the girls' had, when they saw him.

Beside Zack Cassie fidgeted and cleared her throat. "Sorry we're a little late."

"You're fine. Matt hasn't even started the charcoal for the steaks yet," the shorter of the two women said.

With a nervous smile Cassie introduced him to the women. Ellie Harte, Matt's new wife, was an older version of her daughter, small and slender with auburn hair and sparkling green eyes. Sarah, who was apparently brave enough to be willing to marry wild, reckless Jesse Harte, was tall and willowy with a long sweep of wheat-colored hair.

Their expressions were polite and curious but far from friendly. Unless he found a way to break the ice, he could see they were all in for a long, awkward afternoon.

"What can I do to help?" he asked as Cassie moved containers around in the big refrigerator to make room for her salad. "I can fire up the charcoal if you'd like."

"Matt gets a little territorial when it comes to his barbecue," Ellie said.

Then he was probably real testy about breaking bread with the man he thought had taken his wife. Zack winced. Maybe Cassie was right to be so nervous. Maybe they should have put this off a little longer.

No. There was no sense in waiting. He owed Matt an explanation and an apology and he might as well get it over with. Not here at the house, though. If the man wanted to take a swing at him, he wouldn't do it in front of the nervous eyes of the women and Zack didn't want to deprive him of the chance. He figured he owed him that, as well.

"I think I'll just take a stroll around and see how much the ranch has changed in the past ten years."

"I'll come with you," Cassie offered.

He shook his head. "Why don't you stay and visit? I'd rather go alone."

She sent him a searching look, then nodded and squeezed his hand in gratitude or for luck, he wasn't certain.

He found Matt Harte with his elbows resting on the split rail of a corral fence watching a filly canter around inside.

Cassie's oldest brother, the man who had raised her from the age of twelve, narrowed his gaze as Zack approached but said nothing, waiting for him to make the first move.

He had always liked and respected Matt Harte. The man had nerves of steel and the best natural horse instincts of anybody Zack had ever met. It didn't surprise him at all that in the past ten years the Diamond Harte had become world-renowned for raising and training champion cutters.

That didn't make what he had to do any easier.

He joined Matt at the fence. "She's a pretty little thing, isn't she?" he murmured, nodding toward the filly.

"Yeah. She's shaping up to be a real goer. I thought her gait was a little off this morning but she looks like she's fine now. Ellie said as much but I had to check for myself. I guess I should listen to my vet more often."

They lapsed into an awkward silence. Zack didn't have the first clue where to begin.

"I know you don't want me here," he finally said.

Matt turned around and leaned against the fence, elbows propped on the rail and his expression shuttered. "If

I had my way, you'd just ride right on back out of town the way you came."

"I'm not going to do that."

He received only a grunt in return and sighed. This was much harder than he'd expected. "Look, you can think whatever you want about me for walking out on your sister. You couldn't think any worse of me than I do of myself for that. But I didn't leave with Melanie. I swear it."

Matt gave him a sidelong glance as if testing his sincerity. "So you say. But you still left."

He nodded. "I had my reasons. I thought they were good ones at the time."

"And now?"

"I don't know," he answered honestly. "I don't think I was ready to be the kind of man Cassie deserves."

"And I'm supposed to believe everything's different now? That you're not going to get itchy feet in a few days or a few weeks and walk away from her again?"

"To be blunt, Harte, it really doesn't matter what you believe. Just what she believes."

Matt muttered a pungent oath. "I'm not going to let you break her heart again. She grieved over you for a long time. Too damn long. And I know she blamed herself that Melanie ran off and left me with Lucy so tiny."

His chest ached at the words. "I owe Cassie more apologies than I can ever give for hurting her. I'd like to spend the rest of my life trying to make it up to her. And I'm also sorry I betrayed your trust in me. You were a man I liked and respected. Even if I hadn't been engaged to Cassie, for that reason alone I never would have touched your wife."

He paused. "I drove out of town alone ten years ago, Harte. I know you don't believe me and there's not a damn thing I can do to prove it, but it's God's honest truth."

A muscle worked in the other man's cheek as he gazed

at the ranch house. "You're right. I'll never really know if Melanie left with you or not. It doesn't really matter. If not you, she would have latched on to some other saddle bum to take her anywhere but here. All I know is she walked away and never looked back. Just like you did."

Although he felt about as uncomfortable as a short-tailed bull in fly season talking about this with another man—and Cassie's brother to boot—he plunged forward. "I love your sister. I never stopped loving her in all these years. I hope as a recently married man maybe you can understand a little about that."

He paused, feeling his ears redden while Matt appeared to become suddenly fascinated with something on his boots. "I want to marry her," he went on gamely. "But I won't come between her and her family. You and Jesse mean too much to her."

If Matt was surprised by that, he didn't show his hand.

"I know the past is always going to be there between the two of us. Maybe you're always going to wonder if I'm one of the men who messed with your wife. I can swear up and down that I didn't, but if you don't think you can get beyond that, do you think you can just pretend, for Cassie's sake? Hate me all you want on your own time. But can we at least try to be polite to each other around her?"

The other man was silent for several moments then he shrugged. "Let's see how you treat her first. Now what's this I hear about you running a spread near Durango? Cattle or horses?"

Zack breathed out a sigh of relief. He couldn't exactly say Matt had welcomed him back with open arms. But he hadn't shoved his face in the dirt, either.

"Cattle," he answered. "Only a couple hundred head. It's beautiful country there but not as beautiful as Star Valley."

As the conversation shifted from women to the far more comfortable topic of ranching, he relaxed a little.

One brother down, one to go.

With her stomach still snarled into knots, Cassie stood on the wide flagstone patio watching Zack and Matt leaning against the corral fence, deep in conversation. If only they were a little closer, she might be able to read their lips.

"What do you think they're talking about?" she asked Ellie.

Her sister-in-law shaded her eyes with her hand to follow Cassie's gaze. "I don't know. But at least nobody's throwing punches yet."

"It's early in the game," Sarah put in. "Wait until Jesse shows up."

Cassie groaned. "You two are not helping."

The quiet, pretty schoolteacher who had captured Jesse's wild heart was immediately apologetic. "Sorry. I shouldn't have said that. I was only joking. For what it's worth, Matt has too much control to punch anyone, and I made Jesse promise to behave himself. Everything will be fine."

Why did everybody else seem to think that but her? She huffed out a breath. "So, um, what do you think?" she asked, anxious for her friends' opinion.

"About what?" Ellie asked, her eyes dark green with teasing laughter.

"About him," she said impatiently. "Zack."

"He seems very polite," Sarah offered.

"He must have plenty of sand in his gut to walk right out first thing and face Matt," Ellie added.

Sarah cocked her head, her expression thoughtful as she gazed at the pasture where the two men stood admiring the horses. "And I have to admit, I can see why a woman might find him moderately attractive," she said.

Ellie snorted. "Moderately attractive. Right. That's like saying Matt is moderately stubborn. The man's beautiful. Movie-star gorgeous, Cass."

"He is, isn't he?" She smiled as the tremors in her stomach changed from nerves to that familiar achy awareness.

After a moment Ellie touched her arm, her green eyes worried. "But *gorgeous* and *good for you* aren't the same thing at all. Are you sure you know what you're doing?"

Did she? No. She was still scared to death whenever she thought about the future, but she was beginning to feel the first fledgling stirs of hope.

"I still love him," she said simply. "I never stopped."

Ellie studied her, that anxious look still on her face, then it faded away as she smiled. "Then that's good enough for me."

"Me, too," Sarah piped in, with uncharacteristically poor grammar but with a sincerity that brought tears to Cassie's eyes.

"Thank you. Both of you." On impulse, she hugged them both, grateful once more to fate for handing her such wonderful sisters and friends—and that her brothers had been smart enough to snatch them up.

"Just be careful," Ellie murmured.

Oh, it was far too late for that, she thought. She was way beyond careful. When she stepped away from the embrace, she decided her curiosity couldn't wait any longer "I think I'll just go see for myself what they're talking about."

"Tell your brother to get up here and start the coals, or it will be midnight before we eat."

She hummed a little as she walked down to the corral, her heart suddenly much lighter than it had been driving to the ranch. Maybe Zack was right. Maybe everything would be fine, after all.

When she reached the men, Zack's smile of greeting warmed her to her toes. She slipped her hand into his and was met with a look of surprise, then deep pleasure at her gesture that told him she wouldn't hide their relationship behind her fear.

"Your wife sent me to tell you to start the coals," she told Matt. "Those steaks aren't going to grill themselves."

Matt's relaxed grin took her by surprise. She might have expected thick tension between the two men with their history, but they seemed to be getting along like a couple of hogs rolling in mud.

"Yeah, she's a bossy little thing, isn't she?" he answered, looking toward the house and his wife with such an expression of joy and love on his face that tears burned behind her eyes.

Was it happiness she felt for her brother and his bride? Or envy?

Whatever, she blinked them back as he headed toward the house. "What were you two talking about?" Her voice came out a little ragged around the edges, but Zack didn't appear to notice.

"Oh, this and that. I told him I'm interested in buying this little filly for my ranch when she's trained. He told me he'd think about it."

"Did you…did you talk about Melanie?"

"Yeah."

She frowned impatiently at him. "And?"

He shrugged. "I told him I didn't leave with her, but he's a hard man to read. I think he's far more concerned about you than about Melanie at this point. I tried to assure him my intentions toward you are honorable."

"Oh. That's really too bad," she teased.

His laughter sounded rough. "If I had my way, I'd drag you back into that barn over there, find a nice soft pile of hay and then…" He whispered something in her ear that sent heat rushing through her like the blast from a welder's torch.

She shivered in reaction, but before she could answer, raised voices sounded on the patio, destroying the moment. With a groan of resignation, she eased away from the sultry promise of that low voice in her ear.

"That would be brother number two. The hotheaded one. Your hay pile idea sounds like a very smart one. Let's go."

She yanked his hand to lead him toward the barn and outbuildings, but he shook his head, gripping her fingers. "Come on, sweetheart. We've come this far. Don't chicken out on me now."

She blew out a breath. "I was afraid you were going to say that."

Squaring her shoulders, she walked beside Zack toward the house, her hand still wrapped in his. They were almost to the patio when Jesse marched out to meet them.

She had expected him to be angry, but the sheer cold fury in his eyes stunned her.

"Get away from him, Cass," Jesse growled. "Right now. Go on into the house."

An answering anger flared and she stepped forward, chin out. "I haven't taken orders from you since I was fourteen years old. I'm not about to start now."

"Do it, Cassie."

She was dismayed—and disgusted—to see dark violence in his eyes, etched into his features.

"Forget it," she snapped. "You're a little old for settling things with your fists, don't you think? Not to mention the fact that around here you're supposed to be upholding the law, not shattering it."

"That's exactly what I'm doing. Slater, I'm going to have to ask you to come with me down to the station."

Zack's laughter held little humor. "You're arresting me for dating your sister? Don't you think that's a little extreme?"

"I'm not arresting you for anything. I just have some questions to ask you."

Cassie stepped between them. "Stop it. This is ridiculous. We're here to share Sunday dinner with the family, and that's just what we're going to do. If you have a problem with that, Jess, maybe you need to go eat somewhere else."

Zack certainly didn't need Cassie to fight his battles for him but he was absurdly touched that she stood up to her brother, chin up and her hand still in his, clenching as if she was ready to take Jesse on if he made one wrong move.

He wanted to kiss her right there, but he had a pretty strong feeling that that wouldn't go over well given the current climate.

He glanced toward the wide flagstone patio where the rest of her family gathered and the first flickers of unease stirred to life in his gut.

Something was wrong.

Seriously wrong.

Matt and his wife both looked stunned, their faces ashen, and the other woman—Jesse's fiancée, Sarah—looked as if she was ready to cry.

He jerked back to the heated conversation next to him. Cassie was still upbraiding her brother for his lack of manners and his immaturity.

He held a hand out to stop her. "What's going on?" he

asked slowly. "This isn't about some personal vendetta, is it?"

The police chief's voice was hard as a whetstone. "No. I'm investigating a homicide, Slater. And right now you're my prime suspect. I need you to come in for questioning."

Beside him, he felt Cassie jerk her shoulders back. "A homicide? Are you crazy? We haven't had a homicide in Salt River in years."

"Right. This one is about ten years old. Remember that skeleton Ron Atkins found a few months ago in the foot-hills of his ranch? The state crime lab was finally able to make an identification."

A feeling of dread settled over him. "And?"

"And Matt wasted his money getting a divorce in absentia. Apparently he's been a widower all these years. The bones belonged to Melanie."

The color leached from Cassie's face. "Oh, no."

"After her fingerprints were found on some of the items found with her body, the state crime lab ran dental records and they matched perfectly. No question it was Melanie."

She was going to be sick.

The smell of charcoal and starter fluid wafting from the grill suddenly seemed greasy—the heat of the afternoon too heavy and oppressive—and she pulled her hand away from Zack's to press it to the churning of her stomach.

Melanie was dead. Murdered. She could hardly believe it.

She had hated her manipulative, amoral sister-in-law passionately even before she thought Zack had run off with her, but she had never wished her dead.

All these years when she thought of Melanie it had been with malice and hateful anger for the future Cassie thought she had stolen from her. And all these years, the object of her hatred had been dead, buried in a shallow grave just a few miles away from the Diamond Harte.

Her stomach heaved again and she had to breathe hard to battle back the nausea.

She shifted her horrified gaze from her brother to Zack and found him watching her with an odd, stony expression on his features. It was only after she looked closer and saw the deep shadows of hurt in his eyes that she realized she had subconsciously stepped away from him as if she couldn't wait to put as much distance as possible between them.

She wanted to apologize but she was afraid it was too late.

"I didn't kill Melanie." He addressed his words to Jesse but his gold-flecked eyes locked with hers. "What motive would I possibly have?"

"That's something I'm sure we can discuss down at the station."

"I don't think so."

Jesse stepped forward, and she recognized the barely restrained violence simmering under the surface of his calm. "I don't believe that was a request, Slater."

"You really think that gives you enough evidence to arrest me, only because I was the last person seen with the woman a decade ago?"

A muscle flexed in Jesse's jaw but he didn't answer, which she supposed was answer enough.

"In that case, as I said, I'll have to pass," Zack murmured, his voice dripping with irony. "I'm always happy to cooperate with the law. I'll answer any questions, but unless the rules have changed since the last time I heard the drill, I believe I have the right to an attorney present for our little chat. I can send my plane to Denver for him and have him here in a few hours. Would that be convenient for you?"

She recognized his statement for what it was, a not-so-subtle reminder to Jesse and everyone else—including her—that he was no longer the dirt-poor ranch hand he'd been a decade ago, that he had money and influence now and wouldn't be railroaded into a murder charge.

Jesse looked as if he couldn't wait for an excuse to take a swing at him, but Matt stepped forward and rested a warning hand on his shoulder.

The motion jarred her out of the dreamlike, surreal state she'd slipped into.

Matt. And Lucy. Dear heavens How was this going to affect them? Her stomach shuddered again, and she tasted bile in her throat. Poor Lucy. Though she and Matt had tried to shield her as much as possible, children at school whispered to each other. She knew they did.

It had been hard enough on Lucy to believe her mother had abandoned her. Now, when she finally had a real family, all the talk about Melanie would resurface and Lucy would be hurt all over again.

She blinked when she realized Zack was speaking to her in a cold, distant voice she hated.

"I'm sure you can find a ride back to the Lost Creek, Cassie. If you'll all excuse me, I need to make some phone calls."

He turned on his heels, leaving stunned silence behind him. For a moment—only a moment—she was torn by conflicting loyalties. Her family would need her. Matt and Lucy would need her.

But she couldn't let him leave. Not like this. She turned to follow him, but Jesse grabbed her arm.

"Let him go," he ordered.

"Back off, Jess."

She and Sarah both said the words at exactly the same moment, only Cassie snarled like an angry bobcat while Sarah just murmured them in her soft, compelling voice.

She was pretty sure Jesse responded more to Sarah's request than her order, but she didn't wait around to thank her after he let her go. With her heart pounding, she raced around the house and caught up with Zack just as he was climbing into the shiny sage-green pickup she had picked out for him.

She skidded to a stop and stood there for a moment, scrambling for words.

"I'm sorry," she finally whispered, the only thing she could come up with as shock and misery choked her throat.

His expression was grim, closed. "For what? Believing I could be capable of murdering Melanie?"

She wanted to say she didn't believe it. That she could never believe it. But she had to admit that a tiny dark corner of her heart—the raw bruise that had never completely healed, had never been able to completely forgive him for leaving her—raised ugly doubts.

He *had* been the last one seen with Melanie. Jesse and others had seen them kissing outside the Renegade and then they had driven off together. Who knew what might have happened after that?

She'd been tempted to wring Melanie's neck more than a few times herself for what she'd put Matt through in their short, stormy marriage.

No. She swallowed hard. The tender man who painted her toenails and held her so gently and blew raspberries on her stomach would never use violence against a woman.

Never.

She couldn't believe it.

"I know you couldn't have killed her," she said firmly.

"But a part of you wonders, right? Unless your brother

comes up with another suspect in a hurry, part of you will always wonder."

She opened her mouth as if to deny it, then closed it, shattering his heart into a thousand tiny pieces.

How could he blame her? Ten years ago he had broken her heart, had left her without a word. He couldn't blame anyone but himself if she had a hard time believing him after he betrayed her so completely.

He couldn't blame her but he also knew he couldn't live with a woman unable to trust him. They couldn't build a future on something so flimsy, or it would crumble to dust in the first hard wind.

A bitter laugh threatened to choke him. Hard wind, hell. This accusation of murder was a tornado coming out of the blue.

"I told you what happened that night," he said gruffly. "She came on to me, I turned her down. I couldn't let her drive home in her condition and I didn't want to leave her drunk at the Renegade at the mercy of any unscrupulous cowboy who came along. I tried to give her a ride home. When she wouldn't let up, I finally kicked her out of my truck. Whatever happened to her after that is anybody's guess. I didn't kill her."

Even as he said the words, deep down in the pit of his gut, he knew differently. He was as responsible for her death as if he'd been the one who pulled the trigger.

She must have run into trouble after he'd driven away. He should never have left her unprotected and alone on the road, no matter how much she might have provoked him.

A good man, a decent man, never would have abandoned a woman alone in the dark.

A no-account drifter, on the other hand, would do just that.

"Go on back to your family, Cass," he said gently. "This will be tough on them. They're going to need you."

She glared at him, but there were tears gathering in her eyes. His Cassie, who hardly ever cried. His heart wept along with her.

"Damn you, Zack. Don't you do this to me again."

"Do what?"

"Push me away. Make my decisions for me. You didn't give me the choice to stand beside you once. Don't do it again."

He couldn't drag her through this kind of ugliness. He had to push her away, no matter how badly he wanted to yank her against him and bury her head against his chest.

If he listened hard, he could almost hear the sound of his dreams shattering around his feet. The future stretched out ahead of him, bleak and empty. A vast gray expanse without her laughter and her sparkling blue eyes and the miracle of her love.

He had never deserved any of it. All this time he thought the money and power he'd spent a decade accumulating had made a difference, that he would finally be worthy of her.

But she was right all this time. Everything he had accomplished didn't matter at all.

He would always be the worthless son of a drunk saddle bum. And now he was under suspicion for murder.

No. It was better this way.

"Goodbye, Cassie. I didn't say that before and I'm sorry for that. I should have."

He slid into the truck but her outstretched hand kept him from closing the door behind him.

"You're...you're leaving?"

"Not right away. But I'm going to be busy for a while trying to fight this, then I'll be heading back to Denver.

I'm sure you won't want to stay at the Lost Creek anymore now that the sale has gone through. Claire is capable of taking over for you—you've more than fulfilled your part of our deal. I'll send your check here."

"I don't want your money."

Tears seeped from her eyes, trickling down her cheeks into the corner of her mouth. Everything in him cried out to reach for her, but he knew he couldn't.

If he did—if he touched her—he wouldn't be able to let her go.

"Take it. Open your café. Be happy."

At his words, her outstretched hand curled into a fist and she pressed it against her stomach.

He closed the door of the truck and started it up, then drove away from the Diamond Harte without looking back.

This was the sort of day she usually loved.

Cassie stood at the sink in the modern kitchen of the Rendezvous Ranch, gazing out the window at the rain drizzling down outside. The sky was dark for late afternoon, the trees dripping heavily.

When she was a girl, her mother used to call these stormy summer afternoons "do nothing" days and that's exactly what they would do. Curl up on the porch swing with a book or play go-fish at the kitchen table or scavenge through each item in the cedar chest that always graced the foot of her parents' bed, brimming with history.

Those days had been rare and precious, when she could have her busy mother to herself. She closed her eyes, re-membering soft hands, a tender smile, a lap just perfect for cuddling in.

Her parents had died when she was twelve, on the cusp of becoming a woman. She used to wonder if being without her mother during those critical teen years had some-how left her broken, a puzzle with a few pieces missing.

Growing up in a household of big, macho men, she had never had anyone to give her advice about being a girl. About how to talk to boys and what to wear and how to fix her hair. As a result, she had treated most of the boys she went to school with just like she treated her brothers. She hadn't known any better. And they had responded in kind, considering her just one of the gang.

Maybe that's why Zack had so completely swept her off her feet. He'd treated her like a woman, even from the beginning.

No. No matter what had happened in her past, she some-how knew that she would have fallen just as hard for the tawny, dangerous cowboy with the sweet smile.

If her mother hadn't died in that crash, what advice would she give now to her heartbroken daughter?

Forget him and move on? Or go after him, even though he wanted nothing to do with her?

Ten years ago if she had the first inkling where he might have gone, she would have gone after him, no question about it. But she had changed over the years.

This time she knew exactly where he was—still hun-kered down at the Lost Creek since Jesse had ordered him not to leave town until he was either arrested or cleared in Melanie's murder.

She might know where he was, but she couldn't go to him. Not this time.

He didn't want her beside him.

No matter how she tried to convince him she knew he had nothing to do with Melanie's death, he still pushed her away. She thought she knew why—once more his damned nobility gave him some stupid, misguided notion that she deserved better than a man under suspicion for murder.

There was no one better. Why couldn't he see that? Zack Slater was the best thing that had ever happened to her.

She sighed and watched the sky weep while her heart wanted to cry right along with it. The rain she usually loved only reinforced how miserable and off-kilter she felt here.

It was kind of Wade to offer her a job at the Rendez-vous, but she missed the Lost Creek. She missed her little cabin. She missed Jean and Kip and Claire and Greta.

Most of all she missed Zack.

"Something smells good in here."

The deep voice interrupted her reverie, and she looked up to see her new employer in the doorway wearing a long rain slicker and Stetson. He looked ruggedly handsome, like something out of a cologne commercial, and she wondered a little desperately why she couldn't have fallen in love with someone like him.

Despite Zack's claim that Wade might have been involved in whatever he'd stumbled onto the night he left Salt River, she still couldn't believe it.

Wade was nice and safe, and he wouldn't have made a habit of crushing her heart like it was made of toothpicks.

She managed to summon a smile. "Beef and barley soup and homemade bread. I know it wasn't on the week's menu we worked out, but it seemed just the thing for such a drizzly day."

She thought she saw just a hint of irritation flicker across his dark eyes, then he smiled. "That sounds perfect. I'm sure the guests will understand about the change in plans."

She cleared her throat, suddenly uncomfortable. "I'm sorry. I guess I should have cleared it with you first."

"No, it's fine."

At the Lost Creek she had enjoyed full autonomy in the kitchen. If she had wanted to serve cold cereal for dinner,

Jean would have just laughed and gone along with it. But she was learning that Wade liked to have a hand in every aspect of his guest ranch.

She couldn't really blame him. While only a few miles away on horseback from the Lost Creek, the Rendezvous was in a completely different stratosphere when it came to its guests.

Wade's ranch catered to a far more exclusive clientele than the Lost Creek.

While Jean tried to bring in young families and older people—average folks yearning to experience the romance of the Old West for a while—the Rendezvous attracted movie stars and Wall Street tycoons and media moguls. Movers and shakers who wanted to be close to Jackson without the annoying crowds.

Her humble beef and barley soup had probably been a lousy idea. Big surprise there. She hadn't done a single thing right since she came here.

"I'm sorry," she said again.

Wade waved one hand dismissively while he removed his Stetson with the other one. "Don't worry about it. How are you settling in?"

Somehow she managed to find another smile. "Fine. Your kitchen is wonderful."

Wade studied her for a long moment until she began to squirm, then he smiled. "I hope this doesn't sound too forward of me but I designed it with you in mind. I always knew you would end up here, one way or another."

Okay. This was getting a little creepy. What was she supposed to say to that? She didn't have the heart to tell him the Rendezvous was just a brief resting place on her journey to her ultimate goal. As soon as the dust settled from this ridiculous murder charge against Zack and he left again, she would make an offer on Murphy's.

She would, she assured that hateful little voice raising doubts in her mind. She just needed a little more time.

"You made the right decision coming here." Wade moved behind her to grab a bottle of imported water from the refrigerator. "Distancing yourself from that...that son of a bitch Slater was the right thing to do. I tried to tell you he was no-good. Sooner or later, he'll be arrested for murder. That kind of ugliness should never have to touch you."

He reached out and rested his hand on her shoulder, and she fought the instinct to flinch away.

What on earth was the matter with her? Wade had been her friend for a long time. She shouldn't have this edginess around him.

"I'm not so sure about that arrest," she finally said, compelled to defend Slater even though he clearly didn't want her involved. "If Jesse had enough evidence against him, Zack would already be in jail."

"He will be. Just wait. If there was one thing I learned when I was on the force, it's that the wheels of justice roll slowly sometimes. But Slater will get what's coming to him. I guarantee it. He's going to find out we don't let men like him get away with killing innocent women around here."

Melanie? Innocent? A raw laugh almost escaped her throat, but she swallowed it back just in time, somehow sensing Wade wouldn't appreciate the irony. More than likely he would be horrified at her callous attitude toward her late sister-in-law.

Before she could answer, Wade changed the subject. "What are you planning for dessert?"

The shift in conversation so disoriented her that it took her several moments to gather her thoughts. "I, ah, I'm not sure."

A little frown wrinkled his tanned forehead. "Oh. Well,

I'm sure it will be something delicious. I'll check back later. Remember, dinner is at seven sharp."

After he shoved his hat on and left, she gazed out once more at the gloomy late-afternoon sky. Dear heavens, she hated it here. She wanted to go home. Not to the Diamond Harte, to the Lost Creek. And to Zack.

Her fierce longing to see him again—to talk to him, to assure herself he was okay—was a physical ache inside her, grinding away at her spirit.

She forced her attention back to dinner. She needed to come up with something spectacular for dessert to make up for the soup disaster, and she didn't have any time to waste wishing for the moon.

At the Lost Creek she would have served jam and butter with the homemade bread, but she suspected that wouldn't win her very many points here.

What about crêpes Suzette? They were relatively easy to make and always generated excitement, what with all that flaming brandy. It might be a little extravagant as a counterpoint to the soup but maybe a little flash wouldn't be such a bad thing.

So, brandy. Where could she find some? She did a quick mental inventory of the kitchen supplies she had seen throughout her week of working at the Rendezvous. Wade kept the spirits tucked away in one of the higher cupboards, didn't he?

She had to pore through several before she found it. There. Tucked away in a corner of the kitchen, on the top shelf with several other bottles. She pulled a stool over and climbed up, immediately spying the orange liqueur she would also need.

She was just reaching for the decanter of brandy when she spied something else in the rear of the cupboard.

A box, no more than six inches long and maybe four

inches deep. Small and wooden, it seemed out of place amid the richly colored bottles.

The wood was smooth, cool in her hands as she picked it up and she heard a clink and rattle from inside. What might be inside? Someone's forgotten bank stash? Heirloom jewelry? A secret diary?

Her dark mood momentarily gave way to curiosity as she remembered those rainy days spent with her mother pawing through the old cedar chest.

This box was also cedar, the kind a woman might keep treasured letters inside. As she worked the catch and lifted the lid, the evocative smell wafted to her.

She closed her eyes, once more in her parents' bedroom looking at old photographs and bronzed baby shoes and bits of lace pillowcase her grandmother had tatted as a new bride.

This box was lined in red velvet, she saw when she opened her eyes again, the contents obviously precious to someone.

Why? she wondered. It was jewelry all right, but instead of old cameos and pearls that might have belonged to someone's ancestors, at first glance it seemed to be nothing but cheap costume jewelry. A gaudy necklace, spangled bracelets, a pair of dangly earrings.

She had seen these things before. She blinked, racking her mind to remember where. A long time ago. Someone she knew had owned similar pieces.

She couldn't think who or where or when until she moved them aside and saw something else at the bottom of the pile of trinkets. A photograph, facedown, with no writing on the back.

She pulled it out, and nervousness skittered down her spine like a closet full of spiders.

With trembling hands she turned over the picture, then gasped.

It was a Polaroid of a woman she knew all too well, with dark curly hair and troubled gray eyes.

Melanie.

She wore a tight, flashy dress along with every one of the items in the box.

And judging by the pool of blood puddling under her head and the empty look in those gray eyes, she was very, very dead.

Chapter 11

She stared at the box in her hands, vaguely aware of the drumming of her pulse, her rapid, shallow breathing.

Her mind raced, trying to figure out what it meant. Why would this be here, tucked away in the kitchen of the Rendezvous Ranch? Had Wade somehow been involved in Melanie's death? Was this box some kind of grisly souvenir?

Her vision dimmed at the thought, and she had to step down from the stool before she toppled to the ground.

What other explanation could there be?

Zack had tried to warn her about Wade, but she hadn't listened. Now she saw his claims in an entirely different light. Had Wade really been involved in the drug ring Zack said he'd stumbled on the night he left? Had he been one of the men who had brutally kicked and beaten Zack before ordering him out of town?

She had struggled to believe Zack's claims. The idea of a mild-mannered, kind man like Wade—a pillar of the community, active in church and civic responsibilities—wrapped up in something so ugly seemed ludicrous.

It didn't seem so outrageous now.

She stared at the picture in her hand, at that beautiful face with the wide, empty eyes, and her stomach churned.

Had Melanie been linked to the drug activity Zack claimed to have seen? She wouldn't have been surprised to know her sister-in-law had been abusing drugs. It fit the pattern of an unhappy, self-destructive woman.

Melanie hadn't died of an overdose, though, but of a bullet to the brain. Had Wade put it there?

She began to shiver. Why, in heaven's name, would he have left this here tucked away in a back cupboard of his kitchen? He must have known she would eventually find it.

Maybe that's exactly what he wanted.

A chill gusted over her, colder than any January wind. Why? Why would he possibly want her to see this?

No. This must be some kind of hideous mistake. The logical, rational corner of her mind still couldn't imagine Wade could be capable of this. A box full of costume jewelry wasn't proof of anything.

The picture, though. That was a fairly damning piece of the puzzle.

Jesse. She should call Jesse. He would know what to do. Hands shaking, her breathing ragged, she rushed to the phone hanging on the kitchen wall and dialed her brother's cellular number.

She was just punching in the last number when the door opened. She froze, her finger poised above the five, and the box in her other hand just as Wade walked back into the kitchen.

In one quick movement, she shoved the box behind her back and hung up the phone.

"Did you forget something?" she asked, hoping he couldn't hear the panic she tried to hide behind a thin, crackly sheen of false cheerfulness.

He narrowed his gaze at her, looking from the phone and then back to her. "Is everything okay? You're looking a little pale."

"Fine. Everything's just fine." *Breathe,* she ordered herself as her knees started to wobble.

"Are you sure? Maybe you need to sit down."

"No. I promise, I'm fine."

If anyone in her right mind could consider ready to jump out of her skin any minute now at all close to *fine.*

"Am I interrupting something?"

"No. I was…was just trying to figure out what to fix for dessert."

"That's why I came back. I had a couple of suggestions for something to serve after your, uh, delicious soup."

If she hadn't been so terrified, she would have been offended by that not-so-subtle dig.

"I was thinking a cheesecake might be nice. Or some kind of torte. I believe we have fresh raspberries."

She made a noncommittal sound, willing him to leave the kitchen. When she didn't answer beyond that, his gaze narrowed. "Are you sure you're all right, Cassidy? You look as if you've seen a ghost."

Maybe because she had. "No. I…I'm fine. Just a little tired."

"What do you have there?"

"Where?"

"Behind your back. What are you hiding?"

She shuddered out a quick breath, her mind scrambling. "It's, um, a surprise. For dessert."

He fingered his hat. "Please don't take this the wrong way, but I'm not really all that fond of surprises. Why don't you just tell me what you're planning?"

"Crêpes Suzette," she blurted out. "It's one of my specialties."

"Oh." He smiled. "That sounds very elegant. Very French. I don't believe we've ever served that at the Rendezvous. Okay. Good. I'll see you at dinner, then."

To her vast relief he started to walk back out of the kitchen. She forced her breathing into a slow, measured cadence. But just before he reached the door, he stopped, his head turned toward the liquor cabinet.

To her horror she suddenly realized the door to the cupboard was still wide open, the stepstool in front of it. There was nothing she could do to hide either at this point.

If he was indeed the one who'd stashed the gruesome little box there, he would know she had discovered it.

He turned back to her, his mouth suddenly grim, then walked closer. "What are you hiding?" he repeated.

"Nothing. Just…nothing." She was too frightened to come up with anything more coherent than that.

"Oh, dear. This is a problem. You found it, didn't you?"

"Found what? I don't know what you're talking about."

"You were never a very good liar, Cassidy. You shouldn't have gone snooping around. It wasn't very polite."

She tried one more time to bluff her way through. "I'm not lying. I was…was just looking for some brandy for the dessert. For crêpes Suzette you pour brandy over the crêpes and set them ablaze. It's really quite dramatic."

His sigh was resigned. "I'm afraid I can't let you leave, now that you know."

"I don't know anything. I swear."

"You're a smart woman, Cassidy. That's one of the things I've always admired about you. That and your lush beauty. You're like a rare rose blooming in a weed patch." He reached a hand out and traced one finger down her cheek, and it took every ounce of strength to keep from flinching. "We could have made a wonderful team together."

Even though her stomach heaved and she was very much afraid she was going to be sick all over him, she mustered a smile. "We still can."

"It's too late for that. Far too late. You shouldn't have gone snooping."

He was crazy. He had to be. He left the box there in plain sight, where anyone could have stumbled on it, then he accused her of going searching for it. Real fear began uncoiling inside her. He wouldn't let her leave. Not after this.

"You're very much like her."

"Like who?" She barely paid attention to him as her mind chased in circles trying to come up with an escape route. There were two doors in the kitchen, one to the back porch of the lodge, the other to the dining room. She mentally scanned her options and decided her chances were better outside.

He would be on her in a second, though, unless she came up with something to delay him.

"Like Melanie," Wade went on, his voice conversational, as if he were talking about something benign, mundane.

"I loved her. I never wanted to hurt her." His sigh sounded wistful, melancholy. "We were going to leave Star Valley. Make a new start, just the two of us. I was working on getting the money."

"By dealing drugs with Carl Briggs?"

She hadn't meant to say that, it just slipped out. Wade's dark eyes widened with surprise for just a moment, then his expression hardened. "How did you know about that?"

She didn't answer, just tried to focus on escaping.

"That bastard Slater told you, didn't he? He doesn't know how to keep his mouth shut. I knew we should have finished him off that night."

She swallowed hard as his words confirmed everything Zack had said and more.

"Carl and me and a few of the other boys had a good thing going," Wade went on, apparently not expecting any involvement in the conversation from her. "We were the middlemen. It was a perfect setup. Who would have suspected a podunk small-town Wyoming police department was a distribution hub for the intermountain West? We could have gotten away with it forever. Then that night everything went wrong."

He glared at her as if it had all been her fault.

"First that no-account drifter of yours turned up where he had no business, then I came home to find Melanie at my place in town, drunk and acting crazy. She wanted to leave that night. I told her I needed a few more weeks to come up with enough money. She said she couldn't wait, that she had to get out of town and didn't have any more patience for what she called my stupid little schemes. She shouldn't have said that."

His expression darkened until she hardly recognized him as the same kind, decent man she had always believed him to be.

She cleared her throat, compelled despite her own instincts of self-preservation to hear of Melanie's fate. "What happened?"

"I had to prove to her I was onto something big, to convince her to wait just a few more weeks, so I showed her the blow still in the truck. We were delivering it the next morning to our contacts.

"If she had only stayed quiet, everything would have been fine. But she started going on about how she wanted in. If I refused, she said she would go public with the whole thing and expose us all."

A vague plan began to form in her mind, and Cassie began edging toward the stove, hoping he wouldn't notice.

To her relief, he seemed to be too wrapped up in the

past. "I tried to shut her up, but she kept going on and on about how she deserved my share since she took pity on me and slept with me."

He closed his eyes as if to block out the memories, and Cassie took advantage of his distraction to step closer to the stove.

"I didn't know what else to do. She wouldn't shut up. She even picked up the phone and said she was calling the sheriff right then. I knew if she told anybody, Carl would kill *me* for showing her the merchandise. I pulled out my gun, just to scare her. She laughed at me and kept dialing."

"So you shot her."

He opened his eyes as if he were surprised to see her still there.

"I shot her. I didn't want to. I cried the whole time I dug that grave out at the Atkins place. I loved her. I never wanted to hurt her." His lips narrowed. "I don't want to hurt you, either, Cassidy. You shouldn't have gone snooping around."

"You shouldn't have left this in the back of the liquor cabinet, then, where anybody could have stumbled on it."

She held out the photograph, and for a moment he froze, then he reached out and snatched it from her, examining the grisly scene as if it was a Monet watercolor.

"Wasn't she beautiful?" he murmured. "Like an angel."

She chose that moment to move, while he was distracted by the picture. In one motion, she picked up the heavy stockpot of soup—the soup he had been so disdainful of—and hurled it into his face.

As the boiling liquid hit him, Wade screamed a terrible, high-pitched scream and went down on his knees, his hands over his face. She knew this was likely her only chance for survival so she didn't wait around.

In seconds she had rushed out the back door. Although

she knew it was costing her precious time, she quickly hefted one of the sturdy Adirondack lawn chairs on the back porch and wedged it under the doorknob as a further delaying tactic, then took off running.

The sky had darkened even more, and after just a few yards she was soaked and shivering in her jeans and sweatshirt.

A short distance from the house she caught a lucky break. Wade had left his horse tied up to a hitching post near the driveway, obviously intending to ride out again after he finished nagging her about dessert.

The horse was skittish as this strange, dripping-wet woman ran up to him out of nowhere. He whinnied and danced around on his lead, but Cassie hadn't spent her whole life around horses for nothing. She grabbed the reins firmly and wasted a few more valuable seconds trying to calm the animal with soft words.

When the fractious horse was finally under control, she quickly mounted. Although the stirrups were set for Wade's much longer legs, she dug the heels of her sneakers into his side. The horse apparently got the message and the two of them hurtled off through the rain.

She wasn't conscious of any kind of plan beyond escaping whatever grim fate Wade had in store for her. But as the horse galloped away from the Rendezvous, she realized exactly where she was heading.

To the Lost Creek.

To safety.

To Zack.

It was over.

Despite the steady drizzle, Zack nudged his mount a little higher up the trail above the Lost Creek, loath to leave the mountain just yet. He wanted one last look at this place he had come to love so much—at the bright, shining future he had cupped in his hands for only a few precious moments before it had trickled through his fingers.

He was leaving in the morning at first light, Jesse Harte's edicts about not leaving town be damned. His lawyers could wrangle over the particulars. Until the county prosecutor determined there was enough evidence to charge him, they had no legal basis to keep him here.

And he couldn't stay any longer.

It was too painful being so close to Cassie, to know she was just through the trees at her new job working for that son of a bitch Lowry. Just a few miles away but forever out of his reach.

For a few magical weeks she had been his again. The world had gleamed with promise. Possibilities. He closed his eyes, his mind filled with images of her: laughing at something he said, her smile wide and her eyes bright; bustling about the heat of the ranch kitchen with flushed cheeks and that look of concentration on her features; her body taut beneath him, around him, as he made love to her.

He should have known this time with her wouldn't last. It had been a chimera, a fleeting glimpse at something he could never hope to own.

The identification of Melanie Harte's remains—and the subsequent wide net of suspicion cast on him—had effectively shattered that future.

The irony of the past didn't escape him. He had left her a decade ago in an effort to protect her from a no-good son of a bitch like him. He was doing the same now.

Once more he faced charges for a crime he didn't commit—this time for a heinous crime against a member of her own family—and the injustice of it made him want to climb to the highest spot he could find and shake his fists at the sky.

So close. He'd been so close to grabbing the prize, the only thing he had ever wanted. A home, a place to belong, with the woman who had owned his heart since she was just eighteen.

And now he had nothing. Less than nothing. A few memories that cut his heart like a fresh blade.

He drew in a ragged breath and dismounted at a spot where the trees thinned. Below him the Star Valley spread out, little clusters of population surrounded by acres and acres of farms and ranches.

The dark clouds overhead saturated the valley with color. The countryside looked fresh and clean and verdant.

A place where he would always be an outsider.

He couldn't stay anymore. If Jesse Harte wanted him here to face charges, he could damn well charge him with something or cut him free. This had been just a brief, wonderful interlude that ended in disaster, and now he needed to get back to his real life.

His solitary, empty, colorless life.

He sighed, fighting the primitive urge to keep on riding until he reached the Rendezvous, then toss Cassie over his saddle and ride off into the mountains with her.

No. He couldn't. He had to head back to the Lost Creek, to spend one more night at the guest ranch he now owned and didn't know what to do with.

He didn't feel right about turning around and selling it to someone else. Not when he had promised Jean Martineau he would care for her ranch with the same care she had always given it.

He would just have to hire someone to run it. Would Cassie consider the job? he wondered, then discarded the idea just as quickly. She would excel at managing the place, he had no doubt about that whatsoever. But he could never ask her to work for him on a permanent basis, even if he thought for a minute she might even consider it.

What a mess. He'd been so damn sure his plans to woo her again would eventually succeed that he hadn't planned for failure at all.

With another deep sigh of regret, he shoved his boot in the stirrup and swung into the saddle. He spared one last look at the pristine valley below before nudging the horse back down the trail.

He had only ridden a hundred yards when he heard something crash through the undergrowth on the trail ahead of him, hidden from view by the thick brush. Moose and elk often frequented the thickly wooded area. They were about the only thing big enough to make that kind of noise, he thought, then he heard a high whinny and the unmistakable sound of a horse at full gallop.

Damn. What kind of idiot takes a muddy, steep trail like this at such a pace? Either the animal was out of control or its rider had some kind of a death wish.

He spurred his own mount as fast as safety dictated to catch up with the rider. As he burst around the bend, he saw a muscular buckskin being urged hell-for-leather down the trail. At first he thought the rider was a foolish boy who had been caught out in the weather unprepared, judging by the lack of rain gear and the short dark hair plastered to his head.

Then, as the rider turned around to see who followed, Zack had a quick impression of delicate, pale features, and realized the rider was no boy.

It was Cassie. And she looked scared to death.

He thought for a moment she was going to keep hurtling down the mountainside, but she finally reined in the buckskin. The horse skidded to a stop then stood, sides heaving, while Zack caught up with her.

He dismounted and rushed to her, his arms out. She slid almost bonelessly into them, stumbling when she reached the ground. She would have fallen if he hadn't held her so tightly to his chest. He realized she was trembling, from cold or shock, he wasn't sure, and his gut clutched with dread.

"What is it? What's happened?" Urgency sharpened his voice.

Her voice sounded dazed, thready. "He killed her. We have to get out of here. I think I heard him following me."

She tried to pull away from him, her face tight with fear, but he held her fast. "Who? Slow down!"

"Wade. He…he killed Melanie. I stumbled onto proof at the Rendezvous. I tried to hide it from him, but I couldn't and he…I think he was going to hurt me, too. I threw a pot of soup at him and ran. All I could think about was coming here, to the Lost Creek. To you."

His arms tightened around her, and she rested her cheek against his chest only for a moment, then drew back frantically.

"We can't stay here. I think he's crazy. Who knows what he'll do if he finds us. Come on. We have to get to the ranch and call Jesse."

And she needed to get out of this rain and her wet clothes before she caught pneumonia. Already he could see signs of hypothermia in her bloodless lips and dazed expression. He pulled off his oiled slicker and wrapped her in it. She was trembling so much he didn't think she would be able to stay in the saddle much longer. "I think you and your horse are both done for. You can ride with me."

She opened her mouth as if she to argue, then closed it again, obviously deciding there wasn't time.

Grateful for the strength of the big, rawboned bay he'd been riding since his arrival at the ranch, he mounted first, then reached down and helped her up behind him. She clung tightly as he urged the horse down the trail, the buckskin plodding tiredly behind.

She wrapped her arms around him, soaking in the heat that emanated from his powerful back. Although deep tremors still shook her body, for the first time since that gruesome discovery—no, for the first time since the week before, when Jesse had growled out the news about Melanie's death and Zack had pushed her away—she began to feel safe and warm again.

As they rode, she explained her discovery to him, about stumbling onto that terrible box and the story Wade had told her of Melanie's death.

"How did you get away?" he asked, shifting in the saddle so he could see her through the gathering darkness.

She winced. "I, um, threw a pot of hot beef and barley soup on him and ran out the door."

"Soup? You threw *soup* at a man threatening to kill you? A man who has already murdered at least one person who stood in his way?"

Feeling warmer by the second, she clenched her teeth at the stunned disbelief in his voice. "Yeah, I know. It was a waste of good soup. How about the next time a murderer comes after me, I'll ask you first before I make any kind of move to protect myself?"

Before he could answer, they heard a loud rustling in the thick brush twenty yards or thirty yards ahead of them. Both horses alerted, tails raised. With a soft command to the bay, Zack reined in the horse, his head up like a tawny mountain lion scenting danger.

Although there was a good hour of daylight left, the steady rain created a thick, misty curtain that limited visibility. All she could hear was the heavy pounding of her pulse and the musical drip of raindrops plinking off the leaves.

"Is it Wade?" she whispered through the fear in her throat.

He squeezed one of her hands wrapped around his middle. "I'm not sure. Probably not. A man doesn't quickly recover from having a pot of beef and barley soup hurled at him."

He gave her that lopsided grin she loved so much, then it slid away. "Damn. I wish I'd brought a revolver with me."

A revolver? Did he really think he might need a weapon? She had never wanted to put Zack in danger. All she had been thinking about was escape. Now her mind reeled with a dozen scenarios, each more grim than the last.

After a moment they heard nothing else down the trail so Zack cautiously urged his horse on. Before they could make it even ten yards, Wade stepped out of the brush, holding a shiny black handgun aimed right at them.

Cassie swallowed a shriek, and her grip tightened convulsively around Zack.

All signs of the benign, friendly man she had known had disappeared, replaced by an angry stranger. Wade's face was a dusky red, as if he had spent way too much time in the sun. Odd, since it was so cloudy. It took her several seconds to realize he must have been burned by the soup broth.

"Oh, this is perfect," he drawled. "It couldn't be more perfect. I can take care of two problems at once."

Horrified, Cassie stared at him. What had she done? She had led Wade right to them, now here they were unarmed and completely at his mercy. Dear heavens. She should have escaped to the Diamond Harte. It was several miles farther, but Wade wouldn't have been able to storm into the ranch house.

And even if he had managed to catch up with her, at least Zack would have been safe.

"How did you find me?" she asked, and cursed her voice for trembling.

"It wasn't hard. When you stole my horse, I knew you would come here. To him. Slater." He said the name like the vilest curse. "Besides, you left a trail a mile wide for me to follow. I just can't figure out why you're still so hot for him after what he did. I would have been so good to you."

"Like you were for Melanie?"

The words tumbled out before she could swallow them down, and she winced. When would she ever learn to shut her big mouth?

If possible, more color suffused his face. "You don't know anything about that. I loved her." He gestured emphatically with the hand holding the gun, and she held her breath, waiting for the bullet to dig into her flesh. Or worse, for Zack to be hit.

He appeared to be struggling to regain control. A moment later he pointed the gun at them again. "Get down. Both of you."

Inside the circle of her arms, Zack's already taut frame tensed even more. "Why?"

"I'm the one with the gun. Because I said so, damn it. Now get off the damn horse."

Her legs were shaking just like the rest of her, and she had to grip Zack's hand tightly to keep from falling as she dismounted. Once she reached the ground, he climbed down from the horse to join her, then moved in front of her, shielding her body with his.

Wade noted the gesture with a cold smile. "You really think you're going to take me on? It looks to me like I'm the one holding all the aces here. My Colt .45 trumps your bare hands any day."

The bare hands in question clenched convulsively. This must be horrible for Zack. Forced to stand helplessly and do nothing while they both literally stared death in the face.

Wade pointed the gun at Zack suddenly. "Cassidy, you tie up the horses. Mine, too. We wouldn't want them to wander back to the ranch and raise any suspicions. Oh, and make sure those knots are tight, too, unless you want to watch your loverboy die right here."

With cold, shaking hands, she obeyed then stood aside while Wade double-checked her knots.

"All right. Now walk," Wade ordered, his voice hard.

"Where are you taking us?" Zack asked.

She suspected even before Wade answered.

"There's an old, abandoned cabin between the Rendezvous and the Lost Creek," he said. "Jean and I keep it maintained for the tourists to see what an authentic Western homestead was like. It's the perfect place for a lovers' tryst."

His laugh raised her hackles. "And for a lovers' spat."

They walked single file through the heavy timber on what looked like little more than a deer trail, Cassie in the lead, Zack a few steps behind her and Wade coming up the rear, his gun trained on them both. Even with the warmth of Zack's oiled slicker, she was still wet and cold.

What did it matter if she was shivering? She was going to die in a few moments, anyway.

"So you're going to kill us both and make it look like a murder-suicide?" Zack broke the silence, his voice almost casual. She marveled at his grit—how was he so calm when she could barely make one foot move in front of the other?

"That's the general idea."

"You used to be a cop. I'm sure you're aware those kind of crime scenes aren't easy to fake."

"I'll make it look good. Trust me. It won't be too hard. Everyone knows you and Cassie are on the outs now, that she and everybody else think you murdered Melanie. I've got the proof right here."

Eyes focused on the trail ahead of her for some kind of weapon, she barely heard a thump as he patted the pocket of his slicker. He must have brought the box with Melanie's picture and her jewelry.

"Your poor grief-stricken brother will be smart enough to put it together, Cass. The minute the police chief sees this in your cold, dead hands, he'll know you found evidence that your lover killed Melanie. Even he'll be able to figure out you must have confronted Slater with it, forcing him to kill you. Then, unable to live with his crimes, he turned his gun on himself. It's very romantic, really. The perfect setup."

It *was* perfect. Given his overwhelming animosity toward Zack, Jesse would be quick to jump to such a conclusion.

She couldn't let Wade get away with it, she thought fiercely. Not only because she didn't want to die here on this cold, rainy mountainside, but for Zack's sake.

It wasn't fair. He had been unfairly blamed for too many things, only because he was an outsider.

Through a break in the trees she saw the outline of a structure ahead and knew they were almost at the old cabin. They didn't have much time. She had to figure something out.

She was just wondering if she could create a diversion long enough for Zack to get away when he coughed behind her. She surreptitiously turned her head to look at him and their gazes met. The sun had almost slipped behind the mountains to the west but she had enough light left to see him mouth a single word to her.

Run.

She stumbled on the trail, then righted herself with a small, emphatic shake of her head that sent drops of rain flying from her wet hair. No. She wouldn't leave him here at Wade's mercy, even if she had more than the slightest chance in hell of escaping.

Turning her gaze back to the trail for some kind of a weapon, she felt rather than heard his resigned sigh.

An instant later the world erupted into a flurry of motion. She felt something shove her off the trail—Zack, she assumed, trying to get her out of harm's way. She rolled through the slippery grass and looked up just in time to see Zack smash his elbow into Wade's face. The other man sagged to his knees from the impact, blood spurting wildly from his nose, but he didn't drop the gun.

While Wade still reeled from the unexpected attack, Zack dived in low, hoping to catch him off guard. For long terrible moments the men grappled for the weapon. They were evenly matched, both hardened by years of ranch work. Wade was an inch or two taller and maybe thirty pounds heavier, but Zack didn't have an ounce of spare flesh on him.

Besides, he was fighting for his life. For *their* lives.

She crouched in the wet grass for long moments while the two men fought for possession of the revolver. Without even really focusing on it, she managed to pry a rock the size of a frying pan out of the mud and waited for a chance to use it as a weapon if she had to. It was slick and heavy in her hands and she only prayed she could hang on to it.

She wanted to help—do anything—but she was afraid whatever she did might distract Zack enough to give Wade the advantage.

Zack seemed to be gaining the upper hand. They were locked so closely together she couldn't tell exactly what was happening, but she could tell Wade was hampered by the blood still gushing from his nose. With one powerful lunge, Zack tumbled him to the ground, his hand on the wrist holding the gun. They rolled again until both of them were covered in mud and she could no longer see the gun.

Wade was tiring, she realized. Zack almost had him overpowered.

And then the gun went off.

Her breath tangling in her lungs, Cassie could only stare at the two men still snarled together as the echo of the gunshot boomed across the mountainside.

Which one had been hit?

She felt a scream build up inside her an instant later, when Zack slumped over on his back, a crimson stain blossoming across his chest. The breath she had been holding escaped with a hollow gurgle and she swayed, her vision dimming around the edges.

Wade stood over him, wiping the blood that still seeped from his broken nose with the back of his hand. "Stupid bastard," he growled, his breathing ragged.

The words and the angry disdain behind them spurred her to action. Praying for strength, she hefted the stone high above her head and rushed toward him, bringing the heavy weight crashing down against his head with her last ounce of energy.

It struck with the same hollow, thumping sound of a car driving over a pumpkin.

He crumpled to the ground, out cold, and she snatched the gun out of his motionless hand, then rushed to Zack.

The wound was bleeding profusely, seeping out in all directions, and she did her best to stanch the flow with his sweater.

Dear God. Please let him be all right.

"Why did you have to be such a damn hero?" she growled.

His breathing was irregular, and beneath his tan, his face wore an unnatural pallor. He grabbed her hand and his grip was weak. "Cass, I'm sorry."

"For what?" she asked.

"For making you cry. I hate making you cry." He coughed and more blood bubbled out of his wound, then his eyes fluttered shut again and stayed that way.

"You are not going to die," she vowed, only vaguely aware of the tears seeping down her cheeks to mix with the rain. "I'm not letting you leave me again."

She had to get him dry and go for help but she knew she didn't have much time. Wade could wake up any moment. He wouldn't have the gun since the cold weight of it was tucked into the waistband of her jeans, but he could still finish Zack off if he regained consciousness before she returned with help.

Although she knew it would take precious moments, she knew she had to secure him somehow. How? she wondered, near frantic. The horses! Zack's horse and the buckskin both had coiled ropes hanging from their saddles.

With fear for Zack coursing through her veins, she ran down the deer trail, slipping and sliding through the mud in her haste. When she reached the horses, she grabbed as much rope as she could find, then untied the reins of Zack's big blood bay and vaulted into the saddle.

He was much more surefooted than she had been as they rode up the narrow trail toward the cabin.

She wanted to rush to Zack first but she could see that Wade was already beginning to stir. He hadn't regained full consciousness and she contemplated hitting him again with the rock. But it was one thing to bean a man who had just shot the man you loved. It was quite another to strike an inert figure who was still only half-conscious.

Before he could come back all the way, she quickly shoved him over with a knee in his back and trussed his hands together behind him, deeply grateful for all the time Matt had spent with her teaching her how to hitch a good knot.

She left him with his face in the mud while she tied his legs together then used the other rope to bind him to the nearest tree, a sturdy pine.

Only after he was secured could she turn her attention to Zack. She skidded toward him, sick to see how much the angry red stain on his sweater had spread in the five minutes she'd been gone. "Zack. Come on. Wake up. We've got to get you to the cabin so you can stay dry while I go for help. Please! Wake up."

Her breath came out in heaving sobs when he didn't even flutter his eyelids and she whispered a plea for help. What could she do? Even on a good day, she didn't have the strength to drag two hundred pounds of hard-muscled man that far—especially not one bleeding heavily from a gunshot wound to the chest.

And this had *not* been a good day.

She had to get help fast, but she couldn't leave him here like this in the rain. Her mind whirled through her options for a few seconds, then she somehow managed to haul him a few feet until he lay under the spreading branches of a nearby spruce tree.

He didn't move at all while she situated him but she blocked her mind from the very real possibility that his gunshot wound might prove fatal.

She wasn't going to let him die.

Quickly rifling through the bay's saddlebags, she found the emergency survival kit Jean always insisted the Lost

Creek guests rode with. Inside among the other supplies was a thin plastic rain jacket and an emergency space blanket.

She worked as fast as she could, wrapping his own slicker—the one he had lent her—around him along with the rain jacket, then she constructed a primitive rain shelter over his upper body by draping the silvery material of the blanket over the branches just above his head.

That would keep the worst of the rain away from him, at least.

It was only after she finished that she realized her vision was obstructed not from the elements but from the steady tears that still coursed down her cheeks.

The next fifteen minutes passed in a blur as she bowed low over the horse's head and raced through the darkness toward the Lost Creek. Fortunately, Zack's horse was as eager to be home as she and he knew the trail far better.

By the time she reached the ranch, the adrenaline rush that had carried her through the last hour, since that horrible discovery in Wade's kitchen, began to ebb. Every muscle in her body strained and ached and she could barely manage to breathe past the cold ball of helpless dread lodged in her throat.

At the ranch she was baffled to see several police vehicles parked out front, Jesse's Bronco among them. How had he known? she wondered as she burst up the stairs and into the lodge with her last ounce of energy.

Her brother was standing just inside the door, surrounded by what looked like the entire Salt River police force. His face went slack with shock when he saw her.

"Please. I need help." It was the only thing she could manage to say through her racing lungs.

Jesse rushed to her, taking in her bedraggled state and the blood and muck she knew was smeared all over her soaked sweatshirt. "Cassie. What the hell happened? Are you hurt?" His eyes sharpened with anger. "Where is he? Where is that son of a bitch? If he hurt you, I swear I'm going to rip him apart with my bare hands."

She blinked, finally realizing how odd it was to find him at the ranch. He had no way of knowing what Wade had done.

"What are you doing here?" she managed to ask, her voice weak and raspy.

"I've come for Slater. No way in hell was I going to let the bastard skip town. I finally managed to convince the county attorney to file charges against him for killing Melanie."

She gazed at her brother's hard, angry features. Of course, she thought hysterically, what else would he be doing? He was here to arrest Zack, who even now lay bleeding to death because he had stepped in front of a bullet.

For her.

The trauma and terror and terrible fear that had been nipping at her heels finally caught up with her.

She began to laugh, a bitter, grating, horrible sound. "You can't arrest him, Jesse. Not if he's already dead."

Chapter 12

He awoke to grinding, white-hot pain just below his left collarbone and the disorienting sensation of knowing he was in a completely unfamiliar place.

It had to be some kind of hospital. The walls were white, clinical, and he could hear the whoosh and beep of medical equipment. He looked down and saw a bandage wrapped around his chest.

What happened? Where the hell was he?

He closed his eyes, trying to remember what might have brought him here. For a moment he had only brief fragments of memory. Images, really.

Cassie.

A rainy mountainside.

Lowry…

He hitched in a breath as memories tumbled back like hard stones being thrown at him. Lowry. Cassie. A bitter struggle.

Where was she? Had she been hurt?

He had to find her! He struggled to rise, but a steady

hand suddenly held him down. "Whoa there, cowboy. You don't want to move too much, I promise, or you're going to find yourself in a world of hurt."

A man with a steely gray buzz cut and a white coat stood over him writing on a clipboard. He knew this man. He squinted, trying to place him, then it came to him. Old Doc Wallace at the Salt River Clinic.

He swallowed, aware suddenly that his throat felt as if he'd gulped down a plateful of desert sand.

"Cassie," he managed to rasp out.

The doctor gestured with his thumb toward the door, where Zack thought he heard raised voices.

Hers, he realized. Sweet relief coursed through him. She couldn't have been hurt too badly if she was outside his door yelling at someone. He thought he heard the words *owe* and *apology* and *pigheaded*.

"Who else?" he asked.

Doc Wallace rolled his eyes. "Whole damn town, seems like. Her whole family got here right after they brought you in. I believe Chief Harte is the one being, uh, reprimanded out there. Jean Martineau and most of her Lost Creek staff showed up a few minutes ago. I think the police officers who rode up that mountain after you and Lowry are still hanging around. You're quite the hero. Lowry, in case you're wondering, has a concussion but he's being treated at the sick bay over at the jail."

Zack closed his eyes again, remembering those terrible moments on the trail when he was sure the son of a bitch was going to kill them both. When he had known he wouldn't be able to save her.

"Cassie's okay? You're sure?"

"More scared than anything. She had a mild case of hypothermia but she's fine."

The doc finished scribbling in the chart, then closed

it with a wry smile. "Since you haven't bothered to ask about yourself, I'll tell you anyway. You are one lucky cowboy. I don't know how but that bullet missed just about everything important. You lost a lot of blood but you're stable enough now that I can send you on to Idaho Falls for surgery."

Surgery. Great. He grimaced. He hated hospitals, always had. But they sure beat the alternative—bleeding to death in the muddy mountainside above the Lost Creek.

As if he'd read his thoughts, the doc gestured toward the door to the trauma room. The shouting had died down, Zack noted. "That's one hell of a woman you got there," Wallace said. "You never would have made it if she'd had one ounce less grit."

Zack wanted to correct him but he didn't. Yeah, Cassie was one hell of a woman. He would never argue there.

But she wasn't his.

He remembered her kneeling next to him, tears coursing down her cheeks, and his chest felt tight and achy from more than just a lousy bullet hole.

"She's itching to come in," the doc said. "You up to a visitor?"

He nodded and kept his gaze trained on the door for the next few moments, trying not to focus on the pain, until she opened it cautiously, peeking around the door.

He was startled to see a whole crowd milling around outside behind her. What were they all doing there? An instant later she slipped inside the door, then closed it behind her, shutting out the noisy waiting area.

Her eyes looked red and puffy, and smears of shadow underscored them. She looked tired, he thought with concern. If he hadn't felt so weak himself, he would have ripped out this damn IV line and climbed right out of the bed so she could lie down for a few minutes.

Unfortunately, he had a sneaking suspicion he would end up on the floor if he tried it.

For all her fatigue, she moved quickly to his side. "How do you feel?"

"Like I've tangled with a couple of bull moose." His voice sounded rough, raspy, and he cleared it before continuing. "The doc says I should be fine once they patch me up."

"Oh, Zack. I'm so glad." To his dismay, two tears slipped out from her spiky dark lashes and were quickly followed by several more.

He grabbed her hand and wrapped his fingers tightly around it. "Hey. Don't cry. Everything's okay."

"I was so afraid you wouldn't make it."

He squeezed her fingers. "The doc says I wouldn't have if you hadn't been there."

"You wouldn't have been shot in the first place if not for me! I'm so sorry I dragged you into it."

He breathed deeply of her wildflower scent. "Don't say that. I don't want to think about what might have happened if he had found you alone."

"I would have figured something out," she mumbled.

"Yeah. More beef and barley soup."

Although he knew it wasn't wise, he couldn't restrain himself an instant longer. With his good arm he reached out and snagged his fingers in her hair, then brought her face to his. Her mouth tasted sweet and pure and he wanted to stay there forever just drinking her in. "Thanks for saving my life," he murmured.

She sniffled, and more tears slid down her cheeks. "Right back at you."

She edged away, grabbing a tissue off the small table next to his bed. "Jean tells me you were planning on leaving tomorrow."

The hurt in her eyes stabbed at him like a sharp scalpel. "I had to go, Cassie. I'm sorry. It was too hard staying here with the way things were between us."

"The only reason for that was because of your stubbornness! You're the one who pushed me away."

Only because he was trying to protect her, just as he had pushed her off the trail to safety so he could take on Lowry. He didn't know how to answer, so decided to keep his mouth shut.

After a moment she spoke again. "So Doc says you'll probably have to spend a few days at the medical center in Idaho Falls. Will you be heading to Denver when you get out?"

Did she want him to go? Was this her way of telling him to get lost?

"I don't know. I guess that's something I'll have to figure out."

"Well, let me know when you make up your mind."

The scalpel twisted a little harder. "I will."

"Good." She paused. "I just want to know what forwarding address to give my family."

He stared at her, his vision a little gray around the edges. The damn medications must be making his head fuzzy. "What did you just say?"

She gazed back with an innocent expression. "You don't really think I'm going to let you just ride off into the sunset again, do you?"

He cleared his throat. "Cassie…"

"No. I'm sorry, Zack, but this time I'm sticking to you like flypaper. Wherever you go, I'm going right along with you. Denver. Durango. Timbuktu. It doesn't matter."

Dazed by her conviction, he could only stare at her for several long moments. "You would be willing to leave your family?" he asked when he could find his voice again.

"Star Valley? Everything you love here? All for some no-account drifter?"

She shook her head emphatically. "No. But I would leave in a heartbeat for you."

Gripping his hand tightly, she brought it to her chest, where he felt her heartbeat strong and true beneath her shirt. "I love you, Zack Slater. I have never stopped loving you. When I saw you lying so still on that mountainside, I realized nothing else matters but that. Whatever happened in the past can stay there for all I care. We have the rest of our lives ahead of us and we can build whatever kind of future we want."

"What do you see in that future?" He found he was suddenly desperate to know exactly where she was heading with this.

"Simple. We're going to get married and have babies together and live happily ever after."

Oh, hell. He felt the sting of tears behind his own eyes as wave after wave of love for her washed over him, purifying him, healing him. He could see that future vividly, and he wanted to reach for it so fiercely he trembled with it.

"Is that a proposal?" he managed to ask through the joy exploding inside him.

She smiled that slow, sweet Cassie smile that had haunted him for so long, for all the years and miles between them.

"No, Slater," she murmured softly against his mouth. "It's a promise."

* * * * *

We hope you enjoyed reading this special collection from Harlequin®.

If you liked reading these stories, then you will love **Harlequin® Special Edition** books!

You know that romance is for life. **Harlequin Special Edition** stories show that every chapter in a relationship has its challenges and delights and that love can be renewed with each turn of the page.

Enjoy six new stories from **Harlequin Special Edition** every month!

Available wherever books and ebooks are sold.

HARLEQUIN®

SPECIAL EDITION

Life, Love and Family.

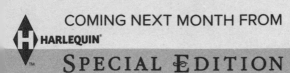
Available March 17, 2015

#2395 THE TAMING OF DELANEY FORTUNE
The Fortunes of Texas: Cowboy Country • by Michelle Major
Francisco Mendoza is having a bout of bad Fortune. Though he's been hired to help
with the new Cowboy Country theme park, Cisco is told to lasso a member of the
famous Fortune clan to help him out. So he courts spunky rancher Delaney Fortune
Jones under the guise of helping him with his project...but falls for her instead! Can
Delaney and Cisco find love in their very own pastures?

#2396 A DECENT PROPOSAL
The Bachelors of Blackwater Lake • by Teresa Southwick
When billionaire Burke Holden enters McKnight Automotive, he gets more than
just an oil change. When beautiful mechanic Sydney McKnight asks him to be her
pretend boyfriend, the sexy single dad happily accepts. But no-strings-attached
can't last forever, especially since Burke's vowed to stay commitment-free. It might
just take a true Montana miracle to give the Big Sky bachelor and the brunette
beauty their very own happily-ever-after.

#2397 MEANT-TO-BE MOM
Jersey Boys • by Karen Templeton
Cole Rayburn's back home in Maple River, New Jersey...but he's definitely not a
kid anymore. For one, he's got sole custody of his *own* two children; second, his
boyhood best friend, Sabrina Noble, is all grown-up and easy on the eyes.
Sabrina has just called off a disastrous engagement, so she's not looking to get
buddy-buddy with any man...but it's soon clear that her bond with Cole is still very
much alive. And he's not planning on letting her go—ever!

#2398 THE CEO'S BABY SURPRISE
The Prestons of Crystal Point • by Helen Lacey
Daniel Anderson is the richest and most arrogant man in town. He's also the most
charming, and Mary-Jayne Preston falls under his spell—for one night. But that's all it
takes for Mary-Jayne to fall pregnant with twins! The devastatingly handsome Daniel
isn't daddy material, or so she thinks. As the mogul and the mom-to-be grow closer,
can Daniel overcome his own tragic past to create a bright future with Mary-Jayne
and their twins?

#2399 HIS SECRET SON
The Pirelli Brothers • by Stacy Connelly
Ten years ago, one night changed Lindsay Brookes's life forever, giving her a
beloved son. But it didn't seem to mean as much to Ryder Kincaid, who went back
to his cheerleader girlfriend. Now Lindsay is back home in Clearville, California, to
tell her long-ago fling that he's a father. Already brokenhearted from a bitter divorce,
Ryder is flabbergasted at this change of fortune...but little Trevor could bring
together the family he's always dreamed of.

#2400 OH, BABY
The Crandall Lake Chronicles • by Patricia Kay
Sophie Marlowe and Dillon Burke parted ways long ago, but Fate has reunited the
long-lost lovers. Sophie's young half sister and Dillon's nephew are expecting a
baby, and it's up to these exes to help the youngsters create a happy family. Though
the rakish former football player and the responsible guidance counselor seem to
be complete opposites, there's no denying the irresistible attraction between them...
and where there's smoke, there are flames of true love!

*To placate her father, Sydney McKnight convinced
Burke Holden to be her temporary boyfriend. But could
a temporary relationship of convenience turn into a
forever love?*

*Read on for a sneak preview of
A DECENT PROPOSAL,
the latest volume in*
Teresa Southwick's miniseries
THE BACHELORS OF BLACKWATER LAKE.

"I don't know why you're willing to go along with this but
I'm grateful. Seriously, thanks."

"You're welcome."

Oddly enough it had been an easy decision. The simple
answer was that he'd agreed because she had asked and he
wanted to see her again. Granted, he could have asked her
out, but he'd already have had a black mark against him
because of turning down her request. Now she owed him.

Sydney leaned against the bar, a thoughtful look on her
face. "I've never done anything like this before, but I know
my father. He'll ask questions. In fact he already did. We're
going to need a cover story. How we met. How long we've
been dating. That sort of thing."

"It makes sense to be prepared."

"So we should get together soon and discuss it."

"What about right now?" Burke suggested.

Her eyes widened. "You don't waste time, do you?"

"No time like the present. Have you already had dinner?"

She shook her head. "Why?"

"Do you have a date?" If not, there was a very real possibility that she'd changed into the red blazer, skinny jeans and heels just for him. Probably wanted to look her best while making her case. Still, he really hoped she wasn't meeting another guy.

She gave him an ironic look. "Seriously? If I was going out with someone, I wouldn't have asked you to participate in this crazy scheme."

"Crazy? I don't know, it's a decent proposal." He shrugged. "So you're free. Have dinner with me. What about the restaurant here at the lodge? It's pretty good."

"The best in town." But she shook her head. "Too intimate."

So she didn't want to be alone with him. "Oh?"

"Something more public. People should see us together." She snapped her fingers. "The Grizzly Bear Diner would be perfect."

"I know the place. Both charming. And romantic."

"You're either being a smart-ass or a snob."

"Heaven forbid."

"You haven't been there yet?" she asked.

"No, I have."

He signaled the bartender, and when she handed the bill to him, he took care of it. Then he settled his hand at the small of her back and said, "Let the adventure begin."